*Adam held her gaze for a long, silent moment suspended between them like a finely spun and equally fragile gossamer thread.*

Callie knew that a very great deal hung on that thread, and that Adam could choose to break it at any time. In her deepest heart she knew that everything rested on his decision: He could choose the future and move on with his life, or he could choose the past and continue to live with pain and regret.

"Callie . . ." he said, his voice hoarse. "I think you had better find the strength for both of us and tell me to go before I do something unforgivable."

"I don't want you to go," she replied, her breath catching in her throat at the odd, almost desperate look in his eyes. Her heart started pounding again, but this time with a deep, unfamiliar physical excitement that left her trembling.

Adam groaned. "Callie, for God's sake, don't look at me like that or I won't answer for the consequences. I'm a man, not a saint."

"You're as far from a saint as I can imagine," she said, finally understanding that there was something more that she could give Adam. She could give him the strength of her body and the embrace of her love to help him remember how to live again. He had spent too long alone in the dark reaches of hell, and it was well past time for him to let the light back in. There was so much that she could give him, and she'd been utterly selfish to hold herself back just because he hadn't said the words she wanted to hear.

Callie didn't think any further. She acted instinctively and with a glad heart, shifting away from him as she pulled her nightdress over her head in one smooth gesture and dropped it on the floor.

He passed a hand over his face as if he couldn't believe his eyes and stared up at the canopy over the bed. "Callie," he said, his voice cracking, "what do you think you're doing?"

"I'm offering myself to you," she said.

"An emotionally stirring Regency romance that reaches deep-down inside and touches the reader's soul. The way in which the story gets the title *In the Presence of Angels* had me so emotionally moved I felt my eyes watering and a tightening in my heart—something a mere book seldom does for me. Katherine Kingsley has done it again—this is a definite keeper." —*STARDUST "Sprinklings" of Romance*

## The Sound of Snow

"*The Sound of Snow* is as lovely a story as its name. It is a timeless tale of the miracle of true love, which conquers all, heals all, and makes all new again. Add interesting characters, unexpected plot twists, and a touch of the supernatural, and the result is a memorable, feel-good read."
—*All About Romance*

"KATHERINE KINGSLEY HAS DONE IT AGAIN. *The Sound of Snow* is a true gem . . . a sheer delight. I treasured every word." —*The BookNook*

## Call Down the Moon

"Fascinating . . . an 'A' all the way!"
—*The Atlanta Journal-Constitution*

"Katherine Kingsley's magic touch once more provides an emotional story that combines enchantment and the wonder of love. . . . A beautiful and uplifting story—the kind that makes readers sigh with pleasure and smile through their tears. Tender, sweet, joyous, sensual and poignant, this novel is simply wonderful." —*Romantic Times*

*Books by Katherine Kingsley*

In the Wake of the Wind

Once Upon a Dream

Call Down the Moon

The Sound of Snow

In the Presence of Angels

Lilies on the Lake

Song from the Sea

# KATHERINE KINGSLEY

## *Song* from the *Sea*

A Dell Book

SONG FROM THE SEA
A Dell Book / April 2003

Published by
Bantam Dell
A Division of Random House, Inc.
New York, New York

ISBN 0-440-23744-0

Manufactured in the United States of America
Published simultaneously in Canada

OPM   10   9   8   7   6   5   4   3   2   1

*To Gary,*
*for bringing me home.*

# *Acknowledgements*

Many thanks to my dear friends Francie Stark and Jan Hiland for careful reading of the manuscript and for general encouragement, always much appreciated. Thanks also to Sierra Raven Wolf for keeping my body (and soul) together so that I could actually *write* the manuscript. Finally, my appreciation to author and lecturer Alan Cohen, from whom I first learned of the African tribal custom of the soul song.

To the readers: I hope you enjoy *Song from the Sea*, for I certainly enjoyed writing it. You can write to me at P.O. Box 37, Wolcott, Colorado 81655, e-mail me at <u>katherinekingsley@yahoo.com</u>, or visit my web page at http://ooourworld.compuserve.com/homepages/kkingsley

*For winter's rains and ruins are over,*
*And all the season of snows and sins;*
*The days dividing lover and lover,*
*The light that loses, the night that wins;*
*And time remembered is grief forgotten,*
*And frosts are slain and flowers begotten,*
*And in green underwood and cover*
*Blossom by blossom the spring begins.*

ALGERNON CHARLES SWINBURNE
—*Atalanta in Calydon*

# Song from the Sea

# Prologue

*October 12, 1817*
*Villa Kaloroziko*
*Corfu, Greece*

"Papa . . . Oh, Papa, please don't leave me," Callie whispered as she watched her father weakening hourly. "I don't know what I'll do without you." She laid her forehead on her father's chest, trying desperately not to cry. She couldn't believe that his time had come after such a long and valiant struggle, but the tumor in his brain had finally taken its toll and she knew there was nothing more she could do. No medicine in the world that she could concoct would bring him back to health.

Magnus Melbourne opened his eyes and his smile was as sweet as ever. "My little Callie," he murmured, lifting his hand with an effort and softly smoothing it over her hair. "How I wish I could see you, my beloved daughter. Your mother and I named you aptly: Callista, 'most beautiful one.' You are all of that, inside and out. You have made me so proud."

Callie choked back a sob. "I am happy to know it, Papa. You have been nothing but the best of fathers. We have had adventures, haven't we?" she said, trying to inject a lighter note into her voice.

"Indeed." He patted her shoulder. "I doubt there's another young lady on earth who is so thoroughly traveled. You must take what you have learned, my darling, and see that my book is properly finished. It's such a shame that I became ill when I did." He released a soft sigh. "Never mind that now. I know I can trust my work to your capable hands. More important, I know I can trust you to Harold Carlyle, who will make you a fine husband and give you a good life in England."

Callie abruptly sat up. Harold Carlyle was her least favorite subject and had been the cause of many sleepless nights. She knew the growing tumor had addled her dear father's thoughts, that he never would have made such a silly arrangement with his old friend Lord Geoffrey to marry their two only children to each other. Her father hadn't even seen Harold since he was a small child, so how could he possibly know what sort of man he'd become?

She and her father had had countless disagreements on the issue, but her father had refused to budge, convinced that his plan was the only way to ensure a safe future for her after he was gone. If she had to go to England at all, she'd far rather have gone to her distant relative, Lord Fellowes, but her father hadn't been in touch with that part of his family for years, so he had refused to consider the possibility. He'd decided that Harold Carlyle was the perfect solution, and that was that, no matter how loudly Callie protested.

But now the time for disagreements was over. She wanted her father to die in peace, and the least she could do was let him believe that she would do his bidding—and she would, insofar as she would journey to England and meet the Carlyles. She owed her father that much, but she simply couldn't go through with a marriage to a complete stranger.

She'd just have to explain exactly that to them. They couldn't force her to marry, after all, and it wasn't as if they needed the money she would bring as a dowry; her father had said the Carlyles were very plump in the pocket, so she didn't think they'd mind not having hers as well. Then, after conducting that piece of unpleasantness, she could return to Corfu and settle back down to life in the villa with Niko, Billiana, Panagiotis, and Sofiya to look after her as they always had.

Her inheritance would give her financial independence, so she needn't ever marry: She welcomed the idea of matrimony about as much as she would welcome a bout of dysentery. As long as she remained a single woman she could control her fortune and her future and that was all she wanted. The idea of some high-handed man ordering her around made her feel positively ill. The only drawback was that she wouldn't have children, for she liked children very much, but she supposed she could always indulge herself with other people's offspring.

"Callie? You didn't answer. I expect you to obey me in this," her father said, looking agitated, and she could see that the little strength he had was fading.

"I know, Papa. I am sure you know best," Callie said, trying to reassure him without lying outright.

"Indeed I do, and I am pleased that you have come to understand that. Lord Geoffrey writes glowingly of Harold and is as delighted as I am at the thought of your marriage. This is what your mother would have wanted for you, just as I do."

Callie brought the back of her father's limp hand to her lips, kissing it and curling her fingers into his. "I know you only want my happiness, Papa."

"I do. I could wish no greater gift for you than the kind of loving marriage your mother and I had. Harold comes from a fine family, even finer than our own. My father was only the younger son of a baron, but Lord Geoffrey is the younger son of a marquess, you know, and uncle to the current marquess."

Callie knew only too well. Her father's mind must be drifting again, for he had produced this piece of information more times than she could count, as if it would somehow impress her into wanting to marry Harold. She was neither impressed nor even interested in his bloodlines, since she had no use for the English aristocracy or their silly customs, customs which her father had tried to drum into her head during the last few months with little success.

"I still have to wonder why Harold Carlyle would want to take on a woman who is not only ancient at twenty-five, but who also has so few social graces, no matter how hard you've tried to instill them in me," she said lightly. "I can easily converse in a variety of languages on the subjects of plants and tribal customs and cures, but when it comes to things that proper young English ladies are *supposed* to speak of, I can't seem to think. I know I horrified poor Miss Margaret Evans when she came to call last Christmas. She couldn't believe that I didn't know the first thing about the latest London fashions, or care."

His brow furrowed. "I have often thought how selfish I've been, keeping you to myself instead of sending you to a proper school, teaching you subjects such as Greek and Latin and botany when I should have had you instructed in the gentler arts that a young lady needs to know."

"Oh no, Papa, please—you mustn't think that at all," Callie said, not able to bear hearing her beloved father berate himself over her unorthodox education, of all things.

She gently smoothed his forehead. "I have loved our life together, the way you took me everywhere and never held me back from learning the things I wanted, even if they weren't things that girls were supposed to be interested in. Never for a moment did I ever wish anything to be different. . . ." She paused, not wanting to lie to him. "Well, I did often wish that Mama hadn't died when I was only eight, but that couldn't be helped."

"Your dear mother," he murmured. "Her lungs were always weak. Even though we left England for a warmer climate, in the end nothing could help her. God willing, I shall soon be with her again, for I have missed her every day since she went."

"I wish you wouldn't go," she whispered, leaning down and kissing his cheek, dry as parchment. "I shall miss you most dreadfully, every bit as much as you have missed Mama."

His mouth curved up at the corners. "You mustn't be afraid of death, my little Callie. It is all a part of living and, in the end, just another beginning and a glorious one. Promise me you will remember this when I have gone."

"I promise," Callie solemnly swore, although her heart was breaking. Hot tears stung at her eyes and trickled down her cheeks, and she hastened to wipe them away with the side of her hand before her father knew she was crying. She rubbed her wet nose for good measure and stared hard at the dappled sunlight that fell through the half-closed shutters, trying to compose herself.

"And I promise that I will watch over you," he vowed just as solemnly, but his words faltered and he had to pause. "If you should feel a breeze on your cheek on a still day or hear a lark singing in the night, you will know I am with you," he finished.

Callie hadn't thought of this. She fervently hoped he

wouldn't watch over her *too* carefully or he'd know that she'd failed to honor his last wish, but in all conscience she really couldn't go through with such an absurd plan, even if he did think it was for her own good. "You will always be in my thoughts, Papa. Always and forever until we meet again."

He squeezed her hand, no more than the lightest of pressure. "I must sleep now, darling girl," he said, his voice now barely audible. "Sit here with me. I haven't much longer." He turned his head on the pillow and fell silent.

Two hours later, as dusk fell and the shadows drew deep into the room, her father opened his eyes again. He clasped the hand that still lay in his, his grip suddenly surprisingly strong. "It's time," he said, his blind eyes filling with a joy she didn't understand. "Sing to me now, Callie. Sing my soul song as I taught you. Sing me into the next life and as you sing, know I love you with all my heart."

"As I love you, Papa," Callie said, thinking she couldn't bear the pain that tore at her heart. "Be free. Go into God's arms with a glad heart." She took a deep breath, said a prayer for his eternal soul, and then began to sing his song in a high clear voice, exactly as he'd taught her, fulfilling the covenant she'd made to him years before.

He died with a smile on his lips.

# 1

Adam Carlyle, fifth Marquess of Vale, seventh earl of Stanton, and ninth Viscount of Redlynsdale was determined to kill himself, and he wasn't about to let a little foul weather get in his way. Indeed, he'd waited for a day when the wind would be blowing from the northeast. What he hadn't planned on was having the wind suddenly pick up into near-gale conditions, nor had he planned on having to fight the angry, churning sea.

Wiping the fierce salt spray off his face with his forearm, he shielded his eyes and glared through the gray haze, trying to work out the best way to navigate the next deep trough ahead. He'd gladly have let the sea swamp the rowboat then and there and put him out of his misery, for his back and shoulders burned painfully from the effort of pulling at the oars, but he had his reasons for forging on:

namely, his cousin Harold. His hatred for Harold was second only to his desire to die, and he'd be damned if he was going to make it easy for Harold to inherit the marquessate after Adam was gone.

Therefore, despite the inconvenience, Adam was going to make good and sure that when he drowned he would do so as far from England as possible. He intended the rowboat to sink to the bottom of the Channel and his body to wash up on the shores of France as another nameless victim of the capricious sea. Harold would be a long time waiting for a final declaration of his cousin's death and the chance to get his grasping, greedy fingers on the twenty thousand acres of Stanton Abbey and the fortune that went along with it.

Smiling grimly, Adam relished the thought of how irked Harold would be. But then Adam had spent nearly an entire lifetime doing everything he possibly could to irk Harold, and for the most part succeeding at it.

Just the thought of Harold and his smug fat face gave Adam renewed vigor. He wrapped his hands more tightly around the handles of the oars and dug the blades back into the water, pulling then forward with all his strength. His only regret about dying was that he wouldn't be around to see that smug fat face when Harold received word from Adam's solicitor that Adam had not vanished for good, which would be everyone's initial assumption, but merely gone on a prolonged trip around the world. By God, Adam had put enough time and effort into planning the ruse so that Harold would be many years chasing down false leads before Adam was officially declared dead and Harold finally got his hands on Stanton.

Adam snorted with disgust at the thought, then renewed his grip on the handles of the oars and pulled again, turning the boat slightly sideways to pitch over the crest of yet another wave, getting a cold slap of water in the face for his trouble.

Peace, he thought, gritting his teeth against the strain and willing his aching arms to dig harder. Peace. A complete absence of pain awaited him, no more guilt; no more sleepless nights spent cursing a God he didn't even believe in. He might just as well have blamed the barn cat for all the good that had done him.

Suddenly exhausted, he slowly laid the oars down inside the rowboat and carefully unclenched his numb hands, lowering his head and wrapping his sore arms around his knees as he struggled to catch his labored breath. He had finished his job. The rest was up to the sea—the sea, and the God he didn't believe in. Maybe for once, mercy would prevail. He counted on it.

The little boat bobbed and rolled as if freed to go where it would. Adam hardly cared as long as it didn't go backward, but there was little chance of that given the strength of the current that pulled them out toward France and toward welcome oblivion, for sooner or later a large enough wave would come along and sink the boat, taking its grateful passenger down with it.

His breathing finally slowed and he gingerly lowered himself into the nest of the hull, leaned his back against the seat, closed his eyes, and prepared to die. That wasn't difficult. He'd been as good as dead these two interminable years past and so had no emotional preparation to make. His last conscious thought was that he rather liked the idea of his mortal remains becoming fish food. As the vicar was so fond of saying, one should always give back. With a little luck the fish would make a feast of his flesh and there would be little left to make possible any identification of his body.

Something jolted Adam out of the deep slumber he'd

fallen into. A song, that's what it was: a faint, lovely, high-pitched song that sounded like a soprano solo in a heavenly choir. Disoriented, he rubbed his eyes, wondering if this was the heaven he'd scoffed for the last two years and now found himself residing in. Just as quickly he banished that notion, for he was wet, cold, and thirsty, and every muscle in his body ached. Worse, he was still in the blasted rowboat, which was proving most annoyingly to be unsinkable. At least the wind had somewhat abated, so he wasn't being blasted on top of everything else.

Rubbing his sore, swollen eyes again, he peered through the fog, looking for the source of this song, and then somewhere in the dim recesses of his blurred mind he remembered the Sirens, the sea nymphs whose song lured sailors to shipwreck. As he recalled, Odysseus escaped them by tying himself to a mast and stopping up his men's ears. Well, he had no intention of stopping up his ears. Here at last was his undoing, and he was going for it hell-bent. He might be an atheist, but he had no arguments with the ancient Greeks. He was just about to settle back to be lulled peacefully to his death when he bolted upright, unable to believe the sight before him.

To his utter astonishment, a clipper ship appeared out of the fog, not thirty feet away from him. In one clear moment he registered not only the source of the song but the singer herself, who balanced precariously on the stern of the ship, hands outstretched as if entreating the sea to take her.

That he understood well enough, but what he couldn't comprehend was why she was singing so joyously.

He didn't have the same feeling about his own impending suicide, but then he didn't really have any feelings about it at all other than sheer relief. Or maybe, he mused, she was leaping to her death to avoid marriage to some overweight windbag like Harold. Yes, that must be it, he decided. An albatross, or a bird large enough to make the image appropriate, winged directly over her head. It was probably a Great Black-backed Gull, but still, he thought it a perfect harbinger of doom, a fitting touch to complete the picture. His Classics tutor would have been most impressed.

What a fine woman, Adam thought, settling lazily back to watch the spectacle of her grand finale. No nonsense with her. A quick leap into the sea and the deed would be done. Of course, she probably didn't have to deal with the complicated problems of trying to keep a large estate from a pesky cousin for as long as possible.

Suddenly the ship lurched as a wave buffeted it from its starboard side and the object of his admiration went flying straight off the stern. The dive was not the swanlike affair that he'd anticipated, but a great business of arms and legs flapping, skirts flying overhead, all punctuated by a loud, prolonged shriek. She struck the side of the ship on her plummet downward, and the force of the impact threw her sideways and out like a rag doll flung carelessly into space. Only a moment later her limp body plopped into the sea.

She surfaced about twenty seconds later, long strands of hair streaming around her face like seaweed, her mouth open and gasping soundlessly like a landed fish, the bird diving around her, making enough noise to rouse an army.

Adam heaved himself to his feet, balancing himself against the rocking of his little boat, wondering if he hadn't been mistaken in her intent. She didn't look like someone who was happy to be consigned to the depths. Instead, the pathetic cries for help she'd started bleating, combined with the wave of her hands over her head toward the direction of the disappearing ship, made him wonder if she meant to be in the water at all.

With a sinking heart he decided probably not, which left him in a most awkward and unpleasant position. Since no one on the ship had noticed the woman's plunge over the stern, that left solely him in the position of rescuer, and he knew he'd better rescue her fast.

"Why can't *anything* ever go right?" he muttered through parched lips as he picked up the oars and dug in, rowing as fast as he could toward the woman whom he'd decided was no more than an utter idiot.

Clearly he'd have to postpone his death. Adam had never been so annoyed in his life.

"Home, sweet bloody home." Adam had never expected to see Stanton again, but he felt an enormous relief when he finally spotted the lights of the house shining like a beacon from the dark stretch of coastline and guiding him safely to shore.

He groaned as he lifted the limp body of his bedraggled passenger from the rowboat. The bird that had made a complete nuisance of itself for the three full hours it had taken to get back to the Stanton boathouse made one last low circle, emitted a loud series of piercing cries, and headed back to the sea, as if now that it had seen its charge safely on land it had consigned her to Adam's care.

"Don't count on it, you mangy excuse for feathers," he muttered. He didn't know what he was going to do with the girl, since she couldn't be bothered to wake up and tell him who she was or where she belonged, but he reckoned his housekeeper could deal with the immediate situation. After that, he'd send her on her way and wash his hands of the creature. The last thing he needed was someone making any sort of demands on him. He'd rescued her from certain death and owed her nothing else.

His position now clear in his head, he readjusted her weight, threw her over his shoulder, and hauled her up to the main house.

The lights shone in the windows as if he'd never left, as if they'd all been expecting him back, which of course they had. The only person to whom his return came as any surprise was himself.

"Mrs. Simpson," he bellowed, grasping with one hand for the brass knob on the back door to the scullery, the last place anyone expected to see him appear given the reaction he received as the door swung open.

Pandemonium broke out in the kitchen but he ignored the shrieks and crashing of breaking china, continuing to shout for the housekeeper as he kicked the door shut behind him. She obliged him by appearing posthaste, as composed as if she were accustomed to seeing him bearing half-drowned women in his arms.

"Goodness, my lord, what have we here?" she inquired in a level voice, carefully adjusting the starched cap on her head as if that might give her an answer.

"What we have is a disaster, Mrs. Simpson," Adam replied shortly. "Take her away, do whatever has to be done. She fell off a ship into the sea, so I imagine she needs warming and cleansing and anything else you do for people who fall into the sea."

Mrs. Simpson shot Adam a look of extreme alarm. "I will send for the doctor at once. As for yourself, my lord? Perhaps you might benefit from a bath and some dinner on a tray?" She eyed him with deep concern, which for some reason only annoyed Adam more.

"I am perfectly well," he snapped. And then, letting his

burden slip from his exhausted arms into some nameless footman's hands, he collapsed, letting the darkness surround him and carry him down into oblivion.


Nigel Dryden, steward to Stanton Abbey and Adam's closest friend since childhood, was trying to concentrate on the ledger, tallying one column of figures against a second, but his thoughts kept drifting back to Adam. Something wasn't right: He'd felt it in his bones all day. He couldn't pinpoint exactly what was wrong, only that Adam had been behaving in an even more distant fashion than usual—or what had become usual since the tragic deaths of his wife and small son. Adam's grief had not diminished with time. If anything he had become more despondent, although he was a master at masking that despondency with a cool, polite detachment.

Nigel was not fooled, but even he had not been able to break through Adam's wall, a wall that had grown higher and more impenetrable as time went by. The saddest part was that the Adam he knew and loved was nothing like the man he'd become. Adam by nature was kind and generous, his heart as big as they came. Despite his mother's dying when he was born, his father's death when Adam was only nine, and the misery of thereafter being raised by his aunt and uncle who were more tormentors than guardians, Adam had always managed to keep a sense of humor and a caring eye on those he deemed less fortunate than himself.

All that had changed. Perhaps the size of Adam's heart and his enormous capacity for love had been his downfall in the end, for the loss of his wife Caroline and little son Ian, both whom he'd loved to distraction, had dealt him a blow it appeared he'd never recover from.

Nigel had despaired for his friend, who had shut the world out so completely that he no longer made the smallest effort to see any of his many acquaintances. He didn't even bother to go to church. Nigel didn't think Adam had set foot in one since the funeral service in the family chapel two springs earlier. He didn't recall his smiling, either, in all that time. All the joy that Adam had taken in life vanished as if it had never been. Worse, he seemed to have given up hope on life altogether.

In the last few months Nigel's concern had grown as Adam seemed to disappear even further into himself, sometimes vanishing from Stanton for days on end without explanation. On his return he would be exhausted and pale, as if he'd been off struggling with demons. Nigel imagined he had, and he had been deeply afraid that one day the demons would win and Adam wouldn't return at all.

Nigel lifted his head as a pounding started at the door of his house. He frowned, wondering who could want him at this hour. Surely it wasn't Adam. Adam never summoned him for anything anymore, save for reports on the concerns of Stanton.

"Mr. Dryden. Mr. Dryden, sir, you're needed!"

*Adam* ... With a sudden surge of alarm, he leapt to his feet and wrenched his door open. Young Albert the footman stood there, looking frantic.

"What is it, Albert?" he said, forcing his voice to remain calm. Dear God, but he hoped Adam hadn't gone and done something foolish. He'd been dreading something like this.

"There's been an accident, sir," he panted. "A near-drowning. His lordship—his lordship ..."

Nigel fought down panic. "What *about* Lord Vale?" he said, ready to throttle the lad. "Catch your breath, calm down, and tell me what's happened."

"A woman, sir. She fell off a ship. He—his lordship rescued her from the sea and brought her to the abbey, and he just collapsed, sir, right there on the scullery floor. Now they're both in a stupor and Mrs. Simpson sent for the doctor and sent me for you. She said you're to come at once."

"And so I shall," Nigel said, breathing a sigh of relief that it was nothing worse. He pushed past Albert and took off out the door at a fast clip. Five minutes later he arrived in Adam's bedchamber where Adam lay on the bed, still clothed, and those clothes soaking wet. Two footmen stood on either side doing absolutely nothing.

"For the love of God, get him undressed," Nigel snapped. "Where is Plimpton?"

"His lordship gave him the day and night off, sir. Mr. Plimpton went into the town to visit friends."

"Not the best timing for a valet to go missing," Nigel said, his tone dry. "Very well, one of you fetch hot, sweet tea, and bring up some cognac while you're about it. You go, Michael, and tell someone to heat water and have that brought in along with warm bricks for his lordship's feet. He'll need bathing and he'll need to be kept warm." He moved over to the bed and took Michael's place, helping Henry to remove the rest of Adam's clothing.

Casting his eye over Adam's muscular body, he saw that Adam appeared to be unmarked, save for a sprinkling of bruises on his forearms and some blisters on his palms and thumbs. The doctor could do a more complete examination, but Nigel imagined that Adam suffered from cold and exhaustion rather than any physical damage.

"Right, let's get him under the blankets, Henry." He lifted Adam in his arms while Henry drew the covers aside, then gently laid him back down and piled the sheets and blankets around him. "Build up the fire, then wait outside until Michael returns." Pulling up a chair, Nigel sat down to wait for the requested provisions to appear. For the moment there was nothing more to be done.

"So, Adam," he murmured. "You actually rescued someone. That's more effort than you've put into anything for a very long time. I suppose as a gentleman, though, you had no choice." He contemplated Adam's face. Still and pale, at least he looked peaceful—or if not entirely peaceful, at least he didn't wear the cold, hard expression Nigel was accustomed to.

For one very bad moment, he'd thought that his fear might have been realized when the footman had appeared at his door so shaken he could barely speak. He could only thank God that was not the case, although he had to wonder what Adam had been doing out on the sea to begin with in this nasty weather.

He doubted he'd get any explanation, but right now that wasn't his concern. He wanted only to see Adam awake and well, if not in heart, at least in body. Adam was strong and fit, and that ought to go a long way toward helping him recover. His emotional injuries were another story altogether.


"What the devil . . ." Adam forcefully pushed away whatever was moving over his face like a warm, soggy stocking. He spluttered and sat up, glowering at the culprit, who turned out to be none other than Nigel, beaming at him as if pleased to be shoved aside. "What in God's name do you think you're doing, man?"

"I was *trying* to wash half of the English Channel off you, but be my guest and do it yourself. Or let it stay for all I care. Here, have some tea. I laced it with cognac, which should put you in a better mood." He thrust a steaming mug toward Adam. "If you will go diving overboard for damsels in distress, the least you can do is take care of yourself after the fact."

Adam took it, memory returning, and it wasn't a pleasant one. He was supposed to be dead by now and out of his misery, but oh, no. Here he was, back in his bed, being treated like an infant in need of scrubbing. The next thing he knew he'd have nursery food shoved down his throat—which was uncommonly dry and rather sore at that. "Bloody woman," he muttered, gulping at his tea. "What on earth was she thinking, leaping into the heaving sea?"

"I have no more idea about that than I have about why you were out in the heaving sea to begin with."

"It wasn't heaving when I went out," Adam said in his defense. "How was I supposed to know I'd run into a squall?"

Nigel regarded him with a complete lack of expression. "For someone who was raised on this coast and can read the weather like the back of his hand, I'd say you've suddenly developed a remarkably blind eye."

"Don't be absurd," Adam snapped, feeling an unwelcome pang of guilt. "I wanted to do some fishing. The weather appeared perfect for my purposes." That, at least, was true. He didn't like lying to Nigel, but he couldn't exactly tell him he'd gone out planning to put an end to himself, could he?

"In the future do us both a favor and confine your fishing to the river. I'd sleep more easily. So exactly what did happen out there? How did the woman come to fall off the ship?"

"She just . . . fell," Adam said, still puzzled about that himself. "God only knows what she was doing out on the stern of a clipper in a howling storm. I don't suppose the idiot's come to her senses yet and explained?"

"Not that I've heard," Nigel said. "I've been in here with

you since you were brought upstairs. Apparently Dr. Hadley's been summoned. Perhaps he'll enlighten us."

"I hope someone does. I have a raging headache and my muscles ache from all that unnecessary exertion."

But Dr. Hadley had nothing to tell them when he eventually appeared to check on Adam's own health.

"The young woman is still unconscious, my lord, and likely to stay that way for some time," the doctor said as he poked and prodded Adam, much to Adam's displeasure and discomfort. "She's suffered a severe blow to the back of her head. I fear that I cannot tell you with any certainty if she'll regain consciousness, let alone survive the incident. Swelling to the brain can often be fatal, and you'll both be fortunate not to develop fevers given the drenching you took."

"I have no intention of developing a fever, Doctor, and I would thank you not to be so pessimistic. Now if you please, cease and desist your infernal examination. I've suffered nothing more than exposure to the elements and some muscle strain from which I shall recover by tomorrow."

"Your diagnosis is correct, my lord," Hadley said with a glimmer of what Adam sourly expected was amusement lurking behind his spectacles. "I am afraid I must insist, however, that you confine yourself to your bed for the next twenty-four hours just to be sure that you make a full recovery. I shall be back to check on the young woman tomorrow morning. I have instructed Mrs. Simpson to summon me if there are any developments in the night— convulsions are not unexpected in a case such as this."

Adam, thoroughly fed up with the subject of "the young woman," who had given them all more trouble than anyone needed, merely grunted.

As soon as the door had closed behind the doctor, Adam turned and glared at Nigel. "Why," he said from between clenched teeth, "did this happen to me? I was going about my business perfectly happily, and now look what I've been landed with. A—a half-drowned, half-brained numbskull," he said, although the truth of the matter was that he was feeling deeply concerned about the girl. He hadn't saved her to have her go and expire on him. As soon as he felt a little stronger, he'd go and have a look at her. After all, she wasn't the one who was supposed to die. That was his job, and he wasn't in the habit of passing his responsibilities off on other people.

Before Nigel could answer, Adam drifted back off to sleep. He didn't feel the hands that gently pulled the covers up around his neck or hear the voice that quietly said, "Sleep well, my friend."

## 2

Callie's eyes flew open in panic as her arms flailed wildly in the air, trying to get hold of something, anything. She couldn't manage to catch her breath to cry out for help—everything was dark, so dark, and she had the horrible feeling that she was suffocating.

"Breathe. Come now, take deep breaths. You can do it."

A low, soft voice came from what seemed like a million miles away, but the reassuring sound steadied her and she obeyed, slowly inhaling, realizing that fresh cool air still rushed into her lungs. She somehow managed to gulp down that precious air, trying desperately to orient. Her head pounded furiously and her skin felt as if it was on fire, but at least she knew she was alive. She was quite sure that pain did not exist in heaven.

Her eyes slowly focused, taking in the soft flickering of

candlelight on a mantelpiece directly across from her, where a fire gently crackled in the grate below. She couldn't think where she was or how she'd gotten there.

"So you're back with us. It's about time," that same low voice said, only this time it sounded nearer, over to her left. Gingerly turning her aching head, she looked for its source.

A man, or what seemed to be a man, sat in an armchair, his hands folded on his lap, his legs propped up on what she realized was the bed she was lying in.

For a confused moment she thought he might be an angel, since a nimbus glowed around his head, backlighting his dark hair. He had the appearance of an angel—or at least what she'd always imagined one should look like: not that absurd blond version most painters tended toward, but rather the valiant fighter against evil. Saint George battling the dragon, sword in hand, determined and dangerous—that was how this man looked to her. Only this man's eyes were a startling blue and trained directly on her in a most unangelic fashion. If anything, he looked irritated.

Still, she couldn't shake off the feeling that she was looking on an angel of mercy. She just didn't expect an angel to look so human—or so bad-tempered.

"Who—who are you?" she croaked, her throat feeling horribly dry and parched. She licked her lips in an attempt to moisten them. "Where am I?" she finished on a whisper.

"You are in England, in the county of Kent. To be precise, you are at Stanton Abbey. As for myself, I am Adam Carlyle. I live here. More to the point, who the devil are you, and what were you doing falling off a clipper ship into the English Channel?"

Callie blinked, not knowing what he was referring to. The last thing she remembered was . . . She didn't remember anything at all, she realized with deep alarm. She knew her name was Callie, but nothing else came to her. Everything was a blank, a confused gray void. "I—I . . ." Her voice trailed off and she swallowed hard. "I slipped," she said, thinking that sounded like the most reasonable explanation, praying that her mind would clear before he asked her any more difficult questions. She tried desperately to suppress the panic that coursed through her veins, making her want to grab at him and beg him to hold her tight.

"That much I believe," he said. "What I'd like to know is what you were doing out on the stern of a ship in foul weather, singing your heart out."

Callie tried to think through the fog in her brain. She couldn't imagine anyone doing anything so foolish, and she wasn't a foolish person—at least she didn't think she was. Apparently she must be, though, for this man had no reason to lie to her about her tumble into the sea. As for singing, that did seem like an odd thing to do in the middle of a storm. She hoped that at least she'd been singing on key. "You were there?" she asked, stalling for time. Oh, *why* couldn't she remember anything? The fear threatened to take her breath away.

"I was out in my boat, yes. I saw you fall and decided that you needed rescuing, since the ship you were on was fast disappearing toward England."

"Well, what were *you* doing out in your boat in foul weather?" she retorted, thinking that a good offense was in order at this point, since she had no defense, no defenses at all.

"Fishing," he said, scowling at her. "I did not expect to land a silly young girl any more than I expected to be subjected to twenty-four hours of unwelcome bed rest for my trouble." He leaned over to the bedside table, poured a glass of water from a pitcher, and handed it to her. "Drink this," he said. "You've been out cold for the last two days and you are feverish on top of that."

She started to sit up, but quickly decided that was a very bad idea since her head started throbbing twice as hard. "I—I need some help," she said, hating to admit it, especially to this foul-tempered man who didn't seem to have an ounce of sympathy for her plight. "My head hurts rather badly."

He quickly slid his arm under her shoulders and held the glass as she thirstily drank, then helped her lie back down. "You have a lump on the back of your head the size of an egg. You must have hit yourself on the way down. It's a miracle that you didn't drown before I managed to reach you, since according to the doctor you managed to brain yourself rather well. You don't seem to do things in half measures."

"I am very grateful to you for rescuing me and bringing me to your home," she said, and that really was the truth. She didn't add that she wished he could be a little more sympathetic about the matter, since she already felt like an utter idiot and utterly, horribly alone.

"I'm sure you are. However, if you wish to express that gratitude in a more useful fashion, perhaps you would now deign to tell me your name and your address so that I might return you to your relations as soon as you've recovered."

Callie bit her lip. Since she couldn't recall her last name or any relations, she supposed she'd just have to make something up for the time being, since she couldn't possibly admit that she'd lost her mind. Surely her memory would return shortly? "My name is Callie," she said, trying to think what to add to that. Callie—that had to be short for something. "Miss Calliope Magnus," she continued, rather liking the sound of that, although she didn't feel the least bit reassured.

"And where does Miss Calliope Magnus hail from?" he asked, pressing his forefinger to his temple.

She strained for an answer, but nothing came. Absolutely nothing. She'd have to come up with something though, since the truth certainly wouldn't serve. *I'm sorry, Mr. Carlyle, but I haven't the vaguest idea.* Oh, that would sound just wonderful. He'd have her out the door so fast that her already spinning head would probably fall off altogether.

Considering carefully where she might possibly have come from, she decided she shouldn't be too specific. The farther away she made it, the better, so that he couldn't track down the details very easily. He'd said she'd been on a ship, so she could have been coming from anywhere. A brilliant idea suddenly occurred. "I have lived most of my life abroad, sir. We traveled often, never settling down anywhere for very long." That scenario sounded perfectly reasonable to her. "My parents were British, but they were expatriates," she added, inventing as quickly as she could. "As they are both now deceased, I thought I might return to the land of my birth and see what it was like." She attempted a smile, hard when she felt like fainting.

"I see." Adam regarded her with what she could only interpret as exasperation. "Where did you most recently live, then, and where did you intend on going once you'd arrived in England?"

"Most recently we resided in . . . in Italy, and I wasn't sure where to go when I arrived, as my parents never talked about their families. I thought that was because they must have had personal troubles and left England as a result. Since I know of no family members, I thought I would apply for a post as a—as a lady's companion." She prayed that sounded like a perfectly logical explanation. Funny, though, she really did have an image in her mind of an Italianate house with brilliant red blossoms pouring over a high wall. Bougainvillea, that was the name of the vine. How on earth could she know that and nothing else?

"You traveled all the way from Italy in order to find a post in England as a lady's companion." He raised his eyebrows. "Could you not have found a position there and saved yourself a great deal of trouble and expense?"

Callie hadn't thought of that. "Really, Mr. Carlyle," she said, hoping to divert him. "You needn't worry in the least. As soon as I'm on my feet and in full health, I'll embark on my original quest. You've been very kind indeed and I shan't trouble you a moment longer than necessary." She fervently hoped that would be the case. If she carried on in this empty-headed fashion she really didn't know what she was going to do. The icy fear in the pit of her stomach made her feel as if she was going to be sick, and she pressed her hand against her middle in an effort to steady herself.

He shot her a look that was far too incisive. "Are you hungry?" he eventually asked. "I can have something sent up from the kitchen."

She barely managed to shake her head, wanting only to fall back asleep. Tomorrow had to be better. With luck she'd have some real answers. She had to have, or she was in very serious trouble. Tomorrow her memory would certainly return, and then, when she felt a little stronger, she could go merrily on her way without his knowing that she'd ever deceived him.

"Sleep then. I will look in on you tomorrow." He rose, and she heard the door close softly behind him.

Sighing, she gratefully closed her eyes. Her last thought before sleep overcame her was whether she had any money to go merrily on her way, but she decided to worry about that later. Everything would come clear in the morning, she was sure of it.

Something was definitely not right. Adam shook his head slowly as he gazed out over the river that meandered out into the sea. The full moon, staring pale and high in the night sky, reflected down into the river's calm surface. He couldn't put his finger on exactly what was wrong, but Miss Calliope Magnus's story didn't ring true to him.

He realized that she was ill and probably confused from her head injury, but nevertheless he couldn't dismiss the idea that she'd thoroughly misled him. If nothing else, he'd always been a good judge of character, and the nagging suspicion that the girl was not who she said she was simply would not go away. If he was correct, the question now was what reason would she have for lying?

His eyes narrowed in thought. She knew nothing about him or his circumstances. She'd only ever seen a portion of the room she resided in, and a dark room at that, so she couldn't possibly know anything of the vastness of Stanton or its land, nor could she know of his title or the fortune that came with it. That eliminated any possibility that she might think herself sitting in a fine situation she had no intention of relinquishing. Therefore he had to believe that she must have secrets she didn't wish anyone to discover. No one, no matter how injured, would be so vague about her background unless she had something to hide.

What he found particularly odd was that she appeared as innocent as a babe. The impression might have been made by the blond hair, the color of sunlight now that it was dry, her finely drawn features, the mouth shaped like Cupid's bow. He knew that her eyes were a soft brown, once she'd finally bothered to open them. As he'd sat vigil by her bed for all those hours he had wondered if she ever would. The doctor had not been optimistic; given the nature of the blow she'd received to her head, the shock to her system from nearly drowning, her raging fever, and her continuing unconsciousness, he'd declared her prognosis grim.

Adam's huge relief when she finally did regain consciousness had surprised him, so much that he'd been annoyed in the extreme at himself—and at her. How could he possibly feel anything as absurd as relief over a silly chit who had seriously disrupted his well-laid plans? Perhaps the unexpected emotion had come from a misguided sense of responsibility for her life, since he'd hauled her from the sea.

That idea was even more absurd, he decided, turning and looking up at the wing in which Silly Miss Magnus resided, the light of the candles flickering faintly through the windows. He didn't indulge in emotion. He hadn't cared about anyone or anything since his beloved Caroline and his precious little Ian had died, a great void existing where his heart had once resided. He certainly didn't care about a girl he didn't even know who was stupid enough to fall willy-nilly off a ship. From the way she'd stared at him blankly when he'd asked her the simplest of questions he had to wonder if she had any brains inside that head at all.

Probably not. Brains were rare enough in a female, especially a pretty one. His wife had been the exception to that rule, thoughtful in her opinions, always tranquil, never prone to histrionics, her beauty never marred by emotional fits and starts, her interests extending far beyond the usual drawing room gossip. He quickly pushed Caro's image away, unable to bear the memories it brought of a time that he'd been happy, when the future had seemed so filled with promise.

What a great joke his life had become, a joke at his own expense. He'd finally found happiness and a certain degree of peace after the nightmare of his childhood, and it had all been snatched from him in a matter of moments, a blind, cruel stroke of fate. On that horrible, dark day, he'd lost all hope that there was a God, let alone a merciful one. Life was nothing more than a series of random accidents. You were born and you died, and most of what happened in between was completely senseless and usually painful.

Adam pressed his hands hard against his temples as if he could somehow squeeze the torturous thoughts out of his head. He couldn't allow himself to feel for fear of what it might do to him. He needed to think of his present dilemma, of how to discharge this latest unwelcome responsibility so that he could get on with the matter of leaving the world he had a strong distaste for.

The strain of pretending to be a living, walking human being had already brought him to near breaking point. He really didn't think he could go on for very much longer.

Squinting painfully against the suddenly bright light that invaded the soothing dark behind her throbbing eyes, Callie cautiously peeped out through her half-lowered eyelashes to locate the source. It appeared to be a large window with an equally large woman standing in front of it; a starched cap perched on top of her head and a starched apron was tied around her girth, from which a cluster of keys hung. One plump hand was engaged in pulling back a plush blue velvet drapery.

For a moment Callie thought she must be in an opulent hotel room somewhere in the Mediterranean. The heat stifled her and the light blazed like dragon's fire into her already burning eyes.

But then the woman turned and spoke, and her thick British accent immediately brought memory rushing back.

A dark room, a dark man, confusion and fear. Not knowing who she was . . . Callie probed her mind as if she were gingerly probing a sore tooth, seeing if the trouble was still there. It was. She couldn't remember a thing about herself before last night. Her heart sank, but she tried valiantly to focus on what the woman was saying.

". . . And I'm happy to find you awake, my dear. His lordship said you'd come to your senses in the night. We're all pleased, so worried about you the last three days. His lordship thought you'd like some nice chicken broth." She beamed like a mother hen. "You should take some nourishment. It can only do you good," she said, ladling a large spoonful of broth from a small tureen on a tray into a cup and carrying it across the room to the bed. "I brought some toasted bread as well, hoping you might have an appetite. The doctor said you should eat as soon as we could coax you to do so. How does your poor head feel?"

"It aches," Callie said, feeling ridiculously weak and not at all inclined to move.

The woman slipped a practiced arm under Callie's back and gently lifted her to a sitting position. "There, there. Of course it does. You're still hot to the touch, but no longer burning up. The fever will soon break, and when it does you'll feel much cooler." She held the cup to Callie's lips. "Come along, my dear, give it a try. Cook makes a most superior broth. You'll be much stronger for it, trust me."

Callie did as she was told. The broth tasted surprisingly good, not greasy as Callie had expected, but clear and flavorful. And oh, the warm liquid felt wonderful going down her dry, sore throat. She drank and drank until she'd finished the whole cup.

The kind woman beamed again and immediately

poured another cup. This time she dipped some toast into it, and Callie ate the dampened bread between sips.

When she'd finished, the woman helped her to lie back down. "Thank you," Callie whispered. "What is your name?"

"Didn't I say? Heavens, I thought I had. I am Mrs. Simpson, my dear, Lord Vale's housekeeper these past ten years. I gather that you are Miss Magnus." She patted Callie's hand. "What a wonderful thing that his lordship was out in the storm when you fell, and managed to pull you into his boat."

Callie frowned, thinking she really had lost her mind. "I—I thought Mr. Carlyle rescued me." She distinctly remembered his saying so. Didn't she?

Mrs. Simpson chuckled. "That's his lordship all over. He probably didn't want to alarm you by using his title. Carlyle is his family name, but he is properly known as the Marquess of Vale."

Callie stared at the woman in horror. A *marquess*? She'd landed on the doorstep of a marquess? She drew in a long, shuddering breath. That was not good news. That was not good at all. Marquesses had power and money, and if this one ever found out that she wasn't who she'd said she was, he could probably have her thrown into jail for . . . for assuming a false identity or something like that. As far as she knew she didn't have a penny to her name or a family to come to her defense. She could be locked up forever, which would probably suit the heartless devil.

Last night he'd looked as if he wanted to wash his hands of her the first moment he could, and jail would be the perfect solution, wouldn't it? Or even better, a lunatic asylum if he found out she had no memory. Wasn't that where they put people who had lost their minds? Tears sprang to her eyes as she contemplated the horrible thought.

"There, there, my dear. There's no need for distress. You

can see why his lordship didn't tell you right away, for fear of just this reaction, which is not good for someone in your fragile condition." She produced a handkerchief from one of her apron pockets and wiped Callie's eyes. "Lord Vale is a kind man, not given to airs and graces, so you needn't worry about your lack of position, if that is what is upsetting you."

*If you only knew,* Callie thought, closing her eyes. *Not only do I lack a position, I lack an identity.* "I beg your pardon," she murmured. "I am not usually given to tears. It's just that my head hurts so dreadfully."

"You poor poppet," Mrs. Simpson said. "I will bring up a nice saline wash that will help to soothe the ache. Dr. Hadley is coming by to see you this afternoon and if he decides it will not be harmful perhaps you can have some laudanum for the pain."

Callie nodded. "Thank you," she said. "Could you please draw the draperies? I find the dark easier to bear."

"Oh, my goodness. How thoughtless of me!" With a series of clucks that sounded like those of a distressed mother hen, Mrs. Simpson crossed over to the window and pulled the curtains across it.

Blessed shadow immediately bathed the room and Callie sighed with relief.

"Rest now, my dear. I will be back shortly to bathe your head. We'll have you feeling better in no time."

Callie doubted that. Nothing was going to make her feel better until she knew the truth about herself, and she saw no sign that her memory was going to return anytime soon.

A light tap sounded at the door of Adam's study. "Come in," he called, placing his pen in the quill holder. He'd been busy composing a letter rescinding his previous orders to his solicitor, who would doubtless be puzzled about why Adam had abruptly canceled his lengthy travel plans.

He'd already written to the man whom he'd hired to periodically withdraw funds in his name at various intervals from banks abroad and told him to await further instruction. Silly Miss Magnus really was proving to be a nuisance. At least he'd managed to remove his instructions regarding the running of Stanton during his absence before Nigel had found them. That would have put him in a pretty pickle, having to come up with all sorts of false explanations for Nigel that he was in no mood to give. In any case, he wasn't in the habit of lying to his friends—or at least not to their faces, he amended, given the nature of the deception he was planning on executing. His one real regret was deceiving Nigel, whom he counted as his closest friend.

He looked up as Nigel walked into the study. Not only did Adam consider him a good friend, but he also trusted Nigel implicitly. "Good morning. Thank you for responding so quickly to my summons."

"Not at all. You look back to your old self, but how is the young woman faring today? Has there been any change?" he asked, his face filled with concern, as if prepared for bad news.

"Amazingly enough, she woke in the night."

"What excellent news!" Nigel said, his bright eyes and broad smile reflecting his delight. "I had prayed, but given what the doctor said that night I hardly dared to hope. I am very relieved."

"Yes, yes," Adam said impatiently, not wanting to revisit the subject of relief. "Apparently the good doctor was overly pessimistic. She has a bad headache and that's little wonder, but she seems to be improving. Actually, she is the reason I called for you."

"How may I be of service?" Nigel asked, looking

remarkably enthusiastic, which surprised Adam. Nigel was loyal and dedicated, but those qualities didn't usually extend to unknown women of unknown origins.

"I would be most grateful if you would go to the shipping offices at Folkestone and make inquiries about a Miss Calliope Magnus. She will have been on a clipper ship, probably coming from France, which arrived three evenings ago. She must be on the passenger manifest of one of them, and I would like to know her point of embarkation and whether she was traveling with any companions."

"I'd be happy to, but is Miss Magnus not able to provide you with that information herself?"

"As I said, Miss Magnus woke with a headache and therefore was able to give me little information other than her name and that she'd been traveling from somewhere abroad. Italy was her last place of residence, but I don't know if she actually sailed from there. She might easily have gone by land as far as the coast of France."

"I see. That is not much to go by." Nigel scratched the back of his head. "Still, a name is at least a start."

Adam stroked the tip of his finger slowly across his blotter and gave Nigel a long look, wondering how much to tell him. He might trust his friend implicitly, but at this point he only had vague suspicions to go on. "Yes. I also think that someone must have noticed she didn't disembark with the other passengers, and there would be the matter of her uncollected luggage. I'd like you to discover as much as possible about her—her behavior on the journey, whether she kept to herself, that sort of thing. If you can uncover nothing at Folkestone, then go on to Dover and do the same there. See if anyone has been inquiring for her."

"Hmm. If all goes well and I find any frantic relations or companions, what would you like me to do? Bring them here?"

Adam considered. He'd been mulling that tricky question over for half the night. He liked to be thorough in his affairs, and the last thing he wanted was to end up with another complication. If the girl needed protecting from something or someone, he didn't want to bring the source of the trouble directly to her bedside. On the other hand, a concerned companion or relative, if indeed one existed at all, might be a blessing and could take his unwanted burden off his hands.

"Use your judgment," he said. "I have always found it to be impeccable. I might as well tell you that I am not at all sure the girl is not in some sort of trouble. People generally don't fall off ships for no good reason. She claims she slipped, which might well be the case, but I cannot help but wonder if there's more to the story."

Nigel slowly nodded. "I confess that I had wondered the same. A woman would have to be mad to go out on deck in such weather. That sort of rashness is only asking for trouble."

"She might be rash, but mad? I don't think anything that extreme, although one never knows."

"Do you think she deliberately meant to fall? She would have to be desperate indeed to do such a thing." Nigel fixed Adam with a look that disconcerted him, almost as if Nigel knew what he'd been planning himself. He pushed that thought away as being an impossible one. He'd been very careful not to give any indication of his intentions.

"I have no earthly idea," he said, feeling more uncomfortable by the moment. This was a subject he definitely didn't care to address. "I didn't think so at the time, given the manner in which she fell, all bleats and cries and hand-waving once she'd hit the water. The point is that nothing makes sense. She says she has no relations that she knows of. By her account she is a young woman alone in the world, and yet she's attractive enough and well-spoken—

or at least so I thought from the little I managed to get out of her. I have to assume she is not ill-bred."

"What has that to do with anything? She could have been brought up in a palace and still be on her own if she'd fallen on hard times. Any number of things might have happened to lead her to her present circumstances. Did she tell you *nothing* else? I would be more effective in my inquiries if I had details of any sort."

Adam made a tent out of his fingertips and gazed down at his desk, thinking. "She said she'd come to England to find employment as a lady's companion. I thought she might have been traveling in that capacity with some elderly woman she neglected to mention. On the other hand, she might have been running away from something or someone."

"Do you mean a marriage gone wrong, that sort of thing?"

Adam looked back up at Nigel. "I honestly cannot tell you any more, other than I estimate she is in her early twenties and I believe her to be unmarried. Oh, and her hair is light blond, her eyes brown with dark, heavy lashes, and her figure slight in build. In any case, find out what you can and do whatever you think best."

"I will make every effort. My, what a mystery this is turning out to be. I am positively awash with curiosity." Nigel grinned. "The girl from the sea. What will she turn out to be?"

"I need none of your misguided, not to mention poor, humor," Adam snapped. "Go now. See what you can discover and come directly back. I want a full report as soon as you have something to tell me."


Nigel's step slowed as he strode toward the stables, and he came to a full stop as an extraordinary thought occurred to him. He turned abruptly and looked back at the imposing façade of Stanton Abbey, but his gaze was not trained on the magnificent house, nor the beautifully landscaped lawns and gardens that surrounded it. He barely registered any of it. He focused instead on the look in Adam's eyes when Nigel had left him.

Something was different. Something subtle, almost indefinable, but he could have sworn he'd actually seen a glimmer of real interest, enough anyway for Adam to send him on this investigation.

He doubted Adam even realized that he cared about the fate of this girl, convincing himself that he was simply discharging a duty, but Nigel had a sneaking suspicion that he did care. Perhaps he didn't care very much, but at least he was interested enough to make an effort. He could just as easily have let the girl recover and leave without making any inquiries at all.

It was a beginning. It was a definite beginning. To Nigel's way of thinking, the longer that Miss Magnus stayed around, the better. She would give Adam something to worry about other than his own troubles. Interesting that Adam had described her as attractive . . . he wouldn't have thought Adam would even notice.

Nigel doubted that he'd be so lucky as to come up empty-handed, but given everything Adam had told him, or rather how little, at least he had a fighting chance.

Callie opened one drowsy eye as she heard a light tap and then the sound of her bedroom door opening. No one in this peculiar household seemed to have much regard for her privacy, let alone her need to sleep. People came and went at all hours and she never knew whom or what to expect. Chambermaids, Mrs. Simpson, the doctor, all seemed to pop up on a regular basis and they all wanted her to do something. Eat, submit to a washing, or worst of all, be examined and poked. She was grateful to be alive, but she really did wish that they'd leave her alone to recover.

Her heart froze in her chest as she took in the tall, imposing figure of the man who'd rescued her. Broad in shoulder, solid in chest with narrow hips and long, powerful legs, he was an altogether intimidating man and not someone she wanted to see in the least. Given the stony expression on his face, he wasn't pleased to see her, either.

Callie licked her lips and forced her other eye open, trying hard to focus. "Mr. Carlyle—I mean Lord Vale," she croaked. "Good afternoon, or is it good evening? I don't seem to be able to keep track of time."

"It's evening, Miss Magnum," he said, taking the chair by the bed that had hosted what seemed like an entire parade of people by now. "I spoke with Dr. Hadley before he left. He is encouraged by your progress, although he does think that you might continue to feel weak and ill for some time to come. He said it's the natural outcome of a nasty head injury."

"I am sorry to inconvenience you," she replied, wondering if he deliberately wanted to make her feel like an imposition, or if he was high-handed, rude, and brusque with everyone who crossed his path. "As I told you, I will be on my way as soon as I am able."

"I have every confidence," he said, regarding her lazily with his startling sapphire eyes, eyes she could read nothing at all from. "The question remains what that destination will be. However, you need not trouble yourself over that just yet. You must rest and regain your strength, and you are welcome to stay here until you do."

Completely at a loss, Callie could find absolutely nothing to say. One moment she felt as if he wanted nothing more than to be rid of her, and in the next she felt as if he had all the time in the world to harbor an invalid who had literally dropped into his life. He was an enigma to her, as much as she'd become one to herself. Struggling to find words she could only manage to say, "Thank you. Forgive me. I am very tired."

"Dr. Hadley said he'd given you laudanum to ease your headache. I won't trouble you any further. I wanted only to see that you were resting more comfortably. If there's anything you need, do not hesitate to ask one of the servants." He rose. "Sleep. We will speak again when you're feeling more clearheaded."

As he left, Callie fought back an irrational desire to weep. How could someone who appeared so distant and cold manage to touch her as if he'd laid a hand directly on her heart? Releasing a long breath she closed her eyes, deciding that she could postpone that question until tomorrow. She was clearly addled and not thinking with any sort of logic.

# 3

Pulling the collar of his coat higher up around his neck as protection against the lashing rain, Nigel picked his way around a large puddle, sidestepped a carriage that barreled down the muddy street without any thought to the pedestrians in its way, and safely made his way to the other side. He stopped in front of a small glass-fronted door emblazoned with the names Rothwell and Gilford, Shipping Brokers. The smallest of the Dover firms, it was nothing more than a little pigeonhole surrounded by other equally modest businesses.

Two long days and happily he hadn't come up with a single lead. He'd asked at every shipping office in Folkestone, and no one had heard of a Miss Calliope Magnus. He'd combed every passenger manifest for clipper ships coming from various ports in Northern France and as far away as Italy. The story had been the same in Dover. This was his last stop before heading back to Stanton, and with any luck he'd come up empty-handed here as well. He felt immensely pleased with himself: God was finally giving him a helping hand in the matter of Adam's recovery.

He pushed the door open and a bell tinkled, announcing his presence.

"Good afternoon, sir." A gnomelike gentleman of middle years with a receding hairline and horn-rimmed glasses looked up from a pile of papers. "Another wet day, isn't it? I am Mr. Gilford. How may I be of service to you?"

"Good afternoon," Nigel said. "I wonder if you could tell me if a Miss Calliope Magnus was a passenger on one of your clippers embarking from a port in France, most likely in the north. She would have been due in Dover on the evening of April twentieth."

"I can certainly look, sir. Won't you take a seat?" Gilford reached for another pile of papers and began to flip pages over.

Gratefully sinking into an uncomfortable wooden chair, Nigel prepared to wait. He knew this business could take some time, so he removed his hat, located a handkerchief, mercifully dry, and wiped his face with it. He wanted nothing more than a hot meal and a tankard of ale to take the chill off his bones, and he'd spotted the perfect posting inn on his way across town.

"Let me see, let me see," the little man murmured, running his finger down a list. "Miss Calliope Magnus . . . No, nothing here. The only clipper we had in that evening was the *Aurora,* coming from Calais. We were that relieved when she arrived safely, given the storm that had blown up." He chuckled. "We had quite a few passengers who were green around the gills when they came down the plank, I can tell you. No, definitely no Miss Magnus here."

"I see," Nigel said, ridiculously pleased at this piece of good fortune. Still, he really ought to ask about unattended luggage. "Did you by any chance have any trunks or valises taken off the *Aurora* that went unclaimed?"

Mr. Gilford frowned. "Unclaimed baggage? No . . . that is to say that we did have three trunks and two cases which arrived without a passenger, but they were collected. Apparently the young lady in question had missed the sailing. Her fiancé was mightily put out, which I could understand." He shook his head. "Imagine being so flighty as to miss a booked passage, not that it doesn't happen. We often get relatives in our office, wringing their hands and making a great to-do. Of course in this business one must be tactful. I remember one instance when—"

Nigel, not interested in hearing the man's reminiscences, abruptly cut him off. He leaned forward, his muscles tight with foreboding. "What was the name of the young lady?"

"Let me see, let me see." Gilford stabbed his finger at the list. "Yes, here it is. Miss Callista Melbourne. Pretty young thing, too. Her fiancé had a sketch of her that he brandished around. He was in quite a temper, quite a temper. I almost felt sorry for the girl, not that it's any of my business."

Nigel blew out a breath. Calliope, Callista. Close enough, unfortunately. "I see. Do you recall the name of her fiancé, by any chance?"

"Yes, indeed I do." Gilford grimaced. "I'm not likely to forget that one. A Mr. Carlyle, Mr. Harold Carlyle of Fawn Hill, outside Smeeth."

Nigel started. *Harold?* Not Adam's ghastly cousin? He could scarcely believe his ears or the way his luck had abruptly turned. "No," he said quickly, although his head reeled with shock. "Those wouldn't be the people I was looking for." He stood and put his hat back on. "Thank you so much for your trouble."

"Not at all. I hope you find your Miss Magnus. Is she a relative?" Behind his spectacles Gilford's eyes sparkled with curiosity.

"No relative of mine," Nigel said shortly. "Good day, Mr. Gilford." He quickly left, the tinkling of the bell ringing as he shut the door behind him.

Twenty minutes later, sitting in front of a steaming steak-and-kidney pie and the tankard of ale he'd been pining for, Nigel pondered what to do. Why, if there had to be a blasted fiancé, did he of *all* people have to be the horrible Harold?

Harold, who had been a torment to Adam for as long as Nigel could remember, Harold, who was so full of his own imagined importance that it was a wonder he hadn't blown up like an overinflated balloon long before—How on earth had Harold managed to persuade anyone to marry him?

He probably hadn't. No doubt the girl had been co-erced against her will. Little wonder she had chosen to jump off the ship into the heaving sea.

Taking a long drink from his tankard, Nigel considered his options, none of them particularly appealing. He could tell Adam everything he'd just discovered and put Adam in the unenviable position of sending Miss Magnus—or rather Miss Melbourne—straight to Fawn Hill where she would be forever tortured by Harold and his equally despicable mother, Lady Geoffrey. That would be the sane and sensible thing to do, but Nigel was feeling neither sane nor sensible.

If Harold's father were still alive, Nigel might have felt a little better about the situation, since Lord Geoffrey hadn't been a truly wicked man, just terribly browbeaten by his wife, utterly myopic about the shortcomings of his son, and completely hopeless with finances—his and others', as

Adam had bitterly learned on reaching his majority. But Lord Geoffrey had died four months before, and he probably wouldn't have been any use to Miss Melbourne anyway. Poor Miss Melbourne would find no support at all.

Nigel played with a forkful of his pie, his appetite having deserted him. He wondered if she might try to take her life again if she knew that she'd been found out and was still going to be sent to marry a man she clearly didn't want to have anything to do with.

He supposed he could always go to Miss Melbourne directly and tell her that he knew the truth about her, but would leave it up to her to decide what to tell Adam.

Too complicated, he decided, and probably far too distressing for a woman in her fragile health and precarious emotional state. No, that was a very bad idea, but it would be equally as bad if Adam did decide to wash his hands of her.

Which he probably would, given his own precarious emotional state. He hadn't looked *that* concerned. Miss Melbourne would probably find something else to fling herself off of, leaving Adam with yet another death on his conscience, as if two weren't already enough.

Wonderful, Nigel thought, looking around at the smoke-filled room as if he might find an answer there. He had two potentially suicidal people on his hands and no idea what to do with either of them. The way he saw it, they might be able to help each other if they had a little time.

He slowly smiled as the perfect solution occurred to him. Time . . . at least he could give them that. Why not? It was what he'd been hoping for, after all. He would simply tell Adam that he'd been unable to discover anything about his Miss Magnus. That at least was true. He didn't like the idea of lying to Adam, but it wouldn't be a lie, exactly, more an error of omission.

Eventually the truth would come out, but with any luck by that time Adam might not be in the frame of mind to consign Callista Melbourne to Harold's care, regardless of their engagement.

Suddenly feeling much better, he wolfed down the rest of his steak-and-kidney pie, drained his tankard, and went back out into the pouring rain to fetch his carriage.

Adam paced up and down his study, wondering what could possibly be taking Nigel so long. He glanced up at the grandfather clock, its steady ticking annoyingly loud. Eight minutes past six, four minutes later than the last time he'd looked.

Striding over to the window, he peered out into the lashing rain that showed no sign of stopping. Maybe Nigel had become mired in the mud, he decided, but whatever the case, he wished the man would get on with it. Impatience burned at him. He was not accustomed to being so thoroughly in the dark, and silly Miss Magnus had been absolutely no help, sleeping the days and nights away as if she hadn't a care in the world. He had half a mind to toss the bottle of laudanum out the window and shake her to her senses, if she had any. He doubted it, given the habit she had of gazing at him blankly with those big brown eyes, like a fawn that had lost its mother.

A knock sounded at the door and he spun around. "Come in," he called with relief, thinking Nigel must have driven around the back way, since he hadn't seen the carriage coming up the drive.

The door opened and he scowled when he saw it was only Mrs. Simpson.

"I brought you some claret and sandwiches, my lord,"

she said, coming in with a tray and placing it on the low table in front of the sofa. "You haven't eaten a thing since luncheon and I thought you must be hungry. This should tide you over until dinner. Cook has made a nice saddle of lamb with spring vegetables and roast potatoes."

"Thank you," he said, forcing civility into his voice. "How is our patient this evening?"

"I am happy to report that Miss Magnus is somewhat improved," she said, seemingly oblivious to his foul mood. "She sat up for a full hour and ate a decent meal for the first time. I believe the pain in her head is easing, although the poor dear is still weak as a babe. At least the fever is finally gone, thank heaven. I was that worried she'd develop congestion of the lungs." She poured a glass of wine from the decanter on the tray and set it next to the plate.

"Is she still taking the laudanum?" he asked, thinking that would be the biggest improvement of all.

"She is, my lord, although in a reduced dosage now. Perhaps by tomorrow she won't need it at all, and wouldn't that be a blessing?"

The blessing would be if Miss Calliope Magnus would pull herself together, give a full accounting of herself, and then take herself off as quickly as possible, he thought sourly. "Very good, Mrs. Simpson. You may leave me now. Oh, and when Mr. Dryden returns have Gettis send him directly in."

As soon as the door closed behind her, Adam sank down on the sofa and cleaned the plate of sandwiches. He hadn't realized how hungry he was. He couldn't remember the last time he'd had such a voracious appetite as he'd had the last few days. It was probably a result of all the strenuous exercise he'd taken rowing halfway to France and back. He still didn't understand how he'd managed to find the strength to haul the girl into the boat and get them both safely back to shore, any more than he understood why the rowboat hadn't foundered in the fury of the storm.

And then there was the matter of the gull, he thought, frowning. What bird in its right mind would fly that distance against a raging wind, and then, instead of resting once it had reached land, turn right back around and go straight out into the storm again? That alone defied reason.

He picked up his glass of wine and turned the stem around in his fingers, watching the deep red of the claret sparkle in the facets of the cut crystal like so many rubies. Well, never mind why, he decided. It had happened and that was that. He needed to focus on the consequence, which at that moment resided upstairs in the best guest bedroom.

He had so many questions and next to no answers. Thinking of that, he couldn't imagine what had become of Nigel. Darkness was drawing down and the roads could be treacherous in this weather. Worry began to replace his impatience.

Putting the glass down, he quickly rose, moving back to the window. There was still no sign of the carriage. If Nigel had met with an accident he'd never forgive himself. Images of Nigel lying injured on the side of the road played through his mind and he couldn't make them go away. He'd just decided to call for a carriage and go out to look for him when he heard the door open.

"Nigel!" he exclaimed, weak with relief to see his friend standing in the doorway, looking half drowned but all in one piece. "Where the devil have you been?"

"To London, to London to visit the queen," Nigel replied with his usual grin.

"Don't start playing the fool with me," Adam snapped. "I've been half out of my mind with worry."

"No need, Adam. I'm a big boy. The roads were not at

their best, and I had to take a detour around Sandgate where a section had been washed out. It was a nuisance, but nothing insurmountable."

"Sit down, then. Have some wine to warm you and tell me what you discovered." Adam fetched a glass from the sideboard and filled it, handing it to Nigel, who downed the contents in two swallows.

"Better," Nigel said, sinking into an armchair as Adam brought the decanter over and refilled his glass. "Lord, but that was a beastly journey. I nearly stopped in Folkestone, but I reckoned you'd be on pins and needles so I decided to forge ahead."

*"And?"* Adam said, his impatience returning now that he knew Nigel was safe. "What did you discover?"

"I'm sorry, Adam. I discovered absolutely nothing about Miss Magnus. Her name wasn't on a single passenger manifest and no one recalled seeing anyone of her description. I checked every single shipping firm and broker in both Folkestone and Dover."

"Nothing?" Adam said with disbelief. "How can that be? We know she was on the ship. She can't have spirited herself on board anonymously. Even if she did manage it somehow, what reason would she have?"

"You'd have to ask her that," Nigel said mildly. "How is she, by the by?"

"Better, Mrs. Simpson says. She's been playing Sleeping Beauty for the most part since you left. See here, Nigel, there must be sense in this somewhere. God knows I haven't managed to get any from Miss Magnus."

"There's plenty of time for that," Nigel said. "She's not going anywhere, and neither are we. Best to let her recover in peace before peppering her with a lot of awkward questions, don't you think?"

"What I think is that this situation becomes more and more peculiar. Either she's lying through her teeth or she's a complete idiot." Adam pushed one hand through his hair, frustrated with the girl for creating such difficulties and with himself for not being able to solve them. "Whichever the case, I have a nightmare on my hands. What am I supposed to do with her, Nigel?"

"I'm sure you'll work something out. You did see fit to rescue her, after all. Maybe a little more rescuing would be in order."

Adam glared at him. "It is not my mission in life to rescue ridiculous young women who don't have the good sense to keep their affairs in order, never mind keeping their feet on solid ground."

Nigel took a sip of wine and glanced up at Adam. "What other option do you have? Do you plan to throw her out into the street with no clothes, no money, and nowhere to go?"

Adam just shook his head. "I'm damned if I know. It's tempting, though, mightily tempting."

"Now that's the Adam I know and love," Nigel said, rubbing his earlobe. "You're absolutely right; to hell with Miss Magnus. Why should you exert yourself in any way over her welfare? You've done enough, that's what I say. Out with her the minute she can stand on her own two feet."

Adam shot him a filthy look. "If you're suddenly going to become holier-than-thou, why don't *you* take her on? I'm not the one with a need to save lost souls."

Nigel raised one eyebrow. "Then why *did* you bother to save her? You could have spared yourself a great deal of trouble. It would have been easy enough to let her sink."

In that moment Adam could happily have throttled his dearest friend, but he settled for clenching his fists. He drew a deep breath and slowly released it, counting to ten. "I saved her," he said, measuring his words carefully, for he was damned if he was going to let Nigel goad him any further, "because it was my duty as a gentleman. You would have done the same. I did not, however, save her because I wanted yet another responsibility in my already complicated life."

"Fair enough, but then life never does deal us what we expect. It simply happens, Adam, as you know full well. All we can do is roll with the punches and do our best. Here endeth the lesson." He smiled. "Maybe I missed my calling. I rather like the pulpit."

As much as Adam didn't want to listen, he had to concede that Nigel had a point. He couldn't help what had happened. All he could do was to fix the situation as best he could. The sooner he did that, the sooner he could put an end to his miserable existence. He shrugged a shoulder and tried to look nonchalant. "How do you suggest I proceed?"

"Let me see . . ." Nigel leaned back in his chair and assumed a faraway expression. "I might start by gaining Miss Magnus's trust. I don't think that browbeating her will get you very far, especially if she's been frightened by something or someone." He scratched his temple. "Maybe you should think of her as a skittish filly. You've always been exceeding talented in gentling skittish horses, thereby getting the best performance from them. Perhaps if you take the same approach in this case you might realize the same results. Some time and patience might be required, but you're familiar enough with the technique."

Adam snorted. "Miss Magnus in no way resembles a spirited filly," he said. "Indeed, she's exhibited no spirit at all." Adam thought again of those blank eyes—well, maybe not entirely blank; more confused, if he was to be entirely fair.

"She suffered a severe head injury, Adam, not to mention nearly drowning. What do you expect? Perhaps when she recovers she might show a bit more vinegar, especially if you persist in grilling her beyond her ability to answer."

"I'm hungry," Adam said in reply, tired of the subject and not wanting to examine his conscience any more closely. "You must be famished. Mrs. Simpson informs me that Cook has prepared a basic but satisfying meal. Why don't you go clean up and join me in an hour?"

Nigel's face reflected his surprise, which Adam tried hard not to notice. He knew full well that he'd badly neglected his friend, and he owed him something for his efforts. He might not have the chance to show his deep regard for Nigel that much longer; he should use the time remaining to him wisely. "I'd be glad for the company," he added lightly. "I've grown exceeding tired of my own."

"I'd be delighted," Nigel said easily enough, letting the moment slide by.

"Good. But no more talk of Miss Magnus. I'd like to enjoy my dinner."

When Nigel had gone, Adam slumped into the chair behind his desk and put his head in his hands, incredibly weary.

If it wasn't for his unwanted obligation to silly Miss Magnus he'd happily have put a gun to his head and ended it there and then, Harold be damned.

# 4

ood morning, Miss Magnus, and a fine morning it is. The rain has stopped and the sun has come out." Mrs. Simpson bustled around the room in her usual businesslike fashion. Callie cautiously opened her eyes as Mrs. Simpson drew back the draperies.

For the first time since she'd regained consciousness she had no stabbing pain in her head, only a dull throb, and even that was slight. Her relief was infinite. She had loathed taking the laudanum which made her feel as if she were swimming underwater, but at least that was better than the horrible ache.

"Good morning," she said, pushing herself upright in the bed. Even that movement felt reasonably comfortable.

"How are you feeling this morning?" Mrs. Simpson asked, peering at her as if she were an interesting physical specimen.

"Much better, thank you," Callie said, and Mrs. Simpson clucked approvingly.

"I am so pleased to hear it, and I know his lordship will be delighted. He's been that concerned about you, and little wonder. Indeed, the entire household has been in a state of worry over your health."

"I—I'm sorry," Callie said. "I didn't mean to cause anyone distress."

"Never you mind that. What's important is that you are recovering nicely. I thought that after breakfast you might like a nice bath if you're feeling well enough. A long hot soak would do you the world of good." She patted Callie's hand and beamed, a mother hen pleased with her chick's progress.

Amused, Callie thought that if Mrs. Simpson had been a hen, she would have been a fine, plump, well-feathered bantam. "That sounds wonderful," Callie said with genuine pleasure. She couldn't remember the last time she'd had a proper bath—Callie caught herself mid-thought. How could she possibly remember something as mundane as her last bath when she couldn't remember anything else? Her head might have ceased to throb, but it was as empty as ever, she realized with dismay.

"Jane will be bringing up a tray for you in just a few minutes with eggs, some lovely rashers of bacon, sausages, toast and jam, all from Stanton's home farm. We're very proud of our produce. Indeed, we sell it all over the countryside."

"Jane?" Callie asked in confusion, sorting through this maze of information and wondering if she'd forgotten something else she should have known.

"Jane is one of the chambermaids, my dear, and a nice, sensible girl. She will be attending to your needs now that you don't need so much nursing. We've organized some clothes for you, modest as they are, until such a time as the dressmaker can arrange a proper wardrobe. I thought you might like to dress after your bath and sit for a time by the window. Would you like that, my dear, or would you find it too taxing?"

"Oh, no, not at all," Callie said. She might feel weak, but having been cooped up in bed for seven days had been tedious, despite how ill she'd been. "I'd like that very much."

"That's a good girl. His lordship would like to visit with you later this morning and he thought you might be more comfortable receiving him if you were up and dressed."

"How thoughtful of Lord Vale," Callie said, her pleasure instantly vanishing. A visit indeed. What he wanted was to interrogate her. He would grill her with questions that she couldn't answer, she would have to bluff as best she could, and the whole thing would end in disaster. Her next place of residence would be Bedlam.

She supposed she could always plead the return of her headache, but then she'd probably be forced to take the laudanum again and that she really couldn't bear. She couldn't go through life in a drugged stupor just because she didn't want to face Lord Vale. She'd just have to keep a level head and be creative. There was nothing else to be done.

Three hours later, having eaten, bathed, and dressed, Callie sat in an armchair in an agony of anticipation. She stared out of the window overlooking a bright green lawn that seemed to run forever until it reached a line of trees far to the east. A river cut through the middle of the lawn, a stone bridge spanning its width. Lush plantings of flowers and shrubs spread out in eye-pleasing arrangements. Lord Vale clearly cared well for his estate, and he had a good eye for color and symmetry—or if not he, then someone he'd hired to do the planning for him.

She begrudgingly had to give him credit, at least for good taste.

Callie started as the dreaded knock sounded at the door. "Please come in," she said in a small voice that sounded more like a squeak. Her heart began to pound furiously in her chest and her mouth went dry as the door opened and her waking nightmare appeared.

She couldn't help staring. Lord Vale in the full light of day was even more imposing than she'd remembered. Tall and magnificently built, he exuded a powerful masculinity with his saturnine dark looks and those startling blue eyes—eyes he had trained on her like a gun on a helpless animal.

"Good day, Miss Magnus," he said. She didn't think it quite right that someone so formidable should have such a rich, melodious voice.

She swallowed hard. "Good day, Lord Vale," she said, trying to keep her own voice steady. "How kind of you to come to see me." That was an absurd comment if ever there was one. Kindness had nothing to do with it, and they both knew it.

"Not at all," he replied as if echoing her thought. "I am very pleased to hear that you are feeling better. Mrs. Simpson has been bringing me constant reports of your progress."

Callie licked her bottom lip with the tip of her tongue. *Cat and mouse,* she thought. She had no doubt as to who was the cat in this game. She'd better seize the advantage before he pounced thoroughly and completely and gobbled her up alive. "Lord Vale...I am very grateful for everything you've done for me. I know I've been a great deal of trouble and I apologize for that."

"There's no need for apologies, Miss Magnus. I am at your disposal for as long as necessary."

"I thank you," she said, "but I think that now I am

feeling so much improved I must start making plans for the future. As I told you—"

"As you told me," he cut in smoothly, "you have no concrete plans other than trying to find a post as a lady's companion. That can wait. May I sit down?"

"Oh . . . Oh yes, of course," she said, nonplussed. "Please do."

He pulled up a straight-backed chair and faced it toward her before taking his seat. She couldn't help but notice the well-defined muscles of his thighs that strained against the material of his trousers. Blushing, she looked away.

"I think, Miss Magnus, that before you start organizing your future, you would be better served by focusing on the present. You still have a period of recovery ahead, so we might as well take full advantage of the time remaining to you here at Stanton."

"I—I don't understand," she stammered. She'd been under the impression that he couldn't wait to wash his hands of her.

"No, of course you don't. Let me make myself clear." He leaned slightly forward, which unnerved her even more. "I see no reason why we shouldn't make a thorough search for your relatives. You must have some, and with the means I have at my disposal, I feel confident that we can turn up someone who might be willing to help you."

"No!" she cried. "I mean, that won't be necessary," she said in a more level voice. The last thing in the world she needed was a futile search for relatives that didn't exist—at least not under the imaginary name of Magnus. Any inquiry at all in that direction would expose her for exactly what she was—a fraud.

"I don't understand you," Adam replied. "Do you not want to find your relatives? Surely one of them would be willing to take you in and provide you with a life far more comfortable than that of a paid companion."

"No—no, I think I would be better off living a life of independence rather than relying on the kindness of people who have no emotional connection to me, for that would be a terrible obligation to them and to me. I am perfectly content with the life of a paid companion, Lord Vale, really I am." This interview was *not* going as she had planned.

"Miss Magnus, I wonder if you have any idea what the life of a paid companion entails. You would be at someone's beck and call day and night. You would not have an iota of independence, let alone any social standing." He frowned. "Why will you not at least let me try to help you?"

"You have done enough already," she said, wanting to cry with frustration. "I do not wish to be beholden to you any more than I already am, or to anyone else for that matter."

"That I can understand. But let us examine the practicalities of your situation."

He leaned back again and she breathed a sigh of relief at the widened distance between them. There was something about Lord Vale that made her feel as if her lungs badly needed air.

"The practicalities of my situation are perfectly clear to me, Lord Vale. I am a woman on my own who needs means to support herself. I am more than capable of discovering those means for myself."

"May I make so bold as to ask you why you are so determined to be stubborn on this matter when I have offered to help you in any way that I can?" He folded his arms across his broad chest and regarded her with curiosity. "Most women in your circumstances would be happy for a helping hand, and yet you refuse anything but my temporary hospitality. I find your attitude difficult to fathom, although I will admit that I admire your tenacity on the matter of your independence. You are a most unusual woman, Miss Magnus. I cannot help but wonder if you have something to hide."

Callie paled and her head began to pound with an agonizing fury. "I have nothing to hide, my lord, nothing at all," she said, clutching her hands on the arms of her chair until her knuckles went white. "I have told you everything that is necessary for you to know. Beyond that, this is my business alone."

Before she knew it, he'd jumped to his feet and gathered her up in his arms. Carrying her over to the bed, he gently laid her down. "Forgive me," he said softly, pulling a blanket over her. "I have thoughtlessly overtaxed your strength. Please don't concern yourself with anything but recovering your health. Everything else can wait, Callie. Don't trouble yourself any further—you have nothing to fear. You are safe here." He smoothed a hand over her hair. "Sleep now if you can. Dr. Hadley will be in later to see you."

Callie managed to nod, then gratefully closed her eyes.

"Would you like some laudanum to ease the pain?" he asked, in that deep, gentle voice.

"No . . . no, thank you," she murmured. "I don't like it."

"Good girl. Nasty stuff, laudanum. I took it once when I broke my arm as a boy and it had to be set. I vowed never to let myself be dosed again. There's nothing worse than not being able to keep one's thoughts together."

*How right you are,* Callie thought. She vaguely registered the draperies being drawn against the light and the relief of the cool darkness that surrounded her.

As she drifted off to sleep she pondered the contradictions in Adam Carlyle's character. In one moment he could be cool and calculating, and in the next, kind and caring. She really didn't understand him at all.

"I tell you, Nigel, I don't understand the girl at all," Adam said, swinging a leg over his gelding and settling in the saddle. The bridge on the road to town had been flooded by the storm and he wanted to see what would be needed in the way of repairs. "Today I saw a completely different side to her. She's stubborn beyond belief, especially where the matter of her independence is concerned. I have to admire her pluck, as foolish as it is under these circumstances—I can't think of another woman I know who would turn down all offers of help, most especially from someone of my station." He turned the gelding's head around and waited for Nigel to finish adjusting his stirrups. "The usual silly miss would have jumped at the opportunity to take what she could, but not this one. She didn't want a thing from me other than to be allowed to recover and go on her way without interference."

"She gave you no reason?" Nigel asked, coming up next to Adam. They left the stable yard at a comfortable walk.

Adam shrugged. "She told me in no uncertain terms to mind my own business. That's as far as I got before she turned white as a ghost and I had to put her to bed."

Nigel glanced over at him. "I sincerely hope you didn't browbeat the poor girl."

"Browbeat her?" Adam said with indignation. "I was perfectly civil. I went so far as to put myself at her disposal. Her *disposal!* I can't think what came over me."

He didn't add that he'd been completely taken aback when he'd entered the room and seen Miss Calliope

Magnus sitting by the window, her hair washed and simply arranged, the sun shining on it so that it appeared the color of spun moonlight. A faint pink tinge colored her pale cheeks, her skin as delicate as porcelain. He hadn't realized until that moment that she was so lovely. He supposed he hadn't expected to see her looking so—so normal. She'd almost behaved in a normal fashion as well. Almost. He still couldn't believe that she'd dismissed him so completely. He was not accustomed to being dismissed, and the feeling didn't sit comfortably.

"I think you were very good to have offered your help," Nigel said. "I cannot think of any rule that mandates she accept it, though."

"The rule of common sense, which is a quality entirely lacking in Miss Magnus," Adam retorted. "I refuse to let her march out of this house into a life which would make anyone miserable when I can do something about it." He urged his gelding into a trot and Nigel did the same.

"I don't think you have any choice, Adam. She's not your ward. You have no legal say over what she decides to do, as admirable as your concern is." Nigel hesitated for a moment. "Tell me, what has changed your mind? Yesterday you were in a hurry to be rid of her."

Adam didn't have a good answer. He didn't really know himself. Mulling the question over, he decided that his reason had something to do with not leaving any unfinished business behind when he went, but he couldn't tell Nigel that. "I thought about what you said," he eventually replied. "I went to all that trouble to rescue her, so I might as well go to the trouble of seeing her safely settled. She doesn't know the first thing about life in England, how things are done here. She has some featherbrained notion that life as a lady's companion will give her independence.

I tried to explain the reality of the situation, but did she listen? Of course she didn't."

Scanning the upcoming bridge with a practiced eye, he decided the damage wasn't as bad as he'd feared, and that came as a relief. Two trees had come down and some cleaning up would be required to remove the mud and debris. Miss Magnus's affairs were not going to be so easy to sort out. "I don't know, Nigel. I still think she's hiding something, but for the life of me, I can't think what it is. I intend to get to the bottom of the mystery, though."

"All in good time," Nigel said. "As I said, you must gain her trust. She has no one else now but you to depend on, and from what you said, she's not the sort of woman who falls apart at the drop of a hat. If you're right about her hiding something, she must have good reason for keeping her own counsel." He pulled his horse to a halt and surveyed the bridge. "Not so bad. The foundation will need some shoring up, but all in all I'd say we were lucky. It's a shame, though. I'm always sorry when we lose elms. They're such a noble tree."

"I begin to believe that you're a sentimentalist," Adam said, dismounting and slogging his way through the mud. "Have Kettridge organize a team to clear this mess away and tell him in future not to be such an alarmist. I want to get back to the house and change my clothes. Dr. Hadley is due soon and I'd like to have a word with him." He looked down at his soggy boots with a grimace. "Plimpton will not be happy with what I've done to his precious leather, but that's the least of my worries."

"I agree," Nigel said in an enigmatic fashion. "You have many other matters to contend with. The foundation will hold, Adam. The foundation will hold."

————

"Where *can* that girl be, Harold? It's been a full week now and still not a word from her!" Mildred Carlyle, who preferred even her closest friends to address her as Lady Geoffrey, glared at her son as if he was supposed to produce Callista Melbourne like a rabbit out of a hat.

"I have no idea, Mama," he said, fed up with the entire subject. His mother had been harping unceasingly for seven days. "I'm not to blame for her missing her ship. She's bound to write and let us know when she's rebooked her passage. After all, we have all her belongings. She can't go long without those." He turned the page of his newspaper and began to study the racing forms.

"But what do you *think,* Harold?" Mildred marched across the room and stood in front of him, her hands planted on her bony hips. "I would be most obliged if you'd look at me when I speak to you. Really, you can be most irritating. Your future is at stake and all you can do is bury your nose in the papers."

Harold didn't respond, busily making a mental list of the horses he planned to back. It was a good thing his mother didn't know about the tidy nest egg he'd made by borrowing from the household accounts for the last five years.

"Pay attention, boy!" Mildred swatted Harold's knee with her fan. "If you want to do something useful, you can find a way to open those trunks. Maybe there's a clue inside as to where she's gone. I couldn't find a single thing inside her valises except hopelessly outdated clothing—one would think her father would have spent some of his fortune on attiring the girl correctly—but perhaps the trunks contain something more fitting for an affianced girl." She tapped her finger against the corner of her cheek. "At the very least there might be a letter."

Harold lowered the newspaper and glared back at his

mother. "I don't think Miss Melbourne would have left a letter inside a trunk explaining that she was planning on missing her sailing. She probably decided to spend a little extra time in Paris or some such place and simply forgot to inform us."

"That's what I meant, you fool, a letter from someone whom she might have stopped off to visit. It's the name and address I want." Mildred tightly pursed her lips. "If your father was still alive, he'd do as I told him. He wouldn't just sit there like a useless bump on a log. Honestly, Harold, anyone would think you didn't want the girl's fortune. I'm depending on it, you know—we could buy a large property far more suitable to our position and live extremely comfortably. My nerves are taxed from scrimping and saving."

"Yes, Mama," Harold said obediently, wishing she would cease her whining. What did she expect him to do? Go haring off to Europe to try to find the girl? "As I said, she'll show up sooner or later and then I can conclude matters. I can't marry her for another two months as it is, not until my mourning period is finished. Don't trouble yourself so. Once we're married you'll have everything you want."

"Everything I *should* have had. If your father had been a more practical man and pursued his business affairs with diligence, we wouldn't be in this predicament. How he managed to lose his entire inheritance I'll never know."

"If Adam had been a gentleman and made a proper settlement on us in return for all we did for him, we wouldn't be in this predicament, either. As it is, I am forced to marry a girl who Papa said was raised with none of the usual social graces." He regarded his mother sourly. "I am making an enormous sacrifice, Mama. Miss Melbourne will probably turn out to be an embarrassment to me and all my friends."

Mildred smoothed down the front of her black bombazine dress and picked an imagined speck of lint from it.

"I should think that you'd be a little more grateful, Harold." She spoke petulantly. "Your father and I came up with the perfect solution to put us back in funds and you only complain. The girl can be managed once I get my hands on her. All you have to do is to bring her to the point, and I expect you to put some serious effort into courting her, for she is under no legal obligation to marry you. All we have is an agreement between your father and hers that the match would suit."

"I do *know* that, Mama," Harold said impatiently.

"Yes, but she might not," Mildred replied equally impatiently. "I am hoping that she believes everything to be contracted already, and if she doesn't, I shall lead her in that direction should she show any signs of balking—*which* she should not, *if* you do your job properly."

"Yes, Mama," Harold said, wishing his mother would stop kicking up such a dust. He knew exactly what he had to do, although the very thought of having to court an ill-behaved nobody from the back of beyond exhausted him. At least the girl would be so grateful that he was gracious enough to overlook her advanced age and lack of manners that she wouldn't put up any resistance to his suit.

"Just you keep that in mind. After you're married you can do whatever you please." She sniffed. "I am the one who will be saddled with her, but I have never shirked my duty."

"No, Mama," Harold said, wondering if it was coming up to teatime. He fancied crumpets and cream and some of those nice seed cakes.

"Look at all those years I raised your ungrateful cousin and never complained, not even when it was your father who should have had the marquessate. If Adam had died at birth as the doctor said he was supposed to, my life would have been entirely different—and yours. You would have been the marquess these last four months. It's all Adam's fault."

"Yes, Mama," Harold said, for once agreeing with her. He might not agree with her on many things, but when it came to Adam, they were of like mind. They both loathed the ground he walked on. Adam Carlyle had been nothing but a thorn in his side for as long as he could remember.

"I suppose it's still not too late," his mother said, perching on the edge of a delicate Louis Quinze chair and fanning her scrawny bosom. "Adam might meet with some misfortune. Bad luck runs in that family: first Anna died giving life to the brat, then Leon succumbed to influenza only nine years later, and just look what happened to Adam's wife and son, if that doesn't prove me right."

"Too bad Adam wasn't in the woods that day," Harold said with a sneer. "He might have met with the same unfortunate fate."

"He might also have prevented it, Harold," Mildred pointed out. "At least Ian's death put us back in direct line of succession. I cannot tell you how perturbed I was when Adam married that ridiculous woman and produced a son, of all annoying things to do. Had I known Ian wouldn't live to see his fifth birthday, I could have spared myself a great deal of unhappiness. Well. It just goes to show that one never knows when disaster will strike. Perhaps Adam won't reach his thirty-fourth."

"One never knows," Henry said, not wanting to discuss the subject any further. Talking about Adam always gave him indigestion, and he didn't want to unsettle his stomach before his tea.

5

What I'd like to know, Dr. Hadley, is how long you anticipate Miss Magnus will be incapacitated by these headaches?" Adam almost hoped that the doctor would tell him weeks, not because he wished a splitting headache on anyone, Calliope Magnus included, but because he was more determined than ever to get to the bottom of her story and he knew he was going to need time.

"I regret that I cannot say with any certainty, Lord Vale. Cases like these can be most unpredictable. It has been my experience, however, that with severe head injuries these episodes can continue for some time. The best one can do is to protect the patient from stressful situations, as those seem to bring on an attack."

"Stressful situations," Adam said. "You mean anything that might cause emotional upset?" He stood and walked over to the window, his back to the study, trying to suppress a stab of guilt.

"Yes. Emotional upset of any kind is most detrimental. Peace and quiet, fresh air, good, wholesome food, and moderate exercise are my recommendations for Miss Magnus's well-being."

"I see . . ." Adam said, thinking that the good doctor might as well be tying his hands behind his back. He turned around. "What you mean is that Miss Magnus should not be pressured to speak about herself."

"Most definitely not at this time. Er, Lord Vale, may I ask you a question regarding Miss Magnus?" The doctor folded his fingers together and regarded Adam speculatively.

"I see no reason why you shouldn't," Adam said. "Whether I can answer is another matter."

"How much do you know about the young lady? I realize that you knew nothing of her when you rescued her, but what has she told you about herself since then?"

"Precious little," Adam said. "If I may be frank with you, Doctor, I believe that she might have fallen into unfortunate circumstances. She is not inclined to speak of those circumstances—if indeed I am correct in my supposition. She avoids any reference to her previous life and has no clear plans for her future."

"Yes . . . yes, that would make sense, if I am correct. Let me propose a theory to you, for I have observed a certain reticence in the woman myself. I believe I might have an idea as to why she is so vague about her life before her accident."

"By all means," Adam said, his curiosity sharply aroused. "I haven't been able to make head or tail of her story from the start."

"Let me begin by saying that instances like these are uncommon but not unheard of. Oh, yes, thank you," he said, as Adam poured him a glass of sherry and handed it to him. "Have you heard of the condition called amnesia? It is one in which the sufferer loses all memory predating a traumatic incident, and is usually incurred by a blow to the head."

Adam stared at him. "In plain language, do you mean to say she has no idea who she is?"

"That is my hypothesis. I have never personally come across a case like this before, but Miss Magnus does exhibit some of the symptoms." He scratched his head. "I wondered about her evasiveness concerning simple questions, so I read a few previously reported histories. I believe the shock to her brain may have erased any memory of her past."

"Good Lord," Adam said, stupefied. That idea had never occurred to him. "Does this last forever or is it a passing condition?" He took the chair facing the doctor and regarded him intently.

"In some instances the memory returns," the doctor said. "In others it is gone forever. The patient has no choice but to start afresh. One case I recall involved a woman who had been happily married with three children and had no recognition of any of them after a bad fall she'd taken. Her husband had to start from the very beginning, introducing her to her family as if she were a complete stranger."

"Did she ever recover her memory?" Adam asked, appalled by the potential implications of Callie's case.

"Not that I am aware of. Nevertheless, she managed to carry on and eventually became comfortable with her family. Mind you, I'm merely speculating about whether Miss Magnus is suffering from the same affliction."

Cold comfort, Adam thought. "If she is suffering from loss of memory, why hasn't she just come out and said it? I cannot see any purpose served by her withholding the truth."

"You must consider this from her position, Lord Vale,"

the doctor said as if he was speaking to a small and rather dim young child. "She would be terrified, do you not think? Imagine not knowing who you were or where you belonged. She has no possessions to give her any clue as to her identity. All she would know is that she was traveling to England for some reason, but no family has stepped forward to claim her, have they?"

"No...I sent Mr. Dryden to inquire at the ports and he came back with no information at all. That would explain why no passage had been booked under her name. She must have made the name up." Adam pushed a hand through his hair, wondering what on earth he was supposed to do now. "How does one generally proceed in these instances? Should I ask her outright?" That would be a fine thing—he could just imagine the conversation: *Tell me, Miss Magnus, if that is indeed your name, have you misplaced your past?*

Dr. Hadley considered. "If I were you, I think I might leave the inquiries for the moment. As I said, any stress or pressure will only bring on one of her headaches and that will get you nowhere. Perhaps when she is more fully recovered you can ask her what you wish—but do keep in mind that my suspicion might be no more than that: The girl might very well be who she said she is and is simply trying to conceal some misfortune. Whatever the truth might be, Miss Magnus is not physically able to deal with distressing questions just yet."

"Very well, Doctor. I will do as you ask." Adam wasn't happy about the man's request, but he saw the sense in it. "I am to indulge her for the moment, is that it?"

"That is it exactly. Let her take the lead. If she has anything she wants to tell you she will. Other than that, I would let her be."

Dr. Hadley finished his sherry and went on to see his

next patient. Adam wasn't so lucky, being stuck with the one he had for God only knew how long.

Nigel was in the middle of going over the household accounts with Mrs. Simpson and Gettis, when Adam burst into the housekeeper's parlor. All three of them looked up with astonishment. Adam was not in the habit of invading the servants' quarters, any more than he was accustomed to storming into rooms unannounced.

"I've been looking for you everywhere," Adam said, and they all jumped to their feet, not sure whom Adam was addressing. Nigel had not seen Adam looking so spirited in a very long time. He wasn't sure whether to be pleased or alarmed.

"A word with you, Nigel," Adam said, practically twitching with impatience. "Forgive the interruption, but this is urgent."

"I'm at your service." Nigel closed the books. "We'll finish this later," he said to Gettis and Mrs. Simpson as he took off after Adam, who had already disappeared.

"What's happened?" he asked breathlessly when Adam finally stopped outside the back door of the scullery, having gone directly through the kitchen, also not his habit.

"Not here," Adam said. "The rose garden is closest. I want to be absolutely sure that no one can overhear or interrupt."

Intrigued, Nigel followed him around the side of the house to the walled garden that extended from the south wing. Adam opened the wooden door, firmly closing it behind them. He went straight to the stone bench that sat under a large oak tree. More surprised than ever, since this had been Caroline's personal preserve and not a place that Adam had spent any time in since her death, Nigel took a seat next to him.

For someone who'd been in a tearing hurry, Adam fell suddenly silent. Nigel waited, not having any idea what to think, although he couldn't help but wonder if Adam had discovered Callista Melbourne's deception. He prayed that wasn't the case, but that would explain Adam's agitation. God help her . . . Adam would most likely dispatch her to wretched Harold in no time flat.

"I spoke with Dr. Hadley," Adam finally said. "He has the most peculiar theory about Miss Magnus. I want to know what you think."

"A theory?" Nigel said, perplexed. "What sort of theory?"

"He thinks the girl probably doesn't know who she is. He calls the condition amnesia." Adam looked as if he wanted to tear his hair out. "She might as well have pudding inside her head instead of brains, Nigel. How am I meant to dispose of her when she doesn't even know where she belongs?"

Nigel stared at Adam, staggered by this piece of information. "She doesn't remember who she is?"

"How am I supposed to know? I'm not even supposed to ask her for fear of bringing on one of her headaches. She needs peace and quiet, Hadley said. No pressure on her. What about the pressure on me, I ask?" He clenched his fists in his lap. "I do *not* need this, but I'm damned if I have any idea what I'm supposed to do."

As appalling as the situation was for Callista Melbourne, Nigel couldn't help being secretly pleased. Adam wasn't likely to toss out a helpless young woman into the street, and as for Miss Melbourne, if she didn't remember her engagement to foul Harold, the better for her. Considering everything, maybe this wasn't such a bad turn of affairs. Adam's agitation was far better than apathy. At least he was behaving like a normal person with a full range of emotions instead of a shadow going through the motions. Nigel didn't see that any purpose would be served by revealing what he knew. "Did Hadley say how long she would remain without her memory?"

"That's the point," Adam said on a near shout. "He doesn't have the first idea. She could be like this forever—it's been known to happen. I ask you again, what am I going to do?"

"Nothing for the moment, I imagine. Follow the good doctor's advice. With luck Miss M . . . er, Miss Magnus's memory will return once she's regained her health. You did say today that you wanted to get to the bottom of the mystery—perhaps if you listen carefully to what she says, you can piece together the puzzle."

Adam glared at him. "You're being very helpful. Why don't you tell me something I haven't thought of?"

"Because I can't think of anything else," Nigel said calmly. "I feel sorry for the girl. If she's been making up a story for your benefit, she must be feeling utterly miserable about lying, but what else is she to do? I'm sure I would do the same in her circumstances." He chuckled.

"What the devil do you find so amusing?" Adam demanded. "This is a disaster."

"Forgive me. I was just thinking that your Miss Magnus is quite resourceful. She did spin an interesting tale—living in Italy and all that. Of course, you still don't know if she made up a history for your benefit or if some of it's true. You'll just have to wait and see."

"Next you'll be telling me to consider this a challenge." Adam sighed heavily. "Very well, Nigel. I can see that you're not prepared to take the situation seriously, but then, it's not your responsibility, is it?"

"No, but I'm willing to help in any way that I can. I would very much like to meet your Miss Magnus."

"She's not *my* Miss Magnus. She's not anybody's Miss Magnus. She's probably not Miss Magnus at all." He stood and walked over to a climbing rose that bloomed on the near wall, running a finger over one deep red flower and pricking his thumb on a thorn as he pulled his hand away. Swearing under this breath, he sucked away the drop of blood that had welled up.

He turned around. "I think you should meet Miss Magnus, and the sooner the better. If she's feeling well enough this evening, I'll ask her to join us for dinner. The more time we spend with her, the more likely we are to be able to find out what we need to know."

Interested that Adam had suddenly included him in his plans, Nigel nodded. Adam might have a challenge on his hands, but Nigel had his own: keeping Callista Melbourne's true identity and her connection to Harold to himself for as long as possible. The poor girl deserved nothing less.

"Lord Vale wishes me to have dinner with him?" Callie sat up and gazed at Jane in horror.

"Yes, miss. He said only if you feel strong enough, but he thought you might like a change from eating on trays in your room." Jane crinkled her brow. "Oh, and he said please to tell you that he promises not to plague you with questions."

Callie closed her eyes for a moment. She didn't want to be forced to endure more of Lord Vale's company, but she couldn't accept his hospitality and then deliberately avoid him for the duration of her stay. She did feel much better, and the four walls of the room, despite its generous size, felt as if they were beginning to close in on her.

"Very well," she said, wondering if she was not making a terrible mistake. Still, he had been very kind to her that morning when her head had started throbbing again. She couldn't help shivering at the memory of his strong arms picking her up and carrying her to the bed, his gentle touch and soft voice. "Please tell Lord Vale that I'd be happy to join him, although I have nothing appropriate to wear."

"Not to worry, miss. Mrs. Simpson has taken care of all that. I'll bring the dress in directly and help you to prepare yourself."

Half an hour later a light tap came at the door and Jane stepped back from the chair where she'd been arranging Callie's hair. "Michael is here to take you downstairs, miss. He's a footman." She sounded slightly breathless and Callie, amused, thought that maybe Jane harbored a secret fondness for the man. And why shouldn't she? Jane was young and passably pretty and probably dreamt of a husband and children.

For an awful moment, Callie wondered if she might have a husband and children of her own, but something deep inside her told her that wasn't the case. She doubted she'd ever had yearnings in that direction, at least not for a husband.

"Thank you, Jane. Oh, dear. I feel as if I'm being sent into the lion's den." She tried not to think about the knot in her stomach.

"You mustn't think that, miss. His lordship is everything that's kind—he helped my family no end when my father hurt his back in the fields and couldn't provide for us. He may seem a trifle forbidding, but then, he's nobility, isn't he? Underneath he has a heart of gold, although he probably wouldn't want anyone thinking so. The nobility's funny that way."

She regarded Callie solemnly as if reviewing her handiwork. "I'm no lady's maid, but you do look very nice. The blue of the dress suits you." Handing Callie a light wrap, she opened the door. "Miss Magnus is ready to go down now, Michael," she said, flushing lightly as she regarded her heart's desire. "She's still weak, so be sure you keep a hand under her elbow."

"Don't you worry, Janie. I won't let any harm come to Miss Magnus. This way, miss. We'll take it nice and slow."

Callie, who was beginning to feel like a small child in the hands of two nursemaids, obediently let Michael support her, only because she did feel slightly wobbly on her feet. As they progressed down the wide hall to the great staircase that led down to a vast marble hall, Callie tried to absorb the grandeur around her. Never in her wildest dreams had she imagined she was residing in such a magnificent house. Enormous portraits of men, women, and children in various period dress lined the walls. Everywhere she looked she saw fine furniture, carvings, tapestries, ceramics, and paintings. Stanton Abbey was fit for a king.

"Here we are, miss," Michael said, finally stopping in front of a double door paneled in rich mahogany. "This is the library. His lordship will be in shortly. Please make yourself comfortable."

He opened one side of the doors and Callie stifled a gasp. The room was immense, sporting a billiards table and a pianoforte as well as a harp and comfortably arranged furniture, but what gave Callie real joy was the library itself. The walls of the room held bookshelves from top to bottom, every inch of available space filled. Callie might not know much about herself, but somehow she knew that she loved books with a deep and abiding passion. Her nervousness forgotten, she slowly made her way around the room, running her fingers down leather-bound spines as if she were reacquainting herself with old friends.

Shakespeare, Milton, Thomas Moore, all the great English

poets lined the shelves, as well as Jane Austen, which surprised her, since Callie had always thought of Austen as an author for women. Apollonius, Plautus, Virgil, and Ovid in the original Greek or Latin were stocked in another. Even Omar Khayyám and Li Po in translation graced the collection and many more like them. And that was just in the small section she'd managed to scan.

Adam Carlyle apparently was a man who enjoyed his literature, or if not he, then one of his forebears—although, if nothing else, he would have to have added the most recent of the books. Really, she thought, the man was becoming more interesting by the moment. She pulled a volume of Horace from a shelf and began to leaf through it, finding familiar passages and scanning them with pleasure.

"I see you enjoy reading, Miss Magnus." Adam's voice came from over her left shoulder and she spun around, nearly dropping the book in her surprise. She'd been so absorbed that she hadn't even heard him come in.

"I—yes, I do," she stammered, flustered by his nearness. Her head came only to the top of his shoulder and she stared at his snowy white cravat for lack of any place better to look. Taking a hasty step backward, she bumped into the bookshelf behind her. In evening dress he was more staggeringly handsome than ever.

Adam took the book from her hand and looked down at it. "You read Latin?" he asked, his tone surprised.

"I do," she said, as surprised by her ability as he was, but too shaken by his presence to dwell on that mystery.

"Hmm. I imagine you speak Italian as well, having lived in that country. The two languages share many of the same roots." He gazed down at her in a most disconcerting fashion, as if attempting to see inside her head to discover what else might be there.

"Italian is a beautiful language," she replied, stepping slightly to the left, wishing he'd give her room to breathe.

*"Credo che La sto rendendo nervosa, il che non era la mia intenzione—all' opposto,"* he said.

"Oh, no, I do not become nervous as easily as that," she lied, for her knees were shaking beneath her dress.

"So you understand Italian. Do you not speak it?"

*"Lo parlo abbastanza per farmi intendere."* The words slipped out of her mouth as easily as if they'd been English. Maybe she really *had* lived in Italy, she thought, her eyes widening with astonishment that she might have actually hit on the truth without realizing it.

"You speak it sufficiently indeed, and I understand you very well. You are a constant source of surprise, Miss Magnus." He slipped the book back onto the shelf. "You must forgive me for being slightly delayed. I had a small but unexpected business matter to see to. May I offer you a glass of ratafia?"

"Thank you," she said, relieved when he crossed the room and put a more reasonable distance between them. She didn't think he had any idea of what a formidable presence he was.

The rain had started again, pattering against the windows, the sound muted by the drawn draperies, but comforting somehow.

He walked back to her and handed her a glass, his fingers brushing hers as she took it. Callie nearly jumped out of her skin at the unexpected contact.

"Please do sit down. My steward, Nigel Dryden, will be joining us for dinner, but I assure you that you'll find him easy and pleasant company. I was most gratified that you accepted my invitation." He rubbed the side of his mouth, looking slightly uncomfortable. "I must apologize again for distressing you this morning. How is your head feeling?" he asked as he took an armchair next to the sofa.

"Very much improved, thank you," she said, gratefully sinking onto the comfortable sofa, grateful also that someone else would be at dinner to deflect Adam's attention from her. "I feel so foolish for being such a trial. I usually enjoy extremely good health." For all she knew that was an out-and-out lie, but she thought it sounded reassuring.

"I am delighted to hear it. I cannot wonder that you flourished in a warm, sunny climate. Our English weather has been known to bring down people with the constitution of an ox. I trust you have not felt the damp too badly with all the recent rain?"

Callie couldn't believe they were discussing health and the weather given their previous difficult conversations, but she was very happy to be on safe ground. "I haven't felt the damp at all. For such a large house Stanton Abbey is surprisingly draft-free. You are fortunate to live in such a splendid home."

"I cannot claim any responsibility for the splendor," he said. "That is the accumulated work of generations of Carlyles." He gestured around him. "The family took possession of the abbey in the sixteenth century and spent their time adding to the structure and collecting as many treasures as they could. My job has been to try to keep up what they amassed in both property and possessions."

"My goodness," Callie said, fascinated. "That sounds an expensive proposition, but a worthy one."

"Expensive? Not really. The land produces enough income to cover the maintenance and then some. The problem is more the expenditure of time that is required. I am not one to leave the running of my property to others, although I could not do without my steward to oversee the daily details." He glanced up over his shoulder. "Speaking of whom, here he is now. Nigel, allow me to introduce you to Miss Magnus. Miss Magnus, Nigel Dryden."

Callie looked up abruptly and took in a tall man with light brown hair and pleasantly arranged features who smiled down at her as if he couldn't be happier to make her acquaintance. He was as different in manner from Adam Carlyle as was possible, and she couldn't help smiling in return as he lightly took her hand and bowed over it.

"Miss Magnus," he said, his bright green eyes sparkling. "I cannot tell you what a pleasure it is to meet you at last. May I also say that I am delighted to see you looking so well after your unfortunate ordeal?"

"You are very kind, Mr. Dryden," she murmured, liking him immediately, something she couldn't say about his employer.

"Not at all; we have all been deeply anxious to see you returned to health, no one more so than Lord Vale. Indeed, your welfare has been foremost on his mind this last week."

"Lord Vale has also been very kind," she said, her smile fading. "I have promised him that I will do my utmost to repay that kindness by making a full recovery as quickly as possible and taking myself off his hands as soon as I can."

Nigel exchanged a quick and inscrutable glance with Adam that Callie couldn't fathom. "One cannot rush one's recovery, Miss Magnus. Nature must take its course, and I know that Lord Vale is in no hurry to see you go." He deftly changed the subject. "Speaking of courses, I understand that Cook has made a superb effort this evening. We are to have turtle soup followed by turbot, roast hare, and all manner of vegetables and puddings." He patted his flat stomach. "I for one have a prodigious appetite. I plan to make a glutton of myself."

Callie sat through dinner in near-silence, content to listen to the two men speak quietly between themselves; she
was left in peace to concentrate on her meal. She sipped a
little claret mixed with water as she ate, and the combination of good food and drink, as well as the lack of attention
on herself, helped her to relax. She absorbed her surroundings, admiring the fine art on the walls, the precise, unob-
trusive service provided by the footmen, the gleaming
silver and crystal and china and starched linen. Stanton
Abbey's household ran like clockwork; she couldn't help
but be impressed at the orderliness of it all.

Somewhere in the dim recesses of her mind she had a
memory of meals that were anything but quiet, of lively
conversation and servants who thought nothing of insert-
ing their views whether invited to or not. The memory,
nothing more than a vague, amorphous wisp, and as impossible to catch hold of, was all tied up with the Italianate
house with the high walls and bougainvillea.

She pressed her fingers against her forehead, trying to
bring the picture into focus but without success. No matter
how hard she tried, it kept slipping away.

"Miss Magnus? Callie?"

She looked up with a start as Adam's voice penetrated
the fog in her head. "Yes?" she replied, blinking as the image disappeared. Callie . . . He'd called her that before, only
this morning, and she'd felt remarkably reassured by hearing the sound of her true name.

"Are you feeling unwell? Has your headache returned?"
Adam's voice held that gentle, soothing note that somehow
always managed to resonate within her whether she
wanted it to or not.

"No . . . no, I am fine." She forced a smile. "A trifle tired,
perhaps. I was just thinking of home," she said before she

realized the words had slipped out. She felt like melting through the floor.

Adam shot her a keen look. "Yes? What were you thinking? You speak so rarely of your past. Perhaps you might feel better if you talk of your home."

Callie released a sigh. "It's—it's painful for me to remember. That time is gone." *Gone in more ways than one,* she thought. She was tired of prevaricating, but she didn't know what else to do. Maybe she'd be better off by weaving an elaborate story, one that Adam would never think to challenge her on. She'd managed to produce some Italian, after all, which would substantiate her imaginary narrative.

"I miss my home," she said, trying to think how best to assuage his curiosity without giving him any reason to question her more thoroughly. Her silence hadn't helped her in the least, only causing him to question her more closely. "I miss the deep blue of the sea, the rosy-tinted fingers of dawn rising over it, the sighing of the wind in the cypress and olive trees, the low cooing of the doves in their cotes and the sweet smell of jasmine on the warm night air. I miss the noise of the market as the fishermen bring their catch in, the teeming stalls of fruits and vegetables, the unfettered enthusiasm of the local people, who always have something to say about everything possible."

Somehow in her heart she knew that what she said was true. She just didn't know why. "Stanton is lovely, at least as much of it as I've seen from my window, but it's not the same—I suppose I'm not accustomed to the scenery of the English countryside. Perhaps when I'm more acclimated . . ." She trailed off, an ache for what she'd just described squeezing her heart. And still she didn't know why.

"I've never been to Italy, but you paint a most charming

picture," Nigel said. "How fortunate you were to live in such a beautiful place. What was it called?"

"Er . . . Ravello," she said, seizing on the first word that came to mind. But even as she spoke, she knew it was wrong. The scene she'd portrayed felt right, but like something she'd read in a book somewhere.

"Ravello. Yes, I've heard of it. Have you not considered returning?" Nigel asked gently, looking at her with sympathy.

"No," she said, feeling alarmingly like crying, as if she'd suffered a deep loss in that sad place in her heart. "I cannot go back."

"Well, then," Adam said, smiling at her, "we must introduce you to the beauty of England. Stanton has much to offer in that regard. Perhaps if the weather has cleared tomorrow, and providing you feel strong enough, you would like to take a stroll around the grounds? I would be happy to accompany you."

Callie felt instant relief that he had changed the subject, but something else as well—she felt a real joy in the thought of being outdoors, of seeing the gardens, examining the plants. "I would like that very much," she said. She didn't relish the idea of strolling in Adam's company, for he made her feel uncomfortable, as if she'd been turned inside out and back in again, but he would no doubt be able to provide her with a great deal of information and insight as to the flora and fauna. "Thank you," she thought to add, addressing herself to her sorbet, but her appetite had fled.

"It will be my pleasure. You do look tired, Miss Magnus. Would you like me to escort you to your room, or would you like to stay and have pudding?"

"Thank you," she stammered. "I think I would like to go back to bed, but I can find my own way. I enjoyed the meal very much," she said, struggling to her feet, and both men immediately rose.

"Are you sure you wouldn't like assistance?" Adam repeated, his brow drawing together.

"No ... I must learn to manage for myself," she said. The last thing in the world she wanted was for Adam to come anywhere near her bedroom again. A walk in the garden was as close as she cared to be, and even that was too close. . . .

She didn't know why, but Adam Carlyle struck her with a strange trepidation, as if he could see straight through her and knew her for the fraud she was.

# 6

Adam couldn't sleep that night. There wasn't anything unusual in that; he hadn't slept a full, peaceful night since Caroline and Ian had died, but what made this night different was the direction of his thoughts, for they weren't focused on his lost family, but rather on Callie Magnus.

They were two of a kind, he and Callie, both of them lost, although in his case he couldn't escape the memories that brought him no comfort, and in her case, she had no memories that might have given her the comfort she needed.

Or did she remember? He rolled over onto his back and stared up at the canopy of his bed, listening to the rain pounding against the windows. He had sensed a genuine emotion in her at dinner as she talked about her home in Italy. Then there was the Italian that had come so smoothly off her tongue and her obvious classical education, unusual in a woman. Yet he couldn't help feeling that she had been making up large parts of her narrative, more from what she hadn't said, and the sad, lost look in her dark eyes as she spoke.

He wondered if memory could be selective, if it was possible to remember the basics of language, for example, but not the emotional content or details of one's own life. He would have found such a trick enormously useful, to be able to wipe out large portions of his past, the parts that gave him such pain. If he could be sure of the effect, he'd gladly bash himself over the head with a large rock, but unfortunately there was no guarantee that he wouldn't end up a gibbering idiot.

Sighing heavily, Adam laced his hands behind his head. He couldn't find his way back to the happiness he'd once known, but he might possibly be able to help Callie Magnus find her way back. All he had to do was keep talking to her, draw her out without her realizing what he was doing. Maybe she would say things that would give him a clue as to her lost identity. He'd have to be patient, very patient, and very careful as well, for she shut up as tight as a clam at the least hint of prying.

Yes . . . that was it. He'd make some use of his final days on this earth, do some good for someone. He would consider it one last act of kindness before putting himself out of his misery once and for all, and if he did a very good job, he'd be able to accomplish that feat sooner rather than later. He'd have to put his own troubles to one side if he was to accomplish his goal, for it wouldn't do to give Callie any hint that he'd long since given up on life, not if he was trying to give her back hers.

Feeling much more settled in his mind, Adam rolled over and fell into a dreamless sleep.

———

The next morning Adam sprang out of bed with uncommon energy. The sun was shining, the sky painted a brilliant blue, and now that he had a plan in mind, he had all intentions of making it work. Callie Magnus was a project, and he enjoyed projects, feeling them challenges to be met and overcome. He had a talent for putting plans into action and making them work, if he did say so himself.

Shoving a piece of toast between his teeth, he let Plimpton help him into his jacket, took a last gulp of coffee, and briefly inspected himself in the looking glass. He looked the picture of innocence, he decided with satisfaction. He'd just have to remember to keep his expression perfectly pleasant.

Nigel had pointed out to him that he'd developed a habit of scowling and speaking curtly that tended to put people off. Adam hadn't been aware of such a habit, but as Nigel was usually observant and didn't tend to make pointed remarks without reason, Adam was forced to believe that he must be right.

Pity—he wasn't accustomed to paying attention to whatever expressions his face might unwittingly assume, and he imagined the effort would be fairly taxing, but whatever he needed to do to ensure the success of his scheme would be worthwhile in the end.

"Thank you, Plimpton," he said, stepping back from the glass. "You have achieved a most satisfactory result."

"Thank *you*, my lord," his valet replied, looking mightily surprised. "You are looking unusually well this morning."

"I slept," Adam said. "Sleep can do wonderful things for the constitution. Sleep, good food, and large quantities of fresh air are what Dr. Hadley has prescribed for Miss Magnus, and I shall therefore be indulging in these myself so as to oblige him and hasten Miss Magnus's recovery—

oh, and Plimpton, from now on Miss Magnus and I shall be taking a full breakfast downstairs every morning, although I'd still like coffee and toast up here while I dress."

"Very good, my lord. I am delighted to know your appetite has finally returned," Plimpton said, glancing pointedly at the breakfast tray which held nothing but empty plates.

"Mmm," Adam said with distraction, thinking about exactly where to take Callie for their walk. He'd be wise to stay close to the house in case she lost strength, but there were gardens aplenty that ought to keep her interested.

Whistling a little tune, he vanished through the door, intending to do some paperwork before their excursion.

"You wouldn't believe it," Plimpton said, his eyes wide as he managed to pull Mrs. Simpson and Gettis off to one side of the vast kitchen. "His lordship was actually *whistling* as he left his room! *And* he finished his entire breakfast." Plimpton's excited speech was so unlike his usually calm and deliberate manner that both Mrs. Simpson and Gettis immediately understood the importance of what he was trying to impart.

"God bless the boy," Mrs. Simpson murmured, producing a large handkerchief from the pocket of her apron and dabbing at her eyes. "Maybe there's hope for him yet, the poor dear. All that grief, suffering for so long—I've feared for his health, I have, ever since the tragedy."

"It is true," Gettis said gravely, "that he cleaned his plate last night as well, and even had second helpings. I haven't seen the like of that since . . . since before the terrible day. Cook was that pleased. What do you make of it, Mr. Plimpton?"

"I think he's coming back to us, that's what I think," Plimpton said, slightly misty around the eyes. He passed a hand over his balding head as if to collect himself. "What's more, I think Miss Magnus has something to do with it."

Mrs. Simpson gasped, her hand leaping to her mouth. "You mean," she squeaked, "you mean there might be something *there*?"

"I mean," Plimpton said, drawing up in a dignified fashion so that his chest puffed out slightly, "that I believe his lordship is interested in Miss Magnus's welfare and that she has given him a reason to move forward. His lordship has always been at his best when worrying about other people's problems, rather than his own."

"True," Gettis said, nodding sagely. "I've known him since he was a boy and I was only a footman in the household, but his lordship always managed to soothe his troubles by tending to a wounded animal or championing a local lad whom his nasty cousin had taken a disliking to. Perhaps his lordship has found a cause in seeing to Miss Magnus's recovery." He pulled his own large handkerchief from his pocket and wiped his eyes and nose, not from any surfeit of emotion, but because he suffered terribly from hay fever.

"Yes—yes, I think you have the right of it," Mrs. Simpson said. "Look at the way he sat by the poor poppet's bed when she was too ill to come to her senses, fretting over her welfare. He's done nothing but ask about her ever since, consulting with the doctor at every opportunity, seeing that she was as comfortable as she could be. That's his lordship all over, isn't it? Dear boy. Dear, dear boy." She blew her nose delicately.

"It is too soon to hope overmuch, but I cannot help but pray that this marks a turning point in his lordship's grieving," Plimpton said solemnly. "It is time for him to return to the living."

They all straightened instantly and with considerable

astonishment when the unexpected sound of Adam's voice came from some distance behind them.

"Oh, er ... good morning, Cook," he was saying in a cheerful fashion. "I wondered if I might have some stale bread crusts. I thought I'd take Miss Magnus to feed the ducks."

The three of them exchanged a long, meaningful look, and without another word they dispersed and went about their usual business.


Callie shot Adam a sidelong, slightly wary look as Gettis helped her into a pelisse that had magically appeared out of nowhere, like the rest of her borrowed clothes.

As usual, she could read nothing from Adam's face, although it didn't seem to hold that shuttered, slightly forbidding expression that she dreaded. He'd been waiting for her in the Great Hall when she'd come down, and said nothing more complicated than "Good morning. Have you breakfasted?"

That told her nothing at all, and she wondered anew if he had tumbled to all her lies and half-truths and was waiting only to spring his trap.

She swallowed hard, trying to remember how happy she was to be going outside into sunshine that she had longed for as a thirsty man longs for water. She refused to let any foreboding spoil her morning out. She'd worry about Adam and his questionable motives later.

As they walked out the door and down the steps of what she assumed was the main entrance of the house, she peeped over at him again. He was dressed in simple buckskin trousers and a linen shirt open at the neck, his jacket an old and comfortable-looking affair of plain broadcloth; his boots appeared equally old and comfortable. He looked more like a gentleman farmer than a marquess and she had to admit that she liked the effect, for she felt far less intimidated by him. He actually seemed like a normal person, his dark hair ruffling lightly in the breeze, his face relaxed, his stride an easy amble that kept pace with hers. The tension slowly ebbed out of her body as they walked, and she relaxed her guard.

"We're fortunate that it's a beautiful day," he said in his mellow voice. "We've had enough rain this last month to drive even the cows to distraction, but the result should be a spectacular May if the weather continues to hold."

Callie was so absorbed in looking about her and drinking in the warmth of the sunshine that she barely heard him. She glanced back at the house, trying to get some sort of perspective of its size and nearly fell over when she saw just what that size was. Stanton Abbey looked more like a palace. The windows of the long, low front were large and mullioned, the towers of the four staggered wings crenellated, and the stone from which the entirety had been built was a lovely, soft gray, and bathed in the morning light.

"Oh!" The gasp escaped involuntarily, an expression of astonishment and awe.

Adam caught her by her elbow and steadied her just in time, for she tripped over her own feet. "It does rather take one by surprise the first time," he said pleasantly, turning her to face the house full on. "It's hard to believe the place started as a Cistercian monastery. Henry the Eighth closed the monastery right after the poor abbot had spent vast sums of money on new building. My family benefited from that piece of good fortune when Henry decided to give the abbey to them for some service or other—that was in 1540, and then one of my ancestors, feeling flush at the time, decided to rebuild it in the mid-1600's, transforming it into what you see now." He smiled down at her. "The style must be some-what familiar to you, given your Italian background."

"I—yes, it is," she said, perfectly and jarringly familiar with the style. "That is, I am not accustomed to palaces, but I do recognize the architecture. I find it strange to see it here in England." That was an understatement. Other than its size, many parts of Stanton Abbey's exterior fitted closely with the image in her mind of the Italianate house with the high walls and the bougainvillea pouring over them in a riot of glorious scarlet. Instead of tall spires of cypress trees, manicured yews framed and defined the outer walls, and massive beds of flowers completed the ef-fect of lush color, lending the English setting the rich, warm look of a Mediterranean landscape.

"Mmm. I have to agree," Adam said. "It's not a common sort of treatment in this country, but I like it. Of course, it's my home, and having grown up here I'm accustomed to it."

"But I like it very much," she said. "I think it's ab-solutely beautiful—truly breathtaking."

Adam chuckled. "How gratifying. I assure you, you will soon become accustomed to Stanton and its glories. The next thing I know, you'll be pointing out all the cracks in the plaster." He steered her toward the river and resumed his slow, steady pace, careful to keep her at his side.

"I would never be so presumptuous," Callie said, but she couldn't resist smiling. She did have a keen eye for de-tail, that much she did know about herself. In the week that she'd been shut up in her bedroom, she'd noticed a great many things. The tapestry hangings on the four-poster bed were in need of mending in the right-hand cor-ner next to the headboard, and the farthest window to the left had a tendency to leak rain from the topmost edge behind the drapery. It was only a very tiny leak, hardly visible unless one happened to be leaning against the window itself and looking up at the sky, as she'd done last night in the small hours when she'd been unable to sleep.

"You do not strike me as being a presumptuous person," Adam said quietly. "I find that an admirable quality. I don't often meet people who do not presume a very great deal."

"Perhaps that is the misfortune of your position, my lord. It is human nature for man to want what he does not have and to expect those more fortunate to supply those needs as a matter of obligation." She glanced up at him. "The trouble is that in general, people have a difficult time distinguishing between what they think they want and what they really *do* need." She covered her mouth with her hand as she heard what she'd said. "Now I really am being presumptuous," she said, her cheeks flushing hotly. "Forgive me—I have no place saying such things to you."

Adam met her gaze evenly enough, but she could see a spark of surprise in his eyes. "To the contrary," he said. "I appreciate your candor. As it happens, I agree with you. It is a wise man indeed who knows that happiness does not lie in material possessions, as pleasant as they can be. One can be the richest man on earth and still the most miserable."

He fell silent, seemingly lost in thought, and Callie wondered why his eyes had suddenly seemed sad before he'd quickly turned his gaze away. For the first time it occurred to her that his life, as privileged as it was, had not been a perfectly orchestrated harmonic symphony without a single discord to disturb the arrangement, that he must have suffered the usual disappointments and losses—that he was, in fact, a perfectly ordinary man who happened to have been brought up in extraordinary circumstances.

Thinking about it, what she might have mistaken for arrogance was possibly the natural bearing of a man accustomed to power and responsibility. Maybe he really didn't have an ulterior motive after all.

He had rescued her at great risk to himself, after all, taken her into his home without complaint, and treated her with kindness. If he tended toward brusqueness at times, what right did she, a complete stranger, have to expect anything else from him? He had gone far beyond the call of duty as it was; really, she must have stretched his patience to the limit with her evasions and stubborn refusal to let him help her find a position for herself.

Callie felt thoroughly ashamed of herself for ever thinking him cold, beastly, and manipulative. In this moment he seemed anything but. She realized that she knew next to nothing about him, but then Adam Carlyle was not the sort of man who invited personal questions. She doubted he would appreciate an inquiry, especially given her reticence in providing him with any of her own details.

A light silvery mist hung over the river as they approached the triple-arched bridge and Adam guided her over to a bench placed on the river's grassy bank under a large beech tree, its outspread branches providing a dappled shade from the warm sun that spilled down.

"This would be a nice place to rest," he said comfortably enough, as if the melancholy she'd sensed in him had blown away with the soft westerly breeze that had come up, bringing with it a faint tang of warm, wet earth mingled with the fresh clean scent of water.

Callie settled next to him, her hands in her lap. The silence between them felt natural, as if there was no need for speech. She focused on the gleam of the water and the shifting mist, enjoying the sense of sunlight and space, of the gentle cooing of doves in the distant wood, and the varied calls of songbirds going about their business.

Adam shifted and drew a small bag from the pocket of his jacket, then gave a series of low, soft whistles. "Watch," he said, smiling over at her. "We shouldn't have to wait long."

He was right. Only moments later she heard a staccato of quacks, and out of the mist came a mother duck trailed by a series of five ducklings, all wagging their tails and paddling swiftly for the near shore.

He handed her the bag. "Go ahead," he said. "They're spoiled silly. Someone sees that they're fed every day, come rain or shine."

Callie took the bag from him, filled with a foolish pleasure. She stood and scattered a handful of bread onto the river's surface and watched with delight as the ducks attacked the treat, making a great deal of noise as they went about bobbing and diving for the crusts, stopping only to shake the water from their backs.

"Save a few last crusts to throw," he said, a hint of laughter in his voice as he watched her toss bread around like a five-year-old child. "You'll need a good arm to get them far enough out."

She looked over her shoulder at him in question. He nodded toward the shadows under the bridge where the mist swirled and parted, revealing two magnificent white shapes gliding silently and regally toward them. Their necks stretched in a long, graceful arch, their black beaks brilliantly contrasted by bright yellow markings on each side. The ducks disappeared as they approached, as if in deference to royalty.

Callie released a long sigh of pure happiness. "Swans," she whispered. "Oh, you beauties, you lovely, lovely creatures!" She crouched down on all fours, oblivious to how she might look, and took a crust sideways between her fingers, extending her hand out as far as she could, holding it perfectly still. "*Ella, kykno mou,*" she crooned softly. "It's not exactly the food of the gods, but it should do in a pinch."

The larger of the two, clearly the male, drifted forward, eying her carefully, making a full circle as he examined her from every angle, his mate hanging back.

"Callie, for God's sake be careful," she heard Adam call softly but sharply from behind her. "They can be dangerous if they get too close." But she knew she had nothing to fear.

The male floated directly up to her and reached his head forward, delicately taking the crust from her as if he'd been doing it all his life. He moved to one side and his mate took his place as Callie took a fresh crust and extended her hand again. The female swan didn't hesitate. She took the bread without haste, as delicately as her husband had. And then they turned and drifted back into the shadows, the silver mist slowly closing over them.

Callie propped herself up on her knees, watching them with pure pleasure, her hands clasped against her chest.

She felt Adam's light touch on her shoulders, then his hands reaching down to help her to her feet. "Wasn't that *wonderful*?" she said, her eyes shining as she rose to face him.

"Extraordinary is more like it," he said, his voice unsteady. He took her by the shoulders again. "Callie . . . you do know that wild swans don't generally let you get anywhere near them? They're apt to attack you if you try, and they can do considerable damage."

"Oh, not those two," Callie said, laughing. "They're far too well mannered."

"Don't you believe it. They went after one of the housemaids and she was twice the distance from them. She was lucky they didn't take out her eye."

Callie shrugged, looking away from his curious, puzzled stare. "She must have come too close to their nest."

He looked at her hard, his expression appraising. "I gather you have an affinity for birds?"

She considered. "I like all creatures, feathered or otherwise."

His mouth curved up in a wry smile. "I gather they must like you, too. Honestly, Callie, you must stop giving me these shocks. My nerves won't stand for it."

"I—I'm sorry," she said, not sure exactly what she was apologizing for, but from the shaken look on his face, she knew she had genuinely given him a fright. "I knew they wouldn't hurt me, you see, but I suppose you couldn't have known that."

His hands still held her shoulders and the warmth of his palms seeped through her pelisse directly into her skin. "Would you mind explaining how you could possibly have known such a thing?" he asked on a note of exasperation. "Next you'll be telling me you could read their minds."

"No . . . not exactly," she said, trying to think how to explain. "I just knew, just as they knew I didn't mean them any harm." She colored, feeling a little ridiculous.

"Mm-hmm. And do you always speak to swans in Greek?" He released her and took a step back, but his intent gaze didn't leave her face.

Callie stared at him. "Did I?" she said, genuinely amazed. "I hadn't realized. I suppose it seemed the natural thing to do. After all, Zeus took on the form of a swan when he seduced Leda."

Adam looked startled, then burst out laughing. "Oh, of course. How silly of me not to have thought of that. The next thing I know we'll have Zeus and Hera and the rest of

Mount Olympus here at Stanton, creating their usual chaos and mayhem and transfiguring chambermaids into laurel trees and God only knows what else. I can just imagine what Mrs. Simpson will have to say about that."

Callie grinned. "Really, my lord, I do think you should take more care with the quality of guest you invite into the house," she said, imitating the housekeeper. "These Dionysian revelries are keeping the servants up until all hours, and the lack of proper clothing is positively shocking! Whatever will the poppet think?"

Adam merely shook his head. "You, Miss Calliope Magnus, are proving to be one surprise after another."

"Am I, Lord Vale? I am sure I don't mean to be," she said uncertainly, wondering if she'd said something she ought not to have. "I believe it's very unladylike to be full of surprises."

"Do you? How very interesting. And I wish you'd stop calling me Lord Vale. I'm perfectly content to be addressed as Adam, unless you find that unladylike as well."

"Not at all," Callie said cheerfully. "I've never been much good at behaving like a lady." She bit her lip and winced. Another thing she knew to be true, but how? A hazy image played somewhere in the back of her mind of a wild girl tearing around in torn skirts, hair tumbling every which way and full of brambles, thin arms and legs unfashionably tanned from the sun, with no care for what anyone thought. "I—I mean I haven't had any real training, not like proper British girls who were brought up to be presented at court and marry lords."

"I shouldn't worry about it," he said. "Your table manners are perfectly adequate, you enter and leave a room without creating a shambles, and you seem to be able to make intelligent conversation—although believe me, that is not a prerequisite for being presented at court, nor for marrying a lord. Indeed, it seems in that area you might be overqualified for the position."

"I don't understand," Callie said, baffled by this last statement.

"To clarify, women who have been educated to the point that they have mastered Greek and Latin tend to horrify the very gentlemen they have been reared to marry. Are you not familiar with the term 'bluestocking'?"

"Oh," Callie said with a grin. "That."

"Exactly: that, as you so succinctly put it. But then perhaps your parents did not wish for you to waste yourself on an English aristocrat, which is why they removed you from the country altogether. I feel sure that you had a much more amusing time growing up abroad than you would have had if you'd been raised here under the rules and regulations deemed fitting for young girls."

"I wouldn't know," Callie said honestly. "One has to have had the experience to be able to make a just comparison."

Adam cocked an eyebrow. "Is that so?" he said, and she could have sworn she detected a note of irony in his voice.

"Yes, that's so," Callie said firmly. "Furthermore, I have no intention of marrying, so whether I was raised as a hot-house flower or a hoyden is of no import."

"Do you have something against the institution of marriage?" He regarded her lazily.

"Not in principle, no. I am sure it is a very fine institution if the two parties are well suited to each other and willing to be tied together for life. I am only saying that marriage would not suit me."

"Why is that, Miss Calliope Magnus? Do you have an aversion to men in general or just marriage in particular?"

"I have no aversion to men that I am aware of. I just—I

prefer to be independent, to make my own decisions and go my own way."

"Hmm. So far going your own way seems to have led you into the English Channel and onward to Stanton."

"Heartless wretch," she muttered, but his grin took the sting out of his words.

"True on both counts," he answered softly, his smile fading, "but that is neither here nor there. We are not discussing my character, but yours, which so far has revealed a stubborn streak aided and abetted by a considerable amount of backbone and determination, a definite degree of whimsy, and an acuteness of mind that would make most men quake in their boots."

"Really?" she said, highly amused, discovering that she liked Adam more and more by the minute. "Do you quake, Lord Vale?"

"Adam, and certainly not. I gave up the habit many years ago." He glanced over at the river, where the sun had burned away most of the mist. "Perhaps that's not entirely true. I had a slight episode of quaking when you put your face in the direct aim of a swan's bill, but I have since recovered and have no intention of repeating the lapse."

Callie cocked her head to one side and regarded Adam closely, taking advantage of his turned head. His profile was strong, the nose straight, the full lips curved up slightly at the corners, the cheekbone finely sculpted, his dark hair curling crisply over the collar of his jacket. She couldn't help thinking of the fine Greek sculptures of Apollo: not just the noble head, but the body perfectly proportioned, the broad shoulders and chest harmoniously balanced by a lean abdomen and hips, strong back, and powerful buttocks, the long, muscular legs carrying the weight of the body easily as if to spring to action at any moment.

Adam Carlyle might have been the model for any one of the Apollo sculptures.

Callie's cheeks burned with fire as she realized the image she'd conjured up. Not a single sculpture of Apollo wore a scrap of clothing, not even so much as a fig leaf, leaving nothing to the imagination.

She might just as well have stripped Adam bare. She put a hand to her face, wanting to sink into the earth and disappear. What on earth could she be thinking? She was—she was positively *wanton*.

Adam chose that moment to look back at her. "Callie?" He quickly caught her under the elbows. "Are you feeling ill? Do you need to sit down?"

"No," she said, trying desperately to regain her composure. "I—I felt warm for a moment, that's all. I'm better now."

"Warm? Is your fever back?" He lightly touched one hand to her cheek, which did nothing at all for Callie's equilibrium. "You are warm. I should take you inside immediately."

"Please, Adam," she said desperately, knowing that if he didn't take his hand away immediately, she really would sink to the earth. Her knees had started to tremble in the most alarming fashion. She quickly took a step away from him and removed her elbow from his grasp. "I am perfectly well. There's no need to fuss."

"Your head doesn't ache, you have no dizziness?"

"I promise you, I am the picture of health. I shouldn't have looked directly up at the sun, that's all. Some people sneeze when they do such a foolish thing. I go hot all over for a moment. It's that simple."

Adam regarded her with disbelief. "You go hot all over when you look at the sun."

"Yes. The solution is simple: I shouldn't look directly at the sun." *Or directly at you,* she thought with a shiver. What on earth had come over her? She was behaving like a silly miss who had never been exposed to a handsome, healthy male before. The next thing she knew, she'd start tittering behind her hand and batting her eyelashes at him.

"As a general rule, it's probably not a good idea." He still didn't look terribly convinced, and little wonder. Adam did not strike her as a fool, and she'd already pushed the limits of her credibility.

"Do you think we could continue our walk?" she asked, hoping to distract him. "I would like to see more of the grounds, if you have the patience."

"It is not my patience that is strained," he said, a flicker of speculation in his eyes.

Callie's heart skipped a beat and her cheeks started flaming all over again. She quickly bent down and made a great show of admiring a clump of flowers at her feet, barely seeing them. "How lovely they are," she said. "Such an attractive shade of yellow."

"Do dandelions not grow in Italy?" he replied in a muffled voice. "They are considered a common weed in England."

Callie winced. "Of course they do, although they tend to be more of a light lemon in color," she said, improvising madly. Straightening, she said, "Did you know that dandelions are medicinally useful for an assortment of ailments? The infused tea makes a very effective digestive aid, and I personally believe a decoction of the root makes a wonderful antiinflammatory." She was babbling out of sheer nerves and she prayed that Adam hadn't noticed.

To her relief he appeared oblivious to her discomfort. "Come, then," he said easily enough, "let me take you over to the walled fruit orchard if you're sure you're not too tired."

"I'd like that very much. The trees must be coming into bloom. Do you keep bees at Stanton? I am very fond of bees."

"As it happens we have some hives in the orchard that you might be interested in communing with. The bee-keeper tells me that he's been having a devil of a time keeping one of the hives from swarming. The queen seems to be unhappy about something or other."

"Oh, that's easy," Callie said in an offhand manner, waving a hand in dismissal. "Somebody probably didn't tell her something about what was going on up at the house. It's most likely a matter of having me introduce myself. The queens are very keen on knowing about people coming and going, you see. . . ."

She didn't see the amused smile on Adam's face, mainly because he took great care to hide it from her.

As soon as Adam had returned Callie to the house and safely into the clucking care of Mrs. Simpson, he went directly to the stables and had his gelding saddled. For some reason he had an overwhelming urge to ride out to the cliffs, as if a good stiff wind could blow the puzzlement out of his head.

"I think we're both in need of some hard exercise, Gabriel," he said, swinging into the saddle and turning his horse's head straight for the sea as soon as they'd left the stable yard. Gabriel, three years old and full of suppressed energy, sensed Adam's mood and tossed his head with a soft whinny, stretching his legs as he moved from a canter straight into a gallop. Adam let him have his way and gave him his head, and they flew like the wind.

The sun danced and dazzled around them, and for a time Adam forgot everything but the feeling of the magnificent horse beneath him, their power joined as if they were one mind and one flesh as they pounded over the fallow southern fields. Adam didn't bother stopping for the gates. He set Gabriel at them and the gelding took each one easily in a smooth soaring motion. Only as they approached the cliffs did Adam sit back in the saddle and check the reins. Gabriel resisted for a moment, leaning against the bit, and Adam let him have it for just a minute, then checked him again, breaking his stride. Putting his head down, Gabriel danced for a moment, then sweetly straightened his hindquarters out and settled into a respectable trot.

Adam couldn't help laughing as he patted Gabriel's withers. "You've needed that, haven't you, my friend? It's been too long since we've had a good run just for the fun of it."

He frowned, trying to remember just how long it had been. He honestly couldn't remember. He looked back to find time had blurred, as if he couldn't distinguish one day from the next, the events of one week or one month from another or even the last two years from each other. They all seemed to run together in one dull, gray blur. The last thing he could remember with any real clarity in terms of time was the funeral . . . a fine spring day just like this one, the sun shining brightly, flowers burgeoning forth with life as he'd consigned his dead wife and son to their dark tombs. He still couldn't bear the smell of comfrey.

Adam drew Gabriel to a halt at the edge of the cliff, his brow drawn together with effort as he tried to push the twisting pain away. Why the hell did he have to go and remember that now? For the full space of a morning he'd actually managed to forget. The realization rocked him. He honestly hadn't had a single thought of Caro or Ian, and he didn't know whether to feel guilty or relieved. Best not to dwell on that at all, he decided.

The cliff fell away to the water, washing gently up on a long, smooth stretch of sand. Gulls circled overhead, their high, wailing cries carried away by the wind as they swooped on the updrafts, then dived like bullets in pursuit of fish. Looking down at the foamy surf that ebbed and flowed in a soothingly rhythmic fashion, he carefully brought his focus back to Calliope Magnus. She was without a doubt the most peculiar woman he'd ever come across, and he had absolutely no idea what to make of her.

After having spent the morning with her, he was still as sure as he could be that she really didn't have any detailed memory of her life, although she certainly had enough details in her head about other matters. That at least confirmed his theory about selective memory.

What struck him as particularly interesting was that even without a wholeness of memory, Callie was nevertheless a complete personality, and one with absolutely no regard for any of the usual conventions. He'd been hard-pressed not to burst out laughing when she'd gotten down on all fours on the riverbank, her little bottom sticking up in the air like an excited puppy. If she'd had a tail, it would surely have been wagging with delight.

A moment later his suppressed laughter had vanished as she'd blithely called the swans over to her. To his horror they'd come immediately, their potentially vicious beaks only inches from her face, and before he'd even had a chance to move and pull her out of harm's way, she'd fed them from her hand as if they were no more than a pair of tame pigeons.

Adam slowly shook his head. He had no explanation. He knew those swans. They'd never let a soul come within a stone's throw of them, not without threatening to attack. He couldn't help remembering the strange behavior of the gull that had followed them back to shore as if it had been protecting Callie, but the idea that Callie had some special affinity with birds was absurd.

And yet there had been the bees. He hadn't been serious about her communing with them—he'd only thought she might enjoy seeing the orchard. But Callie hadn't hesitated, marching straight through the door to the walled garden and over to the hives before he could stop her. Even the beekeeper, being a sensible man, wouldn't go near them without protective clothing from head to toe and a smoking torch to stun the insects.

Not Callie. She'd blithely parked herself at the entrance to the most troublesome hive where the bees darted about, disturbed and angry. He hadn't even bothered to try to rescue her this time, not seeing any point in both of them being stung to death. And then she'd proceeded to chat away to the inhabitants as if they had a long and intimate acquaintance.

Stranger still, the bees seemed to listen, their frantic darting ceasing as they settled down; a lazy hum began to fill the air. If he hadn't known better, he'd have thought they were responding to Callie's soft-spoken words.

All he could think of was that the warmth of the noon sun had suddenly made them sleepy. Then she'd stood with a self-satisfied expression and brushed herself off. "That should take care of that," she said, as if she'd explained everything, and marched straight past him and out of the orchard.

Adam ran one hand over his face. Yes, indeed, Calliope Magnus was going to take some getting used to.

He didn't for one minute believe that she could talk to bees any more than she could talk to birds, but apparently she thought she could.

Maybe the blow to her head had knocked something loose in her brain other than her memory. He'd have to keep a careful eye on her, make sure that she wasn't afflicted with any other alarming aberrations—like looking into the sun. Not that he'd believed that story for a minute, either.

He hadn't imagined the heat in Callie's cheeks that had bloomed red as roses or her suddenly flustered state, and he didn't have the first idea what might have caused either. He hadn't said anything out of the ordinary, had he? He'd been over and over the conversation and could think of nothing objectionable, unless she'd taken exception to his character analysis of her, but that had been half in jest and surely she'd known it.

She'd looked unusually pretty in that moment, all blushes and confusion, making a fuss over a pile of weeds as if they were the rarest of orchids. If she'd been any other woman he would have concluded that she'd been overcome by a sudden fit of awakened attraction to the opposite sex— he being the only target at hand—but as Callie had yet to behave like any of the typical misses who had crossed his path in years past, romantically fancying themselves in love with him, he couldn't credit the notion. Callie had given no indication that she found him anything more than an over-bearing autocrat.

Adam shook his head with a smile. He had to admit that he found Callie surprisingly good company: sweet-natured, undemanding, and unusually intelligent. She'd exhibited not a single sign of airs or graces, thank God, and she possessed a refreshing sense of humor. Thinking about it, he couldn't find a single objection to her company, which was all to the best since he would need to spend a good deal of time with her if he was to gain her trust and succeed at his campaign.

"Do you know, Gabriel," he said, "I actually think I'm going to enjoy myself." He idly stroked the gelding's mane. "All I have to do is let Callie prattle on willy-nilly about whatever subject she chooses, and eventually some sort of picture will come together. It should be no more difficult that putting the scattered pieces of a puzzle together."

Gabriel pricked his ears forward in response to Adam's voice and turned his head slightly sideways.

"I'm delighted to see that you agree," Adam said wryly. "Do let me know if you have any clever ideas of your own. I can use all the help I can get if I'm going to make any sense out of the girl, and I want her whole and gone as soon as possible."

He wasn't sure why, but something in that statement didn't ring entirely true. He chose not to examine the reason too closely. He had too many other things to think about, like the scheduled dredging of the river mouth.

Turning Gabriel back toward the fields, he nudged him into a loping canter, but he couldn't help hearing an echo in his head of something Callie had said as they'd walked to the river.

*People have a difficult time distinguishing between what they think they want and what they really need...*

He forced her words to the back of his mind and returned to the more practical matter of dredging.

# 7

Once Callie had the limited freedom of the outdoors her health began improving by leaps and bounds, as if sunshine and fresh air were all she needed to mend her body. Her headaches came fewer and farther between and her strength increased daily. Her mind was another matter, for that showed no inclination to oblige her with any concrete memories, and at night she slept dreamlessly.

She tried not to be troubled by the void in her brain, convinced that with time and patience some small memory of her life was bound to return, and once the process started, it would be like winding up a ball of yarn that had bolted away. She was infinitely grateful to both Adam and Nigel, neither who had plagued her with any more questions regarding her past. They treated her like a younger sister whose company they took for granted but paid no particular mind to. When he could spare the time, Adam would walk with her and she enjoyed their brief conversations together, but he'd been more and more busy of late with the spring planting, so as often as not she went out on her own.

Over the last fortnight she'd become accustomed to dining with them in the evenings, and although the conversation ranged freely over a number of subjects, the majority of talk centered, as now, on Stanton affairs.

She looked across the dinner table at Nigel, who was debating the subject of crop rotation and which fields best to leave for summer grazing, his hands waving about animatedly as Adam listened in his usual careful fashion to Nigel's opinions.

Callie also listened avidly, drinking in everything she could, although she did her best to create the impression that she paid no attention at all. She didn't want Adam to think that she would presume to pry into his affairs, knowing that he had an aversion to people sticking their noses in his business, but she really was fascinated by the details of running such a large concern. In a peculiar sort of way, by learning as much as she could about Stanton and its running, she felt at least she was a part of *something,* however little she really belonged.

Looking down at her plate, she decided that if she had her pick of anywhere to belong to, Stanton would be her first choice. She'd become fond of the staff, who treated her with kindness and gracefully let her intrude in their inner sanctum. Cook was obliging enough to allow Callie to sit at the huge wooden table in the kitchen and watch her prepare meals, explaining with great gusto the virtues of English cooking and how she went about creating its marvels.

"See here, my dear, a nice light hand with the pastry can be the making of the dish. You must roll the dough out like so . . ." Great clouds of flour flew at this point all over the table, Cook, and Callie. "And fold and roll *again*." More flour flew and the rolling pin progressed like an advancing army over enemy terrain. Callie adored Cook.

Even Gettis, who at first had seemed like a stiff martinet to her, his dignity worn every bit as starched as his butler's uniform, had unbent his reserve enough to reveal that he had a dry sense of humor and enjoyed telling very bad jokes—Callie always knew when one was coming because he'd clear his throat and begin rocking on his tiptoes. "Er, did I tell you, Miss Callie, that I met a farmer in the market the other day who carried an armful of hares? I undertook a bargaining session with him, thinking to present Cook with the hares to prepare for dinner, but discovered during the course of our conversation that I could not possibly bring the *hares* home, as his lordship is a confirmed Tory, and the farmer clearly embraced the *Whigs*. . . ."

As awful as his jokes were, Callie always laughed, mostly because he looked so pleased with himself.

She also adored Nigel, who always had a smile on his face and a kind word on his lips, as well as a highly developed sense of the ridiculous. At times, though, she thought she caught him watching her with an odd, speculative expression, as if he were an entomologist and she a particularly fascinating species of insect. Eventually she brushed that idea aside as sheer fantasy, for whenever she met his eyes he grinned at her unselfconsciously as if he found her a perfectly delightful female and he was no more than an admiring male.

She'd even—almost—become fond of Adam. As long as she kept her physical distance from him, which seemed to require a space between them of at least a foot, preferably two, she managed to keep her senses about her. She couldn't help but admire his powerfully built figure and striking good looks, but she appreciated his physical attributes in the same way that she might appreciate a handsome thoroughbred or . . . or a particularly fine statue. She felt quite sure there was nothing shameful in such an aesthetic admiration, only she wished her cheeks wouldn't burn and her stomach go hollow whenever she indulged in her aesthetic admiration.

As for his character, he couldn't help his acerbic nature, she'd decided, although she did have to admit that he'd mellowed considerably since her first encounter with him. He hadn't scowled at her once in the last two weeks.

Well, that wasn't entirely true, she amended, glancing over at him and quickly looking away before he caught her staring at him. He had put his foot down in no uncertain manner two days before at breakfast when she'd told him that she planned to go walking in the woods that morning.

"You will most certainly *not* go walking in the woods," he said, his face darkening. "You have plenty to keep you busy close to the house." He stirred sugar into his coffee with unnecessary force.

"I think you're being entirely unreasonable," she said stubbornly, for she longed to explore the mysterious forest and discover what wonders it might hold. There were bound to be all sorts of flora and fauna she'd never seen before. "I wouldn't go far, Adam. Couldn't I just go in a little way?"

"You are not to set even one toe in the woods," he replied, equally stubbornly.

"But why? I can't see what harm I could possibly come to. There aren't likely to be outlaws hiding in there. The days of Robin Hood are long gone. In Ravello I used to be able to go where I pleased."

"Do not think to argue with me, Callie," he said, his

expression hardening. "As long as you live under my roof you'll do as you're told."

"You're behaving like a worried mother hen, even worse than Mrs. Simpson," she snapped. "I'm not a child, you know."

"Sometimes you make me wonder," he said. "If you don't wish to be treated as a child, then don't behave like one."

"You are impossible," she cried. "I've obeyed your every wish!" In fairness she briefly paused to run over a list in her mind, and decided that she really had. "I've even put up with the footmen you set to shadow me when I go out on my own—do you think I don't see them hiding behind trees and statues? Michael and Henry must feel every bit as much an idiot as I do, all of us madly pretending we don't see each other."

Adam's full mouth twitched, but the thunder left his face. "Until I am certain that you are done with your headaches and dizzy spells you will have to put up with your watchdogs. However, I do apologize. You were not meant to be aware of their presence. I shall have to instruct them in the art of invisibility."

"Invisibility? A deer could see and hear them coming a hundred yards away."

"I am not concerned about the safety of the deer," he said, spreading a thin layer of marmalade over his toast. "I am, however, concerned about yours."

Callie dug her heels in. "I cannot see how I could get into any trouble."

"I can imagine any number of ways that you could find trouble. You seem to have a talent for it."

"Oh, that is unfair," Callie said, looking down. "Just because I happened to slip and fall off a ship—"

Adam's snort of laughter cut her off. "My point exactly."

"Oh, all right, there was that," she conceded, "but that was an accident. I'm not entirely incompetent."

"No . . . you do seem to have a talent for talking to insects. Harry Orris tells me that the troublesome hive has settled down nicely since you gave the inhabitants a lecture." His eyes danced with amusement and Callie blushed. "The next thing I know you'll be running off with the fairies."

"I might enjoy having a chat with God's creatures every now and then, but that doesn't mean I've gone fey. Lots of people talk to their animals. You talk to your horse all the time. I've seen you."

Adam glared at her, but she knew his heart wasn't in it. She knew because she'd begun to learn his expressions and to see far beyond what he intended her to see. Adam Carlyle might think himself as inscrutable as the Sphinx, but she knew better. Behind that enigmatic façade was a man with a kind heart and emotions that ran deep, she was sure of it, even if at times he could be the most unreasonable man alive.

She sneaked another glance at him. His focus was still entirely on Nigel, his beautifully shaped hands lightly poised on his knife and fork as he murmured a reply, something about turnips and the western acreage. She realized that she'd lost the thread of conversation, but she didn't mind, happy to admire his striking profile. Every inch of his bone structure spoke of breeding, from his straight, narrow nose to his squared chin and chiseled jawline. Of all his features, though, Callie found his eyes the most fascinating.

She could read his mood as clearly as the weather, depending on their shade. So far she'd catalogued azure for sunny skies, a paler aquamarine when frost threatened, a deep sapphire for approaching turbulence, and dark gray for thunder with imminent lightning. Then there was that color she couldn't name, a shade somewhere between slate and navy blue. At that point his lashes usually lowered halfway, giving him the lazy look of a cat that had cornered a mouse and was feigning complete boredom before pouncing. She'd learned to take that as a reliable cue to leave.

Tearing her gaze away from him, she released a little sigh, wishing that his eyes didn't turn that undefined color quite so often. Pretending indifference was a most annoying habit and she always felt as if he'd had the last word, even when he'd said nothing at all. She glared down at her plate, thinking how unfair his tactics could be.

"Is there something amiss with your roast pork, Callie?"

She jumped when she realized that Adam had broken off his conversation with Nigel and was addressing her. "No—no, it's delicious." She hoped he couldn't see her heightened color.

"Then why are you regarding it as if you'd like to kill it all over again?"

"I would *never* kill a pig," she said indignantly, neatly slicing the last of her meat and pushing the remainder of her beans onto her fork for good measure. "Pigs are highly intelligent. I wouldn't expect you to know this, but they make very good pets," she said when she'd swallowed.

"They make very good bacon, too," Nigel said with a grin. "Then again, I am particularly fond of crackling and Cook does such a good job, don't you agree?"

"You are both impossible," Callie said. "The way you talk, birds are only meant for shooting and fish for angling and—and cows and pigs and sheep and chickens for slaughtering."

"I think that's a very unfair statement, don't you?" Adam said, exchanging a look of amusement with Nigel. "We do keep cows for milking and hens for laying and we even shear the sheep for wool many times before we slaughter them. I don't see how you can fault that."

"You might be surprised to learn that there are many people in the world who are content to live on fruit and vegetables and grains," Callie said, placing her fork and knife on the side of her plate, having tremendously enjoyed her roast pork.

"Ah, but they're not Englishmen, are they?" Adam said. "If one's going to rule an empire one must have a steady diet of meat, preferably red. It stiffens the sinews, summons up the blood . . ."

"This is not Agincourt and you are not Henry the Fifth, Lord Vale," Callie retorted, wiping her mouth with her napkin. "Nor are you a tiger."

"I am deeply disappointed," Adam said. "You have cut me to the quick."

Callie looked over at Gettis, who stood at attention by the sideboard. She couldn't tell if his watery eyes were a result of suppressed amusement or a spring cold. "I think you had better bring bandages straight away, Gettis," she said. "Lord Vale is in danger of hemorrhaging from his possibly mortal wound."

"My wound is only metaphorical, Gettis," Adam said. "I think it might be healed by a nice blancmange."

Gettis bowed, motioned to the footmen to clear the table, and vanished into the kitchen, a series of muffled sneezes coming from behind the closed door.

"Poor Gettis does suffer with hay fever this time of year," Callie said, taking a sip of wine. "If you would only allow me to go into the woods, I am sure I could find the proper herbs to make him a nice tisane."

Adam's amusement abruptly vanished and he shot her a look of daggers drawn. "I would thank you to leave the subject alone," he said tightly. "We have a perfectly good herb garden behind the kitchen. If you cannot find what you need there, ask Roberts, the head gardener."

Callie knew she'd gone too far, but she didn't know why. She glanced over at Nigel, who didn't meet her eyes. "I shall do that," she said quickly, immediately regretting her tease. "Roberts is most wonderfully informative. Yesterday he showed me how to transplant geraniums. It is one of my favorite flowers . . ."

A few minutes more of chattering and she had managed to dispel the tension in the room, but as she slipped into bed and blew out her candle later that night, she couldn't help but wonder what dark secret the forest held. She knew she hadn't imagined Adam's deep agitation both times the subject had come up, and tonight Nigel's face might have been carved from stone when she mentioned it. She knew it was none of her business. She was no more than a temporary houseguest. Soon enough she'd be gone and she'd probably never see Adam or Stanton Abbey again. She certainly had no right to go against his wishes.

But what danger could the woods possibly hold to make both men look so grim and Adam so adamant that she stay well clear?

Rolling over on her side, Callie tucked her palm under her cheek and sleepily gazed out the window into the night sky. Mrs. Simpson did not approve of Callie's habit of sleeping with the draperies drawn back and the window pushed halfway open, but Callie would not be moved. Fresh air was life's blood to her, and she refused to be stifled while she slept.

A waxing quarter moon hung deep gold in the horizon as it started its rise into the starry heavens. Its faint light tipped the treetops of the thick forest, where an owl hooted once, twice, and then fell silent.

Walking into his office, Nigel removed his jacket and hung it over the back of his chair, then sat down and rubbed one hand over his scratchy eyes. He'd slept badly, probably the result of a guilty conscience. He was beginning to wonder if his judgment hadn't been seriously flawed when he'd decided to keep the truth of Callie's identity from Adam, even though his reasons for doing so had proved perfectly sound.

With each passing day Callie became more and more a part of the fabric of life at Stanton. She was like a ray of sunshine that couldn't help but brighten everything and everyone around her, Adam included—Adam most especially. Never in his wildest imaginings had Nigel expected Callie to have such a quick and positive effect on Adam's spirits. The most he'd anticipated was for Adam to be diverted from his own troubles by those of an ill, nameless young woman in trouble, and the best he'd hoped for was that Adam would become fond enough of Callie to see to a happier future for her than she'd find with Harold.

What Nigel hadn't anticipated was Callie herself. No longer ill, save for the occasional headache and a gaping hole in her memory that she disguised uncommonly well, she cheerfully busied herself with whatever she could find to do, whether it be in the kitchen, stables, or garden. Nigel never knew where he'd run into her, but always took pleasure from her company when he did.

Callie had that effect on people. Even Adam behaved as if she'd always been around, rather like a comfortable piece of furniture that he didn't particularly notice but would miss terribly if it suddenly vanished.

Which was where the problem lay, Nigel thought, rubbing his eyes again. Adam seemed to have developed his own case of amnesia regarding Callie. Since the first night three weeks before that Callie had dined with them and Adam had decided that she genuinely didn't know who she was or where she belonged, he hadn't once mentioned her lack of memory or what he planned on doing with her in the future. Adam behaved as if he hadn't given the matter another thought. She might have been a piece of lost luggage he'd mistakenly acquired, forgetting that he ought to return it to its rightful owner.

Nigel no more wanted to see Callie gone than anyone else at Stanton did, but he could hardly let the weeks drag on into months until years had gone by and the existence of Miss Callista Melbourne had been forgotten by the world at large—although he knew that wasn't likely to happen, not with what he'd recently discovered.

He glumly pulled open his desk drawer and withdrew the sheet of paper that had arrived by yesterday afternoon's post, wishing he'd never laid eyes on it. He should never have hired the blasted detective in the first place, for the man had done his job far too well.

Nigel now knew every pertinent detail about Callie's past, and he much preferred her own imaginative and far less complicated version, that she was a penniless young woman most recently of Ravello, Italy, with no relatives to worry about her welfare.

Unfortunately the real Callista Melbourne, most recently of Corfu, Greece, was not only not penniless, she was heiress to a considerable fortune whose trustee happened to be Sir Reginald Barnswell, a respected senior barrister and member of the King's Council. Furthermore, her nearest relative, a second cousin, happened to be the fifth Baron Fellowes.

Someone was bound to be looking for Callie, and if neither Sir Reginald nor Lord Fellowes had yet realized that Callie had disappeared, her ghastly fiancé Harold Carlyle certainly knew she had. Given that Callie's fifty thousand pounds would become Harold's upon their marriage, Harold, eternally greedy, wasn't likely to leave too many stones unturned to find her, and he'd sooner or later notify Sir Reginald or Lord Fellowes, if he hadn't already.

Hence the horns of Nigel's dilemma: If he passed on this information to Adam, Adam's sense of responsibility would immediately compel him to contact Lord Fellowes and Sir Reginald and dispatch Callie directly into one or the other's care, whereupon chances were that she would be compelled to go through with the marriage to Harold as arranged, for God only knew what reason. And if Callie was married to Harold Carlyle that would be the end of any happiness for her. He'd keep her under lock and key, spend all her money, and make her life thoroughly miserable. Nigel really couldn't bear the idea.

He hesitated, then made up his mind. Stuffing the damning sheet of paper into the back of his drawer, he locked it and slipped the key up under the raised inside edge of the desk bottom.

If someone was going to be thoroughly irresponsible, thereby saving Callie from Harold's clutches, it might as well be he.

What Adam and Callie didn't know wouldn't hurt either of them for the moment, and what was a little more time in the scheme of things? One never knew how matters might unfold, and maybe Adam would eventually see what Nigel did: Callie was Adam's perfect match.

———

"I'd be happy to take the basket to Mrs. Bishop for you," Callie said, when she overheard Mrs. Simpson complaining to Cook that she only had two hands, two legs, and an entire house to run, and hardly had the time or stamina to go dashing all over God's kingdom to deliver Charity to Those in Need as much as they might need it.

"If you insist, poppet," Mrs. Simpson said, managing to look doubtful and relieved all at the same time, but handing her the covered basket nevertheless. "It's a fair walk to the Bishop cottage, but if you think you can manage, it will save me the journey and I can get on with counting the linens. Jane's gone on her half-day and I can't spare any of the other girls."

"I can manage easily enough," Callie said, delighted for an excuse to go farther afield than usual.

"I don't know, poppet—with your health the way it's been . . ."

"Honestly, Mrs. Simpson, I feel perfectly well—I haven't had the headache in nearly a week now, the weather is fine, and the roads are dry. It's an easy enough errand."

"Yes, but you should really be asking his lordship's permission before you go."

"Lord Vale isn't here to ask. He went into town with Mr. Dryden to do some business and he said they won't be back before five. I can't think why he'd have any objection."

"No, I suppose not," Mrs. Simpson said, still looking doubtful. "Very well, then. The Bishops aren't really his lordship's responsibility as they're not on his land, nor do they lease from him, but Tom Bishop is my brother-in-law's nephew and they do need the help. Now remember to tell Nellie Bishop that the plasters are to be warmed before she puts them on her Georgie's tummy, and he's to have nothing stronger than the beef tea for three days. He has the stomachache something fierce and she's doing him no good by feeding him buttermilk." She clucked her tongue. "Ah, well, he's her first child and she's not to know any better. By the time the second one makes its appearance in a few months she'll be far more relaxed. The roasted chicken and vegetables are for Nellie and her husband, and she's not to be sneaking tidbits to the boy, not until he's stronger."

"I'll tell her all of that, Mrs. Simpson," Callie said with a reassuring smile, relieved that Mrs. Simpson had forgotten to mention the footmen who were supposed to follow her about.

"You keep to the roads, then, like a good girl—no crossing the fields. The bulls are separated out and you're not to know which fields are which. Nasty creatures bulls can be, and you never know when they're going to turn on you."

"Please don't worry about me," Callie said, privately thinking that people had an unwarranted prejudice against bulls, who were only interested in protecting their families just like anyone else.

She left by the back door, careful to make sure she hadn't been spotted by either Michael or Henry, and set off on her way, humming a snatch of song, breathing in the sharp, sweet air scented with blossom and the rich loam of earth from newly plowed fields, ready for sowing. The afternoon sunlight poured down hot and bright, warming her shoulders that were covered only by a light shawl, and she pulled that off and tossed it over the basket.

Callie's heart felt lighter than it had in a long time. She might not have a family or home of her own, but at least she had a temporary refuge, and with each passing day she felt more at home. She liked being useful, as if she was in some small way paying back the kindness that had been given to her.

She enjoyed every moment of the forty-five-minute walk, taking in all the new sights. Picturesque cottages dotted the sides of the road once she'd left the main drive of Stanton behind, some with gardens filled with wintered broccoli and cabbage, baby lettuces and the feathery tops of carrots, others bright with a multitude of flowers.

Wildflowers grew everywhere and she stopped to admire yellow cowslips, blue vetch, and white stitchwort growing in the thick grass along the verges. Chestnut trees danced with pink blossom, lilacs cascaded down stone walls, and as she rounded a corner she spotted a pheasant sitting peacefully in the sunshine. She smiled and called a greeting, and it ruffled its feathers in reply and lazily turned its head to watch her pass.

The Bishop cottage was tucked back behind a neat hedgerow, a thin wisp of smoke coming from its single chimney. Callie pushed open the wooden gate and made her way up the path to the front door. The two-room house was simple, the white paint around the windows trim and the steps freshly scrubbed, and yet somehow an overall air of shabbiness hung about it.

She'd noticed this general decline in the appearance of the cottages in the last half mile and had wondered at it.

Knocking lightly, Callie shifted the basket to her left hand and pulled out a posy of sweet violets that she'd picked along the way.

The door swung open and a woman whom Callie guessed to be in her early twenties appeared, her dark hair pulled back with a frayed ribbon, her dress clean but carefully darned in places. She looked tired; smudges stood out under her eyes and her cheeks looked pale. One hand rested over the slight swell of her abdomen. From the inside of the house Callie heard the thready, fretful wail of a small child.

"Good afternoon," Callie said. "Are you Mrs. Bishop?"

"I am," the woman said, regarding Callie with a subdued curiosity.

"I am pleased to meet you. I am Callie Magnus. Mrs. Simpson sent me from Stanton Abbey with her compliments and asked me to deliver this basket to you."

Nellie Bishop first looked startled, then uncomfortable, as if she felt embarrassed to be accepting charity. "She is very thoughtful, although I have told her time and again that we manage perfectly well."

"I have decided that as Mrs. Simpson has no children of her own, she feels a need to mother everyone else," Callie said, her heart going out to Nellie Bishop. Callie of all people knew how it felt to have nothing and be beholden to other people. "I've been at the receiving end of her maternal instincts for the last month, bless her, but I confess I seized on an excuse to escape for the afternoon. I hope you don't mind a perfect stranger coming to your door." Callie extended the posy. "They were so pretty, I couldn't resist. They probably need water right away or they'll start to wilt."

Nellie's mouth turned up in a faint smile and she buried her nose in the violets. "Thank you," she said, looking genuinely touched. "Please, won't you come in?"

"Thank you. I'd like that very much." Callie followed Nellie into the house.

A fire burned in the hearth where a pot hanging from a rod simmered, and a child Callie guessed to be about two years of age sat on a blanket in front of the protective screen, still crying and rubbing at his eyes. He was heavily bundled in clothing and looked hot and uncomfortable. "This must be Georgie," Callie said, placing the basket on the kitchen table and going to kneel down next to him. "Hello, Georgie," she said softly. "I hear you're feeling a bit under the weather. Tummy-aches are no fun, are they?" She passed her hand lightly over his shock of blond hair.

Georgie stopped crying and looked at her with wide gray eyes, then stuck his thumb in his mouth and started sucking with a vengeance, drool running down his red cheeks.

Callie looked up over her shoulder at Nellie. "What a fine boy you have. Does he take after his father?"

"He does indeed," Nellie said, relaxing slightly and looking pleased. "From the day he was born he's been the very image of Tom. He's big for his age at eighteen months, so I reckon he'll grow into a strapping man just like his pappy."

"It's always nice when sons take after their fathers. What sort of work does your husband do?"

"He's a farmer, miss. He leases fifty acres from Squire Hoode." Nellie began unpacking the basket.

"Squire Hoode?" Callie wrinkled her brow, trying to recall if she'd heard the name but it didn't ring a bell. "Does his land march with Stanton?"

"Aye, miss, although the grange is nowhere near the size of Stanton, nor the house grand like the abbey. West Grange Manor is nice enough, but nothing could compare to Stanton Abbey, could it? I reckon the squire knows it, too." She stopped abruptly, her hand slipping to her mouth. "Begging your pardon, miss. I have no business going on about my betters."

"Oh, I do wish you would," Callie said, knowing she was breeding mischief but unable to help herself. She felt an affinity with Nellie Bishop, for no reason that she could really explain other than they were close to the same age and Nellie had a nice smile and honest eyes. "There's so much I long to know about Hythe, and Stanton in particular, but I don't feel that it would be proper to ask the servants and I certainly can't ask Lord Vale or even Mr.

Dryden anything the least bit personal. I have to be terribly careful about not overstepping my place, being only a temporary guest, but I'm afraid one of my worst failings is an unquenchable curiosity."

"I do know what you mean, miss. I'm the same way myself. I drive my Tom quite round the bend with questions." She grinned. "He says one day I'll have my nose pecked off when I dig it too deep where it doesn't belong."

"It sounds to me as if we both have the same problem. May I pick Georgie up?" Callie asked, when his face started to scrunch up again and tears threatened anew.

"Please do," Nellie said, settling in a chair with a sigh. "He's getting so heavy, and he's still at the age where he likes to be lugged about. Sometimes I think my back is going to break between his weight and carrying this new one here." She ran a hand over her belly. "We've all of us heard about you, of course, miss—no offense intended, but word spreads like wildfire round the village, being so small-like. They say you fell off a ship into the sea and his lordship rescued you. Is it true?"

Callie swung Georgie up onto her hip and sat down at the table, settling the child more comfortably on her lap and absently handing him a spoon that he proceeded to gnaw on. "It is, and I feel like the veriest idiot. I cannot think how I managed to do such a silly thing, either, but I do thank God that Lord Vale happened to be there at the time, or I wouldn't be here now to tell the tale."

"They say it was a miracle, his fetching you out of the terrible sea like that and bringing you safely back, and that your recovery was another miracle, for no one expected you to live." She regarded Callie gravely. "You look right as rain to me."

Callie laughed. "I am right as rain, or near enough, anyway. I've been fortunate to receive such good care. Lord

Vale made sure of that, and I'll be forever grateful to him for looking after me so well."

"He's a good man, his lordship. He looks after his own. Many's the time I've said to my Tom that I wished we were his tenants and not the squire's, but that's just the way of things, I suppose. Tom's father and his father before him all leased land from the squire's father and *his* father before him, and each one was more tightfisted than the last. The present squire would pinch a penny till it screamed if he could—he tries hard enough." She looked past Callie as if not seeing her. "It's not right that my Tom should work day and night until he's ready to drop and never be able to get ahead, all because the squire won't give him his fair due at harvest time, let alone charging rent for the land far above what it's worth."

"That sounds terribly unfair," Callie said, outraged at the squire's injustice. She was absolutely certain that Adam would *never* treat his tenants like that. Even if she hadn't been so sure of his character, she would have known from the conversations she'd listened to between Adam and Nigel, never mind the testimonials from Mrs. Simpson, Jane, and all the others at Stanton.

Nellie shrugged and her smile was touched with pragmatism. "I shouldn't complain, though. All the squire's cottagers are in the same trouble. There's not a one of us who doesn't wish we had Lord Vale for our landlord."

"I can certainly understand why," Callie said, storing this information away to mull over later. She decided that she liked Nellie Bishop very much, for she was forthright and had no qualms about speaking her mind to Callie, which came as a welcome relief. No matter how kind the staff of Stanton Abbey was to her, their loyalty lay completely with their master, and Callie had intuitively sensed that any but the most mundane of questions about Adam would be politely rebuffed. She had the most ridiculous feeling that in some way they were protecting him, although she couldn't think from what. He seemed a most self-sufficient man and more than capable of looking after himself.

"Have you lived in Hythe all your life?" she asked, wondering if Nellie Bishop might be able to tell her something about Adam's history.

"Oh no, miss. I come from Dymchurch, down the coast, nearer the Romney Marsh. I only moved to Hythe when I married four years ago. Tom, now, he could tell you everything you want to know and more than you probably do about Hythe."

Georgie started to squirm on Callie's lap and threw the spoon on the floor with a clatter, and Callie, distracted from her line of questioning, turned him around and bounced him on her knees.

"I'll take him from you, miss. He's been terrible tetchy with his upset stomach these last few days, crying day and night, and nothing pleases him. It doesn't seem to help whatever I do—I've tried cordial of gripe water and warm milk, but it all just goes right through him."

"Do you know, Mrs. Bishop," Callie said, fairly certain that she knew what Georgie's trouble stemmed from, "I might be able to help. I don't want to interfere—"

"I wish you would!" Nellie said. "I've had more useless advice than I know what to do with. You seem to have a good head on your shoulders."

Callie laughed, thinking that statement was a true irony. "I don't know about that," she said, "and I don't have any children of my own, but I do believe that your Georgie is cutting his molars and having a hard time with them." Clear as day an image swam into Callie's mind of another dark-haired woman, this one olive-skinned, with bright black eyes, bouncing a baby of her own on her lap and describing to Callie an old peasant remedy for just this thing.

"An infusion of valerian," she murmured half to herself, as if reciting from memory. "That will calm him and help him to sleep. Cloves, ground and mixed with water to a thick paste, sweetened with honey and applied on the gums will deaden the pain. Hard rusks of bread will help the teeth break through and settle his stomach, which is upset from all the excess saliva he's producing." She thought hard, wondering what she was leaving out. "Oh, yes, and compresses of cool lavender water on his neck and cheeks will work wonders in relieving the inflammation and heat he's feeling from it. He'll be much more comfortable if you keep him cool rather than bundling him up—fresh air works wonders." She planted a kiss on Georgie's hot forehead. "Isn't that right, young man?"

Georgie gurgled at her as if he'd understood her perfectly and patted her cheeks with both hands.

Nellie Bishop looked at Callie with astonishment. "His teeth, miss? Not a single soul mentioned that, nor any of the rest of it, either. How would you be knowing a thing like that?"

"I wish you'd call me Callie," she said, about to make a huge leap of faith, "and to be perfectly honest, I have no idea, other than I just know. I haven't told another living soul this, but if I don't confide in someone, I really am going to go mad. The truth of the matter is, Nellie, that I've completely lost my memory and haven't the first idea who I am."

## 8

$\mathcal{N}$ellie's mouth dropped open and then firmly closed again, and she clasped her fingers together and placed her hands on the table in front of her. "You don't know who you are," she said, not as a question but as a statement.

"I haven't a clue," Callie agreed, thankful that Nellie showed no signs of distress. She hadn't known what to expect, but Nellie's levelheaded reaction was a balm to her spirit.

"And no one knows about this—How is that possible? You must have been asked questions about yourself, where you came from."

"I made up a past for myself," Callie said, coloring. "I know that sounds a terribly wrong thing to do, but I was so afraid of what might become of me if I admitted that I couldn't remember anything, and at the time Lord Vale didn't seem very pleased to have me at Stanton. I suppose he was annoyed that I'd caused him so much trouble, but I truly worried that he would send me away to a hospital or an asylum or somewhere equally horrible."

Nellie didn't say anything, and Callie wondered if she'd made a terrible mistake, but she held her peace, praying that Nellie might be sympathetic to her plight. She busied herself with Georgie, playing a little game with his hands.

"Why have you told me this?" Nellie finally said. "You have no reason to trust me or to believe that I will keep your secret."

"I like you," Callie said simply. "And I'm in need of a friend."

Nellie's face broke into a wide smile. "Reason enough," she said, as if she'd made up her mind. "You have nothing to fear from me. Well, now. This is an interesting situation. What do you plan to do? Do you think you can go on pretending forever?"

"I—I don't know," Callie said miserably. "I've been praying that one day I would wake up and my memory would be back in full, but an entire month's gone by and all that's come to me are a few vague pictures that I can't really place—like just now, when I was telling you about Georgie's teething and what to do for him. I *know* that what I said was right, for I remember a woman telling me in just those words, but I don't know who she is or where we were when we had the conversation."

She gently wrapped her arms around Georgie, who'd rested his head against her chest, stuck his thumb back in his mouth, and showed every sign of falling asleep. "The worst part is lying to all the people who have been so good to me, Lord Vale in particular. I feel terrible about deceiving them, but I didn't know what else to do. And now that I'm so much better, I feel truly wicked for continuing the deception."

Nellie nodded. "Aye, I can understand why you chose to pretend, especially when you were so ill." She looked long and hard at Callie. "I believe you have a good heart, for my Georgie doesn't take to strangers. Children sense things about people the way animals do." She spread her palms flat against the tabletop. "What can I do to help you?"

"You have already helped by letting me unburden myself," Callie said. "Beyond that, I don't think there's anything anyone can do. I have to work out a way to look after myself, find employment of some kind. I can't stay on at Stanton forever, or even for very much longer."

"Where would you go—what would you do?" Nellie asked with a troubled frown. "You have no family, or not one that you know of, and no one to protect you. Why can't you just tell his lordship your troubles and let him help you?"

"I don't think he'd be very pleased with me if I told him the truth," Callie said grimly. "Perhaps if I'd done so in the beginning he might have understood, but now . . . I can't imagine he'd feel anything but badly deceived and ill-used. Anyway, I already told him that I didn't want his help when he offered it to me."

Nellie gaped at her. "He *offered* to help you and you were foolish enough to turn him down? Miss—I mean, Callie, don't you realize that his lordship could open any door for you that he chose? He could make your life so much easier—What in the world were you thinking?"

Callie thought that was a very good question. She didn't know herself. "I suppose," she said, feeling rather silly, "that I thought he was rude and overbearing and I didn't want him to start looking for relatives he couldn't possibly find, since I don't even know my surname and the one I supplied to him is a fabrication. He'd have worked that out in no time at all, and then I'd have really been in trouble."

Nellie pushed herself to her feet and walked over to a large wooden cabinet that sat against the far wall, taking out two plates. She ladled some stew into them, produced two spoons from a drawer, and put one of the plates in front of Callie. "It's only beans and potatoes, but I always think better on a full stomach," she said, gently lifting the sleeping child from Callie's lap and settling him on the blankets in front of the fire.

Sitting back down at the table, she poured two glasses of water from a pitcher, handed one to Callie, then picked up her spoon and began to eat with an abstracted expression. Callie followed suit, finding the stew surprisingly good. She hadn't realized how hungry she was.

"That's better," Nellie said when she was finished. She leaned back in her chair and regarded Callie gravely. "I wonder how much you know about his lordship."

"I don't really know him at all," Callie admitted. "He's not a man who's inclined to show his hand, and he certainly never gives any hint of his emotions. He's usually polite and can often be amusing, but for the most part he behaves as if I'm a silly girl who just happened to land on his doorstep and whose company he's willing to tolerate until I've fully recovered and can take myself away again— not that he's indicated he's in any rush," she added, trying to be fair to Adam. "He's far too polite for that, whatever he might feel."

"I wonder . . ." Nellie said, her face taking on that abstracted expression again. "I think it's interesting that he's been so obliging to you, when he's hardly taken any notice of anyone in the last two years, even Mr. Dryden, and he his lordship's oldest friend."

Callie sat up straighter. "What are you talking about?" she said, mystified. "He's perfectly pleasant to Nigel—Mr.

Dryden, that is. We all dine together every evening and they behave exactly like the oldest of friends. Did they have a falling out at some point back?"

"Do you mean you don't know? No one's said anything to you?" Nellie asked, looking astonished.

"Said anything about what?" Something prickled at the base of Callie's spine, a feeling that Nellie was about to tell her something terribly important that might go a long way toward explaining the mystery she'd sensed at Stanton, all tied up with the reluctance of the servants to talk about Adam, Adam's adroit ability to steer the conversation away from himself, and his adamant refusal to let her go anywhere near the woods.

"I—I don't know if I should say," Nellie said, suddenly looking acutely uncomfortable. "I don't want to go talking out of turn if his lordship doesn't want his business known, but it's not a secret, I suppose. I mean, everyone knows what happened."

"For heaven's sake, just tell me, Nellie!" Callie felt as if she were about to jump out of her skin with impatience.

"Well... you did know his lordship was married?" Nellie fiddled with her plate, turning it round and round in her fingers

Callie stared at her, the color draining from her face. "Married? I—I had no idea." She didn't know why the news hit her like a hard blow in the soft pit of her belly. Adam, married? The thought had never crossed her mind that he might have a wife. The stew suddenly felt like a lump of lead in her stomach. "But if he's married, where is his wife? No one's said a word about her, and there isn't a single sign of a mistress about the house."

"You misunderstand me," Nellie said gently, regarding Callie curiously. "I meant that he was married once. His wife was killed two years ago, and their little boy with her. The poor lad was only four."

Stunned, Callie could think of nothing to say. She found drawing breath difficult enough. "H—how were they killed?" she finally managed to stammer.

"It was an accident, a terrible tragedy, or at least that was the verdict at the inquest. A poacher must have been in the woods and fired his gun believing he was aiming at a deer, not realizing that her ladyship and the child were out walking. Whoever fired the gun never was found—he must have taken off as soon as he realized what had happened and hardly surprising, for he'd have hanged for the offense, accident or no." Nellie shook her head. "His lordship was beside himself with grief. He doted on his family, and to have them taken from him so cruelly nearly undid him, they say." She sighed heavily. "I've heard it said that a broken heart can take some like that."

"The poor man," Callie whispered. "How unspeakably horrible for him." She could barely conceive of the pain he must have suffered—must still be suffering. No wonder she sometimes caught that bleak expression in his eyes when he thought no one was watching.

"It was that," Nellie said, her gaze steadily fixed on Callie's face. "Anyway, they say he changed overnight—cut the world off, refused to see anyone. No one up at the house was allowed to mention his wife or son's name, as if they'd never existed. They say he never set foot again in the family chapel where the poor souls are interred, not even once to pay his respects."

"I'm sure he doesn't stay away from lack of love," Callie murmured, her heart aching for Adam. "Pain is sometimes too acute to let in even the smallest reminder,"

"Well, that must be why he still doesn't want them mentioned, so I suppose I shouldn't be surprised that you haven't heard anything about it. His lordship's staff is loyal as they come, and they wouldn't go against his wishes. But maybe now you see why I think it's interesting that his lordship bothered to take an interest in you, when he hasn't taken an interest in anything else for so long."

"I wouldn't say he's taken an interest in me, exactly," Callie said. "I'm just an inconvenience he feels obliged to house for the moment."

"Humph," Nellie said. "Maybe so and maybe not, but from what you've been telling me, he doesn't sound like the same man who could barely be bothered to give anyone the time of day only a few weeks ago. Not that he ever neglected Stanton or his tenants, mind you," she added loyally. "Not a soul could fault him there—He knows his duty, his lordship does, no matter how heavily his personal troubles weigh on him."

Leaning her elbow on the table, Callie rested her chin on her folded fingers and considered. She was having a hard time reconciling the Adam she knew with the man Nellie had just been describing, although when she ran back in time to her first meetings with him, he had seemed much colder and far more distant to her. She'd assumed that was because he'd been annoyed with her in the extreme for forcing him to rescue her, not to mention her refusal to be more forthcoming with him.

Looking at the situation from this new perspective, though, she could easily put a different interpretation on it. She had invaded his sanctuary, been an unwelcome intruder in his retreat from the world. He had surrounded himself by high walls, built not of stone but of something even more impenetrable. The determination of the human will was a powerful force, and Adam had used his will to shut out all emotion and protect himself from unbearable suffering.

There was only one very large problem with that line of defense: He'd never heal unless he learned to face his pain and accept his loss.

She knew that as clearly as she knew anything, which wasn't saying much, but in her heart she felt the truth, and her heart was the best compass she had to guide her.

"Good heavens!" she said, suddenly realizing with alarm how much time had passed. "I must be going or Mrs. Simpson will get into a terrible fluster wondering what's happened to me," she said, standing. "Thank you for listening to me, Nellie, and thank you also for being so direct with me. I am grateful to have a new friend."

Nellie's tired face lit up with a smile. "I'm happy for it too," she said. "My door is always open to you, Callie, anytime you care to come through it. You just remember that I have a curiosity to match your own and I'll be wanting to know how things are coming along for you—and anything you care to tell me stays strictly between us."

"It had better, or I really *will* find myself packed off to an asylum," Callie said with a light laugh as she walked to the door. "Oh, before I forget . . ." She quickly rattled off Mrs. Simpson's instructions regarding the contents of the basket. "I shouldn't pay them too much mind, but I thought I'd better tell you in case she asks," Callie added. "Georgie will be just fine once those molars emerge."

"Aye, and wouldn't it be nice if your memory was so obliging?" Nellie said, chuckling as she waved good-bye.


The sun slanted from the west as Callie started back, and she walked as quickly as she could, knowing the time had to be past four, which meant she'd already been gone nearly two hours. Mrs. Simpson would be expecting her by now, and Callie still had close to forty minutes to go before she reached Stanton Abbey.

The last thing Callie wanted was for anyone to be alarmed at her absence, and if by some unlucky chance Adam returned to Stanton before she did and found her gone, she'd be in certain trouble for having left without his appointed shadows. Worse, Henry and Michael would be in for a real earful that they didn't deserve.

Ten minutes later Callie stopped. She could see the abbey in the distance, but if she stayed on the winding road she'd be adding an extra three miles or so to her journey. It would be much more sensible, she decided, to cut directly across the fields and make a beeline for home, saving a good half hour. Mrs. Simpson might be worried about bulls, but Mrs. Simpson needn't know that Callie had taken a shortcut. In any case, the fields would be far less dusty than the road, and she knew from listening to Nigel and Adam that most of the land on this side was still in grass.

She turned to the left and climbed easily over the wooden fence that bordered the road. The meadow felt lovely and soft beneath her feet and she hummed as she walked, reveling in the sweet air and the scent of wildflowers. In the distance a herd of cows grazed, and farther to the south she could just make out the faint screech of seagulls circling over the cliffs.

The next fence she came to had a convenient gate built into the far right, and she opened it easily, careful to close and latch it behind her. Ten minutes more and she'd be safely ensconced in the kitchen with a cup of tea and maybe even some rock cakes, if Cook had been baking. Adam would never know she'd been gone.

Adam . . . she still couldn't absorb the enormity of what Nellie had told her, and she felt vaguely guilty, as if she had made herself privy to a deeply personal tragedy that had nothing to do with her. And yet knowing about his terrible loss gave her a deeper insight into his character that she hadn't had before, and that had to be to the good—or was it? She wasn't entirely sure.

At least now she knew which subjects to avoid, since Adam obviously didn't want any reminders of his loss. Just getting through each day without his wife and child must serve as reminder enough. She really couldn't imagine what the last two years must have been like for him, but if what Nellie said was true, and Callie had no reason to doubt her, Adam had shut himself away with his grief and, Adam being Adam, had refused to let anyone help.

He really was impossibly stubborn.

Then again, so was she, and since she owed Adam a very great deal, the least she could do with the time she had left at Stanton was to help him to see that life was for living, whether he cared to be shown or not.

She wasn't exactly sure how she was going to go about her mission, but she felt confident that something would come to her. Maybe he just needed to be taken out and shaken like a rug that had been sitting about collecting dust.

Callie couldn't help smiling. Somehow she didn't think Adam would appreciate a good shaking. She was absolutely sure he wouldn't appreciate her poking into his business any more than she appreciated his poking into hers—and there was a point.

She really didn't have a leg to stand on when it came to keeping secrets or being evasive. For all she knew she had a terrible tragedy in her past and she just didn't remember how grief-stricken she was. It was one thing to suffer the loss of two people you loved to distraction, and quite another not to remember loving anyone at all.

At least Adam had his memories. Despite the pain it had later brought him, he'd loved his wife and child dearly. She would give anything to know love, even if it was just a memory. She would give anything just to belong somewhere, to someone.

*But you do know love,* a voice whispered, as soft as a breeze on her cheek.

Callie came to an abrupt halt, looking around her. She was alone, and yet she'd heard the voice clear as day.

*Look, Callie, look deep,* the whisper said again. *Open your heart and look at what it holds.*

Callie rubbed her eyes, thinking that she really had lost her mind. Now she was hearing voices that didn't exist.

*Listen to your heart, child. Only your heart can show you where you belong . . .* The whisper faded away until it became no more than the light rustle of leaves in the treetops.

Shaken to her core, Callie sank to the ground. She had no explanation for what had just happened to her, only that she'd felt filled with an overwhelming sense of warmth and peace, as if she'd been enfolded in gentle, invisible, but loving arms. That love still resonated in her heart like a chord that had been struck in perfect harmony, shattering the protective shell she'd built around it and leaving her exposed and very, very vulnerable. Yet at the same time she felt completely and vibrantly alive, as if an essential part of her had been sleeping and was now waking, like a flower opening up to the sun and its warmth after a long winter's rest.

Why then did she suddenly also feel as if she'd just lost her best friend?

She realized that tears were streaming down her cheeks, and she reached up trembling fingers to wipe them away.

*Callie!*

She vaguely registered hearing her name again from

somewhere in the distance, and she cautiously peeped up at the sky from between her fingers, wondering if she was next going to see a host of angels floating overhead with harps and trumpets and . . . and drums. She didn't know if angels played drums, but she distinctly heard a rhythmic beating coming closer.

Only moments later very human, very strong arms grasped her from behind and pulled her around, crushing her against soft material that smelled distinctly of crisp linen and sunshine and . . . Adam.

"Thank heaven I found you!" he said, his voice muffled in her hair. "Are you hurt? What happened? Did you fall?"

She managed to pull back from his tight grasp and look up into his face, incredibly happy to see him, solid and real and looking scared half out of his wits.

"I'm perfectly well," she said, trying to collect her thoughts without much success, too many emotions cascading through her to make sense of them all. "I just—I—um . . ." She couldn't tell him about the voice without his thinking her completely mad. "I sat down for a little rest."

"I don't believe you. You've been crying," he said, the two faint lines between his brows deepening as he lightly touched her wet cheek with his fingers.

"Don't be absurd. I never cry," she said, blinking rapidly.

"Callie, tell me the truth—are you in pain?" He leaned back and quickly looked her up and down as if making sure that she still had all her limbs in the right places. "Is it your head that hurts?"

She gazed at him, thinking that he looked just like he had the very first time she'd seen him—Saint George, the valiant fighter, his eyes blazing sapphire and trained on her with a fierce, concerned concentration. "My head?" she said, thinking her head had never felt clearer. "No . . . my head is fine." Her heart was another matter. It was beating so hard it felt as if it might burst out of her chest and she took a deep, shaky breath, trying to steady it. "My head is fine, I'm fine. Everything is fine, Adam." She smiled at him foolishly. "What are you doing out here?"

"What am I—The question is what the devil are you doing sitting in the middle of a field, on your own and at this hour?" he said, his voice rising to a near-shout as if now, satisfied that she'd come to no harm, he was going to take her to pieces himself. "Do you have any idea how worried I've been?"

"Do you mean you came looking for me?" she said in bemusement, but delighted that he had.

"Yes, I came looking for you," he said with exasperation. "I was *not* very pleased to return home only to discover that you had gone marching off all the way to Hythe hours ago—and by yourself, of all idiotic things. Anything might have happened, Callie, did you think of that? By God, when I saw you suddenly go down like that, I thought—I thought you must have hurt yourself." His mouth formed a grim line.

"I'm sorry," Callie said in a low voice. "I hadn't meant to be gone so long, but I enjoyed talking with Nellie Bishop so much, and then when I realized how late the hour had grown I thought I'd better take a shortcut, just so that I wouldn't worry anyone." She bit her lip. "I didn't think you'd be back in time to notice. Please don't blame Mrs. Simpson or any of the footmen. I'm the only person you should be annoyed with, and I'm sorry if I gave you a fright."

Adam blew out a long breath. "You might think of that the next time you choose to disappear." His voice gentled. "Look here, Callie. I don't mean for you to feel as if you're under lock and key, but you are still recovering from a serious accident and you ought not to be overexerting yourself."

"I'm much stronger," she said, but she knew he had a point.

"Perhaps you are, but Dr. Hadley made himself very clear about the possibility of recurring dizziness and headaches. Furthermore, women, even independent, single-minded, infuriatingly willful women such as yourself, do *not* go out unattended in public."

"But in Ra—"

"And I don't want to hear a single word about how it's done in Ravello, because I think you make up anything that suits you in order to try to get your way. I feel very sure that young women are expected to behave the same way in Ravello and other places in the civilized world as they are in England."

"Oh," Callie said.

"Oh, indeed. You didn't think you could continue to try to put that one over, did you? If life in Italy went on as you painted it, women would be running the country."

Callie grinned. "Well . . . maybe I exaggerated a little."

"A little?" he said with disbelief. "Never mind. I won't even attempt to address the issue further." He stood and held out his hands to her. "Come, it's time to go home. Are you strong enough to stand now?"

Callie was about to tell him that a lack of stamina hadn't been what had made her sit down so abruptly, but thought better of it. "Yes," she said, taking his hands and letting him help her to her feet.

"Have you ever ridden a horse?" he asked, turning and whistling.

Only as Gabriel lifted his head with a whinny and trotted over did Callie realize that Adam had ridden, and that the drumbeat she'd heard had been Gabriel's hooves at full gallop.

"Of course I have," she said, thrilled to pieces. She'd

been longing to ride Gabriel since she'd first set eyes on him. He was a magnificent animal, a beautiful combination of grace and strength, not unlike his master.

Belatedly she realized that wasn't what Adam had in mind as he picked her up by the waist and deposited her sideways on the saddle. He effortlessly swung up behind her and wrapped one arm lightly around her waist. Gathering up the reins with the other hand, he nudged Gabriel into a walk.

Callie quickly decided that she didn't mind this unconventional form of transport at all. She leaned her shoulder against Adam's broad chest and let his weight support her. She hated to have to admit it to herself, but she was tired, and something about the easy manner in which Adam held her close against him made her feel safe and protected.

They reached the house only five minutes later, a pity, Callie thought, for she could have happily sat like that for a great deal longer. Adam pulled Gabriel up at the front steps, dismounted, and wordlessly handing the reins to a footman standing at the ready, he reached up and lifted her down, gently depositing her on the ground.

Callie looked up and realized that Mrs. Simpson, Gettis, Plimpton, Jane, and most of the other household staff stood outside the door, all of them looking pale with worry and vastly relieved to see her home safe, Michael and Henry included. She wanted to disappear with embarrassment and shame and cursed herself for her thoughtlessness.

"I really am sorry, Adam," she said in a whisper.

"We won't mention it again," he murmured, taking her arm and leading her up the steps. "Here is Miss Callie," he said to the gathering. "Safe and sound and I imagine longing for a pot of hot tea and something to eat. Which," he said, turning to Callie, "you will take in your bed, where you will oblige me by staying until tomorrow morning.

Mrs. Simpson will take you upstairs and Jane will see that you're comfortably settled. I must go out again and find Nigel, who thought you might have been foolish enough to disobey me and go into the woods."

The blood drained from Callie's face as the full realization of why Adam had been so deeply concerned about her absence sank in. For an awful moment she felt as if she might faint.

Adam didn't hesitate. He scooped her into his arms as easily as if she were a child and carried her directly through the throng, into the house, and up the stairs straight into her bedroom where he placed her on the bed, pushing a pillow behind her head and pulling a blanket over her in two swift, economic movements.

"Adam, I—" She wet her dry lips with her tongue, trying to find the right words to tell him how terrible she felt about alarming him so unnecessarily.

"Not another word," he said firmly. "I daresay you've learned your lesson and if you haven't, I'll take you over my knee the next time, and don't think I won't. Rest, Callie, and regain your strength. I'll be in later to see how you're feeling."

"Thank you," she said, looking up into his concerned face. "You are very good to me," she said quietly, wondering how she could ever have thought him cold and unfeeling.

"I can't think why," he said, suddenly smiling. "You are a disobedient baggage and should be locked in your room for a week with absolutely nothing to read." He glanced pointedly at her bedside table where a pile of books were stacked. "That would bring you into line fast enough. Ah, here you are, Mrs. Simpson," he said, looking over his shoulder and straightening. "You may take over your charge now, and you're not to scold her. I've already blistered her ears and she's repented for her sins."

"Very good, my lord," Mrs. Simpson said, wiping her red-rimmed eyes with her handkerchief. "All's well that ends well, I always say. Isn't that right, my pet? Will you want the doctor called in, my lord?"

But Adam had already slipped out, so Callie set about reassuring Mrs. Simpson that she had no need for the doctor, that she was only tired, that Nellie Bishop had been such good company that Callie had lost track of time, and so on and so on until Mrs. Simpson was finally reassured and Callie really was exhausted.

Finally left in peace after obediently drinking her tea and eating buttered scones and cucumber sandwiches under Mrs. Simpson's watchful eye, Callie heaved a sigh of relief and settled comfortably under the covers, mulling over her extraordinary afternoon.

She felt as if something significant had shifted in her small world, but she wasn't exactly sure what that shift was, only that it was very important. She'd gained a friend and a confidant in Nellie, and that alone gave her huge pleasure, for as much as the staff at Stanton might welcome her in their domain, they always subtly managed to remind her that an indefinable distance existed between them. She was Lord Vale's guest and they were his servants, and an invisible line separated them that Callie couldn't cross.

Nellie seemed to have made no such distinction, wholeheartedly accepting Callie, Lord Vale's guest or no, but then Nellie had no ties of loyalty or obligation to Adam—another reason Callie had decided to trust Nellie with her secret. She didn't regret her impulse for one moment, for not only did she feel confident that Nellie would not betray her, she also felt greatly relieved to have unburdened herself. The weight hadn't gone from her shoulders but it felt much lighter.

She wondered if Adam had anyone to unburden himself to. Nigel would be the obvious candidate, but from what Nellie had said, Adam had cut even Nigel off from his private feelings. Callie doubted that Adam confided in the vicar for spiritual counseling, since the last few Sundays had come and gone without any effort on Adam's part to go to church—indeed, she had to wonder if Adam even paid lip service to God, never mind the vicar. Adam never mentioned the Almighty in any context unless he was swearing, which led her to believe that his spiritual well-being must be low on his list of priorities.

Thinking about it, she realized how little she really knew about Adam. She knew nothing of his childhood, of when or how his father had died, if his mother was still alive or if he had any brothers or sisters, and if so, where they lived. She'd been so careful not to ask any personal questions for fear that she would be asked the same in kind that she'd kept to the most neutral of topics. Adam had obliged her by limiting his questions about her past to general inquiries about life in Ravello, which she was happy to invent, had even come to enjoy inventing for the sheer fun of teasing him. Other than that, they generally discussed philosophy, history, literature, and their day-to-day activities.

As a result, she knew what his opinions were on a variety of topics, but not what had formed them.

Callie considered. What *did* constitute knowing a person? It couldn't be the ordinary details of one's past, for if that were the case, she would have no understanding of Adam at all, nor he of her. But that wasn't how she felt—they were comfortable together, like old friends who marched along easily without the need for explanations and trivial politeness.

She liked Adam. She liked him very much, and she thought that he liked her, too. Surely that was enough? Knowing him too much better would only make her leaving that much more difficult, wouldn't it?

Rolling over onto her stomach, Callie moaned and buried her head in the pillow. She was lying to herself, and pretending would get her nowhere. She'd already done enough of that; only hard, cold truth would serve her, the master of pretense, now.

*Open your heart and look at what it holds . . . only your heart can tell you where you belong.*

The whisper in the meadow came back to her unbidden, serving as an acute reminder of what she had known deep within her from the moment that Adam had found her in the meadow and pulled her into his arms. She had been trying to ignore the blinding realization ever since.

Against all reason, she'd fallen in love with him.

She, a woman with no past and a highly questionable future, had fallen in love with a man who possessed not only a title and a fortune, but a heart bound to the past and his dead wife and child.

# 9

$\mathcal{D}$usk drew down, painting the deepening blue of the sky with long fingers of red and purple as Adam cantered toward the woods in search of Nigel. An icy dread constricted his chest, as if it were yesterday and not two interminably long years ago that he'd gone into the forest looking for Caroline and Ian. He'd expected to find them standing in their favorite spot on the little wooden bridge that spanned the stream, watching for fish and waiting for him. What he'd found instead didn't bear remembering.

A cold sweat beaded Adam's brow as he struggled to fend off the image of his wife's body lying still and bloodied, half covering Ian's small, lifeless form as if to protect him. He discovered later that she must have been carrying Ian and fallen where she stood; she wouldn't even have had time to register any danger. The single bullet that killed them both had pierced her through the back and finished its deadly course lodged in Ian's heart.

Swallowing hard against the metallic taste of bile rising in his throat, he forced himself to focus on the present. He needed to find Nigel—only Nigel. Callie was safe and tucked up in her bed where no harm could come to her. He might not have been able to save his wife and son, and for that he'd never forgive himself, but by God, no careless poacher was going to hurt any more innocents. Adam had seen that the word had gone out far and wide: Any trespasser on Stanton land would be shot on sight.

Bringing Gabriel to a halt, Adam scanned the line of open trees but saw no sign of Nigel. The temptation to turn straight around and ride home nearly got the better of him, and he had to draw on every ounce of his will to move Gabriel forward into the darker tangle where the trees thickened, their branches meeting overhead. The gelding must have sensed Adam's edginess, for he resisted, dancing sideways and snorting before reluctantly responding to Adam's insistent pressure.

Then again, Adam realized, Gabriel had never been into the forest. He'd only been a yearling and too young to ride, and Adam had taken his usual mount that nightmare afternoon. He'd sold the horse soon afterward.

Calling for Nigel as he went, Adam took care to steer away from the path leading toward the stream and the clearing on the other side of the bridge. He needed no more reminders of Caro or Ian and the many happy hours they'd spent together in what had once seemed a magic place. Even now he could almost hear Ian's bubbling laughter and Caro's light, musical voice echoing across it as they called to greet him.

A flash of movement caught the corner of his eye and

he reflexively snapped his head around as if he expected to see Caro running toward him, Ian's hand in hers, his little legs pumping to keep up.

A fox emerged from the thicket, stopped abruptly as it spotted him, and disappeared soundlessly back into the underbrush. Adam released the breath he'd unconsciously been holding.

"Nigel," he bellowed, as much in an effort to break the deafening silence as to summon the man.

To his surprise and immense relief he heard an answering call not far to his left. Another minute or two and he would have gone stark, staring mad. "Over here!" he bellowed again.

"Have you had any luck finding Callie?" Nigel asked when he appeared a minute later, worry lining his face. "I haven't seen a trace of her."

"She's safely home," Adam replied shortly. "Let's get the hell out of here before my nerves snap altogether." He kicked Gabriel into a canter and didn't breathe easily until they'd reached blessedly open space again. He stopped, taking in great gulps of precious air and gazing at his enormous house, its windows aflame with the reflection of the setting sun. Stanton Abbey looked positively cozy after his sojourn into the darkness.

"Thank the good Lord that she's all right. What happened to her?" Nigel asked, catching up to Adam.

"I found Callie sitting in one of the nether meadows. She decided to take the short way back from Hythe and grew tired. She seemed to be surprised that anyone was looking for her." He didn't mention that he'd found her in tears. He would get to the bottom of that mystery on his own.

Nigel flashed Adam a smile of obvious relief. "That sounds exactly like Callie. She's always surprised when anyone expresses concern about her. You'd think no one had ever worried about her before."

"For all we know, no one has. I don't see anyone lining up to claim her, do you?"

"Ah," Nigel said. "And here I was, thinking you'd forgotten that Callie had a misplaced past."

Adam regarded Nigel wryly. "Forgotten? Don't you think one person walking about with no memory is quite enough?"

"Oh, indeed I do, and I am happy to hear that yours has remained intact. Given that it has, I must commend you on your remarkable self-control. You have not once, or at least not once since Callie has been up and about, mentioned your plans for disposing of the unwanted responsibility foisted on you."

"Do not push me, Nigel," Adam said wearily. "I've had enough strain for one day."

"I beg your pardon. I don't mean to push you in the least. I am merely curious as to whether you have come up with any plan for Callie's future, or if you intend to keep her here indefinitely. I think she might age rather nicely."

Adam narrowed his eyes. "I assume you are jesting?"

"Only partly," Nigel said, his smile fading. "I have come to care about Callie, and as sorry as I would be to see her go, I can't help but feel that she deserves a life to call her own."

"She has a life to call her own. She may leave any time she chooses," Adam pointed out with irritation. "She has not expressed any such desire to me. Has she to you?" For some absurd reason Adam was upset that Callie might have confided in Nigel and not in him, and he was even more upset that she might have expressed a desire to leave Stanton when they'd tried so hard to make her feel welcome.

"She hasn't said a word to me on the subject, but you

know as well as I that Callie is highly skilled at keeping her own counsel."

"Callie is highly skilled at all sorts of things, including trying to bamboozle people into believing what she would like them to believe," Adam retorted. "She doesn't realize that she gives away far more than she conceals with her silly stories." He dismounted. "Let us walk back. My legs could use a good stretch, and perhaps it is time to address the subject of Callie and her future." Actually, the subject was the last one he wished to discuss, but he knew Nigel well enough to know that if he didn't provide a reasonable answer, Nigel would wonder why. Adam didn't care to be second-guessed.

He considered a moment or two, trying to put his thoughts into order, not an easy task when they'd been shaken every which way over the last two hours. "First of all," he said, proceeding in as logical a fashion as he could manage, "so far Callie shows no signs of regaining her memory. Dr. Hadley did caution that this might be a permanent condition, so I think that any plans for her future must take this possibility into account. Now—what sort of decent post would Callie be able to assume without a background to call her own?"

"None that I can think of," Nigel said. "I suppose you could supply a personal reference for her, but you'd be putting your neck on the line if you manufactured a false history, and I don't think you want to expose her or yourself to accusations of fraud if she was ever exposed."

"Exactly," Adam said with satisfaction, pleased that Nigel had grasped the point so quickly. "Therefore," he continued, "I very much doubt that any respectable member of society is going to hire Callie as a companion or a governess or whatever other harebrained position Callie might come up with, no matter how well spoken or well educated she is. Not that I think her suited to such a life in any case. She is far too intelligent and independent of spirit."

"I would have to agree," Nigel said, looking very content for someone who a minute before had been so keen for Callie to have a life of her very own. "What *do* you think her suited for?"

"I am not entirely sure just yet," Adam said truthfully. "I don't see any reason to come to a hasty decision, as Callie still has some way to go before she has fully regained her health. The events of this afternoon proved that." Odd, he thought. He really wasn't in any rush anymore. He'd been too engrossed in seeing to Callie's recovery to think overmuch about his own dispatching—or hers.

"I have sometimes wondered . . ." Nigel said, then paused as if he had thought twice about finishing his sentence.

"Wondered what?" Adam glanced over at him curiously.

"Oh, just about what would happen if someone unsavory from Callie's past turned up, someone who had made her deeply unhappy for some reason, or might make her deeply unhappy. I for one would be hard-pressed to hand her over, but as I've said before, she is not my responsibility."

"What are you implying?" Adam snapped. "Do you think I would hand Callie over to someone unsuitable as if she were nothing more than a—a sack of potatoes?"

"I wasn't implying anything," Nigel said mildly. "I was merely speculating. The possibility does still exist that something or someone unpleasant sent her running from her home—or that she might have been forced to come to England against her will and jumped off the ship rather than face the fate that was waiting for her."

Adam halted abruptly. "Don't be absurd, Nigel. Callie

has more appreciation for life in her little finger than most people have in their entire bodies. She doesn't have the temperament to kill herself."

"I wasn't aware that one required a particular temperament to kill oneself," Nigel said, looking down at the toe of his dusty boot as if it held great interest. "And I wasn't saying that *was* Callie's intent. I'm only trying to point out that you don't know anything for a fact, and you don't want to be caught off guard if something unexpected should happen."

"You're beginning to sound like the oracle at Delphi," Adam said dryly. "Very well, to give your hypothetical question a hypothetical answer, I would base my decision on the circumstances. If Callie turned out to be married, for example, and her husband came to claim her, he would have the legal right to take her away. If, however, he turned out to be a bounder with a habit of drinking himself senseless and beating her, I would do my best to settle Callie somewhere far away from him, and the law be damned."

"That answers my question well enough," Nigel said. "I only wish her to be safe and happy, Adam, wherever she ends up."

"As do I," Adam said. "As do I." He quickly turned the conversation to other matters, unwilling to think any longer about the inevitable day that Callie would leave them.

"My nerves are sorely tried from this day's work, Mr. Gettis, they are indeed." Mrs. Simpson sank into her favorite armchair with a steaming cup of herbal tea that she'd brewed to calm herself before bed. "I thought his lordship was going to dismiss me on the spot, I was that worried by his temper—as if I wasn't worried enough about the poppet as it was. Anyone would have thought I'd meant her to go missing."

"You weren't at fault," Gettis said soothingly, but he poured himself a cup of the same tisane, his own nerves fairly shredded. "You weren't to know Miss Callie had gone off unseen by Michael and Henry."

"True enough, true enough. His lordship did say he held no one to blame." She inhaled the steam from her cup and exhaled loudly. "There's nothing like chamomile and yarrow for calming the system," she said. "If I thought his lordship would take it I'd send a pot upstairs with Mr. Plimpton. I declare, he hasn't been in such a state since . . . well, you know since when, and the good Lord knows we don't want to see the likes of that dark mood again, poor man. He's had more than his share of suffering, he has, and that's the truth."

"His lordship was perfectly calm at dinner," Gettis said, before Mrs. Simpson could get started on the tragedy, which inevitably led to a cataloguing of dear Lady Vale's saintly qualities and poor little Lord Stanton's unfulfilled promise. "I thought him a bit preoccupied, perhaps, but other than that his spirits appeared well enough."

"Yes. Yes, his spirits are remarkably improved since the dear poppet arrived," Mrs. Simpson said, producing the inevitable handkerchief with her spare hand and dabbing at the corners of her eyes. She lowered her voice. "I do believe, Mr. Gettis, that his lordship might actually have formed a *tendre* for our Callie."

"A *tendre*, Mrs. Simpson?" Gettis's eyebrows rose skyward. "Have you heard something that the rest of us have not?"

"I only speak as I find, and what I find is that his lordship makes everything Callie does his personal business, and Callie in turn looks at his lordship as if the sun rises and sets in every breath he takes." She sighed happily.

"Miss Callie is a trifle high-spirited for that description," Gettis replied dryly. "I have heard her contradict his lordship any number of times. She doesn't hesitate to take him down a peg or two when she thinks he needs it, and I never heard her ladyship do any such thing." He chuckled. "What's more, his lordship gives as good as he gets. I've watched many a fencing match played out over the dining room table, and I'd say the honors were about even to date."

"Her ladyship, God rest her sweet soul, was as gentle as a lamb and would never think to cross swords with his lordship. She had her own ways to get around him. That doesn't mean that his lordship can't appreciate something a little different."

"A *little* different, you say? You might as well be comparing night and day, Mrs. Simpson. Oh, Miss Callie is pleasing enough to the eye, I'll give you that, and she's bright as a button, but I think his lordship would sooner give her a good shaking than kiss her." He wished his lordship would open his eyes and see what he had, but so far there hadn't been any sign of that.

"For a man, Mr. Gettis, you understand very little about male nature," Mrs. Simpson said with a loud sniff. "You mark my words—a match will come out of this, see if it doesn't. Why else would his lordship have kicked up such a terrible fuss today over the poppet? That was not the reaction of an indifferent man."

"If you must go sniffing April and May," Gettis said with more than a touch of superiority, "I suggest you look at what *is* under your nose. Michael and Jane, that's what, and if you don't keep a firmer hand on that Jane, you'll be presiding over a hasty wedding and counting the months until a blessed event makes an appearance. Where do you think Michael was when he should have been looking out for Miss Callie?" He jerked his head in the direction of the back corridor that led to the storage rooms. "That's where, if I know anything about it, and Henry standing guard for him more than likely."

Mrs. Simpson gasped, her hand flying to her bosom, handkerchief trembling between her fingers. "Janie? Why, that little trollop, I'll blister her backside!"

"If left to itself, nature does what nature must," Gettis said. "So if you're going to go making matches, I suggest you focus your attention where it is most needed."

Mrs. Simpson, thoroughly taken aback with shock and indignation that she could have missed such goings-on in her own domain, forgot all about Callie and Adam and immediately began planning her strategy to see the illicit union sanctified.

Adam paced his bedroom floor, his unsettled thoughts chasing each other around in circles and always ending up back in the same place with the same disturbing question: What *was* he going to do about Callie?

He shoved his hand inside the open front of his shirt, thinking that he could cheerfully punch Nigel for having brought the subject up at all. Adam had been doing very well focusing on the present. The present included Callie. The future did not. Why did that idea leave him with an uncomfortable knot in the pit of his stomach? He *had* no future, so what difference could it possibly make to him if Callie was gone?

Slumping on the edge of his bed, he rested his arms on his knees, scowling toward the window. He didn't know how or when everything had changed, but his life was no longer painted in simple black and white. It had assumed all sorts of different, complex colors while he hadn't been paying close attention, and for the life of him he couldn't figure out why.

He had always known his own mind. He prided himself on making decisions and sticking to them until he achieved the desirable outcome.

Now, twice in a row, he'd faltered, changed course in midstream. It was all Callie's fault, he decided. If she hadn't fallen off her blasted ship he wouldn't be in this position at all. He'd be safely dead as planned. He certainly wouldn't be chasing about the woods ripping open old, agonizing wounds and proving himself a complete coward to boot.

That was Callie's fault too. If she had stayed close to the abbey as she'd been told—and more than once—he wouldn't have been forced to go looking for her and been frightened half to death when he'd seen her fall. For a very bad moment he'd thought another bullet had gone astray and she'd . . .

Adam didn't finish the thought.

If it weren't for Callie, he reminded himself grimly, he wouldn't have been forced to go anywhere near the woods, and Nigel wouldn't have had the chance to pin him down afterward. He certainly wouldn't be sitting here having this absurd argument with himself.

Nigel was right. It was long past time for Callie to have her own life, and the sooner he saw to that the sooner she would be gone and life would return to normal. He was tired of all this confusion.

Adam abruptly stood up. Why should he take everything on his shoulders? Callie could damned well take responsibility for herself, and there was no time like the present.

Not bothering to think about the lateness of the hour or his state of undress, Adam marched across the room, opened his door, and strode down the hallway with determination, straight to Callie's room. He softly knocked on the door.

"Come in," she called.

Adam quickly composed himself. He'd forgotten how her sweet, melodic voice always made him want to smile, and he didn't intend to smile, he intended to be firm. He was going to make concrete plans for her departure, and for once Callie was going to listen.

# 10

Adam opened the door only to see Callie standing at the open window wearing nothing but a nightshift, her fair hair unloosed and tumbling down her back in a cascade of golden silk. The light of a nearly full moon streamed through the window, backlighting her supple form and outlining the silhouette of her body as if she were wearing nothing at all. His breath caught in his throat as his gaze helplessly took in her slender shoulders and back, the graceful swell of her hips, the perfectly rounded curves of her bottom, and her long, shapely legs. She looked like a wood nymph, wild and free and inexpressibly lovely.

Adam couldn't believe that his heart had started pounding as hard as if he were an adolescent looking at a half-naked woman for the first time. He took a step backward, hoping he could slip out unseen, but he didn't move quickly enough.

"I told you I didn't need anything else, Jane." Her voice, low and dreamy, sounded as if she were a million miles away. She glanced over her shoulder, then spun around with a gasp as she saw him, her eyes widening and her hands reaching behind her to grasp the windowsill as if to support her weight.

"Adam! What—what is it?" Her surprise immediately vanished to be replaced by concern. "Adam? Has something happened? You look as if you've had a shock. Come in—here, sit down. Let me pour you a glass of water."

She crossed over to him, her bare feet silent on the carpet, and gently took him by the elbow, steering him to the armchair next to her bed and guiding him into it as if he were an invalid. He watched her lean over and pour water from a pitcher, her small, beautifully rounded breasts straining against the material of her nightdress as she straightened and handed him the glass.

Adam couldn't have spoken if he'd tried. He sipped the water for lack of anything better to do, one hand carefully positioned over his lap where his traitorous body strained painfully against the confinement of his trousers. He couldn't believe he was sitting in Callie's bedroom with a raging erection, drinking a glass of water as if it were high noon and he had nothing more on his mind than a little romp—stroll, he quickly amended—in the garden.

*Callie?* How could he not have seen her before? Dear God, she was beautiful, the most desirable woman he'd ever laid eyes on, and yet completely unaware of the sensuality she exuded from every fiber of her being.

"Why don't you get a shawl?" he croaked, the request made from sheer self-preservation. "I wouldn't want you to catch a chill."

"I never catch chills," Callie said, but she picked up a

shawl from the back of the dressing-table chair obligingly enough.

Adam breathed a sigh of relief. Callie's frontal view was even more alluring than her backside, if that was possible. He really didn't need to be exposed to the delicious sight of her delicate, erect pink nipples beneath the flimsy shift or the darker patch of down that he could just make out beneath her flat belly as he tried to talk to her. He crossed his legs and tried very hard to think of turnips.

Wrapping the shawl around her shoulders, she hopped up onto her bed, sitting opposite him, her knees pulled up and her arms folded around them, bare toes peeking out from the hem of her shift. "Now," she said when she'd comfortably settled. "Tell me what's upset you."

*You have, Callie. You're not supposed to be so damned desirable. You're supposed to be a nuisance, a problem to be solved. I'm supposed to be banishing you, not wanting to bed you.*

"Adam? Whatever your trouble, you can confide in me. I am a very good listener."

Adam tried to concentrate, not an easy task when Callie sat so close to him, her ripe mouth the color of a rosebud about to bloom, her dark eyes gazing softly and steadily into his as if she could see the secrets of his heart reflected in them.

That thought acted like a dose of cold water. He didn't want anyone looking into his bruised and battered heart, most especially Callie. "My trouble," he said, "is you."

"Me?" Callie's gaze wavered and fell to her hands. "I suppose you mean what I did today," she said in a small voice. "I thought you accepted my apology too easily."

"I accepted your apology fully. I do not say what I do not mean. That isn't what I was referring to."

Her gaze crept back up to his, but now he saw uncertainty there, and even, if he wasn't very much mistaken, a touch of fear. "Perhaps you had better just tell me," she said, catching the bottom corner of her lip between her teeth.

She looked so vulnerable, so very much alone, and he had to forcibly keep his hand from reaching out and stroking the flaxen lock of silky hair that had fallen over her shoulder. "Callie . . . I—I've been thinking."

"It's time for me to leave, isn't it?" She thrust her little chin forward in that gesture of determination he'd come to know so well. Brave Callie, pretending she could take on the world, not ever letting on how scared she felt. "You needn't try to find the right words, Adam," she said, the corners of her rosebud mouth trembling slightly. "I've always known that my time here was limited and I'm much better now, really I am. You need to get on with your life and I need to do the same. You have been everything that is kind, but I too am restless and my thoughts have turned to moving on." Her eyelashes quickly lowered, but Adam had already seen the sheen of tears she was trying to hide.

Adam couldn't do it. He didn't even know what he'd been thinking. His grand plan to march in here with an eviction notice and abandon her to the world at large was nothing more than cruel, and the world had already treated her cruelly enough. Callie couldn't possibly look after herself on her own. What she needed was protective, nurturing hands to guide her until she was ready to stand on her own two feet. By God, he had to admire her courage, though, trying to make it easier for him to toss her out. Only Callie, he thought.

"You misunderstand me," he said gently, picking up one of her slender hands in his and holding it lightly in his palm, his thumb stroking over her fingers. "I have no desire for you to leave, none at all."

"No?" she said, her eyes flying open. She stared at him

in confusion, the tears overflowing and rolling down her cheeks, but she seemed unaware of them. "What, then?"

What indeed? "Actually," he said, desperately casting around for straws, "I was thinking that it's time for you to have a proper wardrobe instead of making do with what the village can supply. We can go into Folkestone tomorrow, make a day of it. There's a seamstress there who is very accomplished, perhaps not up to London standards, but adequate for your needs at the moment. Would you like that?"

Callie's eyes narrowed and she abruptly pulled her hand out of his. "Adam Carlyle, you did not come in here at this hour looking as if you'd just been kicked by a horse to tell me that you wanted to go visit a dressmaker."

He couldn't help smiling. Callie—she wanted all or nothing. He should have realized that he couldn't put her off with a flimsy excuse. "No," he said. "I didn't." He reached his hand out and brushed away her tears for the second time that day. "For someone who never cries, you're becoming a regular watering-pot."

"Don't change the subject," she said, pushing his hand away again. "You said I was the trouble. Other than the obvious, what else have I done to upset you so? You looked almost ill when you came in."

Adam remembered why he'd wanted to simplify his life. "I wasn't ill," he said. "I was—I was concerned. You've been much on my mind this evening."

"Why?" she said with a puzzled frown. "I told you then that there was nothing wrong with me."

"Callie, I found you sitting alone in a meadow, crying. People generally don't cry without a reason. Are you unhappy here? Has someone said something to upset you? Please tell me the truth."

"No. Honestly, Adam. I am very happy here. Everyone has been wonderful to me."

"Yes, yes, I know, and you're deeply grateful," he said, before she could start in on that again. "That explains nothing to me. We are friends, Callie, are we not? Good friends, I hope."

She nodded. "I believe we are," she said, but she looked away, studying a point somewhere over his right shoulder, her cheeks turning a dusky pink. As Callie only blushed when she was telling a massive fib, having a fit of embarrassment, or trying very hard to hide amusement, he assumed she was either lying or badly rattled, since she couldn't have looked less amused.

He tucked a finger under her chin and turned her face back to his, forcing her to meet his eyes. "Friends tell each other the truth."

"Oh, Adam, please don't push me, for I would be hardpressed to explain," she said, squeezing her eyes shut.

"Why don't you try? If you run into a stumbling block I will help you over it."

Callie wiggled out from underneath his hand and slid off the bed, padding over to the window, her back to him. "Very well, if you insist," she said, her voice so low that he had to strain to hear it.

He stood and turned toward her. Her hands were pressed flat against the wood of the sill, her head bent as if in defeat or prayer; he couldn't tell which. She looked very young and very vulnerable.

"I had a . . . memory."

Adam's eyes sharpened and he held his breath, wondering if she finally trusted him enough to tell him the truth.

"It wasn't the usual sort of memory—it was like having someone you loved very much whispering to you from very far away, but I could hear the whisper as clearly as if you spoke to me now."

"What did you hear?" Adam asked quietly.

"That I should listen to my heart, that my heart would tell me where I belong." Her hands slipped to her face and her shoulders trembled. "Don't you see, Adam? That's the problem—I don't belong anywhere, and I'm afraid I never will." A shuddering sob escaped her and then another.

Adam didn't stop to think. Crossing over to her in two strides, he gathered her up, turning her and pulling her body full length against his, wrapping his arms around her and holding her tightly, his cheek resting on the top of her head. He offered himself freely, a safe harbor amidst the internal storm that raged in her. Callie slipped her arms around his back, holding him equally close, her slender body shaking as she released the pent-up fears she'd been holding in for weeks.

When her sobs had finally quieted, Adam gently released her without a word and took her over to the chair. He sat down and settled her on his lap as if she were a small child, one of his arms around her waist. With the other hand he reached for the handkerchief on her bedside table and gave it to her. "Dry your eyes, Callie, and then we'll talk."

He needed a moment to compose himself as badly as she did, for his heart ached—but not with the searing, bitter pain of loss, or the bleak, echoing emptiness that had been his constant companion. He ached for Callie's pain and he wanted to cry out that he couldn't carry her burden, that he couldn't even carry his own. But Callie needed him, and he would not turn his back on her, no matter what the effort cost him. She needed reassurance, and he would give it to her.

She wiped her eyes and nose and hiccupped. "I—forgive me, Adam. I didn't mean to be such a wet-goose. I've soaked your shirtfront."

"If tears are as cleansing as they say, you have done a very good job of laundering it. Plimpton will be most pleased," he said lightly, although his throat was tight and he spoke with an effort.

"You are mocking me," she said, looking up at him suspiciously, her eyes swollen and her nose endearingly red.

"Not mocking you, only teasing." Adam ran his finger down that little red nose. "Callie, why have you not told me before how you felt? I might have been able to help." The words sounded empty, foolish, even as he spoke them.

"How?" she asked simply. "You have given me everything you possibly could. You cannot give me back my family or my home."

"No," he said. "I cannot do that. I cannot resurrect the past any more than I can change it. Believe me, if I knew how, I would."

She nodded. "Not even God can do that," she said, wiping her eyes again. "I think He means for us to go on, to find our way no matter how dark the path seems, but oh, Adam...sometimes I—sometimes I lose my faith that I'll ever find my way." She glanced at him guiltily as if she'd just made the most appalling confession, and he had to smile.

"Faith is a funny thing," he said. "One doesn't think much about it when life is going well, but when the tables abruptly turn and life doesn't seem worth living, faith becomes cold comfort. Personally, I've given up on it altogether."

Callie's mouth dropped open. "Adam," she said, looking genuinely shocked. "You're not saying that you've *completely* given up on God?"

"In a word, yes."

"But He'd never give up on you—never! You are His beloved child, and He loves you for all eternity."

"I've given up on eternity, too," Adam said dryly, rather enjoying Callie's outrage. At least she'd put her sorrow to one side for the moment.

"You *can't* give up on eternity," she said, as if she was explaining the most basic concept to a three-year-old. "Eternity is there, just like God, whether you like it or not. And it doesn't matter if you're a marquess or the milkman. God doesn't make any distinction."

"How do you know?" he asked, shifting her to a more comfortable position and brushing the hair back off her smooth forehead. "Do you and the Almighty regularly take tea together and discuss His plans for bringing His wayward children into line?"

"Don't be absurd. I just know, and so would you if you'd shut off your clever brain and open your eyes and ears and heart and listen."

"You make one hell of a theologian, Miss Calliope Magnus. The Jesuits have been looking for someone like you."

She slugged him in the shoulder and he winced. "What was that for?"

"For being stupid," she said.

"For my sins," Adam murmured.

"Your only sin that I know of is turning away from God and the world He made. That's quite serious on the sin scale, you know. It's not as bad as committing murder or adultery, I don't think, but it's a lot worse than jealousy."

"Hmm. Jealousy isn't really one of my problems. What about thinking carnal thoughts? Where does that place on your er, scale of sin?" He was mightily curious to hear her answer to this one—he had some rather detailed and deliciously carnal thoughts running through his head at the moment, and they all concerned Callie.

Callie considered. "I wouldn't worry too much about that one. God wouldn't have made us human and thrown in physical desire if He didn't mean for us to enjoy our bodies."

She slowly tapped one finger against those luscious lips, which sent Adam's temperature up another degree. He could think of much more useful things to do with that lovely mouth.

"I believe," she finally said, "that the trick to avoiding sin is not to act on those thoughts in an inappropriate fashion."

Adam smothered a laugh. "Ah," he said. "That eases my mind considerably. I have behaved in a most exemplary fashion."

"I don't think you should look so self-congratulatory just yet," she replied tartly. "There's still the matter of your misplaced faith."

"Neither you nor I can do anything about my lack of faith. It is firm, and unshakeable, and your playing vicar will get you nowhere," he said, guiding the conversation back to where he wanted it. "Your unhappiness, however, is another matter, and one that I believe can be resolved."

Callie's eyes darkened and she clenched her hands in her lap. "You do not believe in God, and yet you think to play Him?" she asked with a rare note of bitterness.

"I think nothing of the sort. I do think that truth might go a long way toward resolving this particular problem, though."

Callie stiffened against him. "Truth? What sort of truth?"

"Yours, for a start," he said gently. "You told me a very

nice truth a few minutes ago. Do you think you might be able to manage just a little bit more?"

She shifted on his lap again, and he had to close his eyes, for it was a very, very nice shift, but was producing undesired consequences. He inhaled, thought of turnips—rotting, really putrid turnips this time—and exhaled.

"I—I don't know what you mean," she said, her cheeks turning that fascinating shade of crimson roses in deep bloom.

"You know exactly what I mean," he said, knowing he was taking an enormous chance, but willing to gamble on her innate honesty. "You might think me insufferably stupid, but I am not deaf, dumb, and blind in the bargain. Your creative skills are unparalled and you might one day think about writing a novel, for I am sure you would be highly successful at the endeavor, but this is real life." He regarded her steadily. "This is *your* life. I can't help you with both hands tied behind my back, which is how I've felt since the moment you opened your eyes and started feeding me a story that might have come from *The Accounts of Lady M., Adventuress at Large.* I'd far rather hear the real story of Callie, as sketchy as it might be, even if the story only starts from that first moment."

Callie's hands slipped to her cheeks, one hand covering the back of his, her fingers tightening on it. "You knew?" she whispered. "You knew all along?"

"Not all along, but I had my questions from the beginning. I wasn't sure until about three weeks ago when I spoke to Dr. Hadley. He told me he believed that you'd lost your memory."

She shook her head, incapable of speech, her eyes welling with tears. "No," she moaned, jumping to her feet and running to the window, leaning out as far as she could reach.

Adam, deeply alarmed that she might fall, moved like lightening, grasping her tightly around the waist.

She spun around, shoving so hard at his chest that she caught him off balance and he staggered backward.

"Did you think I was going to jump out?" she cried, her eyes flashing. "You might think me all sorts of insufferable things, including a liar and coward, and in that you'd be right, but I have a better sense of self-preservation than to try to kill myself. I only needed some air," she finished, staring at the floor, her face a picture of misery and embarrassment.

"Callie," he said breathlessly, in as much need of air as she. "Dear God, don't scare me like that again. I honestly— I didn't know what you intended."

"Well, I wasn't trying to kill myself, if that's what you thought," she said, chin thrusting forward. "You gave me a shock."

"That's two of us, then, who are in bad need of some cognac." He looked around the room and mercifully spotted a tray on the bureau that held a carafe of red wine and two glasses. Not wasting any time he grabbed it, took the stopper out, prayed the wine hadn't turned to vinegar, and poured two glasses. He took a cautious sip from one, decided it was drinkable, and handed Callie the other.

He raised his glass, his hand still slightly trembling. "To life," he said, not altogether facetiously.

"To life," she echoed, her expression as grim as he'd ever seen it.

She drank briefly and slammed the glass down on the windowsill. He couldn't believe the goblet didn't shatter, given the force it landed with. "Callie? What the devil has gotten into you?" he said, staring at her. She looked like an avenging angel, and he was her direct target. He wouldn't be surprised if he exploded into flames at any moment.

"You have a great deal of spleen, Adam Carlyle, talking to *me* about life. I at least live mine the best I can, even if I don't remember anything before I came here, but you, on the other hand, behave as if life owes you everything and you owe nothing back."

She paused only to draw breath. "I'm deeply sorry that you lost your wife and child in a horrible accident, and I know that you feel their loss terribly and sometimes would like to die yourself, but that's no excuse for turning your back on all the people who love you and need you, not to mention turning your back on yourself and the gift of life God gave you. He *didn't* give you any guarantee that life was all going to be smooth sailing. You take the bad with the good, as Niko always said, and you do the best you can, and that's all that God ever expects or wants, and you have no right to decide otherwise, no matter what. You have no right at all. You should be grateful just to be drawing breath."

Callie abruptly sat down where she stood, which was the cold, hard floor. "That's all I have to say." She suddenly looked exhausted.

Adam stared at her, his emotions in an uproar. He didn't know whether to be merely indignant, or furious with her insufferable cheek, or to laugh himself silly at this woman who dared to lecture him when she couldn't even remember her own name.

And yet . . . and yet Callie had managed to reach a place deep within him where truth resided. Not a truth he wanted to look at, perhaps, but truth nonetheless.

"Who is Niko?" he said, for lack of anything else that came to mind.

She glared up at him, her elbow on her knee, her fingers shoved through her unruly curls. "Our cook and our houseman and one of the wisest men I've ever known, so I'd listen if I were you."

Callie stopped abruptly, her eyes widening. "Niko... Oh—Oh, Adam—I remember! Not anything else, but I can see him clear as day!" She hopped to her feet, smiling as if she'd just been handed the moon, her eyes glowing. "He's not a tall man like you, and he's slighter in build, but he carries himself with the same confidence. He knows himself, Adam, has that wonderful sense of belonging to everything around him, so everyone else feels as if they belong, too." She started to laugh, twirling around in a circle, her arms hugging herself, tears pouring down her face. "I remember!" She ran over to Adam and threw her arms around him. "I prayed so hard today that I would remember someone, that I would remember what it was like to love and be loved, and I do. I really do!" She tilted her head back and looked up at him, her eyes shining so brightly that she might have been handed the sun as well. "Remembering feels very, very good."

"I am happy for you, Callie, very happy." Her happiness must have been contagious, for the radiant strength of Callie's sun shone all the way into the arctic reaches of his heart, stirring a long-forgotten memory of joy.

He quickly stepped away from her. This was Callie's moment, not his. "Maybe this is only a beginning," he said. "You might start remembering more and more, now that you've recaptured something significant."

Callie lifted one shoulder. "Maybe. For now it's enough." She perched herself back on the bed, wineglass forgotten. "Why didn't you tell me you knew?" she asked, regarding him quizzically.

"Why didn't you tell me you'd forgotten?" he countered.

She puffed out her cheeks and released a breath. "I thought you'd send me to an asylum. That's generally what happens to people who can't remember anything about themselves and who have no one to answer for them or support them, isn't it?"

He couldn't deny it or fault her reasoning. "In general, yes, it is. I suppose you didn't know me at all and didn't realize that I wouldn't do anything so cruel or unconsidered."

"No," she said, with a tender smile that went straight to that strange, exposed place in his heart. "I didn't know you. I know you much better now, and I feel confident that my next address will not be Bedlam, whatever happens to me."

"You will be going nowhere near Bedlam, I promise, although I am hard pressed not to give you a severe spanking for having delved into my affairs with no invitation on my part." He took another sip of wine to fortify himself and met her gaze square on. "Truth for truth. Who told you? About Caroline and Ian, I mean. About what happened to them." Just speaking the words felt like a knife plunging into his heart. He hadn't spoken their names aloud since the day of their burial, at least not while awake. His nightmares were another matter.

"I only found out today at Nellie's," Callie said, reaching out for his hand and drawing him to her, picking up his other hand and holding them both tight between her own. "No one at Stanton ever said a word, I promise. I'd never have plagued you about the woods, Adam, or teased you in so many other ways, not if I'd known. Forgive me if I unknowingly upset you?"

"There's nothing to forgive. We have both kept our secrets, and the time for that is past. I failed Caro and Ian, but I don't intend to fail you, Callie. You will have your life back, one way or the other. I swear that to you."

She shook her head, meeting his eyes squarely. "You can't, Adam. You can't swear to something you have no control over, and I would never think to hold you to a promise you can't keep, no matter how honorable your intentions. I thank you with all my heart for wanting to help me, but in the end my life is in God's hands, and only God can see me safely home."

Something in Adam wanted to cry out that her home was here, that it would always be here, but he knew that was no more than wishful thinking.

Callie was already on her way, her memory beginning to return. Some other lucky person would soon be able to reclaim her for his own, and Adam would go back to his solitary life, the sun gone with her.

## 11

$\mathcal{E}$ngland really was a very attractive country, Callie decided as the carriage barreled down the road to Folkestone. The hedge-banks teemed with shiny yellow buttercup and snowy white campion, the roadsides sported pink-tipped daisies and the bright yellow and purple of heartsease along with a myriad of other wildflowers she'd already identified the day before.

Spotting a clump of valerian growing in the crack of a wall, Callie smiled, thinking of Nellie and her fretful Georgie. She'd have to gather some valerian and make a nice infusion to bring to Nellie—she could make all sorts of infusions and decoctions from the plants she'd seen. That would keep her busy and her mind off Adam for a change.

He sat next to her, his gaze fixed on the road ahead. She had no idea where his thoughts had taken him, but she felt unaccountably shy after their late-night conversation, as if she had stripped her soul bare and was now badly feeling the exposure.

She could only be grateful that Adam had made no mention of their exchange. Indeed, the casual way in which he'd behaved all morning would have made her think she'd dreamed the entire interlude if every moment wasn't burned so clearly into her mind. What was it about the night that brought forth the deepest secrets of the heart?

At least she'd managed to keep her feelings about him to herself, and she thanked the good Lord that she had, for she wouldn't have been able to bear him looking at her with shock and horror, and almost worse, inevitable pity.

She really was ten kinds of fool, and given his extraordinary acuity, he was bound to figure that out for himself in no short order if she wasn't very, very careful. She hadn't managed to keep anything else from him very successfully, had she, no matter how hard she'd tried.

"Callie?"

She belatedly realized that Adam had spoken, and for an awful moment she thought he might have read her mind. She had to mentally shake herself back to the present moment. "I beg your pardon. Did you say something?" She schooled her face to reflect nothing more than polite inquiry. They were on their way to visit the dressmaker, nothing more. He couldn't *possibly* know what she'd been thinking about, no matter how acute he could be.

"I did," he said, regarding her with a tinge of curiosity. "I asked if you minded being left at Mrs. Sorrel's shop while she does all the measuring and so on. I'd like to run some errands that would only bore you if you were with me, and frankly, I'd be bored to tears if I had to perch on an uncomfortable chair and make approving noises all afternoon." He smiled. "I apologize, but I can't help being a man. Even my tailor tries my patience."

"He might try your patience, but the results are worthwhile," Callie said. "You are always well turned out. But do you think it wise to leave me on my own, Adam? I know nothing about ladies' fashions, and might very well choose designs and materials better suited to a scarecrow."

"Callie. You could not possibly resemble a scarecrow, no matter how much effort you put into the endeavor. However, Mrs. Sorrel will not allow you to make any mistakes—she is very particular about how her clients reflect on her. I trust her implicitly."

"I am sure she charges you the moon for the privilege," Callie replied dryly.

"Indeed she does, and if the next words out of your mouth are going to be that I should not be buying you a new wardrobe at all, I do not want to hear them. I, like Mrs. Sorrel, have a reputation to maintain."

"Honestly, Adam, the way you talk anyone would think you kept a stable of mistresses." Callie gasped when she heard what she'd said and blushed furiously, wanting to kick herself. "Oh! Forgive me. I—I didn't mean . . ."

Her words were drowned out by Adam's laughter. He laughed until tears ran down his cheeks and he had to struggle to catch his breath. "Ah," he said, clutching his hand to his ribs. "Ah, Callie, I don't think . . ." He collapsed with laugher again. "I don't think," he finally managed to say, wiping his eyes, "that anyone in his right mind would reach such a conclusion."

Callie tried to smile in response, but she felt like an utter idiot for having thoughtlessly made the joking remark. Adam was the least likely man to keep a mistress and all of England probably knew it. He'd been far too busy being happily married to his beloved Caroline and just as busy grieving her loss to give any thought to another woman.

He lightly took her hand in his. "You needn't look so mortified, Callie. I assure you, I'm not in the least offended, and if you're worried that Mrs. Sorrel might leap to the wrong conclusion, I'll make very sure that she doesn't."

Callie only nodded, feeling as if Adam might just as well have slapped her. If she'd held out any fantastic hope that he might find her even vaguely desirable, he'd just effectively quashed it. He thought of her only as a friend—a good friend, perhaps, but nothing more. He'd made that very clear. Anything beyond that was no more than a foolish dream on her part, and she couldn't afford dreams.

"Look, Callie—we approach Folkestone," he said, pointing ahead at the outskirts of the city. He shot her a mischievous smile. "If you'd chosen to arrive on the shores of England by the usual method, you might have arrived over there at the docks." He moved his arm to the right. "See the masts of the clipper? She probably came in last night. She's the *Mirabelle,* if I'm not mistaken."

"Adam..." Callie suddenly sat up straight as something blindingly obvious occurred to her. She couldn't believe she hadn't thought of it before. "Wouldn't there be a record of a female passenger who left France but didn't arrive in England on the day that you found me?" Her mouth went dry with excitement. Maybe at last she would learn something, anything, about who she was, where she belonged.

"I'm sorry, Callie. Nigel made every inquiry imaginable both here and in Dover, but no information came up at all."

"But how is that possible?" she said. "I was on a ship! I fell off it—you saw me. That's one thing we can be certain about." She thought hard. "There *has* to be a record of some kind, Adam. People aren't allowed to board as they please without a ticket and identification, are they?"

"No, they're not. I'm as mystified as you are, and to be perfectly honest, I've wondered if you didn't stow yourself away."

"Why on earth would I do a silly thing like that?" she said. "It sounds both dangerous and uncomfortable."

"You did disembark in a rather imaginative fashion," he pointed out. "Maybe you'd been ferreted out and were afraid of the consequences."

"So I deliberately jumped overboard into the middle of the English Channel in a gale? I might not have any memory, Adam, but that sounds like the height of stupidity. I don't think being charged with illegal passage would warrant such an extreme act." She chewed on the fingertip of her glove, trying to think of another possibility. "Anyway, you said I was singing. Why would I be singing if I planned to leap to almost certain death?"

"You do a great many things that I don't pretend to understand," he said. "For example . . ." He hesitated, scratching the side of his cheek as if reluctant to say anything more.

"For goodness' sake, don't stop now," Callie said with impatience. "I'm already beginning to think myself quite mad."

Adam turned her to face him directly. "Now I'm going to sound mad, but I've noticed that—that you really do seem to have a gift of communicating with . . . well, with birds and beasts and . . . and seemingly even bees," he said. "Do you understand what I mean?"

"Of course," Callie said, wondering why he looked so embarrassed. "What of it? As I've said before, you talk to your horse and he talks back, doesn't he?"

"Mmmph. Yes and no. I don't—that is, we don't communicate in the same way as I'm referring to." He looked away as if trying to find a polite way to say that she really was away with the fairies.

Callie, far more worried about other matters, just patted his arm. "It's all right, Adam. You are very gifted when it comes to running an estate and looking after people who depend on you, and I happen to be good at understanding God's smaller creatures. Really, there's nothing more to it than that."

"Yes, but Callie, there's something I should tell you about the day I pulled you into my boat and brought you back to Stanton, since I haven't been able to make rhyme or reason of it since."

"What?" she said with alarm. She couldn't think why he was being so evasive. Had she done or said something truly crazed? "Please, just tell me, Adam."

"Very well," he said with resignation. "If you must know, a Great Black-backed Gull was circling over your head just before you fell. You had your arms outstretched, and at first I assumed you were preparing to jump, but perhaps you were singing directly to the gull. That seems odd enough, but what truly puzzles me is that the gull seemed to be protecting you." His fingers tightened on her shoulders. "Callie, that bloody bird accompanied us all the way back to shore, fighting against the wind the entire time. It only left once you were safely on land. To be absolutely honest, and this isn't easy to admit, I'm not sure I would have made it safely home if the gull hadn't shown me the way."

Callie, so deeply moved that she couldn't speak, slipped her hand up to his cheek. "Thank you for telling me," she said simply.

"You're very welcome, and by God, don't think you're getting any more admissions out of me for at least six months. I've done enough confessing in the last twelve hours to make me a candidate for Catholicism. But seriously,

Callie, does this mean anything to you, anything at all? Can the gull have been your pet, perhaps? Can you think of any reason that you would have been standing out in the raging elements singing to it?"

"If you're asking me if the story sparked a memory, I wish I could say it had. I have no answer to your question." She dropped her gaze. "I imagine you think me quite mad to have been doing anything of the sort, but I must have had a good reason."

He nodded, lowered her hand, and straightened. "I have come to believe that your reasons for doing anything might be unorthodox, but they're generally sound. Never mind, we'll eventually work through the puzzle and come up with answers, but for now let us focus on the present. We are arriving at Mrs. Sorrel's establishment."

Adam called to the coachman, who pulled the horses over, and Callie straightened her dress, lifted her chin, and set her mind to conducting herself as she imagined a proper lady might behave so as not to embarrass Adam.

"Lord Vale! How nice to see you again," Mrs. Sorrel, a plain woman somewhere in her middle years who wore a simple but beautifully cut gray dress, hurried toward them as they entered the premises, smiling pleasantly. Adam introduced Callie as the sister of an old friend, much to Callie's amusement, and explained why they were there. Mrs. Sorrel listened carefully to Adam's instructions without interrupting, and when Adam took his leave she sat Callie down with a book of fashion plates.

"These will give you an idea of this year's fashions," she said, pointing at two of the samples. "I don't think we'll have any trouble finding suitable styles, my dear, as you are blessed with a lovely figure. You look through this, and then we'll discuss materials and colors."

Two hours later Mrs. Sorrel finally finished compiling her list and Callie, staggered by the size and probable expense of what Adam had meant by a "complete wardrobe," felt badly in need of some fresh air. Adam wasn't due back for another half-hour and she really didn't think she could sit still any longer.

"If you don't need me for anything further, Mrs. Sorrel, I'm going to take a stroll down the main street before Lord Vale returns. I shouldn't be long."

"Very well, Miss Magnus," Mrs. Sorrel said, looking slightly surprised that Callie would venture out unaccompanied, but she quickly schooled her features into neutrality. "I think I have everything I need. I believe Lord Vale will be pleased with your choices."

Callie hadn't had very much to do with choosing; she'd followed Mrs. Sorrel's tactfully phrased suggestions for the most part. "Thank you, Mrs. Sorrel," she replied equally tactfully. "I am sure he will be very pleased, as will my dear brother. He most specifically requested Lord Vale's help in finding a suitable dressmaker, and Lord Vale did not hesitate to suggest you," she added for good measure, just in case Mrs. Sorrel thought Callie might be Adam's recently acquired mistress.

Callie walked out into the sunshine, happy to stretch her legs. The shop windows teemed with all sorts of interesting goods, but she was particularly struck by the display in the bookstore front at the far end of the street. She wished she had some money, for she would have loved to buy Adam a copy of Thomas Moore's *Lalla Rookh*. Adam had mentioned wanting to read it.

"Good heavens! Look, Harold, it's *her*, as I live and breathe! Do something quickly!"

Callie glanced up, wondering what sort of woman possessed such a loud, grating voice. She froze as she spotted the source of the racket, only about thirty feet away. A thin woman with sharp features and dressed from head to toe in black stood staring directly at her, one finger pointing, her eyes looking as if they were about to pop out of her head. The plump and highly unattractive younger man at her side gaped at Callie as if he'd seen a ghost.

Her heart pounding with alarm, Callie's immediate instinct was to disappear inside the bookstore and hide behind a shelf, but she didn't even have a chance to move before the pair had descended on her in a rush.

"Miss Melbourne! It *is* Miss Callista Melbourne?" The bony woman grabbed her by the arm as if Callie might bolt. "Of course it is—you are exactly like your picture. I am Lady Geoffrey, dear. But where in heaven's name have you been? Harold and I have been beside ourselves with worry for the last month!"

"My mother understates the matter," Harold said. "We have been extremely put out by your thoughtlessness, but I suppose one shouldn't expect more from a girl raised as negligently as you have been."

"I—I . . ." Callie, dizzy with shock, couldn't manage to formulate a single coherent thought other than horror that these two offensively behaved people might actually have something to do with her missing past.

"Harold is exactly right. We've been looking high and low for you and have been *very* put out by your thoughtless behavior," Lady Geoffrey cried, her fingers biting painfully into the tender flesh just above Callie's elbow.

"Have you no idea how alarmed we were when you didn't arrive at Dover on the appointed date?"

"I personally went to meet the *Aurora* and when you didn't appear, I collected your trunks and cases, Miss Melbourne," Harold said, glaring at her accusingly from small, heavily lidded eyes. "Perhaps you will explain why you did not make the crossing with your belongings, as you were meant to do?"

Callie desperately tried to pull herself together and think of something, anything, to say. Callista Melbourne was her real name? It had to be. These people recognized her, knew that she was supposed to have been sailing to England a month ago. They more than recognized her—they seemed to think they had some sort of claim on her person, given the way they were demanding answers. *Dear God, please, please let them be a very distant connection,* she prayed as hard as she'd ever prayed for anything before. *A very, very distant connection, for I don't think I could bear being related to them.*

"Well, my girl? What do you have to say for yourself?" Lady Geoffrey demanded. "Why did you miss your sailing?"

Callie forcibly pulled herself out of the woman's grip. "I was indisposed," she said, frantically wondering how to extricate herself from this disaster. Adam—she needed Adam. He'd help her to get away from these dreadful people. Every fiber of her being screamed that something was badly wrong. She didn't care if she never found out another thing about herself if she could only escape from their clutches.

"I am sorry to hear of your indisposition, although hardly surprised, given the filthy conditions on the Continent. You might have had the consideration to write to us and let us know you would be coming on a later ship," Lady Geoffrey said, suddenly sweetening her tone as if she were speaking to a recalcitrant child who needed to be humored. "But never mind that now. You are here at last, and by good fortune we have found you quite by accident. You must be exhausted from your journey. Come, we shall take you home with us where you belong." She graced Callie with a smile so false and cloying that it curdled Callie's blood.

"Oh—oh, no, that's not possible," Callie said, intending to run straight back to Mrs. Sorrel's establishment. "I—that is, someone is waiting for me."

"Naturally, and you must make your farewell to your chaperon. I am sure she will be relieved to see you finally delivered safely into your fiancé's care. Harold, do take your betrothed to her meeting-place while I see to the carriage. Where do you stay?"

Callie's hand crept to her throat. This wasn't happening. It *couldn't* be happening. She knew in the deepest part of her being that she'd never have agreed to marry the revolting man standing in front of her, not ever. She might have forgotten the most basic details about her life, but she couldn't imagine any scenario that would have led her to such a decision. Even if by some fantastic chance she had agreed to marry the dreadful Harold, she couldn't possibly go through with such an arrangement now.

"M-my fiancé?" she stammered, desperately trying to think how to extricate herself from this nightmare.

"Yes, of course Harold is your fiancé. What else would you call my son, given the understanding between our families?"

Callie stared at her.

"Why, I do believe you are shy, child! No wonder you've barely said a word." She pushed Harold toward Callie. "Now then, you needn't worry about a thing. You and Harold will have ample time to get to know each other before the nuptials. You will not know, but my dear husband died suddenly nearly five months ago, so we must observe the remaining month of mourning before you can be married."

Callie finally found her tongue and said the first thing that came to her mind, the only thing she could think of as she quickly sidestepped Harold. "I am very sorry about your loss, Lady Geoffrey, but I cannot possibly marry your son. I am promised to another."

"*What* did you say?" The woman paled, looking as if she might faint with shock, and Harold didn't look any steadier on his feet. "Promised to another? Are you mad, girl? You cannot be—you are already promised to Harold. It's all been arranged!" She glared at Callie as if she'd like to strangle her. "Who is this other person you claim to be affianced to? His name, girl—give me his name and we shall see who this rogue is who thinks to usurp Harold's claim." She poked her finger into Callie's arm. "I expect an immediate answer, Miss Melbourne."

Callie really hoped she wouldn't go straight to hell for the enormity of the lie she was about to tell, but she couldn't come up with anyone else. "His name is Adam Carlyle and he is the Marquess of Vale."

"*Adam!*" Lady Geoffrey gasped in horror, staring at her as if the world had just come to an end. Harold uttered a vicious curse under his breath, and Callie, who wasn't sure whether invoking Adam's name had been such a good idea after all, stood absolutely still, wondering what on earth she was going to do now. *When in doubt, pray,* a small, still voice reminded her.

Closing her eyes, Callie swiftly sent up a prayer to the entire celestial body of angels to somehow rescue her. A split second later, and to her absolute astonishment, her prayer was answered in the form of Adam himself.

"Good afternoon, Aunt Mildred, Cousin Harold. What a surprise."

Adam's voice came from directly behind her and his hands reassuringly closed around Callie's shoulders in a familiar touch. "I see you have met my fiancée. What a peculiar coincidence, but I suppose it saves me the trouble of paying you a call to inform you of my impending marriage."

Callie could barely believe her ears. Adam was actually *claiming* her as his fiancée? Not only that, he was addressing these two awful people as if they were related to him. He tightened his fingers on her shoulders in a clear message to let him deal with the situation. Obviously he had overheard her statement and decided to come to her defense. She was overwhelmed by gratitude.

"You say you are engaged to Miss Melbourne?" Mildred choked. "This is impossible. You are playing a very cruel joke, Adam, and I am not amused in the least. Miss Melbourne is engaged to Harold and has been these many months."

"I assure you I do not joke in the least. We are to be married shortly. Given that I am the head of the family, I confess I am surprised Harold did not inform me he had any plans for marriage. I am particularly surprised to hear that his supposed fiancée is Miss Melbourne, who has only very recently arrived in England. Do you recall agreeing to marry this man, my pet?" he said, speaking softly into her ear.

"I have never met him before in my life and I have no recollection of making any such promise," Callie said honestly, wondering how on earth Adam was going to extricate them from this pickle.

"There you are," Adam said, as if that resolved the matter.

"But—but it was agreed," Mildred sputtered, her face mottled with red splotches. "They didn't have to meet. Your uncle and his dear friend Magnus Melbourne arranged it between them after Magnus fell ill. Ask the girl—Callista was coming all the way from Greece to marry Harold in accordance with her father's dying wish! Go ahead—ask her!"

"Callie?" Adam turned her to face him, his expression betraying nothing but slight impatience. "I think you had better tell Lady Geoffrey and Mr. Carlyle the obvious—that you never had any intention of marrying a complete stranger. Isn't that true?"

"That is the truth," she said, her gaze locked with Adam's, willing him to tell her what to say next. Her head spun with so many colliding pieces of new information that she struggled just to stay upright. Her only safety lay with Adam—Adam might be able to fix this awful problem if she could just manage to follow his lead.

He smiled at her. "Now I see. This is what you referred to when you said in Paris that you had some silly misunderstanding to clear up when you arrived in England?"

"I'm sorry—I should have told you everything," Callie said, trying to look remorseful, "but the whole business seemed so—so ridiculous. My plan was to pay the Carlyles a visit and explain that I couldn't possibly marry a man I didn't know, let alone love, that my father was too ill to know what he was doing when he made the suggestion. Of course, that was before I met you, and . . . well, everything happened so quickly that I just put it out of my head," she continued, trying to think how to subtly tell him everything relevant she'd learned so that he wouldn't be caught short. "I feel terrible, Adam. Mr. Carlyle met my ship in Dover and he even collected my luggage when I didn't appear, and all because I changed my passage at the very last moment. I didn't even remember to write straightaway, but I've been so busy with all the preparations for our wedding, and of course I wasn't in urgent need of my old clothing after all the shopping we did in Paris."

"Well, at least that saves us the trouble of sending to the harbormaster for your luggage now, dearest. My cousin can send it on to Stanton now that he knows your direction." Adam turned back to them. "There you have it. You misunderstood Miss Melbourne's purpose in coming to England. I hardly think she would have agreed to marry me if she thought she was under an obligation to you, Harold." He smiled lazily, and Callie's eyes widened, knowing exactly what that smile meant. Lady Geoffrey and the unfortunate Harold were about to be made mincemeat of.

"You had better have a damned good explanation for this piece of work, *cousin*." Harold's face had gone the color of a ripe tomato. "I think you somehow got wind of my engagement and you—you deliberately went to Paris to find Miss Melbourne, didn't you? You only asked her to marry you just to thwart me."

"Really, Harold. Now you are being ludicrous."

"Well, why else would you want to marry an uncouth chit who has never even been introduced to society? It's not as if *you* need her money."

"Harold, that's enough!" His mother grabbed his coat sleeve, her face turning even more ashen.

"I see," Adam said, looking as if he'd like to take Harold apart limb by limb. "You planned to marry this 'uncouth chit,' you say, because you wanted her money. I'm hardly surprised. I suppose you talked your father into this scheme?"

"No—it was his idea, his and my mother's. I had nothing to do with it. They made me go along with them."

"I told you, it was Mr. Melbourne's idea," Mildred said quickly, her voice rising with what Callie took to be fear. Mildred had good reason to be afraid, given the dangerous way Adam was regarding them both. "We merely agreed to it."

"Did you. Why don't you explain exactly how this 'agreement' came about?"

"Mr. Melbourne wrote to us when he knew he could not live much longer and suggested that his daughter come to us, that Harold would make a fine husband. He said he didn't feel comfortable sending her to her cousin, Lord Fellowes, as the relationship was distant and—and her trustee, Sir Reginald Barnswell, was a bachelor and no longer young, so he would find caring for a young girl difficult."

"Tell me," Adam said. "Does Sir Reginald have any knowledge of this highly questionable arrangement? It would be he who would have drawn up a marriage settlement."

Mildred's hand jerked. "There was not enough time," she said, looking at Adam with true hatred as he unwound the threads of her story one by one. "It is a lengthy process as you well know, and Mr. Melbourne died seven months ago before any details could be properly arranged. However, he made his wishes *perfectly* clear in his last letter, and furthermore informed us of the terms of his will: Miss Melbourne was to inherit his fortune and the money would go directly to Harold upon her marriage." She stopped and looked at him suspiciously. "But you would know her financial particulars, surely, if you *are* engaged to Miss Melbourne?"

Adam ignored her. "What I know, Aunt, is that you and Harold planned to take advantage of an innocent young woman, recently bereaved and a stranger in this country. Unfortunately for you, you did not know Miss Melbourne, or you would have realized that she is not a woman to be manipulated."

"Oh? Then why did she bother coming to England at all?" Harold said nastily. "She could just as easily have written a letter saying that she was defying her father's wishes and re-mained in Corfu. I say she wanted to leave that backwater and live the life of a fine English lady of society, and I was the only gentleman prepared to offer for her. At twenty-five years of age the girl is not in her first blush, you know."

"You seem to forget, Harold, to whom you are speaking," Adam said, his eyes flashing with anger. "Miss Melbourne is shortly to become my wife, and I will not stand here and lis-ten to you and your mother insult her."

"I do not forget to whom I speak. You are a marquess, and therefore my better, which you never cease to remind me." Harold sneered. "You don't think Miss Callista Melbourne is marrying you for anything but your title, do you? She didn't miss the first opportunity to seize a better matrimonial prize—it's little wonder she didn't tell you that she was promised to me. I think your finger points in the wrong direction when you accuse me of being an op-portunist." He turned his sneer on Callie.

Adam moved so quickly that Callie didn't even register his intention. His fist shot out and caught Harold's jaw, the force of the blow knocking Harold to the ground.

He lay there, a trickle of blood seeping from the side of his mouth as his mother screamed and dropped to her knees, covering Harold's body as if to protect him from further harm.

"Get off me, woman," Harold spat, shoving at her and glowering up at Adam. "I'll call you out for this, don't think I won't," he cried, dabbing at his cut lip.

"I wouldn't," Adam said calmly. "You never were a very good shot. I'd get up if I were you—you look more ridiculous than usual. Good day, Aunt, Cousin." He turned his back on them. "Come, Callie," he said, tucking her hand into the crook of his arm. "I think you'll find the air more pleasing at the other end of the street, and the carriage is waiting."

"I'll bring a breach of promise suit against you," Harold shouted. "I'll make you sorry for this, I swear it! I'll—I'll ruin you both!"

Adam paused, then stopped and turned. "If you say or do anything that in any way causes Miss Melbourne or myself the slightest distress, Harold—anything at all—I can promise you that you will come to regret that action very deeply. If you remember, I always keep my promises."

"Damn you to hell," Harold muttered, shooting Adam a baleful glare.

"You needn't bother," Adam said coldly, looking bored. "Oh," he added as a parting shot, "be so good as to have Miss Melbourne's luggage immediately sent to Stanton. I don't believe her belongings are of any use to you."

He led Callie to the carriage without another word, and Callie was very, very grateful for his silence. She had a strong feeling that she was going to be hearing a great many words from Adam in the very near future, and not one of them was going to be pleasant.

# 12

"Adam, I'm so sorry," Callie said as soon as the carriage had started on its way back to Stanton, desperate to clear the air between them, since Adam was obviously so angry that he didn't intend to speak to her at all. "I never intended to put you in such an awful position, and I can't think why I blurted out that you were my fiancé, but please know that I didn't...I mean I wouldn't..." She halted, trying to find the right words to explain, but she felt at a complete loss. "Oh, I've made such a hash of everything," she said, miserably staring down at her hands.

"You certainly made a hash of Harold and Mildred's plans, and very neatly." Adam casually crossed his legs and leaned back in the seat, resting one arm against the green velvet squabs and not looking the least bit concerned that she'd just made liars out of them both. "I must confess that

I enjoyed helping you. The last time I saw Mildred look so put out was the day I reached my majority and ejected her, her husband, and pathetic Harold from the abbey after twelve long years. You might have gathered there is no love lost between me and my charming relations."

"I did gather that, and very quickly," Callie said, wondering when he was going to take her head off. Perhaps he intended to let her stew in her guilt and misery before he struck the fatal blow and summarily ejected her from Stanton and his life. "I cannot think how you have come to have such dreadful relatives, but then I don't know what my own father could have been thinking to want me to marry into that family." She stopped abruptly. "I can't take it all in," she said after a long moment. "There's so much to absorb, my real name, I mean, and where I actually lived, and that my father—well, that he's dead and I can't even remember him." She suddenly wanted to cry and had to bite the inside of her cheek hard. "His name was Magnus. That must be why I gave myself the surname. I remembered that much, at least."

"Callie," Adam said, finally looking over at her, his eyes not dark and stormy with anger as she'd expected but that lovely clear blue of a summer sky, "please don't distress yourself unduly. You will probably remember more with time, and at least we've begun to uncover the details of your history." He rubbed the side of his mouth. "I cannot say that I ever expected it to be tied up in such an unexpected manner with mine, but life has its odd twists and turns."

She nodded. "It does. I never would have invented you as my fiancé if I'd known that those—those people had anything to do with you. What I've been trying to say is that I appreciate your helping me out of a terrible scrape, but that—that naturally I don't expect you to actually *marry* me. You can just tell Harold and Lady Geoffrey that you cried off. Or better yet, that I cried off—I'm sure they already think that I'm in the habit and I don't mind in the least if they think I'm fickle-minded."

"I believe I am feeling wounded," Adam said, the corner of his mouth turning up. "Are you trying to tell me that you *want* to cry off? Really, Callie, I think that most inconsiderate of you. It's not the done thing to propose to someone and then change your mind only a half hour later, you know."

"Please don't tease," Callie said, about to start crying in earnest. "I don't think I could bear for you to poke fun at me right now."

Adam's face grew serious. "But I'm not poking fun. Quite frankly, I think that my marrying you is a perfect solution to your problem. I don't know why I didn't think of it myself. If you don't wish to marry me, that's something else, but at least you might consider the idea before dismissing it out of hand."

Callie stared at him in disbelief. She couldn't possibly have heard him correctly. "You—you're saying that you w-want to marry me," she finally managed to stammer.

"Why not? I remember what you once said about not thinking yourself well suited for marriage, but we get along nicely, you like living at Stanton, and being my wife would be a far more suitable and comfortable position than becoming some demanding old woman's companion." He tilted his head to one side and regarded her dispassionately. "Of course, now that we know you are a woman of independent means, my offer might not be so attractive. Would you like to think it over for a few days?"

Think it over? The man Callie loved with all of her heart had just asked her to be his wife. He offered a fairy-tale ending to the confusion and uncertainty she'd been living with for an entire month, a perfect antidote to the dread she had of leaving him and the only home she knew. Why, then, wasn't she filled with joy?

The answer came to her immediately and from a place in her heart just as deep and honest as her love.

"I don't have to think it over. I can't marry you," she said before she could change her mind and succumb to temptation.

Two deep lines scored his brow and he sat up straight, regarding her with genuine surprise. "You can't? Why ever not? Have I done or said something to offend you?"

"No," she said, feeling a terrible sadness rush through her as she forced herself to let go of her beautiful dream. "You could never offend me. But you don't love me, Adam, and without that, you would never be truly happy and neither would I." She thought her heart might break as she spoke the words.

His reaction was not what she expected: his face cleared as if she'd said something entirely satisfactory. "Ah. I think I understand. You believe that marriage must be based on love. I never thought you, given your well-trained mind, a romantic, but you have proved me wrong. Let me think how to properly explain the logistics of marriage to you."

Making a steeple of the tips of his fingers, he pressed them sideways against his mouth for a moment, organizing his thoughts in a manner with which she'd become achingly familiar. Dear, dear Adam—he always approached a problem with the same thoroughness, like a scholar who had only to apply logic and perseverance to a puzzle in order to come up with the correct solution.

When he lowered his hands and rested them flatly on his thighs, Callie knew he'd found his line of reasoning. She could have told him he was wasting his time, but she at least owed him the courtesy of listening.

"Now then," he said, "given that we're reasonably certain you were not raised as I was, meaning that you didn't have the rules and regulations of society and your duty toward it shoved down your throat as a daily diet, I can understand why you might have formed this romantic attitude regarding marriage. I cannot entirely regret your position, if it kept you from doing the unthinkable and marrying Harold to satisfy your father's dying and utterly perplexing wish."

"I am not entirely stupid," Callie said, beginning to be annoyed by his superior attitude.

"You are anything but stupid, Callie, but we digress. What you might not understand is that marriage in the upper reaches of society is rarely based on love. It is an institution primarily motivated by financial and dynastic concerns. If one is incredibly fortunate, love will follow. Sometimes, and even more rarely, two people do actually fall in love and the marriage is happily deemed suitable. If they are blessed with a plethora of good fortune, they actually manage to keep that love alive and flourishing."

"As you and Caroline did," Callie said, knowing she was treading on dangerous territory, but determined to make her own point.

"As Caroline and I did, yes," Adam replied evenly enough, but Callie could see that she'd knocked him off balance. "We were very fortunate indeed. Our natures were also well suited, which is more to the point. Many times what one believes to be love is nothing more than a strong physical attraction, and when the brightness of that flame dies down, nothing is left on which to build a lasting relationship."

Callie's annoyance grew. She really didn't need a lecture on the emotional and physical joys of his life with Caroline right now, even if she had been foolish enough to bring up the subject. She felt small-minded and petty, but the way

Adam was talking, she might have been a fund he was interested in investing in, not a flesh-and-blood woman with a heart that needed cherishing, never mind a body that constantly ached for his touch. She couldn't help herself. "I gather you didn't have that problem in your marriage. With the flame, I mean."

Adam's eyes narrowed as if he suspected her of being exactly the low-crawling, jealous creature she was, but he controlled himself admirably despite her deliberate provocation. "My life with Caroline is not the matter under discussion. As I said, we were well suited to each other and we were very happy as a result. I miss her more than I can say." His face took on that hollow expression she'd come to know, and he quickly looked away as if to disguise his grief.

"Forgive me," Callie said in a low voice, immediately repentant and deeply ashamed of herself. "I know speaking of Caroline is deeply painful for you, and I should never have mentioned her."

Adam released a barely audible sigh and turned his gaze back to her, his eyes filled with a bleakness that made him look weary and old beyond his years. "Callie, I did ask you to marry me. How can you help but wonder about Caroline?"

"I can't, but I still have no right to intrude. I have no right to ask for anything beyond what you have already given me. I certainly have no right to ask for your love, for that is a gift that has to be given freely and from the heart."

He shook his head, a gesture of helplessness and defeat. "I wish I could give you the answer you want, but something essential died in me the day my wife and son were killed. I don't have that kind of love to give, not any longer. I can give you my friendship and my loyalty, and I can give you my name and my possessions and a place to belong to.

But I can't give you what I don't have, and I respect you far too much to lie to you."

"Thank you for that, Adam," she said quietly. "I'd far rather have the truth than some empty platitudes that would make us both unhappy." But, oh, how she wished the truth could have been different.

He managed a smile. "Well, then. The truth is that I honestly am very fond of you, and if that counts for anything, maybe you could reconsider my proposal, for I'd like very much to see you stay on at Stanton. Being married to me might not be your heart's desire, but it wouldn't be the most miserable of existences, would it?"

"You know how much I've come to love Stanton," she said, not willing to address the dangerous subject of her heart's desire, for Adam would be shocked to his core if he had any idea how much she loved him. Given his overdeveloped sense of responsibility, he'd probably put all the blame on himself for the state of her unruly emotions and end up being forced to send her away for her own good. "I don't suppose we can just go on as we have been, two friends who enjoy each other's company?" she said in a hopeful voice.

"I'm afraid not," he said. "The cat's out of the bag. Harold and Mildred know about your not only being at Stanton, but also about your supposed engagement to me. You can be very sure that if we don't marry and you continue to live under my roof they will do everything possible to besmirch your reputation, and that I will not have."

"Oh," she said, feeling more wretched by the moment. She could see that knowing she was Miss Callista Melbourne had its drawbacks, for Adam hadn't worried at all about her living under his roof when she had no name or reputation to worry about.

"There's another point, Callie, and one that I didn't want

to mention unless I had to, but you haven't given me much choice. Until we know a great deal more about the exact way your father did leave his affairs, you might still be in jeopardy from my relatives unless I do marry you in short order."

"I don't see how," Callie said. "I told Harold I don't want anything to do with him, and I'm well over the age of consent, as he was kind enough to point out."

"It's not a matter of your consent, it's a matter of what your father did actually stipulate in his will, or possibly wrote in a codicil. I don't ever trust Mildred to speak anything approximating the truth, so I'm not clear on whether you actually have to marry in order to inherit. If that is the case, far better that you marry me than some fortune hunter like Harold, who will be sure not only to spend every penny, but also to take away your freedom and make you more miserable than you can possibly imagine."

"Suppose I do have to be married to Harold to inherit? That's how your aunt made it sound," she said. "I don't think I could bear it, Adam. I'd rather be penniless, I really would. Could he bring a breach-of-promise suit against me?"

"As I said, these are things to be discovered, and the sooner we discover them the better so that we know where you stand," he said, reaching over and squeezing her hand reassuringly. "I can't believe Harold has the legal premises for a breach-of-promise suit or he would have kicked up more of a fuss, but he might not have all the information at his disposal yet, either. Harold would dredge through the sewers to get what he wants, and if he wants you, or rather whatever money you might have to offer him, he will go to any length to get it, and his mother will be right at his side."

Callie paled at the thought of being pursued by Harold in any fashion, let alone his ghastly mother.

"Are you trying to frighten me into marrying you?" she said, only half joking.

"Certainly not. I am only pointing out that we don't know all the facts, and I'm putting myself forth as a better alternative to what you might face should you turn me down." He laughed at her appalled expression. "To be serious, Callie, I would never try to coerce you into marriage, but if you do manage to bring the logical part of your brain to bear, I think you will see that my argument does have a certain degree of reason to it. And even if you can't inherit if you don't marry Harold, your money isn't important to me."

Callie saw the reasons behind his argument well enough, and she couldn't see a logical alternative. Her heart and conscience were another matter entirely. She needed time to examine them more deeply, for she still couldn't marry Adam unless both were clear and unburdened. "I will promise to think about what you said, but for now, I'd rather leave the subject alone."

"I understand. You have a great many other things on your mind, and any time you wish to talk about them, please feel free to come to me. I don't care if it's the middle of the night. If you need comfort or reassurance I am always available."

"Thank you," she said softly. "Knowing that I can come to you is a comfort in itself." She hesitated, not sure if she should ask him the one question that presently burned on her mind, and decided perhaps she'd better not.

"All right, Callie," he said, amusement lighting up his face. "You know I can read you like a book. What is it now? You're practically squirming."

She looked down, unable to meet his eyes. "Have I offended you by refusing your proposal?" She couldn't help peeking up to see his expression, but it hadn't changed one iota. He still looked vastly amused, and she felt even sillier.

"*Offended* me? Good gracious, no. I can easily see why you wouldn't want to take me on unless you had to. I do, however, think that I really would be offended if you married Harold instead."

"That will never happen," Callie said fiercely. "I'd kill myself before letting him anywhere near me!" Her hands flew to her mouth in horror as she heard what she'd unthinkingly said. "Oh, no . . . oh! You don't suppose that's what really happened that day? That I deliberately did jump overboard, rather than marry Harold?"

"I honestly don't know," Adam said gently. "If you thought you had no alternative, perhaps. That's certainly what I would have done if I were being forced to marry Harold," he added, trying to inject a note of lightness into his voice. "But given what you said last night about your faith in God and eternity, not turning your back on life, taking the bad with the good, and all the rest? I have to think you would probably face anything rather than give up."

"You were listening!" she said, terribly pleased and forgetting all about Harold.

"I could hardly help listening," he replied dryly. "You didn't give me an alternative."

"I'm so glad," she said simply.

"So am I," he said just as simply, and Callie wondered why his eyes suddenly seemed unusually bright.

He turned his head away before she could ponder the question any further. "There," he said, clearing his throat and pointing. "You can see the abbey. It always looks so beautiful at this time of day when the sun catches the rooftops and windows just so."

"As if it's alight from the inside, offering a warm welcome," she added, and he glanced back at her in surprise.

"I have always thought the same. It's funny how such a

large pile of stone and mortar can seem to have a life of its own completely separate from its inhabitants. We mortals come and go, living but a brief moment in the scheme of things, but the heartbeat of the structure carries on untouched."

"That sounds like a very good description of the soul," Callie said with satisfaction.

Adam looked at her in disbelief. "You're surely not comparing the soul to a *house*?"

Callie grinned. "It's the other way around. The body is the house and the soul is the heartbeat that goes on unchanged."

Adam didn't say anything. He looked out the window again, then up at the ceiling of the carriage, then gazed fixedly at the door handle, his fingers pinching the bridge of his nose. A muffled wheeze escaped him, and then another, and the next thing Callie knew, Adam's shoulders shook helplessly with silent laughter as tears poured down his cheeks. He leaned sideways against the door. "Ah . . . it's too much," he gasped. "You don't stop, do you?"

"Adam!" Callie said indignantly, pushing at his hard shoulder. "I was perfectly serious."

"I know," he said, lifting one hand to fend her off. "But please, please not another word." He hooted and fell back against the seat, clutching his ribs.

His mirth was infectious and Callie caught it. She started to giggle and soon was overcome by lovely, silly, cleansing laughter that eased her aching heart and lifted her troubled spirits.

When Gettis opened the carriage door, he found them collapsed against each other, tears of hilarity running down their faces.

He had to summon every shred of dignity he had to

keep a poker face, but as soon as he was safely alone in the back parlor, he danced a stiff little jig of joy.

Adam stopped in his study to check the afternoon post and to see if anything had been put on his desk that needed his immediate attention, but his mind wasn't on his job and he was relieved that nothing pressing had arisen in his absence. His thoughts were filled with his last image of Callie, her cheeks rosy from laughter, her eyes dancing as she'd alighted from the carriage looking like a child who'd been caught out in a prank, the corners of her lips trembling with suppressed laughter as she'd attempted a composed entry into the house.

He hadn't managed any better at feigning composure than she had, fairly certain that their state of dishevelment hadn't gone unnoticed by the staff, but he really didn't give two figs. He was grateful that Callie had been able to laugh at all, given the series of shocks that she'd received that afternoon, but then Callie had an extraordinary ability to rebound in the most extreme circumstances—or at least to make a good show of rebounding. He'd learned that her emotions ran deep and that she could be highly adept at keeping them to herself.

He'd also learned, having been on the receiving end more than once, that when she did choose to reveal those feelings she had an equally remarkable ability for incisive honesty.

That didn't make the experience any less raw, and if he was to be just as honest with himself as Callie was, he couldn't say that he felt very happy about the day's outcome.

Not that he minded about Harold, he thought as he

closed the door behind him and started across the hall and up the stairs to change for dinner. Looking at that peculiar turn of events, he could almost be amused. He couldn't have planned a better comeuppance for Harold and Mildred if he'd tried, and he had spent a good many years trying.

He just wished that Callie didn't have to be involved, but she was as involved as she could be, and he wasn't about to let her take the consequences for Harold and Mildred's enmity toward him. That there would be consequences, Adam had no doubt. His job was to minimize them as much as possible, but for that, he needed Callie's full cooperation, and Callie's stubbornness wasn't helping matters.

He would need to speak with Sir Reginald as soon as possible and find out exactly what Callie's situation was; he'd be in a much more credible position to do that as Callie's fiancé. As things stood now, he would be hard-pressed to explain the nature of his relationship with her, which he could hardly explain to himself. He knew Sir Reginald would take a very dim view of Callie's living at Stanton without the benefit of matrimony, and her cousin Lord Fellowes would be no happier.

Adam was *not* pleased to be put in such an awkward situation, all because Callie refused to see sense.

Adam paused on the landing. The more he thought about it, the sillier Callie's refusal to marry him seemed. He had saved her life, after all, at the risk of his own. He had looked after her ever since with every generosity, even extending that generosity as far as to offer her his name in marriage, a very magnanimous and unselfish gesture on his part—especially considering that he'd made a solemn vow never to marry again. She was entirely ungrateful to have refused him at all, when it came down to it.

He brought his fist down on the newel post. And why had she refused him? Simply because he hadn't bowed down before her like a lovesick calf and begged for her hand. He should be deeply insulted, although he was far too reasonable a man to waste time with such useless emotions. He was a reasonable man, a levelheaded man who conducted his business affairs with logic and thoroughness, and this was no time to deviate from that course.

He made up his mind. The only way to deal with a headstrong girl like Callie was with a firm hand, and there was no time like the present. She needed to be told what was best for her. He didn't have time to wait for her to come to the correct conclusion by herself or they'd both end up looking like fools.

Walking down the hall to her door, he rapped.

Callie almost immediately opened it, still fully clothed, much to his relief. He wasn't about to have his will bent by her state of dishabille, as he'd been last night.

"Adam?" Her fingers moved to her throat, just above the point where her pulse beat steadily beneath the fragile blue vein. "Am I late for dinner? I was about to change, but I needn't, not if you'd like to go straight down."

"The only thing you might change, Callie, is your mind," he said firmly, trying to ignore the slender, tantalizing curves of her body, the sweet, trusting expression in her questioning eyes. "Now that I've had time to properly reflect, I've decided that we don't have the time to consider any options other than marriage without incurring difficulties that I, for one, do not wish to deal with. According to the rules of proper behavior, we are both in a compromised position, and believe me, that is how people will see it when they learn, which they will, that we are living together without the benefit of marriage. Therefore, I'm relying on your good sense to do the reasonable thing."

Callie's expression immediately changed from sweet

trust to outrage. "If I hear you correctly, my lord, you are insisting that I marry you?"

"I am not insisting, I am merely once again pointing out the obvious." Adam no longer felt quite so sure of his ground, given that she glared at him as if he'd suddenly become the enemy.

"The obvious," Callie said with disdain, "is that you pretended to listen and to actually care about what I might think, and all the while you were thinking of nothing but yourself and your own reputation. I will most certainly not marry you, not under any circumstances, even if I have to live in penury *and* disgrace for the rest of my life. You and your despicable cousin have much in common, as it turns out."

"Do not think to compare me with my cousin," Adam said, cool reason swiftly vanishing to be replaced by quickly rising anger. "We are nothing alike, I assure you, and I do not care to be insulted."

"Nor do I," she said, thrusting her hands on her hips. "I am not a—a piece of property to be allocated as and where it suits you. You seem to forget that I have feelings, Adam, and a mind of my own, and I am perfectly capable of making my own decisions without your help."

"Very well, madam," Adam said icily, wanting to shake her until her teeth rattled. "I shall keep my help to myself and you can wallow in the consequences of your ill-advised decisions all by yourself. I shan't trouble you again with my obviously offensive offer of marriage, since you have made yourself very clear on the matter and I have no intention of making a nuisance of myself."

"Adam," Callie said, dropping her hands and taking a tentative step toward him. "I didn't mean to imply that—"

"The subject is closed," he said, deeply annoyed that he'd let Callie make him lose his temper, something he never did. "I am going to change for dinner and I suggest you do the same. I consider it the height of ill manners to keep the servants waiting any longer than necessary."

He spun on his heel with that satisfactory parting sally and walked with what he thought was admirable dignity down the hallway to his room, a little disappointed when he heard Callie's door close softly instead of with a great slam, for he would have felt much better if he'd managed to upset her as badly as she'd upset him.

Stabbing her needle into her embroidery as if she'd like to poke someone's eye out, Mildred glared at her son, who was at that moment donning his caped box coat in preparation for a night out in town. "Have you no sensibility at all?" she snapped. "Your cousin has as good as ruined our future—our *mutual* future, might I add—and all you can think of is your own pleasure. If you were half a man you would go and call Adam out, or at the very least claim the girl for your own. How could you have just stood there and let him snatch her away from right under your nose?"

"Please, Mama," Harold said, thoroughly out of patience with his mother, who had been carping at him non-stop ever since the disastrous encounter in Folkestone. "We've been over this a hundred times already. There's nothing to be done. Adam has done it already. He never could stand to see me have anything, and he's gone out of his way to make sure of it this time too."

"What I'd like to know is how that blasted man ever got wind of our arrangement with the Melbourne girl—he *must* have known of it, Harold, or he never would have gone to Paris to sidetrack her."

"Adam has his fingers in enough coat pockets that he could have heard of it from anyone—not that *I* ever said a word to a soul, if that's what you're thinking. Maybe he heard about the arrangement from Sir Reginald, or even Lord Fellowes."

"Well, however Adam heard, he has to be stopped. Heiresses don't just fall off trees, so if you're thinking to land another fortune in that direction, my boy, you can think again. That girl is our only hope—I don't see you making any effort to support us properly, and we can hardly live on the pittance your father left."

"I am not responsible for my father's stupidity, Mama. If he had managed his affairs better, we wouldn't be in this pickle, so it's no good blaming me."

"You really are hopeless," Mildred said with a sigh of disgust. "You've always let Adam walk right over you, and now I have to pay the price, and furthermore, it's no good blaming your father for any of this—he was the one who put the idea in Magnus Melbourne's head to marry his very rich daughter to you. What are you going to do about Adam's interference? That is the question, Harold, and I'd like an answer, not another volley of excuses." She flung her embroidery to one side and started to drum her fingers on the arms of the chair. "I don't see why I should always be the one to do the thinking for both of us. I'm exhausted, Harold, really I am, and I wish you'd contribute something useful to this discussion."

Harold turned toward the window and rolled his eyes. His mother never had been able to see when she'd been trumped. Even after Adam in his typical unfeeling fashion had thrown them out of Stanton, she'd refused to accept that they'd never be allowed across the threshold again and had unceasingly harassed her husband to *fix* matters. Well, the truth was that if Harold's father hadn't so badly bungled the running of the estate, he, Harold, would still be living where he belonged by right.

He scowled. This was all Adam's fault, as usual. Adam had been a thorn in his side from the day Adam was born, and he continued to find ways to draw blood. Harold had done his best to remove the thorn, he really had, but this latest scheme of Adam's to deprive Harold of his God-given right to a comfortable life really was the bitter end.

He spun around on his heel, his eyes flashing with renewed anger. He wouldn't be thwarted, not again. "I'll do something, Mama, I will, by God. Just give me time to come up with a proper plan, for it doesn't do to go off halfcocked, not with Adam."

"Very well," his mother said, looking only slightly mollified. "Just don't be too long about it, for time is of the essence."

"I know, Mama," Harold said, puffing his chest out. "Leave the matter in my hands. I will not be bested by Adam, not this time."

So saying, he swept up his hat, placed it firmly on his head, and sauntered out of the room, filled with determination to seize the moment and put his cousin in his place for once and for all.

Two minutes later, he'd dismissed the entire issue. He had other, more important things on his mind.

Nigel looked back and forth between Callie and Adam, wondering what had come over both of them. Since sitting down to dinner, he'd had to carry the conversation by himself and he felt like a jabbering idiot. Adam barely bothered to reply to the simplest of questions, and Callie didn't make the slightest attempt to join in, very unlike her.

Even more perplexing was the way they avoided each other's eyes, and he couldn't help worrying that they'd had some sort of disagreement. He could almost tangibly feel the tension in the air.

Callie barely touched her dinner and she excused herself at the earliest opportunity, giving Nigel a distant smile as she bid him good night. To Adam she said nothing at all, drifting out of the room with a preoccupied expression.

"Trouble?" Nigel asked as soon as the servants had cleared the table and left them alone with their port.

Adam, who dangled his glass of port between his fingers as if he'd forgotten it was there, looked up. "I'm sorry? Did you say something?"

"Adam, I haven't the first idea of what happened between the time I saw you this morning and the time you came back from Folkestone, but you seem to be somewhere else tonight and Callie is just as far away."

"Mmm," Adam said. "We had an eventful day."

"Oh?" Nigel asked, no more enlightened than before. "Do you plan on telling me about it, or are you going to leave me hanging? Or perhaps it's a private matter," he added tactfully.

"Yes and no," Adam said, putting his glass down untouched. "We ran into Harold, who claimed to be engaged to Callie. Her surname is Melbourne, by the by."

Nigel nearly knocked over his port and he had to fumble to catch the glass before it spilled. "You—*what*?" he said idiotically, trying to pull himself together. "What happened? What did you say?"

Adam quickly explained the details of the encounter. "Thank God," he finished, "that Callie admitted to me yesterday that she does have amnesia, or I might really have wondered what the truth was. Given what I've just told you, I'm sure you can understand why we both might be feeling a little upended."

"Indeed," Nigel replied, completely upended as well. He'd been expecting something to happen, but as well as he thought he'd prepared himself, he was no match for the reality—or his own guilt at not having prepared Adam, either. Still, he had to admire Adam's quick thinking, even though he wasn't sure what the outcome was going to be. "You say you claimed to be Callie's fiancé. Isn't that going to be a little bit awkward when Mildred and Harold find out that you're nothing of the sort?"

"It is going to be awkward in the extreme, given that Callie refuses to come to her senses."

"I don't understand," Nigel said, unable to make heads or tails of Adam's statement. "Do you refer to her lack of memory?"

"Her lack of memory has nothing to do with it. I refer to her lack of common sense." Adam pushed his glass around on the table with his forefinger, his brow drawn into a frown. "I, being a practical man and seeing the only logical solution, asked Callie to marry me. She, being inexperienced and idealistic, clung to a misguided romantic sensibility and refused."

Nigel picked up his port and downed it in one gulp. *Callie* had refused *Adam*? He'd never even considered that possibility. If anything, he'd thought that Adam would be the person who was going to create the difficulty. But Callie? He couldn't imagine her turning Adam down. She had to have had good reason, but he couldn't think what it was, for she showed every sign of adoring Adam—although she hadn't looked the least bit adoring this evening, which led him to believe that Adam had somehow put his foot in it.

He couldn't believe that all of his careful planning was going for naught.

"I see," he said simply. "Well, if Callie won't marry you, what do you plan to do next?"

"That's the question of the day, isn't it?" Adam said, shoving his hand through his hair. "I'm damned if I know. I have no choice but to go up to London and speak to Sir Reginald, and I'm going to look like a complete idiot trying to explain how all this came about. No matter how I paint the picture, the facts are still the same: Callie's been living under my roof without benefit of a proper chaperon and there will be hell to pay for that alone, never mind the added complication of Harold's claim and Callie's amnesia."

He stared glumly at his glass. "Quite frankly, Nigel, I'm at a complete loss. I don't suppose you have any helpful suggestions?"

Nigel thought. "Perhaps you might consider telling Callie that you love her?"

"Don't be a damned fool," Adam said. He stood abruptly. "If that's all you can come up with, I'm going to bed. I've had an insufferably long and difficult day and I'm not in the mood for any of your frivolity. Good night, Nigel. Good night and I hope you, at least, sleep well."

Left alone, Nigel poured himself another glass of port, deciding that if anyone was a damned fool, it was Adam.

## 13

Tossing and turning, Callie found no respite from her misery in sleep. Her restless dreams chased each other in quick succession, a jumble of confused images that shifted and changed: Mildred cackling and poking her with her bony finger like the witch in "Hänsel and Gretel," checking her for plumpness before stuffing her into the oven, Harold standing next to her with a large napkin tied around his neck, his piggy eyes glittering with anticipation.

A large black gull swooped down and lifted her away with its feet just in the nick of time, but he released her and she tumbled through space for what seemed like an eternity before she plummeted into water that ran up her nose and blinded her eyes, her lungs starved for air.

Then Adam was there, leaning over her, saying something over and over again. "Breathe, little one, please breathe..."

Cold . . . she was so cold, and gasping and coughing, fighting for life.

A great hole yawned in the earth and she stood at the edge, looking down at a coffin, her eyes filled with tears. She wondered if it was her coffin, but then she heard singing and realized it was she who sang, the notes pouring through her with a tide of grief so profound that it threatened to overwhelm her. The gull came again and whispered in her ear. "You mustn't be afraid of death . . . it's all a part of living."

"No, Papa, please don't leave me!" she cried out, a desperate keen of heartbreak that came from the depths of her soul.

Callie woke with a start, the front of her nightdress damp with tears, the ache in her heart as great as the gaping hole in the earth that she'd seen.

Abruptly sitting up, she gripped the covers so hard that her fingers hurt. Staring into the moonlit recesses of the room, she tried to calm the erratic pounding of her heart, so loud that it echoed in her ears.

Callie thought she might break apart with grief. She covered her face with trembling hands, her head dropping onto her knees. She could no more stop the sobs that shook her body than she could stop the slicing, brutal anguish of the memory that had caused them.

She felt arms come around her, pull her close against a solid, bare chest, a hand stroke gently over her hair. She turned her face into the comfort of that hard chest, barely able to comprehend who held her but infinitely grateful to feel protected.

"Callie? Callie, you're awake now. It's all right. I heard you cry out, but thank God you were just dreaming. It's all over, just a nightmare, that's all."

Callie took a deep, shuddering breath, and then another one, the soft, soothing words reaching deep into the terrible ache and easing it. "Adam?" she whispered, realizing whose arms held her so tightly. She reached up and wrapped her hands around his forearm as if she could draw him deep inside her and keep her safe.

"Yes?" he said. "What is it, Callie? What troubles you so?"

Callie rubbed her wet cheek against the lightly furred skin of his arm, drinking in his warmth, his familiar scent. "I—I remembered my father," she said, taking another shuddering breath. "I remembered his funeral. I couldn't bear it. I didn't think I could go on."

His arms tightened around her. "I know, I do know," he said, resting his cheek on the top of her head. "Funerals are fairly dreadful occasions. One thinks at the time . . . Well. I'm sorry you didn't have a happier memory, but I'm glad at least that you do remember how much you must have loved him. I'm sure he was a very fine man."

"He was, Adam. I know he was." She shifted, sitting up so that she could look into his face. "I thought some terrible things about him today when I found out what he'd planned about Harold, but they can't have been true—I can't believe that he ever wanted anything but my happiness or I never could have loved him so much," she said, wiping her eyes with her fingertips. "I don't understand anything at all."

"I know how that feels, too," he replied, turning his head toward the window. "Grief leaves one with too many questions and absolutely no answers."

She reached her hand up and rested it on the side of his cheek. "I'm sorry. I was so caught up in my unhappiness that I forgot about your own suffering."

Adam wrapped his own hand around her fingers and squeezed them tightly. "I don't know that one ever recovers from such a blow. I have no knowledge of your father, but

I assume he must have been getting on in years, not that your grief should be any less for that."

"No, Adam, but I do think it's different. My father died from illness, not by violence, and he had lived a good portion of his life. Your wife, and especially your little boy, didn't have that chance."

He turned his head back to look at her, his eyes filled with pain. "I suppose that's one of the worst parts. I can't help but think that Ian had his entire life before him, and it was cut off so quickly and unfairly. Caroline, too, was only beginning to experience the joys of marriage and motherhood. What makes it all the harder is the knowledge that I bear the responsibility for what happened. I left them on the lawn that day to go back to the house and look after business, promising to join them later. If only I'd focused less on what I ought to be doing, and instead gone with them then to enjoy a lovely spring afternoon in the woods as they wanted, maybe everything would have turned out differently."

"You can live an entire life of 'if only,'" Callie said, placing her other hand on his cheek and gently cupping his face between her palms. She gazed intently into his eyes, willing him to hear her. "You can't change what happened, Adam, and you can't know what God had in mind when He called them back to Him. You will never know, not until you go home to Him yourself. The only thing you can be sure of is that you are meant to be here now, living your life as you're supposed to. You can make it happy or you can make it miserable, and the choice is yours alone." She smiled into his eyes. "I truly hope that you choose happiness, for that is what you deserve, and I imagine that is what Caroline and Ian would want for you also. I don't think that they'd want to see you suffering endlessly on their behalf, not if they loved you half as much as you loved them."

Adam held her gaze for a long, silent moment suspended between them like a finely spun and equally fragile gossamer thread. Callie knew that a very great deal hung on that thread, and that Adam could choose to break it at any time. She prayed with everything in her that he would not snap the link between them, for in her deepest heart she knew that everything rested on his decision: He could choose the future and move on with his life, or he could choose the past and continue to live with pain and regret. She could do no more.

"Callie . . ." he said, his voice hoarse. "I think you had better find the strength for both of us and tell me to go before I do something unforgivable."

"I don't want you to go," she replied, her breath catching in her throat at the odd, almost desperate look in his eyes. Her heart started pounding again, but this time with a deep, unfamiliar physical excitement that left her trembling.

Adam groaned. "Callie, for God's sake, don't look at me like that or I won't answer for the consequences. I'm a man, not a saint."

"You're as far from a saint as I can imagine," she said, finally understanding that there was something more that she could give Adam. She could give him the strength of her body and the embrace of her love to help him remember how to live again. He had spent too long alone in the dark reaches of hell, and it was well past time for him to let the light back in. What had made her think that he could do it by himself? What had even made her think that he would be capable of feeling love again until he learned to open his heart enough to receive it? There was so much that she could give him, and she'd been utterly selfish to hold herself back just because he hadn't said the words she wanted to hear.

Callie didn't think any further. She acted instinctively

and with a glad heart, shifting away from him as she pulled her nightdress over her head in one smooth gesture and dropped it on the floor. She rose to her knees, facing him.

Adam stared at her, the breath rushing out of his body. "What in the name of heaven . . . Oh, dear God. Callie?" His gaze drank her in, traveling over her body as if he was a starved man who'd just been offered an unexpected feast— a stunned, but definitely hungry man.

Callie smiled. She liked the way he looked at her, devouring every detail of her body that he could see. She liked it very, very much. The dumbstruck expression on his face made her feel like Aphrodite herself, as if what he saw met with his approval in every way.

She repaid the compliment, gazing at his beautiful form with the same careful attention to detail, traveling from his broad and powerfully formed shoulders down to the well-sculpted muscles that lined his ribs and his flat, ridged stomach—or as much of it as she could see over the top of his trousers, which sported an unmistakable and very masculine bulge. The outline of that bulge made her draw in her breath.

Adam passed a hand over his face as if he couldn't believe his eyes and stared up at the canopy over the bed. "Callie," he said, his voice cracking, "what do you think you're doing?"

"I'm offering myself to you," she said. "I want you, Adam, and I know you want me, so really, I can't think of anything more natural." She had a surprisingly hard time getting the words out because her heartbeat seemed to have taken up all the room in her throat.

"You're—you're *offering* yourself to me." He gazed at her in complete disbelief.

"Yes," she said. "And I don't think this is the time to start behaving like a starchy marquess, Adam."

"A starchy...never mind. Callie," he said, looking anywhere but at her, his face pained as beads of moisture forming on his brow and upper lip, "I'm not sure you understand—when I spoke of consequences earlier—I mean, you can't just go *offering* yourself with no thought to the future."

"Oh," she said, wishing that he'd stop talking, for she wanted nothing more than to be back in his arms. "If you mean what I said earlier, Adam, I'm sorry that I was so difficult. I'd be very happy to marry you, if you'll still have me."

Adam's gaze snapped back to her. If possible, he looked even more taken aback. "You will? I mean, yes, of course I will. Oh, *Callie*." He spoke her name with such relief that for one glorious moment she could almost pretend that he did love her. Almost, but not enough to allow herself to enter into that seductive fantasy. Adam had made his feelings—or lack of them—all too clear.

She didn't have time to consider the subject any further. Adam pulled her hard against him with a deep groan, his arms enfolding her as he covered her mouth with his, kissing her until her senses swam and her heart threatened to burst from her chest altogether.

His hands burned with fire as they trailed down her back, up and over her shoulders and down her arms, and Callie's flesh came alive under his touch. She matched his heat with her own, her fingers twining through his thick, silky hair as he claimed her mouth again and again, his tongue lightly thrusting into the soft recesses of her mouth, each lovely stroke giving her unimagined pleasure.

She returned thrust for thrust, touch for touch, tightly wrapping her arms around his back as little moans of pleasure escaped her throat. She couldn't think, could barely even breathe, and when he lifted her up and rolled her over in one smooth movement, laying her down on her back and dropping his head to nuzzle the tender flesh of her breasts, she couldn't help crying out.

"You are so perfectly made," he murmured, his tongue circling one exquisitely sensitive nipple, then pulling it into his mouth and suckling it. "So beautiful, so incredibly responsive," he whispered just before unleashing the same mayhem on her other nipple.

Callie's hips jerked against the tantalizing steel of his erection that pressed against her belly, and Adam impatiently pulled away and sat up, stripping his trousers off. Callie couldn't help staring. She'd never known that the male member could look so powerful and so very beautiful. It jutted out from his body, steel and strength, and she wanted nothing more than to feel it deep inside her, where a desperate throbbing had started low in her belly.

"Oh, Adam," she said in awe as he turned back to her. "You are magnificent."

Adam laughed, a deep, low chuckle. "Is that so?" he said, leaning down and running his tongue down the pulsating vein in her neck, as his fingers slid over the curve of her hips and down into the downy curls at the juncture of her thighs, seeking out the cleft of her most private flesh.

Callie's legs fell apart as he began to stroke her, sliding his fingers up and down, gently opening her to his touch as he found the hard, sensitive bud of nerves at her apex and circled that with the lightest of caresses until Callie thought she really might lose her senses altogether. Her head fell back and her hands clutched at his shoulders as if he could still the shaking of her body.

"Please, Adam, please," she begged, a spark flashing under his fingers that he teased into flames. He slipped one finger inside her in response and Callie's back arched as she lifted her hips to meet his deeply intimate touch, the flames bursting into full-blown fire that threatened to consume her.

She dimly heard a cry, not of pain, but of joy beyond bearing as her body convulsed over and over again before finally collapsing, spent.

But Adam wasn't done with her. He stroked her hair and kissed her again, and then again and more deeply, slowly, slowly bringing her back to meet him in the fire he'd so carefully built. But this time he rose over her, spreading her legs and guiding his shaft to the entrance of her body.

The hard pressure of his tip pressed against her flesh, stretching it until it burned. She wasn't unwilling, but she couldn't help but wonder how she was going to manage to accommodate his magnificence, having seen and felt the scope of it.

"This might hurt, Callie, but only for a moment and only this first time," he murmured, his breath hot and sweet against her cheek. "I'm sorry, but there's nothing I can do but break your maidenhead."

She turned her head and met his gaze evenly. "It is part of my offering," she said. "I give it to you with joy."

"Callie," Adam said very softly. "You are truly an extraordinary woman. I thank you for your gift."

He pushed then, hard, and Callie felt a sharp, searing pain rend her flesh as he broke through her barrier and buried himself deep inside her, holding very still and breathing in deep, hard pants, his damp forehead resting against hers.

*Home,* she hazily thought through the stinging pain that receded as quickly as it had come. *I've finally come home.*

As he began to gently move inside her, Callie relaxed, picking up his rhythm and answering it, taking him into her heart every bit as much as she took him into her body, a radiant happiness filling her. She held him tightly, her legs lifting to embrace his hips and bring him even deeper into her, her head moving restlessly back and forth as she reached for that torch of fire that burned so brightly and felt just out of her reach.

With one last smooth stroke Adam handed it to her, engulfed by the same bright flame as his body jerked and emptied into hers, his groans mingling with her cries, his heart pounding frantically against the frenzied beat of her own.

Callie wasn't sure how long the journey back from that fiery heaven took, but at some point she became aware of her surroundings. A hushed silence filled the room, broken only by the sound of Adam's slow, deep breathing. His head rested on her shoulder and he'd flung one arm across her waist.

She looked down at him tenderly, her fingers idly moving through his damp hair. She felt strangely complete, her body languid and satiated. Sleep pulled at the corners of her mind, but she wanted to savor every moment of the amazing experience she'd just had. Adam clearly didn't have any such need. His eyes were closed, his expression peaceful. He looked endearingly young, and she couldn't help kissing his forehead.

"Lest you think I'm sleeping," he murmured, his voice barely audible, "I'm not. I am recovering from a violent onslaught to my senses."

Callie chuckled. "Am I meant to feel sorry for you? Obviously you need a steady diet of vigorous activity or you shall go to seed."

Adam opened one eye. "Are you insulting me again, madam? I am thirty-three years of age and nowhere near approaching my seed years. However, I'd be happy to take you up on your offer of vigorous activity any time you choose—after we're married, that is."

"I think I'm going to like being married to you," Callie

said, turning toward him and snuggling down into the warmth of his body. "Can we be married very soon?"

"Mmm. The sooner the better, I think. I'll write away for a special license so that we needn't wait for the banns to be called." Adam ran his hands up and down her back and Callie shivered with pleasure. "I was going to go to London to speak to Sir Reginald," he continued, "but now that you've seen sense I think I'll write to him instead and ask him to come here. He should meet you, and I don't want you to have to make the journey to London, not while you're still recovering."

"Are you going to tell him everything?" Callie wasn't sure she liked the idea of too many people knowing about her memory loss. She felt silly enough as it was.

"Not exactly everything," Adam said with a muffled laugh. "I do think we should explain how this all came about, though. He's bound to have questions and the truth, as strange as it might sound to him, will serve us best. Speaking of the truth, I'd be well-advised to return to my own room before one of the servants discovers us—we might as well pretend to be respectable."

"You're so sweet, Adam, always thinking about the servants' sensibilities." She stifled a yawn.

"I was thinking about my own," he said, kissing her lightly as he disengaged himself and sat up, reaching for his trousers and pulling them on. "I'm always deeply upset when one of them looks at me with disapproval." He bent down and kissed her again. "Sleep well, Callie, and dream of nice things. I'll see you at breakfast."

He crossed the room, opened the door and looked up and down the hall, then slipped out, softly closing the door behind him.

Callie turned onto her side and tucked her cheek onto

her hand, her other reaching out to cover the warm spot where Adam had just been. Despite the dramatic events that had unfolded during the course of the day and night, she felt strangely at peace, with not a single regret.

Well, just one. Adam didn't love her, but at least he was willing to offer her his friendship freely. That would have to be enough. She'd been given the moon. She couldn't expect the stars as well.

"You're looking very cheerful this morning, my lord, if you don't mind my saying." Plimpton carefully wiped off the edge of the razor and reapplied it to Adam's cheek.

Adam waited until Plimpton had finished shaving him before he replied. He didn't want to run the risk of having his face nicked, and Plimpton's hands had a tendency to shake when he became excited.

"I have good reason," Adam said, setting about the task of letting the household know that a large change was in the making at Stanton. He knew that Plimpton was the best person to inform about his impending marriage, for he would at least go about spreading the news with a degree of dignity.

"Oh, yes, my lord? What would that be?" Plimpton finished wiping Adam's face with a warm towel, then stepped back to admire his handiwork.

"Miss Callie has agreed to marry me," Adam said, and watched with satisfaction as Plimpton dropped the towel, exactly as Adam had predicted.

"Why—why, that's wonderful news!" Plimpton exclaimed, his eyes practically popping out of his head and his hands trembling like two large leaves in a storm. "Many congratulations, my lord. We all think the world of Miss Callie. When is the happy event to occur?"

"It will occur shortly, Plimpton, and with a minimum of fuss. Be so good as to ask Mr. Dryden to join me in my study after breakfast. I'll tell him the news myself," he thought to add.

"Naturally, my lord," Plimpton said, drawing himself up. "Would you care for me to inform the senior members of the staff?"

"If you'd be so kind," Adam said absently, already in the process of planning his letters to Sir Reginald and to Doctors' Commons for the marriage license. He needed to write to Lord Fellowes as well, as a matter of courtesy, but that could be brief and to the point. He didn't expect any surprises from that quarter. He didn't really expect any surprises at all. Whatever the terms of Magnus Melbourne's will, they became moot once he and Callie were wed, for he intended to look after her and he had more than enough money to do so very nicely without any help from her inheritance.

Probably the person most surprised about his impending marriage was himself. Just a month ago he would have laughed himself silly if anyone had told him he would ever remarry. But just a month ago he'd been on his way to kill himself.

Adam frowned as Plimpton began the job of tying his neckcloth, not entirely sure when he'd changed his mind. He knew that the idea was no longer a consideration, not only because he was taking on the responsibility of Callie as his wife, and wouldn't do something like that to her, but also because life no longer seemed quite so . . . unbearable.

It had its moments, like the ghastly one in the woods the other day, but he had to admit that Callie had brought a certain degree of sunshine into his life—a surprising degree of sunshine, really, when he thought about it. She might have caused him a great deal of trouble, but at least it was trouble that he could manage, unlike his grief.

No matter what Callie seemed to think, grief was not something that could be put aside like an old pair of boots one had worn through. It stayed deep within one, aggravated by constant reminders, wearing down the heart and soul until just the effort of breathing seemed too difficult.

To be fair to her, she couldn't know, never having experienced the joy of romantic love or the all-encompassing love for one's own child. She had a dim memory of a father she'd loved, but nothing more. Oh—there was that man called Niko, but he sounded as if he'd been a friend, nothing more, so that wasn't the same.

No. Callie didn't have the first idea what romantic love was, only some high ideal of what it should be that she'd probably picked up in a book somewhere.

"Ahem," Plimpton said, politely clearing his throat. "Your coat, my lord."

Adam looked over at Plimpton, who patiently stood a few paces away, coat held out for him to slip into. "Sorry," he said. "I was woolgathering." He obediently turned and reached his arms back.

"I am sure you have many things on your mind," Plimpton said kindly, smoothing out the fabric with a practiced hand. "If you have no further need of me, I will attend to the soaping of your boots."

"Thank you, Plimpton," Adam said, completing the same conversation that they had every morning, although this morning he was sure that Plimpton couldn't wait to bolt downstairs and corner Mrs. Simpson and Gettis with his sensational news.

He wondered if Callie was going through the same ritual with her maid. He also wondered if Callie still looked as pleased with herself as she had last night.

By God, she had taken his breath away, her body gleaming like alabaster in the moonlight. If he hadn't been sitting, he might have fallen over when she drew off her nightdress and revealed her small, high breasts with their pink-tipped nipples, that lovely small waist, the slender curve of her hips leading to the soft, light patch of down between her long, shapely legs. Aphrodite in all her glory: That had been Callie, offering herself up to him like a goddess, fair hair tumbling around her back and shoulders, that gentle, alluring smile inviting him to partake of her.

He'd had his share of women, but he'd never seen anything like Callie. He'd never experienced anyone like Callie, who gave of herself with a freedom and an unselfconscious sensuality that made his senses reel just remembering.

Adam looked down at himself with an amused smile, thinking it was a very good thing that Plimpton had already left the room, or he'd be shocked by the badly disturbed line of Adam's trousers.

Marrying Callie might not have been what he'd had in mind, but it was certainly going to have its advantages. His heart might be irreparably broken, but he'd discovered that his body was as whole and healthy as ever. With a little luck, he might even manage to produce a son with Callie, and that would take care of Harold and his aspirations toward Stanton and the marquessate in short order.

The thought gave him immense satisfaction and yet another practical reason for remarrying.

Whistling merrily, he went downstairs to eat a hearty breakfast, gaze some more at Callie's tantalizing curves, and enjoy her conversation before settling down to the day's business.

Plimpton, taking every advantage of the astonishing information he possessed as his lordship's trusted valet, solemnly gathered the senior members of the staff in the housekeeper's parlor after breakfast, being gracious enough to include Cook and Roberts, the head gardener.

"I have an announcement," he said, clearing his throat and pausing for dramatic effect. "His lordship has informed me that he and Miss Callie are shortly to be joined in wedlock."

The stunned silence that followed hugely satisfied him, as did the almost instantaneous applause and cries of "Hear, hear!"

Mrs. Simpson collapsed into her armchair, shedding tears of joy that challenged even her oversized handkerchief, her loud sobs sending Cook, crying just as hard, running for the smelling salts as much for herself as for the housekeeper.

Gettis bowed his head and clasped his hands fervently together, as if he was offering up a prayer.

Roberts grunted. "Well, I'll be blowed," he said, as if he didn't care that there was a lady present. "Good for the girl, I say, and it's about time we had another mistress about the place. She's a good girl, Miss Callie is, and appreciates the finer aspects of my plantings."

Plimpton clapped his hands together, trying to get their attention. "If you will attend for a moment, I'd like to wish both Miss Callie and his lordship happiness. In support of that endeavor, I would also like to propose that we show a quiet and sustained indication of our enthusiasm for the match, as the time for grieving has passed and the time for celebration has come."

"Dear boy. Dear girl," Mrs. Simpson sobbed into her handkerchief and raised a tear-stained, swollen face. "Whoever would have thought when his lordship brought the poppet in that night that it would come to this? Such joy, such joy." She dabbed at her nose. "Now, Mr. Plimpton," she said, immediately turning to practicalities, "will we be having a large wedding or something more subdued?" She waved off Cook's offer of smelling salts.

"I believe the ceremony will be held quietly," Plimpton replied. "We will need flowers, of course, Mr. Roberts, and a small wedding breakfast and a bridal cake would be in order, Cook, but from the little his lordship said, I think that we need not prepare for company. Perhaps later his lordship and future ladyship will want to give a party, but we must remember that this has been a house of mourning for some time and Miss Callie's health is still to be considered."

"Nonsense. I've never seen a sign of delicacy in the girl," Roberts said. "She looks right as rain to me. I don't know what you're all fussing over."

Gettis glared at him. "You are not a doctor, Mr. Roberts, and Miss Callie is not one of your plants. We will continue to keep a careful eye on her until such time as the doctor declares her restored to full health, and I won't hear another word about it."

"Rightly so, Mr. Gettis," Mrs. Simpson said approvingly. "His lordship wouldn't have it any other way, and didn't he make that clear enough to me only the other day? I saw the way the wind blew, given the way he went on when he thought her missing. Yes, indeed, I saw it, didn't I, Mr. Gettis, but you didn't think he'd tumble in love so quickly after all the grief he's suffered since the tragedy."

"As Mr. Plimpton said, let us put the sadness of that time out of our minds," Gettis interjected quickly, not because he minded having been proved wrong—he'd already reached that conclusion the evening before—but because he really couldn't bear Mrs. Simpson bringing up the tragedy now. "I shall inform the footmen of the news, and you, Mrs. Simpson, and you, Cook, may inform your underlings. It is a great day, a great good day indeed," he murmured to himself, returning to the tasks at hand.

# 14

"I am here as summoned, my lord," Nigel said as he entered the study. "Plimpton conveyed your request with the air of a royal command, so I brought my humble and foolish self promptly. How may I serve you this morning? Or perhaps I should be serving myself—a little arsenic, perhaps?"

Adam was in too good a mood to let Nigel needle him. "I beg your pardon if I was short with you last night," he said. "I called you in to tell you that Callie is going to marry me after all, and I wanted you to hear the news from me and not the servants, who are probably already buzzing like bees."

Nigel raised his eyebrows and shoved his hands in his pockets. "Well, well," he said. "This is happy news indeed. It's amazing what a difference a night can make."

Adam, startled by this observation, regarded Nigel sharply, wondering not for the first time if Nigel had the ability to read Adam's mind. They'd been friends for so long that he sometimes felt Nigel knew him better than he knew himself. "The light of day can often bring clarity to a problem," he said, not about to let Nigel know that he'd managed to thoroughly and happily compromise Callie. "She seems content with her decision. I suppose she simply needed time to recover from the shock of yesterday's events."

"I suppose so," Nigel said. "That's a woman for you. One never knows what they're going to do or say next."

"One never knows," Adam agreed, regarding Nigel with suspicion. Nigel's eyes danced with suppressed laughter as if he was enjoying a private joke, and Adam imagined he probably was.

Adam knew Nigel just as well as Nigel knew him, and he was damned if he was going to be a party to Nigel's amusement, not at Callie's expense.

"Why don't you get back to what you were doing before I interrupted you?" he said, thinking that in another minute Nigel would hardly be able to miss the physical evidence of Adam's attraction to his future wife, for just thinking about Callie in all of her abandoned splendor made his groin start to tighten with renewed need.

Looking at her was even worse and had created some serious problems at the breakfast table. He'd never been so grateful for his napkin before. He really didn't know how he was going to get through the next two weeks and still keep his resolution to stay away from Callie's bed until they were married.

Adam decided to put aside his letter to Sir Reginald and write immediately for the special license, so that it could go in the morning post. The blasted license couldn't arrive soon enough for his liking. He had to suppress a strong stab of guilt at his desire for haste, for he couldn't help feeling that his physical attraction to Callie was a betrayal of Caroline's memory and his love for her—even though love didn't enter the equation when it came to his reasons for marrying Callie.

Still, the least he could do would be to behave in a far more circumspect fashion and push his desire to the back of his mind, at least until he was safely married.

Concentrating on her careful pruning, Callie didn't realize that Adam had entered the rose garden until she heard him speak from behind her.

"The roses are almost as pretty—almost—as you are," he said.

Callie dropped her pruning sheers and spun around. "Adam—you startled me!" she said with a breathless laugh.

"I'm sorry. I should have announced myself sooner, but I was enjoying the scenery."

"It's lovely, isn't it?" she said. "Roberts explained all the names of the different varietals, but he's only just today decided to trust me to do the pruning on my own. He's very possessive of his roses." She smiled up at him, happy to be alone in his company.

She'd seen him at breakfast, but they'd eaten with Gettis, Michael, and Henry standing nearby with their customary watchful attention, so she was forced to behave as if nothing had changed between Adam and herself. That had been an exercise in self-control, for she found it very difficult to eat toast and marmalade while thinking about the way that Adam's powerful, masculine body looked without the benefit of clothing.

Adam, being Adam, betrayed not so much as a blink of an eye, behaving as if nothing was on his mind but a second cup of coffee and reading interesting bits of the newspaper to her.

"Roberts," she said merrily, taking a step toward Adam

and resting her hands on his broad chest, "offered his congratulations on our betrothal with an enthusiasm he usually saves for his plants, so I gather that you've informed the staff." She raised her face for his kiss, but he picked up her hand instead and dropped a light kiss on its back.

"I informed Plimpton," he said, quickly stepping away from her and bending over to examine a rosebush. "Plimpton informed the staff—except for Nigel, of course, whom I told myself."

"Oh," Callie said in confusion, wondering why Adam had abruptly moved away. "I hope he was pleased."

"He was very pleased." Adam straightened and faced her again, his face expressionless. "Everyone seems pleased, which is all to the good, although I expected a little more surprise. Anyone would think that they'd been planning this all along."

Callie wasn't sure what to say to that. She couldn't tell if Adam himself was still pleased, for he looked surprisingly uncomfortable, given what they'd been doing last night. Or maybe he was uncomfortable because of what they'd been doing last night . . . Callie bit her lip, wondering if Adam now regretted making love to her, then dismissed that idea as ridiculous.

"Maybe you're right," she said. "Jane didn't actually say anything when she came in this morning, but I think that she must have realized something had happened when she saw the state of the sheets. I made up a story about having started my cycle and she pretended to believe me, but she still looked awfully smug and said she'd take care of the linens herself rather than leaving it to the chambermaid."

"If you're concerned, I wouldn't be. I am sure Jane has the good sense to keep her opinions to herself, if she wants to keep her job," Adam said.

"No, you misunderstand me. I think Jane was pleased

about what she saw. I don't think she is entirely innocent when it comes to the details of losing one's virginity."

Adam no longer looked expressionless. If anything, he looked pained, for his color had heightened. He turned back to the rosebush. "Callie—I think it would be best if we don't discuss last night any further. We have other things to think about, such as preparing for our nuptials."

Callie couldn't believe it. Adam was actually embarrassed? He hadn't looked embarrassed when he'd left her last night, but maybe ladies weren't supposed to talk about such things in the light of day. She had no idea. Thinking about it, she had very little idea of what ladies were supposed to talk about or how they were supposed to behave.

"Very well," she said, but she couldn't help feeling hurt by his cool behavior. "I don't know what you mean by preparing, for I don't really have anything to prepare, have I?"

"I wasn't referring to sending out invitations," he said, looking over his shoulder. "I meant that you might want to start planning what you'd like to do after we're married. Perhaps you'd like to go on a brief wedding trip, although I shouldn't take too much time away during the summer months. Or perhaps there are some changes you'd like to make inside the house—to your bedroom, for instance, for you'll be moving into the one next to mine." He passed a hand over his brow. "Or maybe you'd like to redecorate the morning room for your personal use, or let Mrs. Simpson know how you would like to run the household—whatever you wish," he said, waving a hand as if she knew exactly how to go about such a thing. "I should get back to my letters."

Adam left her standing in the garden, her pruning forgotten, a deep frown of perplexity on her face.

The practical challenges of being Adam's wife were only

just beginning to dawn on her, and she wasn't at all sure she was up to the task.

"I'm sorry I couldn't come sooner, but since I saw you last, life has been wonderful and awful at the same time," Callie said over her shoulder to Nellie as she had a look at little Georgie. His red face had calmed and his constant drooling had slowed to a mere trickle. "Oh, he looks a great deal happier," she said. "Have you tried the remedies I suggested?"

"I have indeed, and thank the good Lord for your advice, for I think I would have lost my patience if I'd had to endure any more of his crying, bless him. He's a fine little lad when his temper is in check, but he's just like his dad when he's out of sorts."

Nellie took the kettle off the stove and poured boiling water into the teapot, steeping the leaves Callie had brought with her in her basket of food. "I'm glad you came when you could manage, for I've been gasping with curiosity to know how it's been going up at the abbey. You were saying that life's been wonderful and awful. Why is that?"

Callie picked Georgie up and gave him a cuddle, then comfortably settled him back on his rug. "I have so much to tell you and hardly know where to begin," she said. "I suppose the most important thing is that Lord Vale and I are to be married."

Nellie nearly dropped the teacups she'd picked up. "You and Lord Vale?" she said, her mouth hanging open. "I don't believe it!"

"It's the truth," Callie said. "I'm surprised you haven't heard, given the way the staff has been going on, practically billing and cooing at us. You'd think no one had ever been married before, Adam least of all, although he was very much married and very happy with his wife, so I don't know what all the fuss is about."

Setting the cups safely on the table, Nellie shook her head in bafflement. "Well, that explains why his lordship's grand carriage brought you to my humble door instead of your own two legs, but how did all this come about? The last time you were here you didn't let on a thing—right round the other way, I'd say. As I remember, you mentioned something about being nothing more than an inconvenience he had to put up with."

Callie couldn't help laughing. "I think I still am to a degree, but everything got very complicated. We bumped into his cousin Harold Carlyle, who insisted that he and I were promised to each other, and I didn't know what to say since I couldn't remember, so I used Adam as a decoy. I, um . . . well, I said that I was betrothed to him, and Adam was kind enough to back me up, and the next thing I knew, Adam had decided that was the way it should be. I think he only decided that because he couldn't come up with any other way out of the predicament I'd put us both in, but I'm very happy and he doesn't seem too bothered."

"But, Callie, does his lordship know the truth? About your bad memory, I mean? You have to have truth between you, even if there's nothing else."

"Oh, yes. He's known almost all the way along but he never told me for fear of upsetting me. The nice thing is that in the course of meeting Harold, at least we found out my true name, which is Callista Melbourne, and that I came to England from Greece after my father died, supposedly to marry Harold. But then I fell off the boat and Adam rescued me, so Harold wasn't able to take me off, and Harold couldn't have been more angry about it."

"You are one surprise after another," Nellie said, shaking her head again as she brought the teapot to the table.

"I know, and as much to myself as everyone else. Nellie,"

Callie said, coming to the real reason for her visit. "I was wondering if you might be able to tell me something about Adam's late wife, Caroline. I don't really know anything, since Adam finds it difficult to talk about her. Can you help me? I daren't ask anyone up at the abbey for fear of upsetting them, but I would be so grateful to know anything at all."

"I don't know how I can help you," Nellie replied, pouring the tea through a strainer and handing Callie a cup. "I didn't rub shoulders with the likes of her ladyship, although I saw her about from time to time. She was a fine-looking woman, always very polite, nodding her head and smiling in acknowledgement and all that if she spotted you. She was as different to you as can be."

"But *how,* Nellie? How was she different?" Callie asked almost desperately. The question had been plaguing her for the last ten days, ever since the morning in the rose garden. In her weaker moments she felt unequal to the task of following someone who must have been such a paragon of virtue that everyone, Adam most especially, worshipped her memory to the point of respectful silence.

In Callie's better moments she wondered how she could smooth the staff's transition from one mistress to the next, never mind easing Adam's acceptance of her as his wife. Either way, she couldn't compete with a faceless ghost. For her own peace of mind she had to find out what she could, and Nellie was the only person she could possibly ask. "What did she look like, for example?"

"Well, let's see. Her hair was dark, for one, and her eyes green, and she was taller than you." Nellie screwed up her face with concentration as she sipped at her tea. "She didn't have the common touch like you have, if you know what I mean. I mean no disrespect, but she was more of a 'Lady Bountiful,' far above us lesser folk, not that she meant anything mean by it. She just had that air about her. You don't have that about you at all." Nellie chortled. "You couldn't, could you, not remembering your past and all that."

"No," Callie said miserably, thinking that she knew exactly what Nellie meant. Adam had that air, as kind and thoughtful as he was to his servants, of somehow being completely removed from their world. Caroline had been born and raised to the same behavior, and it must have been as natural to her as breathing.

Callie, on the other hand, was as comfortable in the kitchen with her hands in the dough as she was sitting here at Nellie's cottage. Perhaps if she knew something more about herself and her upbringing, she might feel more confident, but she knew very little at all save that she'd recently come from an island in Greece and must have spent a lot of time in nature, for she was as comfortable with birds, beasts, and insects as she was with people—more comfortable, sometimes.

That wasn't much to commend her for the life of a future marchioness. It wasn't much, either, to commend her to Adam as his future wife.

She really couldn't think what she did have to commend her. Adam enjoyed talking to her, and he'd certainly seemed to enjoy their one physical encounter, but she was beginning to wonder about even that: She'd started to think that she hadn't conducted herself very much like a lady was supposed to in the bedroom, for Adam had avoided even the slightest physical contact with her ever since. Perhaps she'd shocked him with her enthusiasm. She couldn't be sure, but she could think of no other reason for his turning away every time she got within touching distance.

She'd lay money that Caroline had known exactly how to conduct herself in the bedroom as well.

"Where have you gone to, girl?" Nellie asked. "Oh!" she

exclaimed, looking appalled and clapping both hands against her mouth. "I suppose I'd better get myself used to the idea of your being a fine lady. I can't go on behaving like we're going to be the best of friends, now can I, not with the changes you're about to make?"

"I can't see why not," Callie said, equally appalled that Nellie would think such a silly thing. "I'm no different from the way I was when I first walked through the door."

"But you are, Callie, and you'd better get accustomed to the idea, or people won't know their places and how they're meant to go along, will they? I'm sorry to have to point the matter out to you, but that's how it is and how it's always been—with the lord and lady in their castle and the rest of us milling around bowing and curtseying to our betters while we work for them. You have to know your place and keep it if the world's to go on as it's meant to, and there's nothing in God's green kingdom that can change it."

Callie's eyes stung with sudden tears. "I don't want it to be that way," she said, turning her face into her hand in complete despair. She'd never thought this far along, that she might be cut off from the fullness of humanity just by virtue of assuming a position in society, and just because she'd married Adam. She loved Adam. That was what mattered, not what people thought.

"I don't see why it has to be that way at all," she said stubbornly.

"Then maybe you'd better think long and hard before you marry your lord, girl, for there won't be any changing your mind after the fact."

"I'm not going to change my mind, Nellie. Adam's already lost too much in his life and I'm going to stay right where I am and try to make him happy, even if he is marrying me for convenience."

"Aye, he deserves some happiness, the poor man. He hasn't had much of it in his life, has he? It doesn't seem right that a child's mother should die practically before he has time to draw his first breath, and then his father to follow her only nine short years later." She shook her head.

"Ah, well," she said, wrapping her fingers around her teacup, "I suppose the good Lord knows what He's about. Still, if what my Tom says is true about the nasty relations who raised him after that and treated him like he was nothing but dirt under their feet, then you have to wonder how much a body can take. And then his wife and little boy being killed..." She shook her head. "Never mind that now, for it's all water under the bridge. I'm happy he's found you, Callie, I am indeed."

Callie was so shocked that she couldn't speak. She'd had no idea that Adam's mother had died in childbirth, although she'd worked out that his father must have died when he was young. Poor, poor Adam. She could hardly imagine what his young life must have been like, especially if the horrible Carlyles had been involved in his upbringing. Adam had good reason for despising them, other than the obvious.

"Why, are those tears I see in your eyes?" Nellie said with surprise. "Heavens, girl, I didn't mean to upset you." She gave Callie a long, appraising look. "Something tells me there's more here than you've let on. I don't think you're the least bit indifferent to his lordship, are you?"

"I'm anything but indifferent," Callie whispered. "I love him with all my heart, Nellie."

Nellie nodded sagely. "I thought as much. That's why you were asking about his wife, isn't it? Not so that you could learn to behave like her, but to find out if he can ever love you as much."

Callie wiped her eyes. "But you said yourself that we're as

different as can be. Anyway, I don't think Adam ever wants to love anyone again. He's been hurt too many times."

"It's natural for people to want to protect themselves when they've been hurt," Nellie said in her calm, sensible fashion. "That doesn't mean that he's not capable of finding his way to loving you. The way I see it, it's a good thing that you're so different to her ladyship, for he won't be comparing you, will he?"

"Oh, Nellie, it's I who makes the comparison, not Adam," she said miserably. "Or at least I don't think he does. I can't help but feel that Adam doesn't even bother to think of me in the same way at all, not as a real wife. I'm just someone whom he's become reasonably fond of and doesn't mind having around, a small and fairly insignificant part of his world. I'm a problem to be solved, and now that he's found a reasonable solution, he's satisfied. Next month he'll be back to thinking about the dredging project or—or whether he should have planted hay instead of turnips."

"I doubt it," Nellie said, rubbing her swollen belly with a little smile. "He's a man and you're a woman, and a shared bed can be a nice, cozy place for two people to get to know each other."

"I don't think I was much of a success in that, either," Callie said without thinking. "Oh—I suppose I shouldn't have mentioned that," she belatedly added, blushing fiercely.

Nellie burst into hoots of laughter and slapped her hands on the table with glee. "So it's like that, is it? You're further along than you think, my girl, if he's already bedded you. He wouldn't have bothered if he was altogether indifferent." She raised her eyebrows in question. "Now, why would you say you weren't a success? Were you a virgin and didn't like it, is that it? That passes quickly enough, believe me."

"No. No, it wasn't that at all. I mean yes, I was a virgin, but I didn't mind the pain. Nellie," she said in a rush, too determined to get Nellie's advice to give in to embarrassment. "Are women supposed to be . . . well, are they supposed to be quiet and docile during lovemaking? Is that what a man expects?"

"Quiet and—now, who's been putting ideas in your head?" Nellie said with astonishment. "I can't believe it's his lordship, for the last thing a man wants is a woman lying under him behaving like she had something better to do." She threw her head back and roared. "Ah, my Tom would love to hear that one." She valiantly tried to sober. "Just between you and me and the wall," she said, wiping the tears from her eyes, "the more pleasure you show, the happier your man will be. He's not in it all by himself, you know. He wants to know you're enjoying his attentions."

"No," Callie said, blushing and laughing all at the same time, "you misunderstood me. I thought perhaps I'd shown too much pleasure. Adam's been behaving like—like a country vicar ever since. He's taken pains to avoid touching me."

Nellie grinned. "And so he should until he has a ring on your finger, poor man. He's probably about ready to jump out of his skin if I know anything about it, now that he's had a taste of what's in store for him. Oh, my. I don't know how we're ever going to turn you into a marchioness, for you're far too natural and earthy for airs and graces to sit naturally on you."

Callie, infinitely relieved by Nellie's reassurance, returned her grin. "I'm beginning to think I needn't worry overmuch, at least not about that part of it. As long as Adam's satisfied, the rest of the world is just going to have to take me as I am."

"And I'm beginning to think that they will," Nellie replied. "I'm beginning to think that they will."

Callie returned home in the carriage, deciding that a long talk with Adam was in order. He might not like talking about himself very much, but she couldn't keep discovering important details of his life from other people. It was bad enough not knowing important details about her own—although at least she was beginning to find out bits and pieces, and she'd had two almost full memories already. That was better than none, even though one of them had brought the deep ache of loss and grief with it.

At least now she could better understand how Adam felt. She understood so many more things about him, given what Nellie had just told her about his childhood.

Adam's soul may have been forged by fire, but his spirit had been tempered and defined by loss over and over again. He'd managed to survive everything that had been handed to him by what must have seemed an uncaring God, but when the wife and child in whom he'd invested every hope and all the love he had to give had been taken from him by a cruel act of fate, he'd lost any hope that life had meaning. He'd certainly lost his faith. No wonder he'd said that something essential had died in him that day.

It was a wonder that he'd survived at all.

She couldn't help but love him all the more. She loved him for the fine man he was, she loved him for taking her on and being willing to make a commitment to her, even if he was making that commitment out of nothing more than practicality.

Adam had rescued her in more ways than one. He had saved her life and he had given her a future, and the least she could do with that future was to devote herself to his happiness. She would somehow find a way to show him that the ashes of despair could be sown with new seed and thrive, if tended with devotion and showered with love.

She would not fail him, no matter how much her own heart might ache.

# 15

Adam paced the Great Hall, impatiently waiting for Callie to return. He wanted very much to see her, not so much because of the news he had to impart, but because he hadn't been able to suppress a vague feeling of anxiety when she'd left Stanton without him.

He was being ridiculous, he knew. She'd gone in the carriage, driven by Kincaid, who was more than competent, she had two footmen accompanying Kincaid in the box, and she had gone only as far as the village. Still, he'd feel a great deal better when he saw her safely back home and in one piece. In one very alluring piece, he reminded himself, and he wouldn't have to wait much longer to avail himself of her considerable charms. And thank God for that, because his self-control was nearly at breaking point, and it was everything he could do not to let Callie see what dire straits he was in.

His head shot up as he heard the unmistakable sound of hoofbeats coming up the drive. Gettis mysteriously appeared out of nowhere to open the door, and Adam, vaguely wondering if Gettis had always had this magic ability to materialize in precisely the right spot and moment, walked down the steps, trying to look as if he'd just casually happened to notice that the carriage had arrived. It wouldn't do for the servants to think him overeager.

But as Callie descended from the carriage and took his waiting hand, smiling at him in warm greeting, his heart filled with a very real happiness that he tried to tell himself was nothing more than relief. He supposed he'd become so accustomed to having her around that he wasn't used to her absence.

"I'm glad you're back. Come inside," he said, tucking her hand into the crook of his elbow. "You can tell me about your visit with Mrs. Bishop later, but I have things to tell you and they won't wait. Gettis," he said in an aside as he took Callie into the house, "be so kind as to bring tea and something to eat into the library."

Callie settled herself on the sofa and regarded him with curiosity as he closed the door.

"What has happened, Adam?" she asked, her cheeks lightly flushed, her eyes shining. "Is it good news?"

"It is indeed. For one, our marriage license arrived in the post just after you left, which means we can be wed anytime we choose. The post also brought a letter from Sir Reginald, and he could arrive as early as this evening. Of all advantageous coincidences, your cousin Lord Fellowes was in London and Sir Reginald ran into him at White's— that's a gentlemen's club, by the by—and Sir Reginald explained your situation."

"That's good?" Callie said, looking endearingly unsure.

"It's good," Adam said, sitting down in the chair across from her, "because Sir Reginald said that he'd explain in detail when he arrived, but as long as we can satisfy some questions he has, he thinks the match a fine idea, and Fellowes agrees." Adam couldn't hide his satisfaction. "Apparently they both feel that I am a far more suitable husband for you than Harold, hardly surprising."

"But, Adam," Callie said, squirming impatiently, "did Sir Reginald say anything else—anything about my father's will, or whether I really was contracted to marry Harold?"

"He did not. I imagine that's what he means by details. Don't you see, Callie?" Adam said with equal impatience. "If he'd had any real objections he would have raised them in his letter, for I told him that we wouldn't go ahead with our plans until I'd heard from him and felt sure there were no legal entanglements. So as far as I can see, we're free and clear to marry, although whether you receive your inheritance is still a question—not that it matters to me, as I've told you before, but perhaps it matters to you."

"No, that's not my concern. Are you sure that Harold won't cause any more trouble?" she asked.

"As for Harold and trouble, I've fired off a letter to inform him that we're going to be married immediately. I added that he'd better return your belongings posthaste or I'll go up to Smeeth to collect them myself, and he won't be thankful for the visit."

Callie leaned back with a sigh of relief. "Then it really does look as if we might have a happy outcome, although Harold won't see it that way," she said. "Adam . . . about Harold?" Her expression changed back to uncertainty.

"What about Harold? You look as if you still think he might try to snatch you away, which I assure you is not a possibility."

"If you feel sure that he won't cause trouble, I believe you. I was just wondering about what caused such enmity between you. I know he's not a very nice man, and I still can't understand why my father wanted me to marry him at all, but that's not the point." She leaned slightly forward, regarding him intently. "You were brought up with him, weren't you, for part of your life at least, and he lived here at Stanton with you. What went so badly wrong between you?"

Adam rubbed his finger back and forth over his bottom lip, not particularly wanting to revist the horrors of those years, but owing Callie the courtesy of an answer, for she had every right to it.

"To be honest," he said, considering his words carefully, "I think that everything went wrong the day I was born. Until then my uncle stood to inherit the marquessate, since my father hadn't married at an early age and didn't seem inclined to marry at all. Harold, being older than I by two years, would have been next in line, but all of that went out the window when my father not only married at the age of forty, but also produced a son within the space of a year."

"So Mildred and your uncle's hopes were dashed, you mean?"

"Dashed to cinders," Adam said. "I've always thought that Mildred and Uncle Geoffrey looked at Harold as a miracle child after so many years of a barren marriage, so they not only spoiled him beyond belief, but they also managed to convince themselves that he should inherit the earth, so to speak. I was a massive inconvenience in their plans for Harold's brilliant future. Mildred's visions of her own brilliant future should not be discounted," he added dryly. "Needless to say, they have not been realized, and she has never forgotten that, which has left her even more embittered and angry than she started out being."

Callie nodded. "I think I begin to understand. They hated you just by reason of your existence, and when they took over as your caretakers, they made your life as difficult as they could."

Adam's brow drew down. "How on earth did you work all that out?" he asked, sure that he hadn't mentioned anything of the sort. He avoided the subject of those years like the plague.

"Simple deduction," Callie replied, looking off to one corner of the room, her hands clenched in her lap. "Neither Mildred nor Harold commended themselves to me in any fashion." She turned her face back to him. "What did they do to you, Adam?" she asked fiercely.

"Nothing to concern yourself over. It's a time long over and best forgotten," he said, not wanting to distress her any further with the truth. The truth really didn't bear thinking about.

"Tell me. Tell me, Adam, for I can't bear having these secrets between us, I really can't," she said, her voice holding a note of genuine desperation that he couldn't help wanting to assuage, and clearly only the truth, or a semblance of it, would accomplish that.

"I went through a difficult time at the beginning," he started reluctantly, trying to find a simple way through what had been a very complicated and twisted time. "My father had just died, and I loved him dearly. I didn't know my aunt or uncle at all well at that point, and Harold even less, but they were all I had left to me, so I supposed I had a young boy's hopes and thought they might help me through my grief, and love me a little, so that I didn't feel quite so alone. I was utterly misguided to think any such thing."

Callie's gaze didn't waver. "Go on," she said quietly.

"Oh, everything went from bad to worse," he said, his mind playing back a myriad of distasteful scenes, but seeing no point in going into the details.

"Harold," he said as if the word was a bad taste in his mouth, "was my real nightmare."

"If he was anything like he is now, I can imagine." Callie wrinkled her nose. "I suppose he was just a smaller version of himself: round, rude, and altogether insufferable."

Adam had to smile. Callie had a wonderful way with words. "He was all of that and more. Harold's problem was that he didn't do anything very well except torment people. Nigel, Harold, and I shared a tutor. Nigel didn't like Harold any more than I did, and we both worked twice as hard at our lessons as we had to, just to show Harold up. Need I add that Harold was not known for his cleverness?"

"You need not. A few minutes in his ghastly company told me everything I needed to know about his lack of intelligence."

"Exactly. Harold thought it a particularly good idea to tell his parents whenever I, usually with Nigel's help, had done something forbidden."

"Forbidden?"

"Oh, nothing serious, just the usual sorts of silly things that young boys get up to, but Nigel and I came up with ways to torture Harold in return for my punishments. We did a very good job, if I do say so myself."

Callie beamed. "I'm so glad. And I'm so glad you had Nigel. Did he live at Stanton with you?"

"No, but he might as well have, given the amount of time he spent here. Nigel's family lives not too far from here, so he would ride over nearly every day. He came for the lessons, but he stayed to make mischief with me. We learned everything together, Nigel and I," he said with a fond smile. "My father taught us to ride and fish and shoot, and he taught us about sailing and the sea. Those were good years."

"And the later years?" Callie asked. "When you were older, I mean. Were you sent off to school?"

Adam nodded. "We both went to Eton—I found it a blessing to be away from my uncle and aunt for long periods of the year, but Harold, naturally, had to come along to school with us, so I never really escaped his presence until he left two years before we did. While he was there, he used his seniority to make life hell. There's a pecking order, you see, and younger boys are subjected to all sorts of ragging from the elder ones. Harold—well, let's just say that Harold took advantage of every opportunity."

Adam paused as a knock came at the door and Gettis brought in the tea tray, setting it down on the table between them. "Will there be anything else, my lord?"

"No, thank you," Adam replied. "This will do nicely. Callie, help yourself. In any case," he continued, picking up a crab patty, "Harold wasn't well liked at school. He was no good at games, he continued to be an indifferent student, and he didn't make friends easily. Why he decided that was my fault, I don't know, but he seemed to think that I used my title to turn people against him, an idiotic notion."

Callie shuddered as she poured the tea. "He sounds more dreadful by the moment, and something tells me that you're giving me the expurgated version of the story."

Adam laughed as took his cup from her. "Perhaps I am, but I think you have the general idea. To finish up, Harold went off to Cambridge, where he was sent down after a year. His parents sent him to live in my house in London— did I tell you I have a town house in London? You'll like it, I think. It's on Grovesnor Square."

"I'm sure I will," Callie said, nibbling on a chicken sandwich, looking not the least bit interested in his fine piece of property. "But what about Harold? What did he get up to in London?"

"Everything you can imagine. He was supposed to be meeting eligible young heiresses, but instead he got into gaming and betting on the horses and doing a great deal of carousing. He ran up an amazing amount of debt, which, I discovered when I took over my own affairs, had been steadily paid off by Uncle Geoffrey from my funds, which he was overseeing as my guardian."

Callie gasped. "But that's shocking! Isn't that illegal?"

"Indeed it is, and I imagine I could have caused a great deal of trouble, but I decided to evict them from Stanton instead. Uncle Geoffrey had been siphoning off money for much more than Harold's gambling debts, as he'd made a great hash out of his own inheritance. He'd also made a great hash out of running Stanton."

Callie mutely shook her head. "You must have been truly livid when you discovered all this," she said after a moment.

"I was extremely annoyed, yes. I'd just finished my time up at Oxford, so I came directly to Stanton to live full time. I removed the old steward and installed Nigel in his place, for Nigel knew every nook and cranny of Stanton, and I knew I need never doubt his loyalty. Anyway, farming's in his blood. Together we put the place to rights as it was in my father's time, and it's run like clockwork ever since."

"And then you married and you were finally happy," Callie said, looking down into her cup.

"And then I married and I was finally happy," Adam agreed, thinking for the thousandth time how fleeting and cruel happiness could be. Still, those days had been good, and he found to his surprise that he didn't really mind talking about them. "Caroline was shy," he said with a soft smile, remembering how difficult she'd found being mistress of Stanton at first, not accustomed to giving orders or making decisions on her own. "She was young, and she'd been brought up in a sheltered environment, so she was a little taken aback by all the things that happen on a working estate." He chuckled. "The first time she saw a bull mate a cow I thought she was going to keel over in shock. I had to support her all the way back to the house."

"It sounds as if she had a very sweet nature," Callie said, still gazing into her teacup, and Adam suddenly realized that Callie felt uncomfortable.

"She had a very sweet nature indeed," he said, wondering how to put Callie at ease. He supposed that it was natural for her to feel disconcerted, listening to him talk about his first wife, but he didn't want the subject of Caroline to be a source of discomfort for her any more than he wanted the memory of Caroline to stand between them like a great, unanswered question, for that would only make Callie unhappy. "She was very different from you," he said gently. "She was a self-contained woman, not given to freely expressing her emotions. She disliked any sort of conflict, would avoid it any way she could. Sometimes I felt as if I were pulling teeth to get her to tell me what was on her mind."

"But you like that—someone who's peaceful and doesn't aggravate you all the time."

Adam considered. "Caroline was like a drink of clear, soothing water after all the turbulence of the years I spent living with my relatives, when there wasn't a peaceful moment to be had. But if you mean that you think you aggravate me, let me put your mind at rest. I enjoy the stimulation of someone who isn't afraid to match me word for word, someone who takes a position and passionately sticks with it from sheer courage of conviction. You do that, Callie, and I don't think I've ever known anyone like you. You don't defer to me—anything but—and I know I can trust you to tell me exactly what you think." He laughed. "You'll tell me whether I want to hear it or not, and I find that refreshing."

"Do you really mean that, or are you just trying to make me feel better?" she asked, regarding him anxiously, as if his answer meant everything in the world to her.

"I really mean it," he said. "You mustn't worry that you are so different to Caroline, if that's what is troubling you. Those days are gone, and you and I will find a different way together, that's all." He had no idea what that way would be. How many different ways did he know how to live? He hadn't managed to do a very good job of living at all, not since Ian and Caroline had been taken from him. But now that he had decided to go on without them, he supposed he would have to apply himself to the job, if just for Callie's sake. That was only fair, given that she was going to have to settle for a life without her precious ideal of romantic love.

"Thank you for telling me," Callie said, the corners of her mouth beginning to tremble. "I needed to hear that."

He abruptly put his cup down on the tray and moved over to sit next to her, taking her cup and placing it next to his. "Have you been worrying, Callie? If you have, it's my fault, for I should have put your mind at rest before this. You are a desirable and beautiful woman, and I thought you understood that I found you those things. Perhaps, being a man, I didn't let you know in an adequate fashion, and for that I apologize."

Callie turned her face away. "I only want you to be happy, Adam," she said, her voice muffled. "I thought that maybe I wasn't enough of a lady to make you a proper wife, that I might have said or done things I oughtn't, or omitted to say and do things I should have."

Adam turned her face toward him with one finger. "What's all this about being a lady?" he said, genuinely astonished. "I haven't the first regard for that sort of behavior. I had enough of it in the drawing rooms of London, believe me, where people never say what they mean and rarely behave according to the standards they so smugly hold up to the rest of the world. Let us have no more talk of that, for I couldn't bear it if you turned yourself into the sort of woman who thinks so highly and so completely of herself that she hasn't the time to think of anyone or anything else." He dropped his hand and took her by the shoulder. "A true lady thinks of others before herself, and doesn't behave as if she's better than everyone else around her. In that, you are exemplary."

"Really, Adam?" she said, gazing up at him, looking thoroughly shaken but infinitely relieved.

"Really. I wouldn't say it if it wasn't true. You will make a perfect mistress for Stanton. The servants already think you walk on water, in case you haven't noticed. I've been feeling a tad put out that they don't treat me with the same adoration. Deference, perhaps, but then I pay their wages. But adoration? Definitely not."

Callie sniffled, and he immediately produced a handkerchief for her use. He never knew when she was going to produce tears, but he'd learned to be prepared.

"I think you're wonderful," she said, her voice trembling. She took his handkerchief and wiped her eyes.

"I was under the impression that you thought me a heartless wretch," he said, taking the handkerchief back from her and running it under her sweet little nose for good measure. That was usually the next thing to start dripping.

"You are anything but heartless, and you're certainly

not a wretch," she said indignantly. "Except when you mean to be, but I generally know the reason. It's just that these last ten days you've been so distant, and so I thought that maybe you weren't so happy about marrying me after all, and that you regretted asking me. And then I thought that was because I wasn't anything like Caroline and that I'd behaved very badly in bed by being too enthusiastic, but Nellie said that wasn't the problem, that it was a *good* thing to be enthusiastic."

Adam listened to this torrent of confession in disbelief, but when she came to the part about Nellie, he sat straight up. "You told Nellie Bishop about—about that?" he said in a strangled voice.

"Of course I did. Who else could I ask? She was very sensible and she wasn't in the least bit shocked, and you needn't worry, because she won't tell anyone. I had to talk to someone, Adam, because I was so confused, and Nellie's my friend."

"You might have come to me," he said, feeling a little put out, but recognizing at the same time that he hadn't exactly given her a chance. "Er, what exactly did Nellie say to you?" he asked, unable to contain his curiosity.

"She said that men don't want to have a woman lying under them behaving as if they have something better to do."

Adam couldn't help himself. He threw his head back and roared with laughter. He laughed so hard he thought his sides might split. "Ah—ah, Callie," he gasped, trying to catch his breath without much success. "That's—that's perfect. I think I'd like to meet your friend Nellie. She sounds as refreshing as you are." He burst into laughter again. "Well, just so you know, Nellie is exactly right," he said, making an attempt to sober. "It is a very good thing to be enthusiastic, and you have no problem with enthusiasm, trust me. The day you start behaving as if you have something better to do will be the day that I will begin to think you've tired of me and taken a lover."

"I would *never* do such a thing," Callie said, punching his arm, which he really should have expected, since she seemed to punch him without reservation whenever she was offended by something he'd said.

"That's very good." Adam rubbed his hand over his bruised muscle with a wince, although he had to admire her. Callie had a powerful fist. "I won't be taking any lovers, either. I have a feeling I'm going to have my hands full until the day I'm carted off in my coffin, and you, madam, are going to be either so exhausted that you expire with me or die shortly thereafter from lack of attention."

"Oh, well," Callie said, grinning. "I don't know about that. Should you die before me, I might then consider taking a lover. Now that I've had a taste of physical bliss, I'm not sure I would care to go without it."

Adam collapsed against the back of the sofa, taking her with her. He turned and covered her face with kisses that he'd longed to give her, then took her sweet, soft lips beneath his own, kissing her until they were both breathless.

He didn't hear the knock or the door opening until it was too late.

"Sir Reginald Barnswell has arrived, my lord," Gettis announced.

Without any further ado, Sir Reginald walked straight into the room.

## 16

Thinking she would die of mortification, Callie jumped to her feet, blushing furiously and straightening her disheveled dress. Adam calmly stood and walked across the library, his hand outstretched to greet Sir Reginald.

"You made excellent time," Adam said, not sounding the least flustered that he'd just been caught in a passionate embrace; Callie had to admire his aplomb. "I only received your letter this afternoon. Welcome to Stanton Abbey. Your reputation precedes you."

"Thank you," Sir Reginald said. "I am pleased to make your acquaintance. I, er, I hope I did not arrive at an inconvenient time." He passed a hand over his shiny scalp.

"Not in the least," Adam said smoothly. "I think you for coming with such alacrity. As you can imagine, Miss Melbourne has questions that she is anxious to have answered." He brought Sir Reginald over to Callie. "Allow me to introduce my fiancée, although you must have gathered quite quickly that this is Miss Melbourne."

"Sir Reginald," Callie said, blushing even more furiously as she dropped a curtsy and offered him her hand.

"Miss Melbourne," he said, regarding her gravely, but his eyes, beneath a bushy pair of gray eyebrows, held warmth. "I have long wanted to meet you. Your father wrote last autumn that you would be coming to England at some point soon. Actually, he wrote to me periodically over the years, keeping me informed about his activities, and yours. He was very proud of you."

"Was he?" Callie said, longing to hear more about her father and the life she'd shared with him. She felt slightly overwhelmed, but filled with joy at the same time. Here at last was someone who could actually tell her something about her past, and that alone gave her a sense of connection to Sir Reginald.

"He was indeed. I gather that you are a very well educated and well traveled young woman with many talents."

"I—I confess that I don't really know," Callie said, feeling foolish. "I believe Adam—Lord Vale, that is—informed you that my memory is impaired."

"Lord Vale told a most extraordinary story in his letter. I experienced deep alarm when I read it. Forgive me for being so familiar, but your father was a most gifted correspondent and his letters came alive to the reader. I feel as if I've known you since you were a very small child and couldn't help an avuncular fear, given the nature of your accident and the injury you suffered."

"Thank you for your concern, but as you can see, I am perfectly well, save for my inability to remember much of anything before I fell."

"Shall we sit down?" Adam said. "We have much to

discuss. May I offer you some refreshment, Sir Reginald? We have just had tea, but perhaps you would care for something a little stronger."

"I would be grateful. I am not accustomed to traveling at such a speed, but I felt an urgent need to reassure myself that Miss Melbourne was not only in good hands, but also in good health." He settled his bulk in one of the armchairs with a contented sigh.

Before Adam even had a chance to ask, Gettis appeared with one of the footmen. Between them they whisked away the tea tray, replaced it with another tray containing sherry and biscuits, and vanished as silently as they'd come.

"I imagine," Sir Reginald said, taking a sip of sherry with an expression of pure pleasure, "that you will first want to know the details of your father's will, Miss Melbourne. He mentioned in his last letter that he had made an agreement with Lord Geoffrey Carlyle. The terms went thusly: that should you and Mr. Harold Carlyle wish to marry after a period of acquaintance, your inheritance would pass to Mr. Carlyle. Your father did not, however, make any binding provision that you inherit based on that particular marriage, stipulating only that your money be given into your husband's keeping whenever you did choose to marry. If you do not choose to marry, your money remains yours to do with as you wish. That sum, which your father invested wisely, is now approximately fifty thousand pounds."

Adam choked on his biscuit. "Fifty *thousand* pounds?"

"That is correct. It is not a sum to be taken lightly."

"Tell me, Sir Reginald," Adam said, recovering his equilibrium, "was Lord Geoffrey aware of the amount of Callie's inheritance?"

"Yes, he was," Sir Reginald said shortly.

"Well, well," Adam said with a slight smile. "No wonder

Harold and Mildred were in such a state when they realized that Callie and her money had slipped through their fingers. Is there anything else we should know?"

Sir Reginald inclined his head toward Callie. "That is the gist of the will. In other words, Miss Melbourne, you are free to marry whom you please. You are under no legal obligation to marry Mr. Carlyle, whatever he might have led you to believe. You are under no obligation to marry at all. You are a very well-off woman in your own right."

Adam shot her a broad smile. "What did I tell you, Callie? Harold has no claim on you, and never did. I, on the other hand, have a very serious claim that I intend to exact as soon as humanly possible, and it has nothing to do with your fifty thousand pounds."

"I think I'll exact my claim on you as well," Callie said, lightheaded with relief. "And I give you the fifty thousand pounds with the greatest of pleasure, for I'm sure I don't know what I'd do with such a sum."

"You can try to give me the fifty thousand, sweetheart, but you won't have much success, for I intend to ask Sir Reginald to keep it in a trust for you and our children."

Callie's heart nearly stopped. Adam had mentioned children, and he'd mentioned them as naturally as if he'd been talking about the weather. But then children were a natural consequence of lovemaking, and as he had just assured her that he planned to do plenty of that, maybe he was being practical again.

Sir Reginald took another sip of sherry, ate a biscuit, and nodded with satisfaction. "I confess that I also came down to Stanton to be certain in my own mind that you, Miss Melbourne, had not chosen to marry Lord Vale simply because you felt alone in the world and frightened, given your loss of memory, but I believe I have seen that is not the case."

"It is not," Callie said. "I am marrying Lord Vale of my own free will and because I—" She'd nearly said "because I love him with every fiber of my being," but stopped herself just in time. "Because I think we will have a full life together." She glanced over at Adam, who regarded her with a quizzical expression, as if he'd expected her to say something very different. "I might not remember my past," she added, "but that doesn't mean that I cannot create a bright and happy future."

"Well said," Sir Reginald replied in a gruff voice. "In that case, I give the marriage my blessing. You don't legally need it, as you have reached your majority, but I'd like to think that I may act in loco parentis. I believe your father would have been happy with the match."

"Sir Reginald," Callie said, "have you any idea why my father would have wanted me to marry Harold Carlyle in the first place? Lady Geoffrey said that my father and her husband were old friends, but my father couldn't possibly have known what sort of man he really was, or how awful his wife and son are."

"I can tell you that your father and Lord Geoffrey were at university together. I can also tell you that your father never returned to England once he'd taken you and your mother to Italy. Your mother suffered from ill health, you see, and could not tolerate the English climate."

"I don't suppose," Adam said, his lips twitching with amusement, "that they lived in Ravello for some years?"

"How on earth did you know that?" Sir Reginald asked. "Yes, they lived in Ravello until Mrs. Melbourne died seven years later. At that time, Mr. Melbourne, who was heartbroken by the loss of his wife, took his eight-year-old daughter and moved to the island of Corfu, where they settled in a villa called Kaloroziko."

"Kaloroziko," Callie said softly. "It means 'good roots.'"

The villa was Italian in style, and had a high white wall with scarlet bougainvillea tumbling over it."

They both looked at her in surprise. "I sometimes remember images," she said. "That was the first image I had after I woke up. Did we live there from then on?"

"Yes. Your father, who was an accomplished botanist, used it as his base, making his travels from there and nearly always taking you with him. You have visited many interesting places, Miss Melbourne. Your father came to rely on you as his assistant."

She nodded. "You've explained so many things—why I seem to know about plants and how to use them for healing, for example, and why languages like Italian and Greek come so easily to mind."

"Your father made every effort to educate you as fully as he could, but he wrote that you were a natural linguist and picked up languages as easily as if they had all been whispered to you by the angels at your birth. I know that sounds fanciful, but your father was like that, a man of deep spirituality who took what he learned from various cultures and religions and applied them to his own life. He also once mentioned—and forgive me if this sounds odd—but he said that you had an extraordinary ability to communicate with God's creatures, that they never showed any fear around you, or you around them. I was curious about that."

"The gull, Callie," Adam said quietly. "And then the swans and the bees."

"Yes," she said. "I know. I suppose it does seem a curious talent, but it's as natural to me as breathing. My father sounds as if he was a fascinating man."

"He was one of the most unique men I have had the privilege to know. You have much of him in you."

Callie, deeply touched, blushed. "Thank you, Sir Reginald.

I would like to think so, for I believe that we carry the legacy of those we loved inside us, that it connects us to them forever, even after they are gone. Would you mind telling me how he died? I know only that he became ill."

"Yes. He developed a tumor of the brain. I know nothing more, as the last communication I had from him was the letter I told you about. He wanted to put his affairs in order while he still could, for he knew he didn't have much time left to him. And to answer your earlier question, he made the arrangement with Lord Geoffrey to put his mind at ease about your future. He loved you very much and was concerned about your being left alone and far away from the land of your birth."

"Given what you have told us about Mr. Melbourne, I cannot believe that he knew anything at all about Harold Carlyle's true nature or reputation," Adam said. "If anything makes sense, it is that my uncle likely painted a completely false picture of his son, not to mention his own financial position. Mr. Melbourne would have had no reason to doubt his friend's word, would he?"

"That is a logical supposition. I cannot say that I was happy with his plan, but given what I knew of Miss Melbourne, I hoped that once she met Mr. Carlyle she would discover that he didn't suit her."

Callie couldn't help smiling. "You were correct. From the moment Mr. Carlyle and his mother accosted me in the street I felt very sure that neither of them suited me in any regard. You have put my mind at rest in many ways, Sir Reginald, and I thank you for your candor."

"Not at all, but if I might continue to be candid, may I ask if you have acquired the special license, Lord Vale? Although you cannot be faulted in any regard for keeping Miss Melbourne here at Stanton—"

"The sooner we are married, the better," Adam finished

for him. "I am aware of the need for haste, and as it happens, the license arrived today."

"Excellent. I am not one to hold with gossip, but you know the damage wagging tongues can do."

"Having lived with wagging tongues in the form of my aunt and cousin, and for too many years, I do know full well. Furthermore, if tongues are going to wag, they are sure to come from that quarter. I would be honored if you would act as witness at our wedding, Sir Reginald. You are as close to family as Miss Melbourne has, discounting Lord Fellowes, of course, but he doesn't know her as you do, even if you only know her through her father's letters."

"I would be honored," Sir Reginald said, looking terribly pleased. "What a delightful idea. Shall we say this evening, if it's not inconvenient and you can arrange for the vicar? I'm afraid that I must start my journey back to London tomorrow, for I have to appear in court at the end of the week."

"Callie?" Adam said, turning to her. "Is this evening too soon?"

The next minute wouldn't be too soon as far as Callie was concerned. She wanted to be Adam's wife more than anything in the world, and now that they knew for certain no impediment to their marriage existed, she was fully ready. "How quickly can you organize the vicar?" she asked, her heart thumping with excitement.

Adam grinned at her, his eyes the color of the summer sky and just as bright. "Give me an hour or so. He shouldn't take too long to persuade. The butler will show you to your room, Sir Reginald. You, Callie, will want to prepare yourself. I'm off to the vicarage, and I'll be back before you know I've gone."

He was as good as his word. Callie had just enough time to wash, change her dress, and let Jane dress her hair.

"It's so exciting, miss," Jane said, cleverly weaving in

roses and baby's breath that Roberts had produced from the garden. "I'm sure you're as lovely a bride as ever was, even if you didn't have time to manage a proper wedding dress. I think the pale green ever so becoming on you, and his lordship's eyes will light up when he sees you, for you have roses in your cheeks every bit as pink as the ones in your hair. Just so you know, Cook is flying around the kitchen organizing a dinner worthy of the great occasion, Mrs. Simpson is already in floods of happy tears and seeing to the linens, and Mr. Gettis is instructing the footmen on what he expects from them, my Michael included." She paused only to draw breath. "I'm to be wed soon, too, miss. I think you and his lordship's happiness must have put ideas into Michael's head, for he asked me just the other day and I was that thrilled to accept him."

"That's wonderful, Jane," Callie said, only barely hearing her, preoccupied with her own imminent nuptials and the upcoming prospect of her wedding night, which was just as exciting to contemplate. She couldn't wait to be back in Adam's arms where she belonged. "Oh!" she said as Jane's words finally sank in. "That's the best of news! I'm very happy for you both."

"Thank you, miss. There. That should do it." She gave Callie's hair a last pat. "Have a look at yourself in the long glass."

Callie floated over and briefly examined herself. Jane was right, she did have roses in her cheeks, and she thought the sea-green dress as pretty as anything that she might have chosen for her wedding. All in all she decided she looked presentable enough, but she would just have happily married Adam wearing a sheet if there'd been nothing else available.

Mrs. Simpson breathlessly appeared in the doorway, her eyes swollen. "His lordship is ready for you at any time," she said, flapping her hand on her large bosom. "The vicar is downstairs with him, and Sir Reginald and Mr. Dryden, and his lordship was good enough to ask Mr. Plimpton and Mr. Gettis and myself to observe the ceremony. Oh, but you do look like an angel, poppet, a true angel. Well, then. If you're ready?"

"Could I just have a moment alone?" Callie asked, needing it very badly.

"Certainly, my dear. I am sure your nerves are altogether on edge, which is as it should be. I'll just go down and tell them you'll be coming along shortly."

"Thank you." Callie waited for the door to close behind Jane and Mrs. Simpson and gratefully sank onto the edge of the bed. Mrs. Simpson was wrong. Callie's nerves were in perfect order. She just hadn't had a minute to herself to assimilate everything she'd learned from Sir Reginald, let alone Nellie and then Adam. For a head as empty as hers was, it felt completely overstuffed with information. But right now, that wasn't what she had on her mind.

She squeezed her eyes shut. "Father," she whispered, "if you can hear me, know that I thank you for loving me so well. Thank you for sending me to England, for if you hadn't, I never would have met Adam. I know he wasn't the man you had in mind for me, but I love him. I will trust him and honor him, and by doing so I also honor you and all that you gave me, for I feel sure that I wouldn't have known how to love Adam so well if you hadn't taught me. It doesn't matter so much that he can't love me, it really doesn't. It's enough for me to have someone to love and a life to call my own."

Callie opened her eyes as she heard a faint knock. At first she thought Mrs. Simpson had returned to fetch her, but the knocking came from the opposite end of the room. She turned her head toward the near window, trying to locate the source of the sound.

A dove sat on the exposed sill, peacefully regarding her, its head turned sideways. It tapped its beak against the wood, then tapped again and cooed, a soft low croon, as if beckoning to her.

Callie stood up and walked over to it, instinctively reaching her hands out. The dove didn't hesitate. It walked straight into her cupped palms and settled there as comfortably as if it was in its nest, its bright eye steadily fixed on her. Extending a finger, Callie stroked its soft head, and the dove easily accepted her gentle caress.

"Hello, dove," she murmured. "Have you come to wish me well?"

The dove cooed again and stepped back out of her hands. In the next moment it turned, spread its wings and took flight, beating a smooth line toward the woods, its melodic song echoing after it.

Callie looked down into her hands where a single pale feather had fallen.

She couldn't have asked for a finer blessing for her marriage. A tear slid down her cheek and fell like a single bead onto the feather, shining like a dewdrop.

Callie tucked the feather deep down into her bodice, a talisman of love, and went downstairs to take Adam as her husband, her heart as light as the feather that rested against it.


Adam couldn't help drawing in his breath as Callie came through the door into the drawing room. The setting sun backlit her so that she seemed surrounded by a shimmering radiance, and her gaze found his and stayed fixed intently on him as if there was no one else in the room. The expression in her eyes was one he'd never seen in them before and couldn't define, and he wondered at it. She stopped, took a deep breath and released it, then walked up to him without a word.

He stretched his hand out to her, completely forgetting to introduce her to the vicar. "You look beautiful," he murmured so that only she could hear. "Are you very sure, Callie, that this is what you want?" He didn't know why he asked, unless he was secretly hoping for a last minute reprieve, for he was fully aware that by making this set of vows, he was betraying an older one that he'd made to himself on Caroline's behalf.

"I am very sure that this is exactly what I want, and I most certainly am not going to change my mind," she replied. "Are you having second thoughts, my lord?"

"I've gone to far too much trouble to have second thoughts," he said lightly, unwilling to examine why he felt so shaken. He was marrying Callie out of simple practicality, nothing more, he reminded himself firmly. "Let us be wed without further ado. Callie, Vicar Dale. Vicar, Callie. Shall we proceed?"

"We shall, my lord," the vicar said, starting to recite the opening words of the Anglican marriage ceremony and proceeding hastily along, which Adam could only put down to a determination to complete his appointed duty and get back to the vicarage as soon as possible to eat his dinner. Adam didn't really care. They were only words, after all, not a commitment of his heart, as his vows had been when he'd married Caroline.

"Wilt thou, Adam, have this woman to thy wedded wife, to live together after God's ordinance in the holy estate of Matrimony? Wilt thou love her, comfort her, honor and keep her in sickness and in health; and, forsaking all others, keep thee only unto her, so long as ye both shall live?"

"I will . . ."

". . . I, Callista, take thee, Adam, to my wedded husband,

to have and to hold from this day forward, for better for worse, for richer for poorer, in sickness and in health, to love, cherish, and obey till death do us part, according to God's holy law, thereto I give thee my troth."

Adam doubted that Callie would ever entirely obey him, but then that was one of the reasons he liked her so much. He never knew what to expect.

Having thought far enough ahead to find his mother's wedding ring and give it to Nigel to produce at the appropriate moment, Adam slipped the simple gold band onto Callie's slim finger and impatiently recited the rest of his vows. Callie responded, and the vicar swiftly said all the usual prayers and gave the blessing.

"I pronounce that they be man and wife together in the name of the Father, and of the Son, and of the Holy Ghost," he finally said, which was all Adam really wanted to hear. At least he could now indulge in slaking his passion with a clear conscience. He was, after all, in the business of getting an heir. "Amen."

*Amen*, Adam thought with satisfaction as he dropped a light kiss onto Callie's mouth. He raised his head, and she smiled up into his eyes.

"Hello, wife," he said, waiting to see what Callie would say to that.

"Hello, husband," Callie replied, her eyes shining, and he could see that she really was pleased to be married.

Nigel thumped him on the back and kissed Callie's cheek. "I'm glad *that's* taken care of," he said in an echo of Adam's exact thoughts. "I wish you both every happiness."

Adam, with Callie by his side, received more of the same good wishes from the rest of the small party, Mrs. Simpson's being miraculously short and to the point.

"Congratulations, my lord, felicitations, my lady," she said. "It was a lovely ceremony, simply lovely. I must get back to my duties. Dinner will be ready shortly."

Gettis and Plimpton made their bows, both looking extremely pleased, and hurried after Mrs. Simpson, leaving Adam and Callie alone with Nigel, Sir Reginald, and the flustered vicar, who took his leave as soon as he'd downed the obligatory glass of sherry.

"Odd," Adam said. "Did anyone else notice that the vicar seemed a little—nervous?"

Nigel chuckled. "Are you really surprised, Adam? He hasn't seen hide or hair of you in a very long time, and you suddenly appear at the vicarage and demand that he marry you instantly to someone he must know perfectly well has been living at Stanton for some time. I can understand why he might have felt a little unsure of the, er...the *exact* situation. I don't suppose you bothered to explain as you dragged him away?"

"I can't think why I should have explained anything," Adam said. "I just told him to do his job and I gave him some money for his church fund. Anything beyond that is none of his business. Isn't that right, Callie?"

Callie rolled her eyes. "I can see one of my first duties as your wife is going to be to pay a call to the vicar and smooth over his ruffled feathers. Really, Adam, no wonder he kept surreptitiously looking at my waistline."

"I can't think why the vicar should be looking at anything but his prayer book," Adam said cheerfully. "He certainly shouldn't be admiring your waistline, but if he was, he has very good taste. Shall we go in to dinner? Marrying you seems to have given me an enormous appetite."

# 17

Callie didn't know how she managed to get through dinner that night. The courses kept coming; the glasses were recharged, and the toasts made. Despite her happiness and the pleasure she took in the company of Sir Reginald, who was a wonderful raconteur, and Nigel, who was in even finer humor than usual and kept them all laughing, she couldn't wait for the evening to be over so that she could go upstairs and ready herself for bed—and for Adam.

She knew the same thought was in his mind, for the heat in his eyes when he looked at her, which he did often, practically scorched her flesh. It certainly made her want to squirm in her seat, and she had to exert all the self-control she had to sit still and try to keep her mind on the conversation that jumped easily from subject to subject.

But finally, when Cook's lovely cake had been cut and

served and eaten, Callie excused herself. "I will leave you gentleman to your port and bid you good night," she said. "The day has been long, and I—I think I'll retire. Perhaps before you depart tomorrow, Sir Reginald, you might find time to sit with me and tell me more about my previous life?"

"I would be delighted, my dear. Once again, my felicitations on your marriage, which I am certain will be a great success and bring you enormous happiness."

"Thank you," she said. "I am so happy you were here for the ceremony."

The three men politely stood as she rose, but Callie didn't miss Nigel's mischievous grin or Sir Reginald's merry twinkle, and she certainly hadn't missed the brush of Adam's warm hand against her thigh just before she stood up.

The day might have been long, but she had a delicious feeling that the night was going to be even longer. She would learn far more about herself in Adam's embrace, and he about her as well, than either of them had learned from Sir Reginald.

"It was a lovely wedding," Plimpton said as he hung up Adam's jacket and laid out a fresh nightshirt. "You were so kind to invite us to observe the ceremony. Miss Callie, that is, her ladyship, looked radiant, if I might be so bold. We were deeply moved to see her in such glowing health and looking so happy after the ordeal she went through, and I speak for Mr. Gettis and Mrs. Simpson as well as myself."

"Thank you," Adam said, not really paying much attention. "I hope you all enjoyed the rest of the cake and the champagne."

"The dining hall was a scene of great merriment, my lord. We ate the cake, and a delicious cake it was, and we drank to your good health and happiness. We drank many toasts, my lord, for everyone wanted his turn."

Adam shot a look a Plimpton over his shoulder, wondering if the man wasn't a little tipsy, for he wasn't usually so talkative.

"Very good, Plimpton," Adam said. He turned back to the bowl of warm water and splashed his face and neck, then reached out for the towel that Plimpton obligingly put into his hand.

"I took the liberty of putting a decanter of cognac next to your bed, my lord."

Adam straightened and lowered the towel. "Do you think I am in need of fortification, Plimpton?"

"No, my lord," Plimpton replied smoothly. "But her ladyship . . . a young lady's nerves, you know . . . perhaps a small glass to fortify her?"

Adam regarded Plimpton dryly. "Have you ever seen her ladyship display nerves of any sort?"

"I cannot say I have. Her ladyship appears to possess a most sound, even-spirited temperament."

"Exactly. Her ladyship would not thank me for putting her into a stupor. I thank you for your thoughtfulness, but my wife will manage her wedding night very nicely and every night thereafter. That will be all, Plimpton."

"Yes, my lord," Plimpton said with a bow. "I wish you good night, my lord. Er, would you like your morning coffee and toast brought to your room in the usual manner?"

"I see no reason why you should not bring it. Whether I shall be here to take it is another matter. Good night, Plimpton. You may direct the rest of the household to go to bed as soon as they've finished downstairs. We need nothing more up here tonight."

"Yes, my lord," Plimpton said, vanishing through the door like the tactful and well-trained valet he was.

Adam gave Plimpton five minutes to clear the hallway of all extraneous servants. He didn't need any curious onlookers watching him go to Callie's room.

He had to admit that if anyone was nervous, it was he. As desperately as he wanted Callie, he equally wanted to be sure that he gave her the best possible experience and didn't rush her in any way. At least they'd dispensed with her virginity, for that was never a pleasant experience.

His wedding night with Caro had been difficult, for she had been terrified, poor girl, and little wonder, given what her mother had put into her head about the horrors of the sexual act. He'd felt like a beast when he'd penetrated her stiff-limbed, trembling body, and he'd spent much of the rest of the night trying to calm her tears and reassure her that he really wasn't a monster.

Months passed before Caro was able to welcome him with open arms instead of fear, and then when she'd become pregnant with Ian, he hadn't been able to go near her at all, for she was certain that he'd do the child harm. Three months after Ian's birth he'd finally persuaded her to let him back into her bed, but he had to start from the very beginning again, for as much as Caro enjoyed being a mother, childbirth had nearly undone her, and he'd begun to wonder if he was going to have to live a life of celibacy.

Callie had no such fears, as natural with her body and her sexuality as she was with everything else, and he thanked God she hadn't been brought up in England. Her unorthodox life and her father's equally unorthodox teachings had done her a world of good.

Adam couldn't wait another minute. He slipped down the hall and knocked on her door. "Callie? Are you alone?"

He'd expected to open the door and find her demurely sitting up in bed, covers pulled up to her chin, but instead Callie opened the door herself, wearing her usual night shift and an enormous smile.

"Adam," she said pulling him into the room. "I thought you'd never come! Look—you're not going to credit what Mrs. Simpson put on my night table, for it could only have been she who would have thought of it." She held up a vial of smelling salts. "Can you believe it?" she asked with sheer delight. "I'm surprised she didn't leave a feather for you to burn and wave under my nose. Oh, Adam, just when I think life couldn't get any better, it does."

She slipped into his arms and gazed up at him, her eyes dancing with laughter. "Do you suppose maybe Mrs. Simpson left the salts for you? But don't worry, I promise not to hurt you or make you swoon."

"You had better not," he said, returning her smile, and grateful beyond belief for her sweet, unaffected nature. "If you hurt me I shall scream, and then you'll have some explaining to do to Mrs. Simpson."

"I will try to be gentle," she said merrily, opening the buttons on his shirt with facile fingers and pulling the material out of his trousers, exposing his chest and running her hands lightly down its expanse, then slipping them around his bare back. "Oh," she sighed in contentment. "You have no idea how much I've longed to do that. You feel wonderful. You smell wonderful too, just exactly of yourself. I think it's the nicest scent in the world." She reached up and pulled his shirt back off his shoulders and down his arms and tossed it to one side. "That's better," she said. "You are wearing too many clothes altogether."

"Am I?" Adam wrapped his arms around her, savoring her own sweet scent that made him think of attar of roses and the earth after a good rain. He relished the feel of her slight, warm body against his own, the soft press of her rounded breasts against his naked chest. Kissing her temple, he ran his mouth down her cheek and claimed her mouth, so soft, so giving, tasting of honeyed wine.

His senses swam as she returned his kiss, her tongue lightly twining with his, her hands restlessly moving on his back, pulling him even closer, and he couldn't help cupping one lovely, perfectly shaped buttock.

"Callie," he murmured, raising his head. "I think I might need those smelling salts if I don't lie down very quickly."

Callie danced away from him and reached her hands out for his, pulling him toward the bed. "You look fevered, Adam. Your face is flushed and your eyes are overly bright. Here, let me help you." She positioned his back against the bedpost and unbuttoned the flap of his trousers, releasing his aching erection. "There, that's better," she said. "You have developed a mighty swelling, my lord, and I know just the cure." She knelt, pulling his trousers down to his ankles. Adam quickly stepped out of them before he lost his balance, which was already precarious. The sight of Callie on her knees, her face only inches away from his erection, nearly undid him altogether.

"Callie . . . oh, Callie," he groaned, reaching down for her, but she held his hands away.

"Is it permitted to kiss you there?" she asked, looking up at him. "I should so like to see how you taste."

Adam couldn't believe his ears or his good luck. "It's permitted," he managed to say, "but be little careful, for I need to keep up my stamina for what's in store. And it's only permitted if I am allowed to taste you as well."

Her mouth curved up. "Fair is fair," she said, then lowered her head and delicately ran her tongue over his exquisitely sensitive and engorged flesh, circling the blunt tip and drawing it between her lips, one hand supporting the weight of the shaft and intuitively moving on it in a slow and perfect rhythm.

Adam thought he might die with pleasure, and Callie's innocent eagerness made the experience all that more intense.

He gently disengaged her, knowing that he couldn't take very much more. "That was very, very nice, but I believe it's my turn now," he said, his voice hoarse.

Pulling her to her feet, he ran his hands up her hips and waist, taking her night shift with him and pulling it over her head. The shift landed on top of his trousers, and he quickly lifted her in his arms and laid her on her back, straddling her hips with his own.

"Ah, Callie, you are so beautiful, so very lovely," he said, running his hands up the sides of her ribcage and cupping the delicate mounds of her breasts, his thumbs teasing her nipples until she gasped and twisted under him in pleasure.

Adam didn't think his groin could take any more direct stimulation for a while, so he moved her knees aside and shifted a little lower between them, then bent his head and took her mouth with his, kissing her until they both gasped.

Faced with such a cornucopia of delights, Adam decided to start at the top and work his way down. He nuzzled her ears with his mouth and then her neck, sliding his tongue down the silken skin and over the notch of her throat, which Callie had obligingly arched back for him, relishing her little sighs of pleasure.

Her breasts were next on his list of feasts, and he circled his tongue around the outside of one creamy orb, honing in on the nipple and drawing it in between his lips. He knew he was doing it right when she writhed under him and tangled her fingers in his hair, moaning in a highly satisfactory fashion, so he moved to the other breast and subjected it to the same delectable treatment.

"Oh, *Adam,*" she cried, and he rubbed his mouth back and forth on that taut peak and suckled it again until she sobbed and dug her fingers into his shoulders.

Having completed his first course, he shifted his weight and edged down on the bed, his mouth tracing a line of fiery kisses over her soft belly as he went, his hands trailing up the soft inner flesh of her thighs and pushing them further apart.

He could smell the lovely, musty scent of her arousal as he approached that sweet nest of damp curls and he kissed her there as well, his tongue slipping lower to slide over the slick, honeyed flesh of her womanhood, that mysterious delta of female wonders, so soft, so wet, so absolutely perfect, a peach in full bloom. He filled his mouth with her nectar, using his tongue to lap up her dripping juices, suckling the tight little kernel of flesh that eagerly quivered beneath his touch, just as her body quivered and trembled beneath his own, her heat matching his.

He glanced up to catch sight of her face and reveled in her excitement, for her eyes were closed and her head moved frantically back and forth on the pillow, little moans and gasps escaping from that rosebud mouth.

Slipping his hands under her thighs, he lifted them higher and drove his tongue home, feeling her muscles contract as she received him. He stabbed it into her again and again in a hard, fast rhythm, and Callie's body tightened, her hips pressing up against his mouth as if she could draw him even deeper.

Callie shook as every muscle tightened, and she suddenly jerked and cried out, a sharp, high keen that went on and on until all she could do was gasp for air.

Adam softly kissed her one last time and lifted himself up over her. "Now, Callie?" he asked, positioning his hips back over hers, supporting his weight on his forearms.

She nodded, her breath still coming in short pants, and murmured something he couldn't quite make out.

Adam didn't waste another moment. He didn't have another moment to waste, for he was ready to explode. Using one hand he guided himself to her entrance and he slid slowly inside her tight, heated flesh until he was fully buried in her. He waited a moment to make sure she was comfortable, but he didn't even have to do that, for Callie immediately wrapped her legs around his waist and began moving her hips back and forth in a languorous rhythm that Adam was happy to match.

He kissed every available piece of her flesh that his mouth could find as he loved her fully and without restraint, Callie giving back to him everything she received and more. He was consumed by her, lost in a mutual passion and need as the world diminished behind them until it consisted only of this bed, their bodies locked in a frenzied dance, their skin sliding across each other as they spiraled higher and higher into oblivion.

He felt Callie's body tense, her arms tighten around him, and he drove into her, holding her shaking body hard against him as her inner muscles tightened and then released, Callie's frantic cries echoing inside his head as her body convulsed around his in great spasms of release, sheathing the steel of his flesh with molten fire.

Adam gritted his teeth against the flood of sensation that threatened to overcome him, a tidal wave that rushed through his blood, gathering height and speed until it crested and broke, and he helplessly fell with it, his body pouring into Callie's, shattering his senses, his groans torn from his body as he surged into her again and again, washing him back and forth on the shores of home. The wave finally released him, leaving him helplessly gasping in its wake.

"Dear God," he murmured, collapsing onto his side and drawing Callie against him as if he were helping her back onto the safety of the shore with him.

He turned his head. "Are you all right?" he asked, still struggling for breath.

"Callie?" he said, when she didn't answer.

He raised himself onto his elbow and looked down at her. Her eyes were closed and her face still, her hair tangled around her arm and shoulders and falling over her naked breasts as if she were a mermaid, which seemed perfectly appropriate, although he hadn't realized that mermaids were quite so dangerous. Maybe she was a Siren. Ah, yes. He should have remembered the Sirens, who would lure you to death on the rocks with their seductive song. He had taken her from the sea, after all.

"Callie? I didn't hurt you, did I?"

Callie opened her eyes and hazily regarded him. "Hurt me? Don't be silly, Adam. That was wonderful. Why would you think such a thing?"

"Because I nearly broke myself," he said with a grin, relieved he hadn't done her any damage.

Callie sat up abruptly. "Adam—you're teasing me, aren't you? You can't break that wonderful appendage, can you?" She glanced down at his groin with alarm. "It doesn't *look* broken, just a little limp."

Adam hooted with laughter and flopped back down on the bed. "No, I don't think you can break it, or at least I've never heard of such a thing." A very wonderful idea had just occurred to him though. "I think I just tired the poor devil out. Maybe I even bruised it a little. Do you think you could have a look?"

"Certainly," Callie said, and leaned over, picking up Adam's limp flesh as gently and tenderly as she might a bird with an injured wing. "I don't know much about it, mind you," she said, giving her subject the gravest attention, "but I don't see any signs of damage. Actually," she said, shooting Adam a look of suspicion, "it seems to be recovering all by itself."

Adam looked down in pretended surprise, for he knew perfectly well he was already stirring again. Callie's touch apparently was irresistible, no matter how worn out he thought he was. "Look at that," he said. "Well, that's a relief. I thought we were going to need to administer Mrs. Simpson's smelling salts."

"I don't think you or your appendage are in need of smelling salts in the least, Adam Carlyle."

"Perhaps not," he said, wrapping a lock of her hair around his hand and gently pulling her down to him. "Perhaps I just need a little more of your own special brand of medicine. You say you know how to ride, Callie?"

"Yes, of course," she said, her eyes lighting up. "Are you saying that you will finally let me? I'd love to give Gabriel a try, for he seems a most amenable horse."

"Absolutely not," Adam said with alarm. "I'm not putting you in any danger of falling. But if you want to ride," he said, relaxing again, "you can always practice on me. I'll catch you if you lose your balance."

Callie ran a finger over his mouth. "Ah, I see. You would like to be mounted, my lord?"

"I would like to test your equestrian skills," he said, "and I can think of no better way." By now he was fully standing, for the thought of Callie riding him like a stallion had stirred his blood. He regarded Callie speculatively, waiting to see what she would do.

Callie sat up, turned around, and swung one leg over

him, settling onto his hips with her knees resting on either side. She reached back and guided him directly into her. "I've always preferred riding astride," she said with a smothered laugh. "Giddiyap, my lord, and show me your paces."

Adam was more than happy to oblige.

## 18

*H*arold was in a very bad mood. He'd been up half the night playing cards and drinking, and he'd been too foxed to get home, so he'd had to spend what little money he had left on a room at the inn, a complete waste of resources.

His head hurt, his mouth tasted like the bottom of a bog, and the sun shone far too brightly for his liking. The last thing he needed was to have to listen to his mother start complaining about Adam and bloody Callista Melbourne.

He was already livid enough that Adam had snatched a fortune out from under his nose, once again taking what he, Harold, was supposed to have, and he didn't need constant reminding. He stayed away from the house as much as possible, but as hard as he tried, he couldn't avoid his mother entirely, for she always seemed to be lying in wait for him, ready to start her nagging all over again.

He really didn't know what she expected him to do. Kidnap the stupid girl and carry her off to Gretna Green before Adam could marry her himself? He hardly thought so, and frankly, having had a dose of Miss Melbourne, he'd decided that he didn't particularly want to be married to her anyway. Therefore he'd done his best to put the entire matter out of his mind, but his mother refused to let it alone.

He quietly let himself in through the front door, hoping that his mother had stayed in bed with another one of her headaches. She'd been working up to one when he'd left the evening before, and they usually worsened during the night. But he had no such luck. Her voice shattered the stillness of the hallway, coming from behind him just as he'd reached the staircase.

"Harold! Where have you been? Come in here immediately!" She stood in the doorway of the sitting room in a state of high agitation, waving a sheet of paper in her hand.

He turned. "Good morning, Mama," he said with a resigned sigh. "I trust you are feeling better?"

"How could I be feeling anything but deeply distressed when my only child has stayed out all night, doing heaven knows what, and I am left alone in this dreadful house where anyone could come in and murder me in my sleep?"

Harold really wished someone would. "I am sorry, Mama. I became involved in some business and I decided to stay over in town to see it completed early this morning."

"Business?" she said. "Ha! What more important business could you possibly have than restoring our lost fortune? Have you done anything, I ask you? No. And here, just this morning, is a letter from that unfeeling, deceitful thief of a cousin of yours. He says that he is marrying Miss Melbourne immediately. *Immediately,* Harold," she said, her voice rising.

"I don't know what *immediately* means, but I don't like it, and I want you to do something about it."

"Do what?" Harold said, wishing he'd never left the inn.

"Find out what he's planning—if he really intends to marry her or if he's only baiting you. I have seen no engagement notice in any of the papers, and nothing would surprise me coming from him, for he likes nothing better than ruining your life. He might be planning to thoroughly compromise her and throw her out into the street, in which case you will have to step in and pick up the discarded and sullied pieces." Mildred narrowed her eyes in thought. "Hmm. That might work out quite nicely in the end. But never mind that now. If he is intending to marry her, I want you to put a stop to it. Right away, Harold, if you understand my meaning."

"I don't understand you at all," Harold said, wanting nothing more than his bed. "How am I supposed to stop Adam from doing exactly as he pleases? I've never managed it before," he added sulkily.

"I wish you'd use your brain for once. Just think about the consequences, Harold. If he marries, he'll probably get her with a brat, and if it's a son again, back you go down to the bottom of the succession. If he doesn't marry, then he can't produce a legitimate heir, now can he?"

"I know that," Harold said impatiently. "I ask you again, what do you expect me to do?"

Mildred smiled, looking like a cat in the cream pot. "I want you to do as he asks in this letter and take Miss Melbourne's belongings over to Stanton."

"Mama, you know as well as I that I'm not welcome at Stanton. He'll toss me straight out, and if not he, then one of his minions."

"He made the request—it's right here in writing. You

are being kind enough to comply. He asked for immediacy; you will give it to him, and you will go now, Harold, this very morning. When you're at Stanton, I want you to find out what you can, however you can, and I want you think very carefully about what you discover. You mustn't miss any opportunities to turn the situation around. I am confident that you will come up with something, anything."

Harold could see his mother would not be dissuaded, and he had to admit, she'd had a clever idea about how to get onto Stanton land and do some investigating.

Once there, he was bound to find some sort of opportunity to get his own back at Adam.

Sleepily opening her eyes, Callie took a moment to orient. The sun brightly streamed in through the window and she realized with a small shock that the hour was late, probably close to noon. She rolled over but Adam was no longer beside her. He must have woken at his usual hour and left her to sleep. They'd been up until very late, and Callie smiled in memory, thinking of Adam's amazing stamina and versatility. She'd never even imagined there were so many interesting variations to the sexual act, but Adam's imagination knew no bounds and she'd been happy to be educated by such a willing and attentive master. She wasn't such a bad student, either.

She sat up and stretched, feeling in excellent health and spirits, surprised that she didn't seem to be the least bit tired. Actually, she felt amazingly vital and fully alive, all of her senses singing.

She looked down at the gold band on the ring finger of her left hand, a symbol of her love and commitment to

Adam. Rubbing her thumb over it, she wondered if Adam saw it just as a badge of office.

But she wasn't going to dwell on that now. She wasn't going to let anything spoil her happiness. If Adam couldn't love her, well—at least he seemed to like her very much. He'd said himself that they'd just find a different way, and so they would.

She heard a scratch at the door, which could only mean that Jane was outside.

Callie quickly slipped out of bed and recovered her night shift, pulling it on. "Come in," she called.

"Good morning, my lady. Did you sleep well?" Jane asked, carrying in a tray of tea and steaming muffins and setting it on a side table.

She looked remarkably demure. Jane usually started chattering away first thing and didn't stop until she'd finished her duties and left, which Callie always enjoyed, for she discovered a plethora of interesting and useful information about what was transpiring in the house, the grounds, the village beyond, and everywhere in between. Maybe Jane had developed a new sensibility now that Callie was formally the mistress of the house, and Callie thought that would be a real pity.

"I slept very well, thank you. Where is everyone?" she asked as Jane brought in a pitcher of hot water and poured it into the bowl on the washing stand.

"Well, let me see," Jane said, forgetting her demureness. "Sir Reginald is in the study with his lordship. They've been in there most of the morning." She considered. "Mr. Dryden is outside with Mr. Roberts, going over some sort of plans, or at least that's what Michael said. Anyway, he said they had a big sheet of paper with drawings on it and were talking a mile a minute, if Mr. Roberts can talk a mile a minute, which

I doubt, so I imagine Mr. Dryden's doing most of the talking. Everyone else is where they belong at this time of the day, except that Mrs. Simpson is airing out the connecting bedroom to his lordship's so that we can move your belongings in later." She turned from the wardrobe. "Would you like the blue walking dress with the white lace trimming and little green flowers, my lady? I do think it ever so pretty."

"Thank you, Jane," Callie said, looking up from the basin where she was giving herself a thorough wash. "That would be perfect. Anything else?"

"Oh—his lordship said that he'd join you and Sir Reginald for a cold luncheon, and then he asked to have the carriage brought around afterward, since he has to go into town on business for an hour or so, and he's taking Mr. Kincaid and the grooms with him to have a look at some horses he's thinking of buying. Or at least that's what he told Mr. Dryden before he went into the study with Sir Reginald."

Callie did like being well informed, she thought with a smile as she dried herself off and let Jane help her into her dress. Jane was as good as having a private secretary.

"And your hair, my lady? Would you like me to put it up, or will you wear it down in your usual way during the day?"

"I'll brush it out and leave it," Callie said. "I don't plan to turn into a grand lady just because I'm married. No one would recognize me."

Jane grinned. "No, my lady. I'm happy that everything will go on just as before—well, almost, anyway. Do drink your tea and have your muffins before they go cold. Cook made them especially for you."

"I'll do that, and then I'll come straight down. What a fine day it is. I think I might do some gardening this afternoon."

"Yes, my lady. If you don't need me for anything else?"

"No, nothing else, thank you." Callie ate her breakfast in peace and then left to join Adam and Sir Reginald, but before she closed the door behind her, she took one last look around the room in which she lived for the last month and in which so much had transpired.

It was odd, she thought. She had both lost herself and found herself within these four walls. She had learned to conquer fear and despair and she had learned to love. Her life would never be the same again.

Tonight she would sleep in a different room, Caroline's old room, and she would sleep there forever after. That was fitting, though, for today she properly began her new life as Adam's wife, a life in which she had left her ghosts behind, and Adam's as well. She wasn't so sure that Adam's ghosts would ever entirely leave him, not unless he regained his faith in God and could finally lay his wife and son to rest.

She was fully aware that she was wishing for a miracle.

"There you are," Adam said, looking up as she came down the staircase. "I'm so pleased that you managed to sleep the morning away, for you look well rested and very pretty as well, I might say."

Callie paused on the landing, gazing down at him. He looked so handsome, so different from the frightening, remote man she'd first met whose imposing good looks had startled and unnerved her. Now he looked just like—just like Adam, easy and relaxed, his eyes that brilliant color of the sky filled with sunshine, his smile just as warm, his hand reached up to her in welcome.

She descended the last flight of steps and slipped her hand into his, and he squeezed it. "I've had a most elucidating conversation with Sir Reginald, but it primarily concerned the financial details of your funds and working out how to draw up the trust that I mentioned. I can't change the disposition of ownership now that we're married, but I can keep the money protected for you."

Callie put a hand on his arm, for she'd had an idea while she was eating her breakfast, and she wanted to see what Adam might think. "You said that you didn't want or need the money," she said, wondering just how to put her proposition.

"That's true. Why? Have you suddenly decided that you want to spend it all?" His eyes teased her.

"Not exactly," she replied seriously. "Adam, Squire Hoode owns the land that marches with Stanton, isn't that right?"

He frowned. "You mean West Grange Manor? He does, but what has that to do with anything? He's a filthy land-lord and should be horsewhipped for the way he treats his tenants."

"Yes, I know, and that's my point. Do you think he'd sell his land to you?" she said in a rush. "I don't know what fifty thousand pounds will buy, but if it's a good enough price for him, you can buy the property and take over as landlord, and that way all the people who suffer because of Squire Hoode's greed and indifference will be free of him and can live a much better life."

Adam stared at her, his gaze sharpening. "By God, Callie ... by God, you might have hit on something. Hoode's put out feelers in my direction for some time, but I've never had enough free capital to buy him out, preferring to put my money back into Stanton." He took her by the shoulders and looked her hard in the eyes. "Are you sure this is how you'd like to see your money used?"

"It's our money now, and I think it would be a superb investment, Adam. You are very good at what you do, and you'd improve the land and its production no end.

Anyway, if you're worried about me and my future or our children's, well—the property won't be entailed to Stanton if you're careful about how you manage to buy it, and that way one of our younger children can have it—or something like that." She shrugged. "I haven't worked out the details, but it will bring in its own income, won't it? The point is that if you can buy the grange, so many people's lives would be improved."

Adam laughed, kissed her soundly, and picked her up in his arms, swinging her around before he set her back down on solid ground. "Yes, they would, and you are amazing, Callie, absolutely amazing, and kind and good and generous and very, very clever. You've come up with a brilliant idea, and I see no reason why we can't make this work. Sir Reginald's gone into the dining room and we should join him, but we can discuss this over luncheon, and perhaps he can come up with some good ideas about how to tie this all up neatly so that everyone's happy." His face alive with excitement, Adam drew her into the dining room and started talking before he'd even sat down.

By the end of lunch, the three of them had put together a workable plan. Sir Reginald, who was all in favor of the idea, seeing it as a wise investment, agreed to have his staff organize the preliminary paperwork and come up with a fair market value. "Even if you have to buy slightly over market price in order to close the sale," he said, "you'll still have a great deal left over to invest in improvements."

"I'd like the cottages to be one of the first things on the list of improvements, if that's possible," Callie said.

"Absolutely," Adam said. "I think I'm very happy that you went into Hythe to visit Nellie Bishop that day, even if you did scare the life out of me. That's what put this idea into your mind, isn't it?"

"It is," she said. "Nellie never complained, not really, but I could see how things were, not just for her, but for everyone. Nellie said there wasn't a single one of them who wouldn't jump at the chance to have you as their landlord. If we could make this a reality I'd feel as if we'd accomplished something important."

"Then we'll see it does become a reality. You are going to make a very fine Marchioness of Vale, Callie. I'm very proud of you."

Callie blushed furiously. "I didn't *do* anything," she said. "I just had an idea. It's you who agreed, and that makes you even more wonderful in my eyes."

"Hmm. Well, enough of this mutual admiration. I have to take my leave, as I have to get into town for a horse sale, but I'll be back a little later." He stood. "Sir Reginald, I can't tell you how grateful I am that you came down when you did. Meeting you has been a very great pleasure, and I feel sure that we are going to enjoy a long and mutually satisfying friendship."

"You can be sure of it," Sir Reginald said gruffly. "I already feel rather like a member of the family, if I might be so presumptuous."

"You make no presumption," Adam said, shaking his hand. "You are welcome at Stanton any time you care to visit. We shall count on you to attend Christmas and christenings and all those sorts of family occasions. I'd like to think that both Callie and I have gained an honorary godfather."

"I should be honored to play the part. On your way now, young man, for your wife and I have much to discuss, and I intend to bore her with a detailed history of her past."

When Callie walked Sir Reginald to his waiting carriage two hours later, she couldn't help the tears that filled her eyes as she said good-bye. He had given her so much just by virtue of his warmth and acceptance, but his most precious gift had been a beautifully told story of her life that had painted a clear and richly defined picture and made her feel as if he had given her the next best thing to her memory—his own, as told through the eyes of her father.

She waved until the carriage disappeared into the distance, then turned and walked back up the front steps, her heart filled to overflowing.

Harold couldn't believe his luck when he saw Adam's carriage barrel past him on the road, made unmistakable not only by the Vale crest emblazoned on the side, but also by the fineness of the four matched bays and the livery of the coachmen and grooms on the box and the footmen who rode behind. But most unmistakable was the man who held the reins, for it was Adam himself.

Harold quickly turned his head so that Adam wouldn't recognize him, not that Adam would even bother to look at an old carriage like his, with only two horses that had seen better days to pull it.

So. Adam had left Stanton and taken a full complement of his stable hands with him, which meant he was probably off to the horse sale; he'd be gone for hours. At least he wouldn't have to contend with Adam directly, and that suited him just fine. He had no desire to tangle with the arrogant bastard.

If his luck really held, Harold thought, he might find nasty Miss Melbourne out walking on her own and he could simply grab her, throw her in the carriage, and make off with her. If he had to, he *would* go to Gretna Greene. He'd do just about anything for those fifty thousand pounds, including marrying that harridan, and just let Adam try to stop him.

His confidence rising with every mile, Harold pulled into the front gates of Stanton and drove straight up to the front door.

He wasn't very pleased when Gettis immediately appeared. He hadn't seen the crotchety man in twelve years, but his sour expression hadn't changed one iota. Harold descended from the box. "Good day, Gettis," he said in his haughtiest manner. "I have come at Lord Vale's request."

"Good day, Mr. Carlyle," Gettis said, his nose in the air as if he detected a bad smell. "His lordship said nothing to me about your paying a visit, and even if he did expect you, which I seriously question, his lordship is not at home."

Harold was prepared. He produced Adam's letter from his coat pocket and thrust it into Gettis's gloved hand. "Read that, if you can. It says that he wished for me to bring Miss Melbourne's belongings immediately, which I have done."

"There is no Miss Melbourne here," Gettis said, and Harold could see he'd taken him by surprise.

"Come now, Gettis, there's no need to play the fool with me. I know Lord Vale's been keeping her hidden away here for the last month."

"If you are referring to Lady Vale," Gettis said, recovering his poise as he read Adam's letter, "she is not receiving visitors. Furthermore, there is nothing in this correspondence that mentions that your presence was requested. Lord Vale states that you were to send her ladyship's belongings. He says nothing about bringing them yourself."

Harold paled and licked his lips. Lady Vale? That meant they were already married? A sweat broke out on his brow. He hadn't counted on that. He hadn't counted on that at all. Oh, his mother wasn't going to be pleased. *Damn* Adam to hell!

Gettis inspected the interior of the carriage where Harold had placed two of the trunks and the two cases, then walked around the back of the carriage to where Harold had strapped the last trunk with great effort. The damned thing had weighed a ton, and little wonder, since it was filled with books, as he'd discovered when he'd forced the lock last month. He ran after Gettis.

"I meant Lady Vale," he said quickly. "I referred to her maiden name from long habit. We are acquainted, you fool, or I wouldn't have her belongings, now would I?"

"And how do you come to have her ladyship's belongings?" Gettis said coldly, regarding Harold with deep suspicion.

"Not that it's any of your business, but I collected them from Dover when she missed her sailing. She was meant to be paying my mother and me a visit, and I was kind enough to keep them for her until she arrived in England. Well, here they are, and I would like to deliver them to her personally."

"That will not be necessary," Gettis said, gesturing to the two footmen who stood at the ready by the front steps. "Albert, Charles, attend to the unloading of her ladyship's things and take them upstairs to her room. Stand back, if you please, Mr. Carlyle. Your assistance is not needed."

Harold glared at him, feeling thoroughly humiliated, but there was nothing new in that. Gettis had always gone out of his way to make him feel like an insignificant and unwelcome intrusion. But there was nothing he could do, absolutely nothing, and the realization that he'd been completely outmaneuvered made his blood boil.

He was forced to stand back and watch as the baggage was removed piece by piece, and piece by piece carried into the abbey. Gettis never took his stern gaze off Harold.

"Now that you have discharged your duty, so to speak,

Song from the Sea   299

you may leave, Mr. Carlyle. I can assure you that his lord-ship will not be pleased to find you here when he returns."

Harold didn't bother to reply to this insult. He was shaking so hard with rage that he couldn't have spoken if he'd tried. He climbed back onto the box, gave Gettis one last filthy look, and turned the carriage around, starting down the drive again feeling like a dog that had just been kicked and was running away with its tail between his legs. As if that wasn't bad enough, he knew his mother was going to kick him just as hard when he got home. She'd told him to do something, hadn't she? She'd told him to take care of things. What the devil was he supposed to do now?

As he rounded the corner that led past the stables and then down the rest of the long drive, he drew the horses to a walk, a brilliant idea occurring to him. He pulled off the driveway and into a small clearing and hid the carriage behind a copse of trees.

He'd be damned if he went home having done nothing at all to get his own back. Harold thought hard. Adam had gone off with the coachman and the two head grooms. There'd be hardly anyone about.

He smiled maliciously as he slid off the box and made his way over the small path that led to the back of the stables. Crouching down behind some bushes, he looked carefully. There was no sign of any activity. He ferreted around in the bushes and found exactly what he was looking for: a dried burr. Perfect.

He made a dash for the door of the tack room and gingerly opened it, peering around. All was quiet. It took no time at all to find the peg where Adam's saddle hung, for it was clearly marked, and he would have recognized the make of Adam's favorite saddle anyway. The man never varied in his habits. The saddlecloth had been neatly folded under the saddle, ready to pick up in one easy movement.

Harold lifted the saddle and carefully tucked the burr between the folds of the saddlecloth where it wouldn't be seen. All that was needed was the pressure of Adam's weight coming down on the saddle and the burr would go straight into the horse's tender flank. That would be that. No horse would sit still for that sort of treatment, and with any luck, Adam would be completely off guard when the horse went berserk.

If Harold's plan worked, Adam would be badly thrown. With any real luck, he'd break his miserable neck.

Next stop for Harold: Stanton Abbey, the marquessate firmly in hand.

Harold replaced the saddle exactly as it had been, and crept back out of the tack room. He tittered all the way back to his carriage and laughed himself silly most of the way home.

$\mathcal{G}$ettis finally tracked Callie down in the rose garden. "My lady, I am sorry to interrupt you, but your, er, your belongings have arrived. I thought you might like to know."

Callie jumped up. "My trunks?" she said with delight. "My cases? Oh, Gettis, how absolutely wonderful—Where are they now?"

"They have been taken upstairs to your new room. I asked that they not be unpacked, as I wasn't sure if you wouldn't rather go through them yourself and decide where you'd like everything put."

"Thank you, Gettis," Callie said, deciding the day couldn't get any better. "I'll go straight up and have a look." She brushed the dirt off her gardening gloves and pulled them off, dropping them into her basket next to her pruning shears. "Will you tell his lordship when he returns that I'll be upstairs?"

"Certainly, my lady. Allow me to take your basket for you. I will put it in the solarium."

Callie handed it to him and practically ran into the house and up the stairs, and she had to remember to turn left instead of right as she was accustomed to doing.

The trunks sat to one side of the large, sunny bedroom, and the cases were neatly laid out on the bed. She looked at them with anticipation. *Her* trunks. *Her* cases. She could scarcely believe it. Here was something concrete from her past. She had no idea what lay inside them, but whatever they held, whatever she found, those things would belong to her and tell her about the person she'd been.

With shaking hands she opened the first case and gently laid the lid back. Clothes, she saw, the outline of clothes wrapped in tissue; a pair of horn-backed hairbrushes lay tucked between the top folds. Something flat and oblong, also wrapped in tissue, lay next to the hairbrushes, and she picked the little package up and unfolded the tissue with trembling fingers. It was a pen-and-ink sketch of a man with long side-whiskers, and a serious but gentle face, whose eyes seemed bright and intelligent behind his wire-rimmed spectacles. He held a book in one hand, and his expression seemed to be one of good-natured patience for the artist.

Callie choked back a sob. She knew without a doubt that she was looking at her father's image. Her heart felt as if it had just been sliced open, and all the grief she'd felt in her dream came pouring back as if a dam had broken.

"Papa," she whispered, running her fingers down his likeness as if she could somehow feel his essence. "Oh, Papa . . . how very fine you look. And oh, how—how I miss you." She held the sketch against her heart for a long moment, taking deep, slow breaths as if that could quiet the pain.

When she felt a little calmer, she carefully laid aside the

precious picture and slowly began to go through the cases, poring over each piece of clothing, each little trinket, everything a treasure to her, everything with a story to tell, no matter how small, and no matter how little she remembered. But that was the problem: she held her past in her hands, and instead of the joy that she'd expected, she felt nothing but a hollow, aching emptiness.

Maybe she hadn't left her ghosts behind her after all.

Adam found her an hour later.

Callie sat on the floor in the middle of the room, surrounded by piles of books and clothes and pictures. He watched her from the door for a few silent minutes, not sure whether to trespass on what was obviously a very private time.

She looked so young and so lovely, so innocent and yet wise beyond telling, peaceful, and yet . . . sad, as if beneath her happiness she couldn't help feeling her loss. He couldn't imagine how he might feel if he held something tangible in his hands but couldn't connect it properly to its importance.

But he did know, he suddenly realized. How many times had he felt the same way? Even now, in a rare, unguarded moment, he would hear something and he'd instinctively turn, his arms reaching out to catch Ian, but his arms found only air and emptiness.

He knew exactly how she felt.

He walked over to her and dropped down next to her. "Are you all right, Callie?" he asked quietly.

She looked over at him and smiled, but her mouth trembled at the corners. "Yes—yes, I'm fine. Look, Adam. All my things. All my memories."

"I know. All your memories, and yet you feel as if you're clutching at straws, is that it?"

She looked down and nodded, her fair hair falling forward to cover her cheeks. "How did you know?"

"Because I just realized that I often feel the same way."

"Oh, Adam," Callie said, reaching out for him and pulling him close. "Of course you do. We're an odd pair, aren't we? I don't remember anything, and you remember too much."

"Maybe we can meet somewhere in the middle," he said. "I'll give you all sorts of new memories and you can help me put aside some of my old ones. How would that be? We can start right away, this very day."

"I think that would be very nice," Callie said, nuzzling her face into his neck as if she could find comfort there.

"All right, then. I know just where to start. I need to take Gabriel out for a quick bit of exercise, for I've neglected him badly the last two days and he becomes impossibly feisty if I don't give him a good run, but after that we can take a walk out to the cliffs. There's something I'd like to show you, if you have the patience to bear with me. I know you haven't gone out there yet, and I completely understand why, but will you come with me if I ask you?"

She gazed up at him, her eyes completely trusting. "Of course I will."

"Good. I'll come back to fetch you. I shouldn't be too long."

"No—wait. I'll walk down to the stables with you, for there are some plants there that I noticed the other day and would like to collect. We can go to the cliffs when you're done with Gabriel. I think I could use as much fresh air as I can drink in just now, and I'm done in here. I'll ask Jane to tidy everything away."

"That sounds like a good idea." Adam stood and helped

Callie to her feet, and together they left the room, hand in hand.


"I'll admit I'm mightily confused, Mrs. Simpson, but there it is." Gettis wiped his brow with his handkerchief. "I know I didn't mistake what Mr. Harold said, and I read the words in his lordship's letter. Miss Melbourne, it said, clear as day."

"I don't understand, Mr. Gettis. His lordship *said* Miss Callie's surname was Magnus. Why would he say that if it wasn't true?" Mrs. Plimpton sat down in her armchair, where she always took her troubles.

Gettis scratched his ear. "I don't know. Now Mr. Harold also said that Miss Callie—her ladyship—was on her way to Dover to pay a visit to him and that mother of his. He said she missed her sailing, so he collected her baggage, and we know that's true since he just brought it over. He claimed acquaintanceship with her, and I find that very strange indeed, because we all know how much his lordship dislikes that branch of the family, and for good reason. What was Miss Callie doing going to visit the likes of them, I ask?"

"That's beside the point," Mrs. Simpson said. "We know something that Mr. Harold doesn't, don't we, Gettis? We know the poor poppet fell off her ship right into the sea and his lordship rescued her. *I* think that his lordship found out that Mr. Harold had designs on our poppet and his lordship gave her a different name to protect her, just in case Mr. Harold got wind that there was a Miss Melbourne staying here at Stanton."

Gettis narrowed his eyes. "Designs, you say? Why, that arrogant, miserable piece of vermin! I should have—I should have taken the whip right off the box and given him a good lashing with it."

"You sent him away with a tongue-lashing, and that was good enough for now. His lordship will see to the rest, you can be sure of that. There's going to be a proper dust-up when he discovers that Mr. Harold had the effrontery to come right to the front door and demand to see the poppet. Cheek, I call that. You did well, Mr. Gettis, in dispatching him right back to where he came from."

"But I told his lordship as soon as he returned home, and he didn't say a word. Not a word, Mrs. Simpson. He just nodded, and then went straight upstairs to see her ladyship."

"That's his lordship all over, the dear boy. He keeps his own council and acts when he sees fit. You can be sure that he'll keep our poppet safe. He married her, didn't he?" Her eyes suddenly widened and her plump hand flew to her bosom. "Good heavens, Mr. Gettis! You don't suppose the poppet actually jumped off that ship to avoid being handed over to Mr. Harold? Oh, the poor, poor dear. She must have thought that a watery grave was a better fate than—than being consigned to that dreadful man." Mrs. Simpson pulled out her handkerchief and blew her nose soundly.

Mr. Gettis abruptly sat down, the shock taking his breath away. "Oh, my goodness. Oh, my dear goodness gracious. Yes, of course ... She had no one in the world to protect her, did she? The poor, brave soul—she must have been truly desperate. Thank goodness that his lordship happened along when he did or it would have ended very badly, very badly indeed."

"That's Fate, Mr. Gettis. Fate sent his lordship out into the raging sea to rescue our poppet, and Fate sent our poppet leaping off that boat and straight into his lordship's arms to bring happiness back into his life. Didn't he fall in love with her right from the beginning and she with him? It's a Great Romance, a truly Great Romance, written in the stars to be sure. I declare, I've never been so moved." She mopped her eyes. "You see, Mr. Gettis, it only goes to show that One Never Knows."

"One never knows what?" Gettis said, thoroughly confused. Mrs. Simpson had lost him when she started on about Fate.

"One Never Knows Why Things Happen or What Is Meant to Be," Mrs. Simpson replied impatiently.

"The only thing I know is that I could use a large glass of cognac. My nerves are badly shaken. Just the thought that we might have lost Miss Callie like that, never had her here at Stanton to brighten all our lives—it really doesn't bear thinking about. And it's all that Mr. Harold's fault that it was such a near thing. He always was a troublemaker, that one. I sincerely hope we've seen the last of him and his nasty tricks."

"The Lord will provide, Mr. Gettis. The Lord will provide."

Adam left Callie gathering herbs outside the stable yard entrance. She looked content, so he felt comfortable leaving her to her work. It would give her something to think about other than her lost past. It was ironic, he thought. He could give her nearly anything material, and he could give her safety and security, but the one thing she truly wanted was completely beyond his ability to provide. He felt both saddened and frustrated, for without her memory, Callie would always carry an empty place in her heart, and she was a person whose heart should be whole and filled with happiness. It seemed so unfair—Callie gave so generously of herself to everyone around her, and she did it without a second thought. Her gesture today when she'd asked that her inheritance be used to purchase the grange had been the perfect example of that, and that gesture had nearly leveled him. He couldn't be any fonder of her if he tried.

He had a quick word with Kincaid, wanting to know how the two new mares were settling in. He'd bought one just for Callie, a nice, placid bay. He intended to give it to her as a surprise, at some point in the future when he felt more confident about her recovery—not that she'd exhibited anything but the best of health in the last two weeks, and given her performance in the bedroom last night, she did seem to have an abundance of strength and stamina.

Adam grinned as he waited for Gabriel to be saddled up. He'd make this a very short ride, for he wanted to get back to Callie as soon as possible. He was anxious to take her out to the cliffs, for he thought that maybe he could help her overcome one of her fears. She couldn't live on the coast of Kent and avoid the water forever—not that she'd ever mentioned being afraid, but being Callie, she wouldn't. He'd made the assumption because he knew full well she had gone in every direction but that one, and she'd never once asked him to take her out there himself— odd for a woman who delighted in every form of plant and animal life, which the cliffs abounded with.

Haskins brought Gabriel out of the stables, his hand tight on the reins. "He's a bit nervous today, my lord," Haskins said as Gabriel released a high whinny. "It must be the new mares, for he's been sidling and pawing since I took him out of the stall. I had the devil of a time just doing up the girth."

"He'll be all right once he has a good run," Adam said. "You're probably right, though, Haskins. The smell of new female blood has probably gone to his head. Isn't that right, Gabriel," he said, running his hand down the gelding's neck. "I imagine you probably feel ignored on top of it all, but I've had a female of my own to attend to."

Gabriel snorted and shook his head, his nostrils flaring and his eyes rolling.

"Come on, then, my lad, let's stretch your legs." He took the reins from Haskins and put his foot into the stirrup and his hand on Gabriel's withers and swung his other leg over the saddle, abruptly freezing in mid-motion at the sound of Callie's panicked voice.

"Adam! Adam, no—something's wrong!" Callie cried, tearing into the stable yard and running directly up to him. "Get off him—get off him now, he's in trouble!"

Adam didn't hesitate. He immediately started to dismount, but he was a fraction too late. Gabriel reared with an ear-shattering scream, and Adam, already off balance, had no way to recover. Instinctively he released the reins and pulled his foot free from the stirrup as he was catapulted backward through the air, twisting sideways to take the force of his fall off his back. To his horror, in that last split second he registered Callie standing directly in his path. There was nothing he could do. As he landed he knocked her over with the force of his weight, and it was Callie who fell backward, hitting her head on the packed earth.

In the worst of all possible ironies, Callie's body cushioned his fall.

Pandemonium broke out around him. Adam immediately rolled over to protect Callie from Gabriel's flailing hooves, using his body as a shield.

"We have him, my lord!" someone cried, but he barely heard through his panic.

"Callie?" He lifted himself up on his forearms and looked down at her still face, her eyes closed as if in sleep. "Callie?"

It was his nightmare all over again, only this time it was Callie who lay unmoving, Callie who didn't respond to her name, Callie whom he'd failed to protect.

"God, please, please, no," he moaned, slipping his hand under her head and pulling her limp body up into his arms. "Please don't leave me, please open your eyes." He felt her chest to see if she was breathing, but his hand shook so badly he could feel nothing but his own trembling.

"Dear God, you can't let her die," he whispered, praying with all his heart and soul. "Punish me for having doubted in You, but she's never doubted a moment in her life. You can't take her now, not now." He bent his head and pressed his wet cheek against her hair.

"You're—you're s-suffocating me."

His head shot up, only to see Callie looking straight at him, her eyes a little dazed, but otherwise very much filled with life.

"Callie—oh, thank God! Thank God," he repeated with a sigh of infinite relief.

She didn't say anything, just continued to stare at him with an expression of complete and utter surprise, then blinked, and blinked again.

The most appalling thought occurred to Adam: If she'd lost her memory the first time she'd hit her head, what if she'd lost it again now? He didn't know if he could bear it, not having her know him, thinking him a complete stranger, the entire last wonderful month wiped out of her head. His heart jerked in his chest in renewed fear, for the way she was looking at him made him think he might very well be right.

"Callie?" he said hesitantly. "Do you know who I am?"

A laugh escaped her throat, and then another, and then she started laughing as if she'd never stop, clutching his arm, tears running down her cheeks.

Adam didn't know what to do or what to think. Maybe the blow to her head had damaged her brain beyond repair.

"Stop," she said, when she finally caught her breath. "Stop looking at me like that. I remember everything."

"You know who I am?" he asked tentatively.

"Of course I do. You're my husband. How could I forget something as important as that?" she said with a grin. "Help me to sit up properly, for you're half crushing me."

Adam, relieved all over again, instantly complied, turning her to face him. "Don't move," he said. "Let me make sure you haven't broken anything."

"I'm fine," she said, pushing his hands away. "Adam, honestly, I'm not a china doll. I don't break that easily. I'd think you would know that by now."

"Why on earth didn't you get out of the way?" he asked, furious with her now that his immediate alarm had passed.

"There wasn't time. Is Gabriel all right?" she asked, looking around.

"I don't know, and I don't care. I'm in half a mind to shoot the damned animal. I can't think what got into him." He frowned. "What made you come running into the stable yard like that? You *knew* there was something wrong. What was it?"

"I'm not exactly sure," she said, her brows puckering. "Something was hurting him. He was in a horrible panic. Thank goodness you got off when you did, or I think he really would have gone mad with pain."

"Can you stand?" Adam asked.

"Of course I can. Really, I'm fine. My head doesn't even ache—well, maybe just a little, but it's nothing serious, not like the last time. Please, go see to Gabriel."

"Oh, Callie, I'm so glad you're back," Adam said,

helping her to her feet and hugging her tightly. "You scared the life out of me."

"I know," she said, "and I'm sorry about that, but I'm not sorry that it happened. I'm glad I was there to break your fall, for you could have been badly hurt."

*He* could have been badly hurt? He could have *killed* her. Just the thought scared him all over again. He didn't know what he'd do if he lost her. *Dear God,* he realized, shock jolting through him like a bolt from the blue. *He loved her.* He loved her with all of his heart and soul, and he hadn't realized until this moment how very much and how completely. The realization rattled him to his core.

When had it happened? He knew that he'd slowly grown fond of Callie, but he'd been so sure that his heart would always belong irrevocably to Caroline that he hadn't even considered the possibility that he might learn to love again. Then again, he wasn't the man that he had been when he'd fallen in love with Caro, and his needs and outlook had both changed.

Perhaps if Caro had lived, and Ian with her, Adam would have continued on the same path, but that path had been drastically altered, and he would never be the same man again. His essential nature had changed as a result of his loss, and that nature now demanded someone very different. Someone like Callie.

He still loved Caro with all his heart, but that heart, so badly broken, seemed to have mended, the pieces coming back in a different configuration, but coming back nevertheless, despite the scars that would always reside inside. Callie had been his cure, and in curing him, she had given him a second chance at life—and at love.

All this time he'd been falling in love with her, and he hadn't had the first idea. He couldn't believe that he'd been that blind, but he supposed he'd been so busy blaming himself for Ian and Caroline's death, and despising himself for living when they had not, that he hadn't been able to see anything beyond that, including this essential, all-important truth. Callie had spoken to his heart from the very beginning, as shattered as his heart was. She'd spoken to his soul as well, directly as well as indirectly, addressing his lack of faith, forcing him to open his darkened eyes and slowly accept the truth of God's greater plan for him. Apparently part of that plan was Callie, for He'd taken the trouble to put her directly in Adam's path, thereby turning him from a disastrous course.

Not once had she asked anything for herself, and in not asking, she had given him the freedom to find his own way to her. And he had, oh, how perfectly he had. He just hadn't seen what was right under his nose.

He'd even ignored his feelings when he'd proposed to her and she had refused him.

*You don't love me, Adam.*

He'd been stupid enough to agree with her. And she had married him anyway.

He had to tell her how he felt about her—He owed her the truth, and he needed to know if she loved him in return, not that he deserved it. But now was not the time. That conversation would have to keep. Right now he had to get to the root of Gabriel's problem.

"Come, Callie, sit over here on the mounting block. I'm going to go speak to Haskins." He settled her on the makeshift seat, gave her one long look, satisfied himself that she really didn't look any worse for wear, and went storming into the stables.

Five minutes later he came out again, his blood boiling. "You were right," he said, holding out his hand. "We found this stuck in Gabriel's saddlecloth. Haskins swears that he put out a clean cloth last night, and that he washed and dried it and folded himself. He would have noticed a burr if there'd been one, even one this small."

Callie picked it up from his palm and examined it. "No wonder Gabriel was in agony," she said. "They're hard to see, but this variety has very fine little thorns, almost like invisible needles. Any pressure on the blanket would have pushed the thorns directly through and into his flesh." She handed the burr back. "Haskins had better have a very close look at Gabriel's hide to make sure all the thorns are out, and then bathe the area with an infusion of lavender and angelica if he has any. If he hasn't, I have a bottle up at the house. Some balm wouldn't hurt, either. Would you like me to have a word with him?"

"No, I can do that. I'd like for you to return to the house and rest while I take care of some business that will not wait." He reached down and handed her the basket. "Are you well enough to walk back on your own?"

"Yes, but what business do you have now?" Callie asked in surprise. "Can't you leave it until tomorrow? I'm fine, really. What about the cliffs? I was so looking forward to going."

Adam turned to her, wondering why Callie was so anxious to go to the cliffs. Perhaps he'd been wrong and she didn't fear the water at all. There was something else, too. Callie looked different, somehow. He couldn't put his finger on it, but she seemed to be more confident of herself, freer, perhaps. For the life of him, he couldn't think why, and he wouldn't be able to find out until later.

"I'm afraid the cliffs will have to wait until I return," he said grimly. "Callie, do you remember when I told you that I broke my arm as a boy?"

"Yes . . . but what has that to do with anything?"

"It has everything to do with what happened this afternoon. I broke my arm then because Harold was ill-advised enough to put a burr under my horse's saddlecloth, and I fell when the horse bolted and threw me in the process. Harold paid us a visit today when he delivered your luggage. Putting two and two together, I think I can be fairly certain that he was stupid enough to repeat the same trick. He had both motive and opportunity, given that I'd taken almost everyone with me from the stables so that I'd have people to ride home any horses I acquired. Do you see?"

Callie paled, her fists clenching. "I see well enough. Harold could have killed you out of petty spite, and he deserves whatever you have in store for him. Harold has a debt to pay to Gabriel as well, and I'll be more than happy to see it exacted. What are you going to do?"

"I'm going to go to Fawn Hill, and I'm going to see to it that Harold never poses any kind of threat again."

## 20

"Harold? Harold, there's a carriage drawing up," Mildred said, pausing in the middle of buffing her nails. "Who can be calling?" Her head shot up. "You don't suppose . . ." Her eyes suddenly gleamed. "Go to the door—this could be the news we've been awaiting." She straightened her dress and stiffened her back.

Throwing down the paper, Harold jumped to his feet, his heart quickening with excitement. He practically ran for the door as a banging started. Stopping for a moment to compose himself, he straightened his jacket and schooled his face into a neutral expression, ready to express shock and grief when he received the news of Adam's untimely death.

Harold opened the door, and his mouth dropped open at the same time that his heart dropped into the pit of his stomach. "Adam . . ." he said, the word coming out like a squeak.

"Surprised, Harold? I can't think why. Or perhaps you were expecting someone else—Nigel, perhaps, bearing the sad tidings of my demise?"

"I don't know what you're talking about," Harold said, pulling at his collar, which had suddenly become too tight.

"Naturally you don't," Adam said, pushing past him and striding into the sitting room. "Good evening, Aunt Mildred. My goodness, you looked as horrified as Harold. May I sit down? I think I shall anyway." He turned his head toward Harold, who had come dashing into the room behind him. "You had better sit down, too, Cousin, for you're about to have another shock."

Harold turned a shade whiter as he sank into the chair next to his mother.

"Now that I have your full attention," Adam said, pulling his handkerchief from his coat pocket and unfolding it, "I thought I would return this to you." He placed the damning burr on the side table. "Nasty things, burrs. They can do some real damage if they happen to lodge in the wrong place, like a horse's saddlecloth."

Harold shook his head back and forth, intending to deny everything, but for some reason no words came out.

"Do you know, Harold, you really ought to break the habit of repeating yourself. It becomes tedious, and has a tendency to give you away. Oh—and if you're planning on denying this latest episode, don't bother." He crossed one leg over the other. "Now the way I see it, I can have you up for attempted murder, which would not be very pleasant for you or your mother, and since you've been placed at the scene of the crime, you really wouldn't have much of a chance of getting off."

Cold sweat broke out on Harold's brow and his hands clenched the arms of the chair, his knuckles turning white.

He cast a frenzied glance at his mother, waiting for her to say something to get him out of the mess she'd put him in, but she didn't meet his eyes. Her gaze was fixed on Adam and her lips were drawn into a tight, bloodless line, her skin stretched tightly over the bones of her face. Harold saw that he'd get no help from that quarter. She'd send him to the gallows before admitting any complicity, the bitch. She always had looked after her own best interests.

"Good," Adam said. "I'm glad you both have the sense to keep quiet, because protestations and denials will not improve my temper. There's just one thing I'd like to know before I decide what to do with you." He leaned forward and he looked very, very dangerous. "Did either one of you have anything to do with Caroline and Ian's deaths?"

"No!" Harold blurted. He was damned if he was going to let Adam pin the blame on him for that one. "I swear, Adam, it was an accident. I *know* it was an accident!"

"And how would you know that?" Adam asked lazily. "I didn't ask if you shot them. You couldn't hit a cow if it was standing three feet in front of you. I did, however, wonder, since you seem so eager to get your hands on the marquessate, if you might have hired someone to kill me, and he just got it a little wrong."

"N-no, Adam. No, it wasn't anything like that—it really was a poacher," Harold said, shaking like a leaf. "I heard about it at the Fox and Hound in Smeeth."

Adam's eyes sharpened. "What did you hear exactly? I want it all, Harold, every last word."

"There's nothing much to tell—I just heard some of the boys talking about it," Harold said. He couldn't get the words out fast enough. "They said a man had come in early that evening. No one knew who he was, but he was in a terrible panic, wanted to know who owned the land down near

Hythe. They told him it was either Squire Hoode or you, and why did he want to know, but he didn't say, he left immediately. No one thought anything of it at the time, but that was before the word got out that there'd been an accident."

"Oddly enough, I believe you," Adam said, and Harold breathed a huge sigh of relief. "To return to the earlier matter, however, you will take responsibility for your actions. I don't take kindly to people who trespass on my property, injure my animals, and try to injure me. Quite frankly, I've had enough of both of you."

"What are you going to do?" Mildred said, speaking for the first time. "Please, Adam, the shame, the disgrace of a trial . . ."

"I agree entirely," Adam said, standing. He reached into the inside of his coat and pulled out a piece of paper. "This is a bank draft for five thousand pounds. In the light of the circumstances I consider this extremely generous of me. You will take this money and you will move to Scotland."

"S-Scotland?" Mildred cried, both hands flying to her neck, but her gaze was fixed on the bank draft. "But why Scotland? We know no one in Scotland, and the climate—"

"You will move to Scotland, because I want you as far away from Stanton as possible. You can move to the Continent or the South Pole, for all I care, but I know how much you despise foreign parts and their inhabitants. Somehow I don't think penguins would suit you, or you them. Sell this house and use the proceeds to bolster your funds, but move you will, and you will move immediately. Good evening, and enjoy your new home." He started to walk out of the room, then stopped and turned around. "Oh, one last thing: If I should hear that either of you has put so much as one foot over the border, I will personally make you rue the day you were born. The same will apply if I hear anything even vaguely scandalous about my wife or myself, so I strongly advise you to keep your tongues firmly between your teeth."

Adam left the room, and they heard the front door close.

"You *idiot!*" Mildred shrieked at Harold. "This is your fault! If you hadn't gone and done something so unbelievably stupid, none of this would have happened. Scotland—my life is ruined!"

"Your life—what about *my* life?" Harold said in self-defense. "In case you've forgotten, it was you who told me to *do* something. Well, I did, didn't I, and you thought it a brilliant idea when I told you about it, so it's a little late to be blaming me for following your instructions..."

Adam, who could hear the shouting all the way outside, wearily shook his head.

He really couldn't wait to get home. He had to find out why Callie was so anxious to go to the cliffs. Far more important than that, he had to tell her he loved her.

Callie looked like an angel, Adam thought as he quietly slipped into her bedroom. She was sound asleep, her mouth curled up in a smile, her fair hair tousled, one hand tucked under her chin, her other arm flung out in front of her. As usual she had the draperies drawn back and the window half open. Late afternoon sunlight streamed through it and slanted across the bed, falling on Callie's outstretched hand and catching on the gold of her wedding ring so that it shimmered like a star.

She'd already made the room her own, her treasures carefully arranged on the bureau and dresser, and he knew how much those treasures meant to her even without the fullness of memory. On one chair she'd propped a sketch of a man, and Adam walked over to look at it. Magnus Melbourne, Adam was sure of it—he saw the similarity to Callie, not so much in the features, but in the expression of intelligence and gentle good humor.

"Thank you," he whispered. "Thank you for giving me Callie. Thank you for loving her so well while she was in your care. I promise you I will always look after her, and you will always be in our thoughts and prayers."

He moved over to the bed and bent down, softly kissing Callie's hair. "I love you," he murmured, trying out the words, feeling the power of them inside him. As he straightened, something on her bedside table caught his eye. It was a feather, a dove's feather if he wasn't mistaken, the light gray vanes delicately etched. An errant breeze ruffled over it, then picked it up. It drifted upward in a slow spiral and floated down again, landing in the palm of Callie's hand.

Adam smiled. Whatever the feather signified to Callie, it looked fitting where it was, and he left it there.

Adam still had one last thing to do before waking Callie for their walk on the cliffs.

Going back through the connecting door into his own bedroom he picked up a candlestick, then headed down the stairs and through the house, past the gallery and down the hallway on the other end until he came to the chapel door. The handle turned easily and he pushed the heavy door open. Tomorrow he would bring Callie here, but this moment was for him alone.

He was surprised to see candles burning on the altar, but he supposed he shouldn't have been. He might have neglected the chapel, but the staff had not.

Adam walked over to the two marble crypts that rested side by side, one large, one small. Fresh arrangements of flowers sat at the foot of each one, their sweet scent gently filling the air. Kneeling, he tenderly placed a hand on the front of each crypt and bowed his head.

"My dearest Caro, my sweet little Ian," he whispered. "Forgive me for having lost my faith, forgive me for holding onto you long past the time when I should have let you go. I will always love you, always hold you close in my heart, but I know that the angels hold you in their embrace now and you are at peace."

Peace. He'd never thought to find it again, never thought to feel joy and claim it as his own. He had been through the fires of hell and he had survived. He had experienced loss, and in losing, had gained. He had grieved, and through grieving had learned the healing power of love. He would never be the same, but in changing he had grown, and that growth had given him an inner strength that would carry him through the rest of his life. For the first time he understood that life was not a random series of accidents, but a divine design, and that design so intricate and unfathomable that all one could do was surrender to it. And believe.

He *did* believe. He believed in life and in life ever after. Perhaps that was the greatest gift he'd been given of all, and he had Callie to thank. Callie and God, for neither had given up on him, even when he'd given up on himself.

"Thank you, Lord," he said. "I will not fail you."

Adam stood. He bent down and kissed the top of each crypt. "Good-bye, my darlings. Rest in peace."

Adam left the chapel, softly shutting the door behind him, and headed back upstairs to wake his sleeping and most beloved wife.

The sun was setting as they approached the bluff of the cliff, the sky streaked with blues and vermilions, punctuated by fat, white, lazy clouds that gently scudded along in the mild breeze. Callie had brought her basket and busily picked up plants along the way, many of them new to her, for the topography closer to the sea was very different from that even slightly inland and yielded a lovely variety of flowers and herbs.

Adam was surprisingly quiet. He had hardly said a word the entire way, seemingly lost in thought, but she didn't mind in the least. His silence gave her time to gather her own thoughts, and she was grateful for the opportunity. She had much on her mind.

He stopped as they reached a particularly fine vantage point that overlooked the sea and stepped behind her, holding her close against him, his hands resting just below her shoulders. "Look, Callie. It's a nice sight, isn't it?"

"It's a very nice sight," she replied, leaning back against him. "The sea holds such amazing power, doesn't it? It gives and it takes, but it never compromises. It is simply and perfectly itself. It is we mortals who are buffeted about by it. That seems a good metaphor for life, does it not?"

"You don't mind looking at the sea, then?" His voice held a note of real question, and mixed in with that, concern. "It doesn't hold any bad memories, frighten you in any way?"

She shook her head. "I don't mind at all. The sea brought me to you, Adam. How can I fault it for that? As for memories . . ." She paused, looking for the right words, for they were so important.

"I remember a very brave man who reached down into a turbulent sea for me when I was half drowned and pulled me into his boat," she said softly. "I remember a man who whispered words of encouragement to me, a man who reminded me to breathe when I'd nearly forgotten how, a man who used his fading strength to bring me safely back to shore.

I remember a man who was there for me when I was able to open my eyes again, and who accepted me for the woman I was without judging me, a man who gave me a home and a sense of security, even though I had nothing to give back."

She turned and rested her hands on his chest, looking straight into his eyes. "That man was you, Adam. You gave me back my life, and you nurtured me and protected me until I was able to stand on my own. Even then you protected me. You kept me safe, even after you knew that I no longer needed your protection." She bowed her head. "You asked if I feared the sea. I honor the sea. I always have and always will."

"Callie," he said, lifting her chin with his hand, his voice very gentle, his eyes the color of azure as he gazed into hers, his expression intent. "What are you telling me?"

"I remember, Adam," she said, tears filling her eyes. "I remember."

He didn't say anything for a long moment. At first he looked stunned, and then a smile slowly lit up his face, reaching all the way into his eyes. "Callie . . . my sweet, sweet Callie," he whispered. "You really do remember, don't you?"

"I remember everything," she said, her heart filled with gratitude and joy and boundless relief to feel whole again. "I think it must have happened when I banged my head again, because when I opened my eyes I felt as if everything had come back into place with a great rush. I remember the villa, and my father, and—and I remember the lush beauty of my island, and all the people I loved. I feel as if God has given me the most precious gift in restoring my memory. It's the strangest thing, but I have no regrets that for an entire month I had no past to connect to, for I don't know if I ever would have fully appreciated what a wonderful life I had until I knew what it was like to have nothing at all."

"I am very happy for you," he said, but his eyes were

filled with question, and behind the question a sadder expression that Callie didn't understand.

"What is it?" she asked. "Tell me, Adam, please. You know that you can ask me anything." She reached for his hand and held it tightly.

"Yes, I know that. And I know you will tell me the truth. My question is this: now that you do remember, do you wish for your old life back?"

Callie's breath caught in her throat. "Oh, Adam— Adam, no," she said, pulling him tightly against her, her cheek resting against his shoulder. "That's not what I meant at all. I could never leave you, not ever."

He pulled back and looked down at her. "Are you sure, Callie? Do you really mean that?"

"I mean that with all my heart. I—I know that you don't want to hear this, for you've made your position very clear . . ." She trailed off, not sure that she should say anything else.

"What is it that you think I don't want to hear?" he said, his voice very low.

Callie gazed up at him, silently praying that she wouldn't drive him away, but he expected truth from her and so she would tell it. "I love you, Adam. I can't help myself. I just do, and I have for a long time."

He exhaled, a long, deep sigh of relief. "That's good," he murmured, resting his forehead on hers. "That's very, very good."

"It is?" she said in confusion.

"Oh, yes," he said, lifting his head and smiling down at her tenderly.

"But you said that—"

"I know what I said. I said a lot of idiotic things, most of which I hope you'll put out of your head. Callie, when I told you that an essential part of me died when Ian and Caroline were killed, I was speaking the truth. What I didn't realize at the time was that a new and different part of me was coming alive. I believe that the beginnings were sown the day that I pulled you from the sea." He released a deep sigh. "I don't know whether it was because I was so worried about you, wanted so much for you to live, but I found myself truly caring about something, about some-one, for the first time in two very long years. And then when you started to recover and I began to know you, I slowly began to recover, too. It took some time before I re-alized what had happened, but one day I realized that I was enjoying life again, that the crushing pain and despair had receded. I have you to thank for that—I have you to thank for a great many things, but the greatest thing of all is for giving me back my life. You did that with your love."

Callie was so overwhelmed she could barely speak. "I am so grateful," she whispered.

"As am I. But there's more I need to say. I can't tell you when or how, but I fell in love with you, Callie. I fell in love with you, and I realized that it was a very different kind of love than I'd felt for Caroline, that I was a very different man and you were a very different woman, and what we had between us was unique and complete. I felt as if I'd fi-nally come home."

Callie stared at him in complete shock. "I didn't know," she said, her voice choked, the tears she'd been holding back streaming unchecked down her cheeks.

"How could you have?" he said, drawing his finger down her nose. "God knows I haven't made myself very clear, but I wasn't very clear myself. Perhaps I didn't realize the complete truth until today, being the stubborn, thick-skulled dunderhead that I am, but today, when I thought . . . let's just say that I have no doubt in my mind about how very much I love you and cherish you. I'd be utterly and entirely lost without you."

"Adam," Callie said, "I'd be lost without you, too." The joy in her heart threatened to overwhelm her. Adam had learned his lesson, and it had freed him—and her.

"I'm glad to hear it," he murmured. "I've been an utter fool, Callie, and I'm sorry. I was so caught up in hanging on to the past that I neglected to realize that the past had stopped hanging on to me."

Callie managed to laugh through her tears. "I'm so glad—I can't tell you how happy I am to hear that. But I've also learned something through this experience, Adam, and it's that the past lives in you, that it defines you and makes you who you are. The people whom you have treasured and who have treasured you are never really gone. They live on in you and continue to give you happiness, and you can only be grateful that they graced you with their presence for whatever time you had with them—the imprint they leave behind stays with you forever, and you can best honor their memory by living your life to the fullest, the way they would have wanted you to."

Adam ran his hands up and down her arms. "Callie—how did I ever have such good luck as to find you? You make life so sane and so simple." He closed his eyes for a brief moment and then opened them again. "I have a confession to make. I never thought I'd tell another soul this, but you have a right to know." He blew out a long breath as if steeling himself. "The day that I found you in the sea—I hadn't gone out fishing. I'd gone out to drown myself. I honestly felt as if I couldn't go on." He looked away, as if waiting for her to lambaste him.

Callie's eyes widened and she pressed her hands against

her mouth, but instead of dismay, she felt only amazement. "Adam—oh, Adam, I'm so sorry that you were in such pain that you wanted to take your own life, but don't you see?"

"See what, exactly?" he said, looking back at her in confusion.

"See God's hand at work? Adam, if you hadn't gone out to—to kill yourself, then you couldn't possibly have rescued me, and we wouldn't be standing here now, either of us, loving each other so well." A hiccup of laughter escaped her. "You may have *thought* you were going to kill yourself, but God had something else entirely in mind. He put you exactly where you needed to be so that both of us could start a new life, and start it together. Oh, that's *wonderful!*"

Adam grinned. "You always have had a unique way of looking at things."

"Oh, but it makes perfect sense. There's something I have to tell you, too. I didn't jump off that ship, Adam. I really did fall." She started to laugh, and then couldn't stop.

"Callie—what on earth do you find so hilarious?" he said, starting to laugh as well.

"No—no, listen, I'm serious." she said, trying to get a grip on herself, holding on to Adam for support. "This is going to sound ridiculous, but the reason that I was standing out there in the storm was because I was singing to my father. I was singing his soul song, Adam, so that he knew I was bringing a part of him back to England. It was the gull, you see . . ." Her face screwed up, her entire body shaking with mirth. "It was the gull that did it—it had been following the ship, and something deep inside me told me that my father was watching over me and had sent the gull, so I went out onto the stern and I started to sing, hoping that my father could hear me. I knew that he'd recognize his song. But then the boat suddenly tilted, and the floor was so wet that I lost my footing, and over I went. He really *was* watching over me, don't you see? He didn't mean for me to go to Harold at all, he meant for me to go to you." She tried to catch her breath, but without much success. "Oh, it's so perfect!"

"Wait, Callie. What do you mean by his soul song?" Adam said, holding her by the waist.

Callie clutched her aching sides. "His *soul* song, Adam," she said, trying to sober, because it was important that Adam understand. "My father taught me his when I was very young. He'd come back from visiting a tribe in Africa, and they'd taught him their custom. When a woman is pregnant, she goes away with her friends, and they all pray until they hear the song of the unborn child, and then they return to the tribe and teach the song to all the members so that when the baby is born, that's the first thing he hears."

"They sing the baby a song they've made up?" Adam said, looking baffled, but at least listening.

"Yes. Every soul has its own unique resonance, and that's what the women listen for when they go out into the wild. Anyway, all through that person's life whenever he goes through an important rite of passage, the village sings him his song. And then finally, when the time comes for that person to die, everyone sings him into the next life. Isn't that lovely?"

Adam rubbed his forehead. "Clearly you believe this."

"Of course I do. I sang my father to his next life when he died, and he was very happy."

"So you mean that even I have a soul song?" Adam asked, one corner of his mouth turning up in a smile.

"Every living being has a soul song, Adam, *even* you, whether you choose to believe it or not, and our children will have theirs, and I will sing it to each one, and you will just have to go into another room if you don't choose to listen."

Adam chuckled. "I can just see you going off pregnant into the wild, which will probably be the nether fields, with Mrs. Simpson and Jane and Nellie, all of you clucking like hens."

She thwacked his arm. "If I were you, I'd pay close attention, or I won't even bother to try to learn your soul song."

"I think you've already heard it," he said with a wicked grin. "Seriously, Callie, I think it's a lovely story, and that does make an interesting explanation for why you fell and why the gull followed us home in that awful weather. I don't mean to make light of you or your beliefs in any way, but for a woman who spouts on about God all the time, you're beginning to sound like a downright heathen."

"You can't box God into any particular religion," she said. "He is everywhere and in everything, whatever interpretation you choose to put on the matter. You don't have to believe, Adam, you just have to pay attention and He will show His face. He brought us together, didn't He, and in the most unlikely fashion. You can argue the point until you're blue in the face, but I defy you to come up with any other explanation."

"But I do believe," Adam said. "I really do, my love. I just need to become more accustomed to your version of God and His mysteries, for it only vaguely resembles the version I was brought up with. Yours is much more... lively. I look forward to my continuing education, but God help the vicar when you get your hands on him."

"I do love you," Callie said with a blissful smile.

"As I love you," Adam replied, kissing her soundly. He lifted his head and cupped her face in his hands. "I always will, sweet Callie, just as I will always be grateful that you fell off that bloody ship and saved us both."

# Epilogue

"Name this child," the vicar said, gingerly holding the squirming infant in his hands while Adam looked on nervously. He never had trusted the vicar not to muddle things, and he really didn't want to watch him drop his daughter.

Nigel stepped forward and said, "Flora Melbourne Carlyle."

"I baptize thee Flora Melbourne Carlyle in the Name of the Father, and of the Son, and of the Holy Ghost. Amen." The vicar dipped his finger into the baptismal font and made the sign of the cross over the baby's forehead. He said the obligatory prayers and handed Callie little Flora, who beamed with pleasure to be back in her mother's arms.

"If you'll indulge me for just a moment," Callie said, smiling at the small group of people in the chapel. "There's something important I have to do."

Adam knew in his bones what was coming, but he didn't

mind in the least. Callie had not only blessed him with a little girl, but she'd also sailed through pregnancy and childbirth with an ease that had alarmed Mrs. Simpson, delighted Plimpton, Gettis and the rest of the household, and thrilled him, especially because she hadn't banned him from their bed for one instant. Whatever Callie chose to do now was just fine with him. The vicar might be taken aback, but Adam doubted anyone else who knew Callie would be the least surprised.

Callie untucked Flora's blankets and held her daughter out in front of her, Flora's weight resting on Callie's forearms, her little head resting in Callie's hands.

Callie looked into Flora's eyes and began to sing, a soaring, complex, and beautifully harmonic series of notes.

She sang Flora her soul song, and Flora's little fists danced joyfully along, her eyes fixed intently on her mother's face.

The chapel echoed with Callie's final notes, throwing them back as if in angelic refrain.

Adam walked over to Callie and took Flora from her, cradling her in one arm as naturally as if he'd been born to cradle infants. "That was beautiful, my love," he said, kissing Callie's cheek. He lowered his voice. "I think you'd better have a word with the vicar again. He's looking a little faint."

"Sherry," Callie said with a grin. "I've noticed it's always worked wonders. Let's take our guest out onto the lawn. We're lucky it's such a beautiful day and we're able to serve luncheon outside."

After lunch when they were all milling around and chatting, Sir Reginald took Callie to one side. "Excuse me, Mrs. Bishop," he said to Nellie, who was engaged in a lively conversation with Callie about the planting of the garden outside of Nellie's new cottage. "Might I interrupt for just one moment?"

"Certainly," Nellie said, going off to find her husband,

who was engaged in an equally lively exchange with Nigel about the crops he planned to put in that spring.

"I wanted to give you these, my dear," Sir Reginald said, handing Callie a bundle of letters tied in a blue ribbon. "I wanted to wait for just the right occasion, and this seemed suitable. Perhaps you will pass them on to Flora one day."

Callie looked down at the bundle, instantly recognizing her father's handwriting. "These are Papa's letters to you," she said, overcome with a flood of emotion. "Oh, thank you, dear Sir Reginald. Thank you so much." She stood on her tiptoes and kissed his whiskered cheek, trying very hard not to cry, for she didn't want to embarrass him.

He cleared his throat. "I thought they might help you finish your father's book, once you have time to begin the endeavor properly. There is much detail in them about his findings."

Callie blinked through the clouds in her eyes. "Yes. Yes, they will be most useful. You are too kind, for I know how much they meant to you."

"Not at all, my dear. You and your husband have given an old man great happiness in the last year. I hope these letters will give you equal happiness." He mumbled something about helping himself to another piece of Cook's excellent cake, and wandered off in the direction of the river. Callie knew that cake was the last thing on his mind.

She watched him for a moment, infinitely grateful that he had come into their lives. He'd become a fixture, visiting them often and always giving enormous pleasure when he did, acting as friend, advisor, and father figure, and she was happy that Flora and the future children that she and Adam planned would have a grandfather of sorts.

Her life was blessed, and she counted those blessings each and every day. The grange had become an enormous success even in its fledgling year under Adam's control, the tenant cottagers thriving now that they were being treated fairly. They worked hard and the land reaped its rewards as a result and gave back those rewards to them. She and Nellie were firmer friends than ever, Nellie's fears about Callie becoming a grand lady having come to naught. Callie hadn't changed her ways one iota, and no one seemed to mind, least of all Adam.

Callie was most especially blessed there, for Adam loved her well and truly, and their lives were rich with love and laughter and shared endeavors. Even when she received letters from her friends in Corfu, usually written by the village priest, she didn't ache to return. She'd go back to the Villa Kaloroziko one day and take Adam and their children with her, but she was in no rush, knowing that Niko held it in good hands. Her life was here now, and it was a good one.

Nigel wandered over, a glass of champagne in one hand, the other wrapped around Adam's shoulder. "There's something I've been meaning to tell you both for some time," he said, raising his glass to them. "As Flora's godfather, I want you to know that I take full responsibility for her arrival on this earth."

"How is that?" Adam asked, raising an eyebrow. "I don't recall your being around for the conception."

"Not that conception. It was the other conception that was my brilliant master plan, and I must say, Adam, as your friend and steward of all your affairs, I did an admirable job. I think you should both congratulate me."

"What are we congratulating you for?" Callie asked, knowing from the twinkle in Nigel's eyes that he planned to unleash one of his incessant jokes.

"You are congratulating me for having made all of his possible," he said. "I have a confession to make, and I hope that you will receive it in the spirit in which it was intended." He took a sip of champagne, grinning.

"Confess then, friend, and why not?" Adam said, returning his grin. "What sin have you committed that needs confessing and should earn our gratitude? The two seem in direct opposition."

"I lied," Nigel said with enormous satisfaction. "Actually, I didn't lie, I merely committed a sin of omission. I knew about Callie's true identity all along, at least from the day I returned from Dover. I knew her name, Adam, I knew that Harold was supposed to be her fiancé, and I kept my mouth firmly closed because I also knew that she was the perfect woman for you. I was right, was I not?"

Adam stared at his dearest, closest friend and looked as if he was sorely tempted to knock him flat.

Callie covered her mouth with her hand, trying terribly hard not to laugh. She couldn't help herself. Her laughter overflowed and she crowed with delight. "I do love you, Nigel," she said, laughing so hard that she thought she might fall over. "You are very wonderful. Thank you—oh, thank you, because if you had told Adam the truth—"

"He would have immediately consigned you to the hell of Harold, given the state of mind he was in," Nigel finished for her. "I know I behaved very badly, but I just couldn't bring myself to be forthcoming. Forgive me for my sins, but I knew exactly what I was doing."

Adam's mouth twitched as if he was wrestling with himself, and then he chuckled. "I should have known," he said. "Damn and blast you, and thank you very, very much." He shook his head and shook it again, then burst into laughter. "I suppose that is the meaning of a true friend," he said, wiping his eyes. "He's the person who loves you enough to save you from yourself. Thank you,

Nigel, on behalf of Callie and myself. You acted as a true steward."

"I did, you're most welcome, and may you live a long a happy life together."

Adam wrapped his arm around Callie's waist. "We shall, Nigel. Oh, we most definitely shall."

# About the Author

Katherine Kingsley is the author of seven historical romances for Dell: *Song from the Sea, Lilies on the Lake, In the Presence of Angels, The Sound of Snow, Call Down the Moon, Once Upon a Dream,* and *In the Wake of the Wind.* She has won numerous writing awards, including two career achievement awards from *Romantic Times.*

Katherine lives in Southwest Florida with her husband. They spend a few weeks every year on the Greek island of Mykonos while their two Jack Russell terriers entertain the neighbors.